Susanna Gregory was a police officer in Leeds before taking up an academic career. She has served as an environmental consultant, worked eighteen field seasons in the polar regions, and has taught comparative anatomy and biological anthropology.

She is the creator of the Matthew Bartholomew series of mysteries set in medieval Cambridge and the Thomas Chaloner adventures in Restoration London. She now lives in Wales with her husband, who is also a writer.

Also by Susanna Gregory

The Matthew Bartholomew series

A Plague on Both Your Houses
An Unholy Alliance
A Bone of Contention
A Deadly Brew
A Wicked Deed
A Masterly Murder
An Order for Death
A Summer of Discontent
A Killer in Winter
The Hand of Justice
The Mark of a Murderer
The Tarnished Chalice
To Kill or Cure
The Devil's Disciples
A Vein of Deceit
The Killer of Pilgrims
Mystery in the Minster
Murder by the Book
The Lost Abbot
Death of a Scholar
A Poisonous Plot
A Grave Concern
The Habit of Murder
The Sanctuary Murders
The Chancellor's Secret

The Thomas Chaloner Series

A Conspiracy of Violence
Blood on the Strand
The Butcher of Smithfield
The Westminster Poisoner
A Murder on London Bridge
The Body in the Thames
The Piccadilly Plot
Death in St James's Park
Murder on High Holborn
The Cheapside Corpse
The Chelsea Strangler
The Executioner of St Paul's
Intrigue in Covent Garden
The Clerkenwell Affair

SUSANNA GREGORY

The Pudding Lane Plot

SPHERE

SPHERE

First published in Great Britain in 2022 by Sphere

1 3 5 7 9 10 8 6 4 2

Copyright © Susanna Gregory 2022

The moral right of the author has been asserted.

A CIP catalogue record for this book is available from the British Library.

ISBN 978-0-7515-8189-8

Typeset in Baskerville MT Std by Palimpsest Book Production Ltd,
Falkirk, Stirlingshire
Printed and bound in Great Britain by Clays Ltd, Elcograf S.p.A.

Papers used by Sphere are from well-managed forests
and other responsible sources.

Sphere
An imprint of
Little, Brown Book Group
Carmelite House
50 Victoria Embankment
London
EC4Y 0DZ

www.littlebrown.co.uk
www.hachette.co.uk

For Thalia Proctor and Liz Hatherell

With love and gratitude

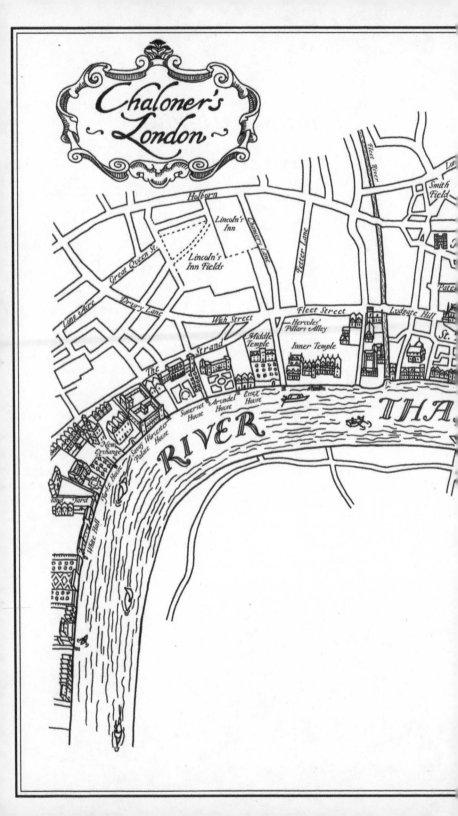

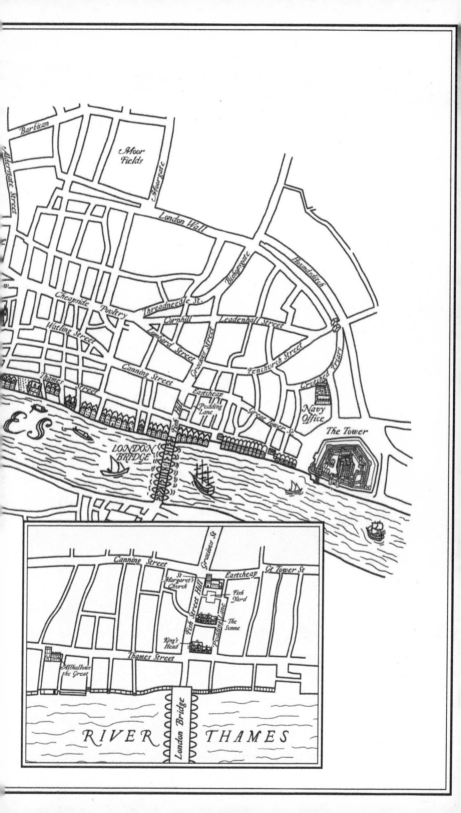

Prologue

The harbour of Gorey, Jersey; late July 1666

It was done. The killer watched the formidable bulk of Mont Orgueil fade into the darkness as the boat carried him away, and heaved a heartfelt sigh of relief. When he had first seen the castle, he had been daunted, afraid he would never manage to broach its defences and claim his victims. He had had to keep reminding himself that he was not there to take it by storm, but rather to gain access by stealth and cunning.

Even so, it had not been easy, and it had been weeks before he had devised a workable plan. To his surprise, it had worked like a dream, not once but twice. He could hardly believe his luck. He had expected the authorities to tighten security after he had murdered Gilbert Millington in his cell, but, incredibly, the governor had deemed the prisoner's death a natural one. True, the killer had been careful, placing the body on its side to give the appearance of peaceful sleep, and there had been no blood to reveal the truth, but he had assumed there would be some manner of investigation, given

1

Millington's importance. Yet not so much as an eyebrow had been raised.

It had been a month before he had dared to rekindle his 'friendship' with the castle guards, sure they would remember exactly who had last seen Millington alive and draw the obvious conclusion. But they had been more interested in the free ale he offered than making uncomfortable connections – namely that Millington had been found dead the morning after the killer, disguised as a cleric, had bribed them to allow him to visit.

His second target had been Sir Hardresse Waller, who was pathetically grateful to the kindly vicar who came bearing gifts of books and fresh fruit. It had been ridiculously easy to dispatch him as he knelt with his eyes closed, waiting for a priestly benediction. Again, the killer left his victim curled on his side, as if sleeping. As he had left the castle, he had been terrified, sure cries of murder would follow within moments, but there had only been amiable nods from the guards, and a hopeful question about whether he would be in the tavern later.

Now, a week later, he was on a ship bound for England. By chance, one of the other passengers was the prison chaplain, a short, fat gentleman in a greasy black coat who rarely set foot inside the gaol, although he was happy to claim the stipend that accompanied the post. Tentatively, the killer raised the subject of two dead inmates within a month, keen to know if there was any worrisome speculation as to what had happened to them.

'No one will miss that pair,' declared the chaplain in distaste. 'They should have been executed as traitors years ago. They both confessed their crimes, did they not?'

'Yes,' acknowledged the killer carefully. 'But surely it

is odd that they should breathe their last within a few weeks of each other?'

'Not really.' The chaplain settled himself more comfortably against the aft rail as the lights of Gorey harbour disappeared into the evening gloom. 'Neither was young, and both suffered from bouts of ill health. They died in their sleep – I saw their corpses myself.'

The killer allowed himself a small smile of satisfaction. The chaplain's words confirmed that the plan was proceeding perfectly, and it would not be long before all came to pass exactly as he intended.

Pudding Lane, London; Tuesday 21 August, 1666

James Hadie had uncovered evidence of something dreadful and he was terrified. The previous afternoon he had confided all he had learned about it to his friend John Bowles the grocer, desperate for advice on what to do. Bowles had listened with horror, and had promised to help him devise a way to unmask the culprits. But that morning, the grocer had been found dead in his shop.

The parish constable's verdict was natural causes, but Hadie knew he was wrong, and that Bowles was just the latest victim in a long and bloody trail of them. For a start, there were all the smashed eggs around the body. The constable maintained that Bowles had knocked them down as he flailed about in his final agonies, but Hadie thought it suspicious that *every* egg in the shop had been broken. Surely, one would have survived intact?

He stood in the shadows outside Skiner's Coffee House, struggling to control his trembling. He needed to find another confidant, but who? Clearly, the killer knew he had spoken to Bowles, which meant that anyone else he approached would be in danger, too. Moreover, who could be trusted? Anyone might be involved, and Hadie was now wary of men he had previously considered to be incorruptible.

He had written everything down, though, and lodged the report in a place where it would be made public in the event of his death. It would not save his life, but exposing the perpetrators would be revenge of sorts, should he suffer the same fate as Bowles and so many others.

Then he saw two familiar faces: Elsie Henwood and Dorcas Eades, fellow freemen of the Company of Poulters. He sagged in relief. They were unlikely to be part of the evil, because their male counterparts were jealous of their talents, so tended to exclude them from any important business.

He started towards them, calling their names, but even as they looked in his direction, he sensed a shadow slithering from the shadows behind him. Before he could turn to defend himself, he felt three hard thumps in his back. There was no pain, but suddenly he could not catch his breath. He dropped to the ground, aware of a warmth beneath him as blood poured from his wounds.

'You will not . . . succeed,' he managed to croak to the sinister silhouette that loomed over him. 'I wrote . . . letter. Your game . . . exposed . . . you . . . will die . . . as . . . traitor.'

He was aware of his attacker freezing in horror. 'You did *what?* Where is it? Tell me!'

But Hadie had no more breath, and could not have replied even if he had wanted. He barely managed a gasp as his assailant grabbed him by the front of his shirt and shook him, frantic to make him talk. As the fellow moved, light from the coffee house illuminated his face. Hadie gaped at the familiar features. He would never have guessed *he* was behind it all!

His attacker dropped him and melted into the darkness when the two women ran towards them. Dorcas barked an order for Elsie to stay with the dying man while she gave chase, but Hadie made an urgent gesture to keep her at his side – he did not want another victim added to the killer's tally.

Unable to speak, he used his hands to convey what he wanted them to know, but he could tell by their bemused faces that they did not understand. He died praying that his message would make sense when they had had time to reflect on it. Then, combined with the information in his letter, the plot would be exposed and its ruthless perpetrators stopped before it was too late.

Chapter 1

London, Wednesday 22 August, 1666

Thomas Chaloner, Gentleman Usher to the Lord Chancellor, was sorry to see John Bowles lying in the Westminster charnel house. He had not known the grocer well, but had often visited his shop in New Palace Yard, as the spices he sold were useful in summer, when food spoiled fast and something was needed to disguise the taste of victuals past their best.

'It is difficult to tell anything at all,' grumbled Richard Wiseman, who exulted in the title of Surgeon to the Person, meaning he tended the King.

He was a large gentleman in every respect: tall, muscular, and self-assured to the point of arrogance. He always wore red, which his detractors said was to disguise the copious amounts of blood he spilled – he had accrued more critics than most *medici* because of his unsympathetic bedside manner and unendearing habit of denouncing his colleagues as inept and stupid. But Chaloner thought his fondness for scarlet was just because he liked to be noticed.

The surgeon was in a foul mood that morning, because Chaloner had woken him very early with a request to examine Bowles. Wiseman had a full day ahead of him, so he had been obliged to forgo breakfast in order to accommodate Chaloner's demand. He would have refused anyone else, but Chaloner was not only his lodger – he rented the top floor of the surgeon's Covent Garden house – but virtually his only friend.

'Why is it difficult?' asked Chaloner obligingly, sensing the surgeon's need to rant.

Wiseman glared at him. 'Because he is covered in egg, which the heat has turned bad. The stink is distracting me.'

Chaloner regarded him incredulously. The aroma of rotten eggs was nothing compared to the stench of what else lay in the charnel house that day. The place was much smellier than usual, because the country was in the grip of the hottest summer anyone could remember and the dead decomposed quickly. They were not all that was affected by the intense heat – trees and crops withered in the fields, a blistering sun blazed down on man and beast alike without respite, and the mighty Thames ran at less than half its normal volume due to the lack of rain.

'Shall I fetch water to rinse the eggs away?' he asked, aiming to appease.

The surgeon shook his head with a sigh. 'There is no need. I have found what I imagine you were expecting – evidence of foul play.'

Chaloner was sorry to hear it, even if he was not surprised. He had bought ginger and cloves from Bowles on Monday afternoon, and had chatted to him while he had closed up his shop. The grocer had been fit and

8

healthy then, and while Chaloner accepted that people sometimes did drop dead with no warning, it rarely happened to men in their prime. Thus he had been sceptical about the parish constable's verdict that Bowles had suffered a fatal apoplexy while stacking boxes of eggs.

'Was he poisoned?' Chaloner asked. 'I saw no pools of blood in the place where he died, and there is none on the body.'

'Oh, yes, there is,' countered Wiseman with his customary haughtiness. 'Although I would not expect a mere layman to spot it. Spillage was kept to a minimum, because the blade was unusually long and thin. When I open him up, you will see he was subjected to a fatal penetration of the heart.'

'There is no need to put yourself to that much trouble,' said Chaloner hastily. 'Your opinion alone is enough for me.'

'You aim to explore the murder?' asked Wiseman, reaching for a blade anyway, as no self-respecting anatomist passed up an opportunity to dissect a nice fresh specimen.

Chaloner nodded. 'He seemed distracted when I last met him, and although the constable assures me that the mess in the shop was caused by his death throes, I am disinclined to believe it.'

'And what gives you the authority to probe the matter?'

'The fact that Bowles supplied White Hall with eggs and spices,' replied Chaloner promptly. 'Ergo, my Earl will want to know what really happened to him.'

'So will the Navy Office,' predicted Wiseman. 'Bowles provided the fleet with victuals, too, and his death could delay our ships putting to sea. Word is that the Dutch sailed yesterday, and if we are not ready to defend our coastline, we shall have Hollanders marching down the Strand before the month is out.'

England was currently at war with the United Provinces of the Netherlands, an asinine conflict that served the interests of neither country. Rumours had been flying all summer about the enemy being poised to invade London, although Chaloner knew the Dutch and their politics, and felt they had more sense than to embark on such a recklessly ambitious venture. However, lightning raids were another matter entirely, so it was indeed urgent that English ships were ready to fend them off.

When Wiseman descended on Bowles with an anatomy knife the size of a small sword, Chaloner took his leave. The surgeon could tell him later if he found anything else of relevance, and he had no desire to watch the grocer dissected. Besides, he needed to tell the Earl what had happened, and obtain permission to investigate and bring the killer to justice.

First, though, he had arranged to meet another friend, this one at his favourite coffee house, the Rainbow on Fleet Street.

The journey from Westminster was hot and dusty, even though it was only mid-morning and the real heat of the day had yet to build. Chaloner had hoped to ride in a hackney carriage, but no one else wanted to walk either, so demand exceeded supply. The shortage of coaches was compounded by the fact that so many drivers had died during the previous year's plague, and had not yet been replaced.

The streets were busy, as many of the tradesmen who came to the markets before dawn had finished their business and were eager to get home. They were noisy, too, as itinerant street-sellers advertised their wares in stentorian tones – new-baked pies, plump onions, fine candles, sweet pastries, best leather and anything else that could be hawked to the city's population of nearly three hundred thousand souls.

During the plague, weeds had grown between the cobbles around Charing Cross, because human footfall had not been enough to trample them away. There were no weeds now, and London seemed as frenetic as it had ever been. Even so, grim reminders of the terrible sickness that had claimed so many lives could be seen on any number of cross-painted doors, showing where the disease had struck but no one had yet scoured the mark away.

As always, Chaloner overheard plenty of gossip as he walked, the most unsettling of which was the news that Wiseman had mentioned – that the Dutch fleet was at sea and poised to strike. Then there was the usual talk of omens and portents of doom, including strangely shaped clouds, talking animals, miraculous cures, and sightings of Satan. The whole city seemed to be waiting with bated breath to see what dreadful calamity would befall it next – over the last twenty years, it had endured civil wars, a beheaded king, a Commonwealth led by a man many had considered a tyrant, and a devastating plague. And now it was in the unlucky year with three sixes, so what else did fate have in store for it?

As Chaloner passed the church of St Mary le Strand, two clerics emerged laughing. One was showing the other a broadsheet. These had become popular since the wars, as they provided an easy way for people to air their opinions. A few were clever, some dull, and others downright treasonous, but all circulated unimpeded in

11

public places, like churches, coffee houses, markets and taverns. Recently, one especially verbose writer had been active, and Chaloner recognised the distinctive red ink that characterised his work. When the cleric tossed it away, he stooped to retrieve it.

As he had thought, it was another tirade by the pamphleteer who called himself 'the Paladin', and this time it was an attack on the Worshipful Company of Poulters. Chaloner liked birds, so tended to agree that the industry was a 'vile and noisome horror which abus'd the Trust that God gave Man when he mayde us Stewards of the Earth'. There followed a vivid and horrifying description of life for hens on purpose-built egg farms, and ended with a series of brutal but amusing caricatures of the Master and his officers.

Over the past few weeks, the Paladin had published upwards of a dozen attacks on people or institutions he did not like. Most were parodies of the many lunatic religious sects that had proliferated after the wars, particularly Fifth Monarchists. The government approved of his rants because he ridiculed the fanatics who itched to overthrow it, while the general populace enjoyed them because they were funny.

The piece on the poulters was typical of the Paladin's style: a serious condemnation of the trade's less laudable antics, but written with a sharply humorous wit that kept his readers' attention until the end. However, it was the first time he had targeted an organisation that might hit back, and the Company of Poulters certainly *would* object to being singled out for such vigorous censure.

When Chaloner had finished with the broadsheet, he left it on the front steps of St Clement Dane, where a verger swept forward and grabbed it with an exclamation of delight. Clearly, it would not be long before the entire city was acquainted with the Paladin's views on the way the poultry industry conducted itself.

At last, he arrived at the point in the road called Temple Bar, where the Strand met Fleet Street. This was a narrow archway that spanned the highway, manned by guards who controlled who came from and went into the city. There were always queues, and the current spate of hot weather was doing nothing to soothe the ragged tempers of those forced to wait.

That day, there was a vicious exchange of insults under way between the owner of a cart loaded with crates of overheated chickens and a courtier named Henry Catline. Catline was an arrogant, smug individual who thought that being a favourite of the King entitled him to do whatever he pleased. His supercilious manner had evidently alienated most of the onlookers, because there was a resounding cheer when the carter decided he had had enough of bandying words and made his point with a punch instead. Fortunately for all concerned, Catline did not draw his sword and run his assailant through, because he was intelligent enough to know that if he did, he might not escape alive himself.

'Remember *that* when you make your damned syllabub!' the carter yelled, emboldened by the crowd's approval. 'You selfish bastard! While honest Londoners starve, you waste food on foolery.'

'What is this?' demanded a butcher's lad, identifiable by his striped and bloodstained apron. He sounded ready to be outraged, no matter what the reply.

'White Hall is making a special dish for the King next week,' explained the carter. 'It is to be the size of a lake, and he and all his mistresses will frolic stark naked in it.'

13

Chaloner had not heard this particular rumour before, although it would not surprise him if it held an element of truth. His Majesty had been restored to his throne six years ago, but did not have the sense to live a sober and dignified life, so new stories about his debauchery surfaced on a daily basis. It was reckless behaviour for a man whose father had been beheaded for falling out with his subjects.

When the crowd growled angry disapproval, Catline prudently decided to abandon his attempt to push through the Bar without waiting his turn, and rode back the way he had come. A hail of small stones followed him, although all missed, and he did not deign to acknowledge the barrage by looking back.

Chaloner took advantage of the situation by darting through the gate while everyone else was busy jeering at Catline's ignominious retreat. In Fleet Street beyond, a wall of heat hit him like a physical blow. The road was narrower than the Strand, and its houses more tightly packed together, so they blocked any breeze there might have been. Sweating and uncomfortable, he wondered how its residents could bear it.

The Rainbow Coffee House was a shabby building just past Temple Bar, opposite St Dunstan-in-the-West. Chaloner could smell the stench of burned beans and pipe smoke long before he reached it, even stronger than the reek of the open sewers that ran along the sides of the road, currently clogged by the weeks of rubbish that had accumulated with no rain to wash it away.

Coffee houses were places where men went not only to sample the beverage that had been virtually unknown in the city ten years ago, but also to expound views that would normally see them arrested or executed. Naturally, the government itched to close them all down, but they were very popular with the people, and more opened every week to meet the growing demand.

Chaloner was not sure why he liked the Rainbow. Its benches were uncomfortable, it was patronised by bigots of the worst kind, and its coffee was barely drinkable. He supposed it was because the place never changed, and continuity was something that had been sadly lacking in his life. He opened the door and stepped through it, grateful to find the place cooler inside than out. The owner, Thomas Farr, stood ready with the long-spouted jug that held his poisonous brew, sporting an apron that was stained black-brown from the greasy smoke that billowed from his roasting beans.

'What news?' he called, using the traditional coffee-house greeting, although he was invariably dissatisfied with Chaloner as a source of intelligence; the spy's training meant he tended to be reluctant to part with any information, no matter how innocuous.

'*He* will tell us nothing of import,' scoffed Stedman the printer, then looked hopeful. 'Unless he knows something about the King's syllabub?'

Chaloner shook his head apologetically, not about to repeat the rumour that it involved His Majesty frolicking naked in it with his mistresses.

Farr addressed Stedman in disgust. 'We know more about White Hall than he does, despite the fact none of us have ever been inside. As a source of interesting stories, he is worse than useless. But what is this about syllabub?'

'Well, word is that the King will have a massive one for his Adrian Masque,' supplied the printer, delighted to show off his superior knowledge to an interested audience.

15

'For his what?' asked Farr, bemused.

'It is a ball to commemorate Pope Adrian the Fourth,' elaborated Stedman. 'He died a little over five hundred years ago, you see.'

'The King aims to celebrate the death of a pope?' asked Chaloner in alarm, thinking it was a sure way to offend Catholics. Then it occurred to him that the King might be Catholic himself – it was his mother's religion, and she exerted considerable influence over him – in which case it was Protestants he aimed to goad. Either way, it was imprudent.

'Adrian the Fourth is the only Pope of English birth,' explained Stedman. 'He is a national hero, so our country should be proud of him. The fact that he was Catholic is irrelevant, and I applaud His Majesty for honouring this long-forgotten man.'

Stedman was a devoted Royalist, who followed all the doings at White Hall with eager approval, so Chaloner was not surprised to hear him speak in support of the King. However, there was a rumble of disapproval from all the other patrons, who clearly felt that, English or not, a pope was hardly someone for a Protestant monarch to fete.

'Did this Adrian have a particular liking for syllabub, then?' asked Farr warily.

'Who knows? But one will provide the centrepiece for the masque anyway,' replied Stedman. 'It is being made to a new and secret recipe devised by the Poultry.' For the benefit of his avid listeners, he added helpfully, 'That is a department in the Royal Household. It is under the Lord Chamberlain's authority.'

'Under the Lord Steward,' said Chaloner, pleased to be able to correct the Royal-worshipping printer.

16

Unfortunately, he should have known better than to think Stedman would make a mistake about a subject with which he was so passionately obsessed.

'The Lord Steward is away, so Lord Chamberlain Montagu is doing his work at the moment,' Stedman flashed back. 'And the Poultry Department, as I was saying before you interrupted, will make the syllabub. Apparently, it calls for some very unusual ingredients.'

'But why choose a syllabub for the centrepiece?' asked Farr, frowning. 'It does not sound very medieval.'

'It is symbolic of the Vatican's biggest lake, where Adrian drowned,' explained Stedman confidently. 'And I have it on good authority that everyone will jump in it at the end of the night, to eat and wallow at the same time.'

'Goodness!' breathed Chaloner, wondering if the dissipated courtier who had devised the entertainment was aware that the Vatican had no lakes. Moreover, he was fairly sure that this particular pontiff had died peacefully in his bed.

Of course, it would not be the first time that a rumour involving White Hall had been grossly exaggerated. And yet, there was no smoke without fire, so the chances were that some wild jape *was* in the making. He only hoped the King knew what he was doing. Unfortunately, he suspected that whatever was afoot was just the latest in a long series of misjudgements that would alienate His Majesty from his subjects even further.

When the conversation moved to omens and their meanings, Chaloner stepped away, loath to listen to more uninformed nonsense. He looked around for the man he had agreed to meet, his friend Captain Salathiel Lester.

17

Lester was sitting alone in a corner, in defiance of coffee-house etiquette which expected visitors to sit with everyone else and contribute to whatever subject was being aired.

Lester was a tall, bulky man with an open, honest face, and the rolling gait of the professional sailor. He was a navy 'tarpaulin', which meant he was a bred seaman who had learned his trade from practical experience. Thus he knew ships and how to sail them, as opposed to the navy's 'gentlemen' – nobles who had never been to sea, but who were given command of a vessel anyway, as a perk. Lester's length of service meant he had served both the Commonwealth and the King, which made him suspect in the eyes of some. Until recently, he had been Master of HMS *Swiftsure*.

'I do not know why you like this place,' he said, looking around the Rainbow with a disparaging eye. 'It reeks of burning.'

'Most coffee houses do,' Chaloner pointed out.

'Not this strongly,' argued Lester, uncharacteristically sour. 'I can barely breathe, and this awful heat does not help. Do you think the doom-mongers are right when they say it will never rain again, and we shall all be slowly roasted to death?'

Chaloner was beginning to wonder if they were, as the only other time he had experienced such temperatures was when he had ventured into a desert. 'Perhaps.'

'It will be cooler at sea – not that I shall ever experience it again,' said Lester bitterly. 'Not after *Swiftsure*. Damn Admiral Berkeley! Why could he not have listened to me? Or better yet, chosen another vessel as his flagship?'

Chaloner patted his arm sympathetically. Berkeley had been a 'gentleman' in his twenties, who had been

18

promoted to the rank of admiral because he was a crony of the Duke of York. His bad decisions and abysmal seamanship had led to *Swiftsure* being captured by the Dutch during the encounter known as the Four Days' Battle. He had been killed in the action, leaving Lester to take the blame for the consequences of his ineptitude.

'Have you heard from the Navy Office yet?' Chaloner asked, knowing that the only way his friend would recover from the humiliation of losing his ship would be if he was given another, preferably one that was free of superior officers who knew nothing about naval warfare.

Lester nodded glumly. 'They told me that they only appoint captains who have *not* handed their previous commands to the enemy. My life as a sea-officer is over, Tom.'

'I have a passing acquaintance with the Clerk of the Acts,' said Chaloner. 'Samuel Pepys is no fool, and will understand exactly how *Swiftsure* came to be lost. Perhaps he can do something to help you.'

Lester sighed. 'I doubt he has the authority, and even if he does, it will cost more than you or I can afford to make it worth his while.'

Lester was almost certainly right: he was living on half-pay, while Chaloner sent most of his wages to his family in Buckinghamshire. Chaloner hailed from a clan of devoted Parliamentarians, who were being taxed into oblivion now the Royalists were in power; his siblings needed every penny he could provide to prevent vengeful cavaliers from marching onto their property and seizing whatever took their fancy.

'Well, I will try anyway,' said Chaloner, hating to see his normally ebullient friend so low. 'Perhaps he will accept something other than money.'

19

'Such as what?' Lester did not look convinced.

'Information,' replied Chaloner. 'We passed all the intelligence we recently gathered in Holland to the Spymaster General, but perhaps Pepys will appreciate his own copy of our report. It may help him to do his job more effectively.'

Lester brightened. 'It might! Perhaps he would like to hear the truth about Holmes's Bonfire, too. I read what was written in the newsbooks, and it was all brazen lies.'

When *Swiftsure*'s captain and officers – and Chaloner, who had been aboard representing the Earl – had been taken prisoner and transported to a gaol in The Hague, they had decided to turn the situation to their advantage. Picking locks was just one useful skill Chaloner had acquired during his life as a spy, so he and the others had escaped the very same day. Then they had embarked on an exhaustive circuit of every Dutch settlement with a port, making notes on all the enemy's ships and defences.

Their last stop had been a village on the Vlie Estuary called Ter-Schelling, where one hundred and thirty Dutch merchantmen bobbed peacefully at anchor. Even as they watched, English ships appeared on the horizon. These were led by Admiral Holmes, more pirate than naval officer, who was noted for his daring raids. He destroyed the merchant ships, then burned Ter-Schelling in a venture that promptly became known as 'Holmes's Bonfire'.

Chaloner and *Swiftsure*'s officers had included the incident in their report, although they had given Holmes a less heroic role than the one he had claimed for himself – attacking the homes of unarmed civilians was hardly noble, after all. The completed document had been presented to the intelligence services three days ago, which was when they had finally returned to London.

'I must go,' said Chaloner, finishing his coffee. 'I need to tell the Earl about Bowles and get his permission to investigate.'

'I will come with you,' said Lester, morose again. 'I have nothing better to do.'

Seeing his friend's misery, Chaloner saw he had better corner Pepys as soon as he had a spare moment.

Again, there were no free hackney carriages, so Chaloner and Lester were forced to walk to White Hall. Unwilling to stand in the queue of people waiting to be waved through Temple Bar, they cut through Lincoln's Inn, then followed a series of narrow alleys that eventually emerged on the Strand. As they walked, Lester talked about the omens that 'proved' the city was headed for yet another disaster of monumental proportion.

'I am surprised at you, Sal,' said Chaloner, after being regaled with an account of a cow that had assured her owners that the Dutch would be masters of White Hall by Christmas. 'You are a rational man – you cannot possibly believe this nonsense.'

'I would be sceptical of one or two portents,' replied Lester. 'But there are dozens, and they cannot all be wrong. Besides, I have good reason to fear an invasion – namely that our defence is in the hands of inept gentlemen, instead of qualified tarpaulins.'

They turned down King Street, which bisected the vast, sprawling complex that was the King's main London residence. White Hall was alleged to have more than two thousand rooms, although the term 'palace' was a misnomer, as there was no central house, but rather a random collection of buildings that had been erected as and when money had been available. There was nothing grand or imposing about it, other than Inigo Jones's Banqueting House, and the best that could be said about the place was that it was handy for Westminster and the city.

Chaloner and Lester were about to walk through the Great Gate when there was a flurry of activity, followed by a rumble of wheels and hoofs clattering over cobblestones. A cavalcade began to emerge, the King and his latest mistress on prancing stallions at the front, and his favourite courtiers behind, some in coaches and others riding.

'Speaking of inept gentlemen, here come a few of them now,' growled Lester. 'They should be in Deptford, overseeing the provisioning of their ships, not larking about here.'

'They should,' agreed Chaloner, although he suspected that the victualling would go a lot more smoothly without the interference of men who had no idea what they were doing.

'And there is the Duke of York,' said Lester, pointing at a tall, haughty man in a massive light-brown wig. York was the King's brother – and his heir, given that the Queen remained childless. 'As Admiral of the Fleet, *he* should be in Deptford, too. Good God! No wonder all our ships still languish in port! He should be leading by example.'

'The Court must be moving to Greenwich,' said Chaloner, watching the bright, noisy throng flood through the gate and turn towards Charing Cross. 'It is supposed to be cooler there.'

'Well, this intense heat *is* uncomfortable,' muttered

Lester sourly. 'And God forbid that His Majesty should stay and suffer with his people, most of whom do not have the money to decant to more agreeable lodgings.'

After the coaches and horsemen came wagons bearing the paraphernalia essential to maintaining the Royal household's lavish lifestyle – crates of clothes, kegs of wine, musical instruments, fine foods and even a cart of prostitutes. Passers-by stopped to gawp, and there were angry mutters about His Majesty abandoning the city in its time of need yet again – he had not stayed during the plague either.

'Perhaps we should *ask* the Dutch to come,' Chaloner overheard one apprentice mutter to another; they were poulters, judging by the feathers that stuck to their aprons. 'They might be more sober – and cost less – than this worthless horde.'

'Butter-eaters?' asked his crony archly. 'I would sooner cut my own throat.'

'There goes the Poultry Department,' said the first, nodding to a group of very well-dressed courtiers led by the arrogant Catline, who sported a swollen nose from his encounter with the carter not long before. 'Famous for its selfishness, greed and corruption.'

'Yes, and you see the man behind him, dressed all in black?' asked the second. 'That is Jeffrey Crookey, who was appointed solely to undermine our Company. I heard him say as much when he visited Poulters' Hall last week.'

'He was there?' demanded the first. 'Why? I cannot imagine he was invited.'

'No, he just arrived, but Master Farmer was too flustered to send him packing.'

Chaloner watched the elegant men of the Poultry

23

Department attach themselves to the back of the cavalcade with the clear intention of abandoning the city with the rest of the Court, but within moments, one of the King's pages was sent galloping down the cavalcade to speak to them. There was a brief exchange, after which they turned around and trooped disconsolately back inside the palace.

'The King probably wants them to stay here to oversee the preparations for his Adrian Masque,' surmised Lester. 'According to your coffee house, it will be the social event of the decade, attended by all manner of ambassadors and luminaries, every one of them dressed in medieval costume.'

'There is also a rumour that he will jump in a syllabub with all his paramours,' murmured Chaloner. 'Let us hope it is untrue, because that will be unlikely to impress these important people.'

'I heard that they will be expected to leap in as well,' said Lester. 'Then they will all eat the stuff. God save us, Tom! I must get a ship soon, because the affairs of landsmen are beyond my comprehension. We do not do that sort of thing at sea.'

'Most of us do not do it ashore,' said Chaloner, aiming for the gate once the way was clear. Then there was a yell of warning and one last coach rocketed out, the driver lashing his horses in order to catch up with the rest. Chaloner glimpsed two people inside as it hurtled past, and recognised one as Edward Montagu, the current Lord Chamberlain.

'*He* should not be careering off to enjoy himself either,' muttered Lester. 'Another thing I heard in your coffee house today is that his wife died yesterday. But there he is, sitting merrily in his coach with another woman.'

24

'He did not look very merry to me,' countered Chaloner. 'Nor did she.'

'No,' conceded Lester. 'So perhaps I am being unfair. I hear good things about him – he is kind to his servants and loyal to his friends, which is unusual in White Hall.'

Once Montagu's coach had gone, Chaloner and Lester walked through the gate and stepped into the vast open area of cobbles known as the Great Court. It was mostly deserted now that so many courtiers and their servants had left, and the few who remained moved listlessly, enervated by the heat.

Unfortunately, Chaloner and Lester arrived at the Earl's rooms only to be told that the great man had decided to work at home that day. With weary sighs, they left the palace and traipsed towards Piccadilly instead.

Chapter 2

Chaloner had not seen Piccadilly since April, and was astonished by how much it had changed in that short time. In the place of fields and hedges were half-built houses. Some were mansions for nobles, while others were more modest. London, it seemed, stood still for no man, and not even the plague or dire predictions for the future could curb its expansion.

Clarendon House occupied the best location, with nice views towards St James's Palace. It was a stately, ostentatious edifice that was grand enough to attract a lot of anger and hostility. The Earl had recently commissioned high stone walls to protect it, but while these ensured more privacy, they also provided convenient surfaces on which to daub anti-Earl slogans. He was unpopular for many reasons, not all of his own making – as Lord Chancellor, he was blamed for any controversial legislation that was passed during his incumbency, which included laws to suppress nonconformist religion and selling the port of Dunkirk back to the French.

'"King Jesus will Reclaime Dunkirke when He comes to Reign",' said Lester, reading aloud one piece of graffiti that was painted in large black letters on the section nearest the gate; two servants were trying to clean it off, although it was evidently too hot for the vigorous scrubbing required, because they were making scant progress. '*King* Jesus?'

'The Fifth Monarchists must have written that,' surmised Chaloner; he saw Lester's bemusement and elaborated. 'The sect that believes the Son of God will come in person to sit in White Hall and run the country.'

'Do folk really think that?' asked Lester, startled. 'Goodness! These radicals have some very strange ideas.'

'They staged a serious rebellion five years ago,' Chaloner went on, 'but their leader and his captains were caught and executed before it could spread too far. The sect still has about two hundred followers, though, and they all expect Christ to relieve our King of his crown in person.'

'Lunatics!' sniffed Lester. 'But what is written next to it? I cannot make it out.'

'"Let the Sonne follow the Father to the Headman's Blocke",' read Chaloner. 'Crikey! I am surprised the Earl did not order that one cleaned off first.'

'Perhaps he did,' said Lester darkly, 'but his staff secretly agree with the sentiment. I certainly do. At sea, it did not matter whether I sailed for a lord protector or a king, but now I am ashore, it is patently obvious that Cromwell was a much better leader.'

'He was,' acknowledged Chaloner, who had also been happier when Parliamentarians were in control – when he had been a valued and respected member of the intelligence services, reporting to Spymaster Thurloe, a man he trusted and admired. By contrast, the Earl considered his talents unsavoury, and deplored both his own need for them and the man who plied them on his behalf.

'Indeed, I can think of nothing good to say about our King at all,' Lester went on sourly. 'Our country deserves better.'

'Well, he did see the Statute of Tenures through Parliament,' said Chaloner, after wracking his brains for a moment. He saw Lester's frown of incomprehension and explained. 'The laws that abolished the last of the old feudal system. It includes outlawing purveyance – the right of nobles to take virtually anything from their subjects without paying a fair price. It was good to see the back of that unjust practice.'

Lester snorted his disdain. 'Purveyance still exists, Tom, but it just has a new name – taxation. It is all money extracted from the poor to benefit the rich. Perhaps it is time for a new set of regicides.'

'Here is no place for this sort of discussion,' said Chaloner firmly, as they walked through Clarendon House's gate. 'And I especially cannot risk being heard speaking of such matters.'

One of his uncles, another Thomas Chaloner, had signed the old King's death warrant, and would have been executed at the Restoration had he not fled the country first. A second uncle, James, had also been involved in the monarch's trial, although his attendance had been patchy, and he had contrived to be away for the session when the warrant had been circulated for signatures. Because he had played such a minor role in the proceedings, most people had forgotten about him, for which Chaloner was grateful, as it was bad enough having one infamous kinsman to remind people of his family's political allegiances.

If folk remembered he had two, his position at Court would be untenable.

Lester ignored him, although he did lower his voice. 'Do you think any of your Uncle Thomas's old cronies would be willing to try again?'

'Most are dead now, while the remainder are either in exile or in prison. They will not be causing more trouble, thank God. I have had enough upheaval and conflict.'

'Then it is a good thing you are not in the navy,' quipped Lester with a sudden grin. 'Upheaval and conflict are our bread and meat.'

Clarendon House was not a pleasant place to live. It was striking from the outside, built on classical principles with pediments, balustrades and a central cupola, but inside it was more mausoleum than family home. It was full of marble, which meant it was never warm, although this was an advantage that day, and Chaloner was sure it was the coolest place in the city. The servants obviously thought so, too, because the hallway, with its lofty ceiling and sweeping staircase, was full of people who had contrived to find work there, sweeping, dusting and scrubbing. It had never looked so spick and span.

'My word!' breathed Lester, when he saw how every available scrap of wall had been covered by expensive paintings, while priceless statues stood in serried rows like a petrified army. 'Your Earl certainly knows how to cram in the art! Do you not find so much of it in one place rather vulgar?'

Chaloner did, but was not about to say so somewhere he might be heard, so he ignored the question and led the way to My Lord's Lobby, the cold, unwelcoming space that the Earl used as an office. Before he reached the door, he was intercepted by Matthew Wren, the Earl's current secretary. Wren was a quiet, likeable man, slight of build and dark haired.

'It is good to see you home again, Tom,' he said, clasping Chaloner's shoulder. 'We were dismayed when we heard your ship was taken by the enemy – and glad when we learned you had not shared Admiral Berkeley's fate and lost your head to a cannonball.'

Chaloner introduced him to Lester, but then their attention was snagged by two servants who were toting a large crate towards the pantry. They should not have been carrying kitchen supplies through the main house, although Chaloner appreciated why they had flouted the rules – it was quicker and considerably more pleasant than lugging heavy boxes around in the heat outside.

'There must be two hundred eggs in that,' remarked Lester. 'And those are scarce at the moment. I learned in the Rainbow – that fine source of useless facts and gossip – that extended periods of hot weather puts hens off their lay.'

'Eggs *are* becoming rare,' agreed Wren. 'We use a lot of them here, as they are in all manner of dishes that the Earl cannot do without – pastries, pies, tarts, cakes. We also need them for cleaning leather, making tonics, and sticking his wig to his head. But speaking of eggs, have you heard that Bowles the grocer is dead? Poor man. I shall miss him.'

'He was murdered,' stated Chaloner baldly. 'I have come to tell the Earl.'

Wren's hand flew to his mouth in horror. 'Murdered? But he was such a nice fellow – and a member of the Company of Poulters into the bargain. Was it robbers, wanting his money? He was very wealthy.'

'I will find out, if the Earl allows it,' said Chaloner, and nodded towards their employer's lair. 'How is he today?'

'Unhappy,' replied Wren ruefully. 'The King went to Greenwich today, but our master was not invited to accompany him. He has fallen even further from favour now that Lord Bristol is home. Bristol struts around White Hall like a peacock, regretting none of the harm he did to our master with his nasty plots and lies.'

Lord Bristol, sworn enemy of the Earl, had tried to impeach him three years earlier, but the scheme had failed because the 'evidence' he produced was so patently fabricated. As a result, he had been exiled to France, from where he had bombarded his friends with letters, begging them to intervene on his behalf. Some had, and he had raced home the moment the King had let him. His return was a disaster for the Earl, because Bristol had vowed not to rest until Clarendon had been parted from his head. Chaloner fully believed he meant it.

'Had he made any hostile moves yet?' he asked worriedly.

'Lots, although only insults and rumour-spreading so far. However, I am sure he is planning something worse, and this time he may succeed, given that our master has so few friends left these days.'

'So few friends?' echoed Lester, startled. 'But he is such a decent soul.'

'Quite,' said Wren drily. 'There is no room for those in White Hall, where everyone would rather have fun than do his duty. Bristol aims to destroy him, and when he falls, his entire household will fall with him.'

'Then we had better make sure Bristol does not succeed,' said Chaloner with more confidence than he felt.

*

31

Chaloner had been in the Earl of Clarendon's employ for almost four years. They had an uneasy relationship, because the Earl deplored the fact that Chaloner hailed from a staunch Parliamentarian family and had been a Commonwealth spy to boot. By contrast, Chaloner disliked serving a man who, while upright, was also selfish, prim and difficult.

The Earl might be contemptuous of Chaloner's skills, but he also knew he needed them to stay one step ahead of the enemies he had amassed during his fifty-seven years. He had been a tower of strength to the King during the Commonwealth, when they had had no country to call home, but had failed to adapt to changing circumstances – now the King was in his thirties, he no longer appreciated being lectured like an errant schoolboy.

'There you are,' he said snappishly, when Chaloner walked in, although he smiled when he saw who was with him. 'And Captain Lester! What a pleasant surprise.'

The Earl thought highly of Lester, considering him a hero for risking his life at sea. Chaloner, operating in the shady world of espionage, was not nearly so easy to admire.

'I thought I would pay my respects, sir,' said Lester, in the amiable manner that made so many people like him. 'I assume you heard what happened to *Swiftsure*?'

The Earl was sympathetic. 'I am sure its loss was not your fault, Captain. I did my best to prevent that young fool Berkeley from being made an admiral, but I was ignored. Of course, now he is dead, no one will hear a bad word spoken about him, so you will never convince anyone that *he* was to blame for the disaster.'

Lester winced as he recalled what had happened. 'He knew his orders would see us isolated from the rest of the fleet, but he thought one English ship could best twenty Dutch ones. It was arrogance at its very worst.'

'I agree,' said the Earl. 'Unfortunately, if I were to speak out in your favour, it would likely do you more harm than good. My enemies oppose me in everything.'

'Speaking of enemies, I am astonished that Bristol is back,' said Chaloner. 'I thought he was banished for life – lying to the House of Commons is no small crime.'

'Not to mention wrongfully accusing me of high treason,' put in the Earl. 'Every scrap of his "proof" was flagrantly false, and he revealed himself to be deceitful and malicious. But now he is home again, braying that he did nothing wrong.'

Chaloner was disgusted that such a dangerous individual should be unleashed on British politics again. Bristol was undoubtedly brilliant and charismatic, but he was also spiteful, untrustworthy and irresponsible. He plotted and schemed without considering the consequences, and was as much a menace to his friends as to his enemies.

'He is Catholic again, you know,' the Earl went on bitterly. 'He recanted when he thought he would fare better as a Protestant, but now he openly attends Mass with the Queen.' He grimaced. 'Perhaps we should get *him* a boat, in the hope that he will suffer the same fate as the detestable Admiral Berkeley.'

That might solve some of the Earl's problems, thought Chaloner, but the navy could not afford to lose a ship while the country was at war. He changed the subject.

'Have you heard the news about Bowles, sir?'

The Earl nodded. 'His death came as a terrible shock, because he brought me some China pepper on Monday evening, and he seemed well enough then, if a little distracted. And by Tuesday morning he was dead . . . '

33

'Distracted?' pounced Chaloner, recalling that he had thought the same when he had met Bowles earlier that same day. 'In what way?'

'Distant, as if his mind was elsewhere. He was usually very chatty, but that night, he was all business. Why? Are you about to tell me that his death was unnatural?'

'He was stabbed, although there was very little blood, so the wound was missed by the parish constable.'

The Earl shuddered. 'I suppose you had better look into it, then. He was a decent man, and a good Royalist. However, there is something else I need you to do first.'

'Yes?' asked Chaloner warily. The Earl delighted in giving him demeaning, stupid or dangerous tasks, and he had hoped for a respite from them after his recent hard work in Holland.

'It is for a friend,' the Earl went on. 'Edward Montagu.'

'Montagu?' Chaloner was surprised *he* was considered a friend – the Earl had an unforgiving streak when it came to politics, and Montagu had sided with Cromwell during the civil wars and the Commonwealth that had followed.

'I am prepared to overlook his past allegiances now he has sworn fealty to the King,' the Earl went on, reading Chaloner's mind. 'However, the poor man has just lost his wife – Eleanor. She died in her sleep.'

'Poor man indeed,' murmured Chaloner, who had lost two wives himself, and was familiar with the raw anguish of it. He recalled the glimpse he had had of Montagu in his coach not long before, and the man's obvious unhappiness.

'She was his fourth wife, and he was her fourth husband,' said the Earl, slipping easily into gossip mode. 'She had married a baronet and two other earls before she finally settled on him. She was also his second wife's stepmother.'

'Goodness!' muttered Lester, scratching his head. 'That is complicated. Is it legal?'

'Oh, probably,' replied the Earl airily. 'He is expected to marry Margaret Hay next. She is certainly interested, and they are often in each other's company.'

'We saw her in his coach just now,' put in Lester, although Chaloner had not recognised her. 'Perhaps she was there to stake her claim.'

'What do you want me to do for him, sir?' asked Chaloner. 'It cannot be to look into Eleanor's death – not if she died in her sleep.'

'Her death was perfectly natural. She was ten years Montagu's senior, and people in their eighth decade do have a tendency to slip the mortal coil. But tongues are wagging in White Hall, and he is distressed by it.'

'Why are they wagging?' queried Chaloner. 'Because Margaret Hay wants to take Eleanor's place, and there is suspicion that matters were hurried along?'

'Yes, and guess where the rumours originated – with *Bristol*, because Montagu sided with me in trying to prevent his return to Court. I told Montagu that you would prove these vile and hurtful stories to be a pack of lies.'

'I see,' said Chaloner, hoping he would not discover anything to the contrary. Montagu might be charming and affable, but that did not mean he had liked being lumbered with an elderly wife when younger alternatives were on offer. Moreover, who was to say that Margaret Hay was happy waiting for nature to take its course?

The expression on the Earl's face turned calculating. 'Besides, if I help Montagu, he has promised to continue defending me against Bristol. Having a popular man like him on my side does me much good.'

'What exactly do you know about Eleanor's death?'

'Just that she died in her sleep. Unfortunately, when her servants came to wake her in the morning, they found she had been reading a book by John Downes the regicide – it was lying across her chest – which is why Bristol screeches foul play.'

Chaloner was bemused. 'You mean it crushed her? Or the pages were poisoned?'

The Earl regarded him with distaste. 'What a lurid imagination you have, Chaloner! No, it was a treatise on poultry, which others have handled with no ill effects. What caused Bristol to spew forth his nasty allegations is the fact that its author is a king-killer.'

'I do not understand, sir. Is this poultry book allegorical, then? Or political?'

'It is about hen-keeping,' snapped the Earl, growing impatient. 'Downes has an interest in the subject, apparently, although it is not one he can practise himself, given that he is a prisoner in the Tower. But the subject of the book is irrelevant. The point is that Eleanor breathed her last after reading words penned by a regicide.'

Chaloner was still confused. 'So does Bristol claim she died because she liked reading books by enemies of the state? Or because Montagu is ready for a younger wife?'

'He has started rumours about both, although there is no truth in either. Ask Montagu why she had this wretched tome – there will be an innocent explanation. You cannot do it today, though, because he has gone to Greenwich with the King. Unlike me.'

'Bristol was not invited either,' said Lester consolingly.

'At least, he was not in the cavalcade that just left. I would have noticed.'

'What else do you know about Eleanor?' asked Chaloner, watching the Earl give Lester a grateful smile.

The Earl considered. 'Her third husband owned vast plantations in Virginia, and as he left them all to her in his will, she liked visiting them. She had not long returned from her latest foray. Ergo, she and Montagu did not meet very often, which is why they were happily married for so many years – you cannot quarrel if you live on different continents.'

'That is why women love a sailor,' put in Lester. 'We are away for months at a time. Of course, being at sea makes it difficult to meet suitable ladies in the first place . . . '

'Then perhaps you should take the opportunity to look for one now you have some time on your hands,' suggested the Earl. 'You can find one for Chaloner, too.'

'No, thank you,' said Chaloner shortly. 'I am finished with all that.'

'One can never predict what God has in mind for us,' said the Earl piously, then grimaced. 'Although I do wish He had kept Bristol in France.'

Chaloner and Lester left the Earl, and were just crossing the cool expanse of the hall, bracing themselves for the sweltering heat outside, when they were hailed by a familiar voice. It was Wiseman, who had forgotten to don an apron while anatomising Bowles, so his scarlet long-coat was liberally flecked with stains of a darker, more sinister hue.

'My new lodger,' he boomed, giving Lester an affectionate thump on the back that almost knocked him over.

When news had reached London of *Swiftsure*'s fate, Lester's original landlord had assumed he was dead, so had let his house to another tenant. When Lester had reappeared alive and well, only to find himself homeless, Wiseman offered to lease him rooms in his own Covent Garden mansion, on the floor below Chaloner's.

'Yes,' sighed Lester. 'Although I would rather be at sea.'

'So would I, on occasion,' averred Wiseman. 'I am far too busy on land. Take the rest of today, for example. First, I have the Earl's gout, and then I must race to Greenwich for the King's bowels, then I am expected in Westminster for the Lord Privy Seal's bladder. Such is the life of a popular royal surgeon.'

He might complain, but the truth was that he revelled in the number of wealthy clients who clamoured for his services. They hired him not for his compassion or gentle bedside manner – both of which were woefully lacking – but because he really was one of the best practitioners in the city, and patients stood a better chance of survival under his care than anyone else's.

'Did you discover anything more about Bowles after we left?' asked Chaloner.

'Only that he had an unusual extra lobe on his liver. You can see it later, because I have put it in a jar to display in my laboratory.'

Chaloner was horrified. 'You *kept* it?'

'Why not? He no longer needed it. Poor Bowles. He deserved better than death from an assassin's blade, so I shall not mind you bringing the culprit to justice. And when you do, I shall anatomise *him*.'

He meant it quite literally: the Worshipful Company of Barber-Surgeons always had first dibs on the bodies of executed felons.

'Will you settle for examining Eleanor Montagu instead?' asked Chaloner. 'There is no reason to suspect foul play, but her husband and my Earl want to quell some rumours.'

'Rumours arising from the fact that she will soon be replaced by Margaret Hay?' asked Wiseman, and shrugged at Chaloner's wince of this proof that the gossip was circulating fast. 'Lord Bristol told me while I was trimming his corns. He also said she died while reading a seditious tract.'

'Will you look at her now? It would be helpful to know—'

'The soonest I can manage is Saturday afternoon,' interrupted Wiseman shortly. 'I have appointments with the King and other important customers until then, most of them in Greenwich.'

'But that is three days,' objected Chaloner in dismay, 'and Bristol's gossip needs to be nipped in the bud now. Please look at her before you go.'

Wiseman fixed him with a beady eye. 'I cannot put your demands for the dead above those of the living.'

'Then recommend another anatomist,' ordered Chaloner crossly. 'Because we need an incontrovertible verdict of natural causes fast, or Montagu is never going to be free of Bristol's accusations.'

'If you want a judgement that everyone will trust, you must wait for me,' declared Wiseman haughtily. 'No one else owns my reputation as a man who never makes a mistake, so hire someone else at your peril.'

'But—' began Chaloner.

Wiseman cut across him. 'However, I am always doing favours for you, so it is time you did one for me. A patient of mine has a problem, and I want you to solve it for him. I like the fellow, you see.'

39

Wiseman did not like many people, and there were times when Chaloner wondered why he had chosen a career in medicine, given that it was a trade that required a lot of interaction with them.

'Who is he?' Chaloner asked warily.

'Symon Farmer, Master of the Company of Poulters. You know what they do, I assume – regulate trade pertaining to the sale of eggs, small game and birds. What is the matter, Chaloner? You look sullen all of a sudden.'

Chaloner *felt* sullen. He kept a small flock of hens, ducks and a goose in Wiseman's garden, which gave him almost as much pleasure as music, his other great love in life. They had preyed on his mind when he had been in Holland, afraid that Wiseman's servants might tire of caring for them and put them in the pot. He had been touched and grateful to return home and find they were not only alive and well, but spoiled rotten.

However, his fondness for birds meant he disliked what was done to them by the Company of Poulters – stuffed into crates and sent to Scalding Alley to be beheaded, plucked and dressed for the table, or kept in cramped, unsanitary conditions for eggs. Thus he was disinclined to feel much sympathy for the man who led their Company. He knew his opinions flew in the face of convention, but he did not care.

'Farmer is having trouble with higglers,' said the surgeon, when Chaloner made no attempt to explain himself.

'Is it contagious?' asked Lester.

'Higglers are unlicensed traders,' explained Wiseman impatiently. 'They bring eggs into the city, and hawk them at reduced prices. Farmer wants them stopped.'

All commerce was controlled by the City Companies,

which determined exactly what could be sold when and where. The Poulters licensed its members to sell their wares at one of three city markets, between dawn and noon on Mondays, Wednesdays, Fridays and Saturdays. By contrast, higglers' eggs were available at other times and places, and were usually cheaper. However, because they were unregulated, the buyer had no legal recourse for any sickness – or worse – that came about from eating them.

'I appreciate that Farmer dislikes the competition,' said Chaloner coolly. 'But ousting higglers would be like trying to stem the flow of the Thames. Every villager for miles around smuggles eggs to sell in the city on occasion, and while those might be swept away one day, others will be back the next.'

'He knows the problem will never be eliminated completely,' said Wiseman. 'But, until now, it has been kept within acceptable levels. However, over the last month or so, higglers have increased tenfold. Farmer says rebels are responsible.'

'Rebels?' echoed Chaloner warily.

Wiseman grinned. 'I thought that would snag your attention. I refer to men in taverns and coffee houses, who urge folk to ignore the Company's rules and do what they please. They bray that only God has the right to tell men when and how to earn a living, and a lot of Londoners agree.'

'I doubt God has the time to tell people how to sell eggs,' put in Lester doubtfully. 'Not when He has a universe to run.'

'Farmer thinks the rebels' real aim is to remind folk that they live in an unjust world,' Wiseman went on. 'And we all know how fast petty grumbles can erupt into outright insurrection. Anyway, I told him you would investigate.'

Although he resented Wiseman promising his services to all and sundry, Chaloner supposed he *had* better speak to Farmer, because the murder of Bowles and the gossip about Eleanor Montagu's death paled into insignificance when compared to the city in the grip of another bout of civil unrest.

'I do not envy you the tasks you have been set, Tom,' said Lester as they left Clarendon House. 'None of them are work for a respectable man.'

'No,' sighed Chaloner. 'However, if rebellion is in the offing, then someone needs to look into it, while we cannot let Bowles' killer go unpunished.'

'And Bristol's mischief-making?'

'Wiseman will prove that Eleanor Montagu died of natural causes,' replied Chaloner. 'Until then, we will just have to hope that her strange choice of bedtime reading will soon be forgotten by the scandal-mongers.'

Lester regarded him soberly. 'You seem very sure her death was innocent. Why? Because her husband is likeable? Even good men kill, and *that*, my friend, is why I do not envy you the waters in which you have been ordered to swim. So, where will you start?'

'Well, not with Eleanor, given that her husband has left the city and Wiseman will not examine her until Saturday,' replied Chaloner sourly. 'So I think I had better visit Poulters' Hall, and talk to Farmer about these so-called rebels. Perhaps he can tell me more about Bowles, too – Wren mentioned that he was a member of that particular Company.'

'After that, you can go to the Navy Office and demand

an interview with Pepys about getting me a ship,' said Lester. 'That is the most pressing matter, as far as I am concerned.'

They parted ways at Charing Cross, Lester to go home, and Chaloner to visit Poulters' Hall. It was a long, hot walk, so the spy was irked to arrive only to be told that the Company headquarters closed early on Wednesdays. With an irritable sigh, he returned to White Hall, aiming to listen in person to Bristol's rumours about Eleanor Montagu.

But although he lurked in the palace until the small hours, he learned nothing new. The most influential courtiers were in Greenwich, and those who remained behind were either too lowly to know anything useful, or were not the kind of people to gossip anyway. Eventually, hot and weary, he trudged home through the stifling city, wondering if the soothsayers were right to claim the world was in the process of being burned to a cinder.

Chapter 3

It was difficult to sleep when there was not so much as a whisper of a breeze, and Chaloner wished he had not chosen to live in an attic. His rooms were sweltering, even with the windows open, and he was sure that every biting insect in London had moved in with him. By the time the sky began to lighten in the east, he had barely slept a wink, and had been stung so often that he feared he would look as though he had a pox.

He washed in the water the servants had left for him, then donned a loose linen shirt and his thinnest breeches, although he was sweating again even as he tied the laces. He considered going coatless, but suspected he would not be allowed inside Poulters' Hall if he arrived too casually attired. He drew the line at putting on a wig, though – not only was it itchy and attractive to lice, but wearing it in hot weather made him feel as though his head was being boiled.

He filled a large bowl with water for the wild birds and went to the window. Sparrows came to drink immediately, but scattered in panic when a kite flew in to join them. The huge raptor took a short but vigorous bath that flung most of the water out of the basin, then flapped away to preen on next door's roof.

Although it was only just growing light, tradesmen were arriving to set up store in the piazza below. Technically, this was illegal, as they had no licences, but the people who lived nearby found their services convenient, and the vendors themselves did a roaring trade. The authorities had turned a blind eye for years, with the result that once-temporary stalls were now regarded by their owners as permanent fixtures.

The market folk bellowed cheerfully to each other as they worked, shattering the silence of early morning with their banging and crashing. They sold a range of foodstuffs, from cheese and butter to fresh fruit and vegetables, although meat, fish and eggs were only available at the official outlets. At least, that had been the case before Chaloner had left in April. Now, he could see one man with baskets of eggs, and another with rabbits. Clearly, they were higglers, although he suspected that would not stop customers from snapping up their wares anyway, almost certainly at bargain prices.

He moved away from the window and looked around his rooms, surprised by the realisation that they felt like home. It was the first time he had experienced a sense of belonging since his regicide Uncle Thomas had dragged him away to join Cromwell's New Model Army shortly after his fifteenth birthday. Since then, he had never lived anywhere long enough to feel settled.

His domain comprised a bedroom, a parlour and a tiny pantry. In pride of place were his viols, the only items he owned of any value. Then there was a shelf of books, and framed sketches of his two wives, which he had drawn himself. He did not want to forget their faces, even though neither marriage had been perfect.

He grabbed a wide-brimmed hat to keep the sun out of his eyes, and went down to the garden. All the piazza houses had grounds at the back, and Wiseman's was attractive with a small orchard, vegetable plots and a paved area for sitting. In the middle of the fruit trees was the sturdy coop where Chaloner's hens, ducks and goose roosted. He let them out and scraped their overnight droppings on to the compost heap. Then he scattered some grain and sat on a bench to watch them forage. While he did so, he began to plan his day.

Most pressing was Poulters' Hall, where he would ask about the 'rebels' who encouraged the unlicensed sale of eggs, and also see what he could learn about Bowles. Hopefully, someone there would have information about both, after which he would spend the rest of the day following up on it.

And Eleanor Montagu? He had done as much as he could for her the previous evening, and was now stuck until Wiseman gave his expert opinion – or until Montagu and Margaret Hay returned to the city and could be questioned.

Finally, there was Lester. Chaloner hated to see him unhappy, and resolved to visit Pepys that day, even if it meant neglecting his other duties. His friend's predicament had no more crossed his mind when he looked up to see him approach, wearing the blue long-coat and white breeches that comprised the unofficial uniform adopted by all tarpaulins. Lester's face was drawn, suggesting he had slept badly, too.

'Are you ready?' he asked.

Chaloner blinked. 'Ready for what?'

'To begin your investigations, of course. I cannot sit around pining for the ocean all day, so I have decided to help you.' Lester gave a wry smile. 'And it will allow me to make sure you do not forget to petition Pepys.'

'I will not forget, Sal,' promised Chaloner. 'But I do not need help today.'

'Nonsense,' said Lester briskly. 'Now, do I hear some of your hens announcing the arrival of fresh eggs? Good. We shall break our fast with them, and then be on our way.'

Chaloner suppressed a grimace. He preferred working alone, and Lester was far too bluff and honest for the kind of ruse he was invariably obliged to deploy while conducting the Earl's business. But then he looked at the tired, sad eyes, and could not bring himself to say so. He handed Lester the eggs, and indicated that he should precede him to the kitchen.

Poulters' Hall was on a tiny thoroughfare named Butcher Hall Lane, a short distance north of St Paul's Cathedral and within spitting distance of Newgate Market. Although not as grand as some of the more ancient foundations, like the Goldsmiths, Mercers and Fishmongers, it was nevertheless impressive, with a façade that had been carved with a variety of birds, all of which Company members were licensed to trap, kill and sell.

Chaloner and Lester were admitted to the main chamber, which comprised a large, airy room with plain glass windows that allowed light to flood inside. There were woollen carpets on the floor, dyed to match the upholstery on the benches that ran at right angles to the dais at the far end. The poulters' coat of arms was carved into the wall above the massive fireplace – an elegant creation of cranes, swans and pelicans, all picked out in gold, blue and red.

Within moments, they were joined by the Company's beadle, a tall, thin, stooped man in a black and grey coat, who put Chaloner in mind of a heron. He introduced himself as Charles Collins, and proudly claimed that he had held his post for twenty-six years. When the beadle eventually paused for breath, Chaloner told him that he and Lester were there because Wiseman had offered their services to Master Farmer regarding the sudden rise in illicit egg sellers.

'But *I* am working on the higgler problem,' Collins cried angrily. 'I am managing perfectly well by myself and I do not want any help, thank you very much.'

'We have no wish to step on your toes,' said Chaloner apologetically. 'But—'

'I have kept higglers within acceptable levels for years,' the beadle went on, 'but suddenly, just these last few weeks . . . well, they are everywhere. He blames me, of course.'

'Who does?' asked Chaloner, bemused. 'Farmer?'

'No, his deputy – William Drinkell.' Collins all but hissed the name. 'He thinks I am too old, and itches to replace me with one of his cronies. But being a beadle is more than just running around after higglers, you know. It is about spotting who flouts Company rules in other ways, and then dealing with the matter quietly and discreetly.'

'What other rules have been flouted?' asked Lester curiously.

'Well, one of our members has been overcharging for speciality produce – bittern and stork, mainly – while another was caught selling wares that were well below

48

Company standards.' Collins puffed himself up importantly. 'Indeed, it is because of me that the city's poulters are so highly regarded.'

Personally, Chaloner had always been under the impression that poulters were rather unsavoury – some were rich and finely dressed, but most were grubby and smelled of chicken muck. It was not the place to say so, however, so he settled for asking exactly how the higgler situation had recently changed. Collins's face turned dark and angry as he replied.

'Rebels are calling on anyone with a laying bird to come to the city and sell their eggs whenever and wherever they please.'

'Why do you call them rebels?' asked Chaloner curiously. 'Do they combine their message about eggs with one to take up arms against the government?'

'Well, no,' conceded Collins. 'But what would you have me name them?'

'Agitators,' suggested Lester helpfully. 'It does not sound quite so . . . turbulent.'

Collins sniffed. 'Well, these *agitators* stand in taverns, ale-shops and coffee houses and urge folk to ignore the law – that if a man wants to sell eggs, then he should do it. They also say that higglers should trade any day of the week that suits them, because birds lay when they lay, so why not sell eggs whenever they happen to pop out?'

'Do you know these agitators' names?' asked Chaloner.

Collins scowled. 'No, I do not, because every time I get word of their whereabouts, they contrive to disappear before I can catch them.'

'Then can you describe them?'

Collins's scowl deepened. 'All I can tell you is that

there are two of the rogues. They spout their poison at night, when it is dark, and they are careful to stand in the shadows. I have not met anyone yet who has seen their faces.'

'What about their clothes?' Collins looked puzzled, so Chaloner elaborated. 'Are they like yours, or ones worn by poorer folk? Are there feathers stuck on them, suggesting they are poulters themselves? What about the quality of their footwear – expensive or cheap?'

Collins raised his hands helplessly. 'They dress like any Londoner. There is nothing to identify them from their attire.'

'Then is there a particular tavern or a coffee house that they favour?'

'Yes – the ones between Pudding Lane and Fish Street Hill, especially the Sunne Inn, the King's Head and Skiner's Coffee House. I have tried lying in wait in each, ready to pounce when they start their poisonous tirades, but if I choose the King's Head, they go to Skiner's, and if I go to Skiner's, they pick the Sunne . . . '

'So they know you,' surmised Chaloner, thinking that Collins was tall, thin and stooped enough to be distinctive, even if he tried to disguise himself. It would not be difficult to evade him. 'And if they spot you, they go somewhere else to preach.'

'We are more vulnerable to rogue traders than other Companies,' Collins went on unhappily. 'Most farmers have a few chickens, so it is easy to smuggle eggs into the city to sell. The same is true of game birds, hares and rabbits. The butchers do not have this problem – you cannot sneak a dead cow into London without someone noticing.'

'I imagine not.'

'Of course, customers love higglers,' said Collins bitterly. 'They charge less than us, so folk think they are getting a bargain.'

'Have you considered lowering your prices?' asked Chaloner, aware that the Company kept them artificially high, so that a dozen eggs or a rabbit were well out of the reach of many Londoners. 'The competition would drive the higglers out of business.'

'Impossible! Our goods are produced to the highest standards, and quality costs. The higglers' wares might be cheaper, but they are inferior. Unfortunately, their customers do not appreciate the dangers of shoddy goods until they are poisoned by them and spend days in the latrine.'

Chaloner continued to ask questions, but Collins could tell him nothing more, so he supposed he would have to visit the taverns and coffee houses around Pudding Lane and Fish Street Hill himself. He changed the subject to Bowles.

Collins smiled sadly. 'He was one of our nicest freemen. He always slipped me a stick of cinnamon or a twist of pepper when he came to meetings. I shall miss him.'

'He was murdered,' said Lester baldly. 'Stabbed.'

Collins's jaw dropped in shock. 'No! Was he killed by robbers, then? There would have been lots of money in his shop, because he had plenty of wealthy customers. For a start, the navy bought his spices to disguise the taste of the rancid meat they feed to their sailors.'

'True – we could never sail without spices from Bowles on board,' acknowledged Lester. 'The fleet would mutiny if our salted pork and beef were served up as they are.'

'He sold eggs, too,' Collins went on. 'He bought them from Drinkell, who has a huge farm north of the city.'

'Did Bowles have any enemies in the Company?' asked Chaloner. 'Anyone who was jealous of his success and riches?'

'Not that I ever heard,' replied Collins. 'But I shall fetch Master Farmer for you. Perhaps he will know. Wait here.'

Collins was gone for some time, and when he eventually reappeared, it was not with one man in tow, but three.

The first was Symon Farmer, a tall, anxious person who kept wringing his hands in agitation. He spent the first ten minutes of the conversation explaining that he was under Wiseman's care for a nervous complaint, one exacerbated by the stress of higglers. He exuded a sense of fluttering inefficiency, and Chaloner was not surprised that illegal trade had proliferated under the leadership of so weak and ineffectual a man.

The second was William Drinkell, who held the post of 'Renter Warden', which made him Farmer's deputy. He was smooth-faced, black-haired and possessed a beak of a nose that made him look like a crow. He oozed confidence and authority, and could not have been more different from his Master if he tried.

The last was a freeman named Henry Newdick, whom Chaloner disliked on sight. He had long, oily hair that he wore parted in the middle, and a face that was lined and leathery. His clothes were well made, but grubby, and he stank of chicken manure. There was an air of cold ruthlessness about him that made Chaloner pity any bird in his care.

'Newdick manages my egg farm,' explained Drinkell, and smiled with pride. 'It is the largest in the country, and has three thousand laying hens, all housed in specially designed barns. This method of production is the way of the future, and in time, all poulters will follow my example.'

'*Three thousand?*' breathed Chaloner, unable to imagine it. However, he doubted Drinkell's prediction would prove to be right, as even the most ignorant of farmers would know that birds performed best in small flocks, and that such vast colonies ran contrary to nature.

'I plan to double that number next year,' Drinkell bragged on. 'Newdick has a rare talent for the work, and together, we shall change the face of egg production for ever.'

'So you claim,' said Farmer, regarding him unhappily. 'But I am not convinced that your new system is very nice for the birds.'

'Very nice!' sneered Newdick, and turned to Chaloner and Lester. 'The Master's business is rabbits, so what can he know of the egg trade?'

'By "mass producing" eggs,' Drinkell continued, 'we can churn them out so cheaply that anyone can afford them, not just the rich. How can that be a bad thing?'

'At a penny apiece, they are prohibitively expensive at the moment, see,' said Newdick. 'And the cost will rise even more as the hot weather continues to affect supplies. But with our methods, prices will remain much more stable, and paupers will love us.'

'But you sacrifice quality for quantity,' objected Farmer. 'Your eggs taste bland compared to those from the little farms with freely wandering hens.'

'A small price to pay,' shrugged Drinkell. 'Besides, people will soon grow used to the milder flavour, and in time they will find all other eggs overly strong. The future lies with places like mine, not ones that fret over maintaining standards.'

53

Chaloner was astonished that a poulter should dismiss the quality of his produce as immaterial, but Farmer changed the subject before he could say so.

'Collins told us that Bowles was murdered. Are you sure it was not an apoplexy?'

'Quite sure,' replied Chaloner. 'And the Lord Chancellor has ordered an enquiry.'

'How dare he!' cried Drinkell angrily. 'It is none of his business. And anyway, if – *if* – Bowles was unlawfully killed, we are quite capable of looking into it ourselves.'

'It most certainly is his business,' countered Chaloner, irked by Drinkell's presumption. 'He is responsible for law and order in this land, so he can order an enquiry into anything he likes. And he wants me to find out what happened to Bowles.'

Drinkell regarded him furiously. 'I do not care! We do not want outsiders prying into our affairs, thank you very much.'

'Quite,' put in Collins. 'I am perfectly equal to catching a killer *and* suppressing higglers. As Company beadle, I—'

'Neither task is within your abilities, Collins,' interrupted Drinkell contemptuously, and turned to Farmer. 'So, if you want these matters resolved, I recommend you dismiss this bumbling ancient and appoint Newdick instead.'

'Do not worry, Collins,' said Farmer, eyeing Drinkell reproachfully as the beadle gave a whimper of distress. 'No one will replace you as long as I am Master. However, as Chaloner carries the Lord Chancellor's authority, he can explore Bowles' death *and* the higglers for us.'

'But—' began Collins in dismay.

Farmer raised a hand for silence; it shook with tension.

'You can pursue those who break our other rules, Collins. No, do not argue! I have made my decision.'

'What you have made is a grave mistake,' said Drinkell between gritted teeth. 'I shall not allow strangers to interfere with Company business when *I* am in charge.'

'But you are not Master yet,' said Farmer with a small spurt of defiance, and turned his back on his deputy to address Chaloner. 'Is it true that a lot of eggs were smashed when Bowles died?'

'Every one of them, which makes me suspect it was deliberate,' replied Chaloner. 'Do you know of anyone who might have done it? Someone jealous of his success, perhaps?'

'No Company man would stoop so low,' averred Newdick unconvincingly. 'So I imagine a higgler is to blame. They are a dangerous horde, which is why it needs a qualified poulter to find out why they are suddenly so abundant.'

'Quite,' agreed Drinkell. 'Higglers are not only violent, but devious, too. Just look at the way they have run circles around poor foolish old Collins.'

'They have not!' objected Collins, stung. 'And for your information, I recruited Mr Hill to help me today. He is prowling around Pudding Lane as we speak.'

'Then let us hope he does not go the same way as the last fellow you hired,' said Farmer worriedly. 'Poor James Hadie – dead to an assassin's blade.'

'Wait a minute,' said Lester uneasily. 'Are you saying that this Hadie was murdered while investigating higglers – the task that you expect Tom and me to carry out for you?'

'He was brutally slain on Tuesday night,' said Drinkell before Farmer could reply. 'So you might want to think again before meddling in our affairs. Two other freemen

55

were within spitting distance when it happened, but that did not deter the killer.'

'So there are witnesses to the murder?' asked Chaloner, ignoring Drinkell's efforts to unnerve him. 'Were they able to identify the culprit?'

'It was dark, so no,' replied Farmer. 'One wanted to give chase, but Hadie begged her to stay. He was a good man, thinking of her safety even as he breathed his last. He was Bowles' friend, so it would not surprise me if their deaths are connected.'

'We should speak to these witnesses at once,' said Chaloner.

'Why?' demanded Collins. 'They saw nothing useful – I interrogated them myself.'

'They will be in the pantry, sorting eggs,' Farmer told Chaloner, overriding his beadle's objections. 'Their names are Elsie Henwood and Dorcas Eades.'

'Women have no place in an honourable Company,' put in Newdick sullenly. 'They are societies for *men*, and admitting females is unnatural.'

'Rather like you creating flocks of three thousand chickens, then,' muttered Chaloner under his breath.

But Drinkell disagreed with his friend. 'Elsie and Dorcas know almost as much about eggs as we do, Newdick, and their birds are healthier, stronger and more productive than any I have ever seen. We should learn their secrets and apply them to our own hens. It will make us a lot more money.'

'And they gave us a new bench as part of their admission fee,' put in Farmer. 'A very *nice* bench with rabbits on it. Shall we speak to them before any more of the day is lost?'

*

56

The 'pantry' transpired to be a vast cellar beneath the hall, in which were stored a huge number of dressed birds, along with countless trays of eggs stacked on purpose-built shelves. There were also items that Chaloner would not have expected to see in a domain of poulters – several large hams, boxes of fruit, and five huge casks of wine.

'For our feast tomorrow,' explained Farmer. 'We shall celebrate Holmes's Bonfire, which was a great victory for our country and a poke in the eye for the Dutch. Admiral Holmes is a true and brave hero.'

'Right,' said Chaloner, wondering what was 'true and brave' about setting fire to the homes of unarmed villagers.

'We shall have fifty boiled eggs, too,' put Drinkell. 'From my own farm.'

'Fifty *tasteless* eggs,' muttered Farmer disparagingly.

'And a hundred fat ducks,' added Newdick. 'I shall wring their necks later today.'

His grin suggested he was looking forward to the task, and Chaloner was hard-pressed to mask his distaste for the man. Then there was a gasp of shock from Lester.

'Is that a *human* corpse?' he blurted. 'Lord, it is! I hope you do not intend to eat *that* tomorrow, as well.'

'It is Hadie,' explained Farmer sheepishly. 'He will be buried tonight, and we put him down here because it is cooler than the hall.'

Personally, Chaloner felt that food and dead people were best stored apart, and wondered how many of the following day's feasters would be put off their victuals if they learned what had been in the cellar with them. He peeled the covering away from the body.

Hadie had been about forty years of age, with long

57

brown hair and a pleasant face. He was naked under the blanket, and blood had dried on his skin.

'I have not had time to dress him for the grave yet,' explained Collins apologetically. 'I will do it later.'

'Let me,' offered Newdick keenly. 'I have no objection to handling corpses.'

Farmer regarded him with dislike. 'I am sure you do not.'

Newdick took umbrage at this, and Collins made matters worse by laughing. To prove his point, Farmer began to cite other examples of Newdick's unsavoury pastimes, so Drinkell stepped in to defend him. While they were occupied with each other, Chaloner indicated that Lester was to help him roll Hadie on to his side. Lester obliged, and neither needed Wiseman to tell them the cause of death: there were three small but deep puncture marks in Hadie's back.

'I have never seen wounds like those before,' whispered Lester, frowning. 'Not that I have great experience in sly murder, of course.'

'They *are* unusual,' agreed Chaloner. 'However, I saw an identical one yesterday on Bowles the grocer.'

Lester regarded him uncertainly. 'You think this man and Bowles were dispatched by the same culprit?'

'I think they were both murdered with long, thin blades.' Chaloner glanced around him. 'Or perhaps some slim, pointed tool used specifically by poulters. If that is true, it will narrow down any list of suspects.'

'Then you keep Farmer and his cronies busy,' instructed Lester, 'while I scout around to see if I can spot anything to match Hadie's wounds.'

Chaloner opened his mouth to stop him, but Lester could move with surprising speed for a man of his size, and was gone in a flash.

'Where is he going?' demanded Newdick as the captain disappeared around the end of a rack of shelves.

'To admire the eggs,' replied Chaloner, and changed the subject before they could take issue with him. 'What more can you tell me about Hadie?'

'Well, he was a spy during the Commonwealth,' supplied Newdick. 'He monitored the fanatical religious sects that met in Allhallows the Great on Thames Street.'

'I hardly think *that* will have a bearing on his death,' said Farmer archly. 'Not after so many years.' He turned back to Chaloner. 'When Cromwell died, Hadie became a clerk.'

'Not a poulter?' asked Chaloner.

'Not all our members are in the small game and egg trade,' explained Farmer. 'Bowles enlisted in order to build on his business contacts, while Hadie joined to contribute to our charitable work.'

'We are noted for our generosity,' put in Collins proudly. 'We feed the poor *and* fund schools.'

'Although that will stop when I am Master,' muttered Drinkell. 'We have far more worthy schemes to finance – like investigating how to improve productivity in hens.'

Farmer ignored him. '*Please* find Bowles' killer, Chaloner. Hadie's too, if you can. Then look at our higgler problem. If you succeed, I shall be eternally grateful.'

'I will try,' said Chaloner, aware of Drinkell and Newdick exchanging the kind of glance that said he would have no help from them. 'May I speak to the two witnesses now?'

At the very back of the cellar, two women were sorting eggs into boxes of straw, ready to be taken to market the following day. One was tall with gold hair bundled under a clean white cap. The other was shorter, plumper and wore a red scarf over her dark curls. Despite his vow to avoid romantic entanglements, Chaloner could not help but notice that the fair one was unusually pretty.

He also saw that Lester had not spent long looking for possible murder weapons, and was talking to them, smiling at the dark one in a way that suggested he was rather taken with her. It was fortunate for the investigation that Chaloner had discreetly assessed the poulters' tools while he had been talking to the others, and was able to say with confidence that none could have caused the victims' injuries.

'I am afraid there is not much to tell,' said fair-headed Dorcas, after Chaloner explained what he wanted to know. 'It happened on Tuesday, at about ten o'clock at night.'

'We had been in Southwark, visiting kin.' Elsie took up the tale. 'We had crossed the Bridge, and were walking up Pudding Lane to our lodgings in Fish Yard, when we heard James Hadie call our names. We started towards him . . . '

'But a man darted from the shadows around Skiner's coffee house, and stabbed him,' finished Dorcas. She shook her head. 'It happened so fast! We ran to help, but Hadie was already dying when we reached him.'

Elsie frowned. 'Before he fled, the killer grabbed Hadie by the front of his shirt. He shook him, as if trying to make him reveal something . . . '

Dorcas disagreed. 'It looked to me as if he was hunting for valuables. Regardless, the rogue had slithered away into the darkness by the time we arrived. I was ready to give chase, but Hadie begged me to stay – he could not speak, but he made gestures.'

'He *tried* to talk,' said Elsie. 'I think he wanted to tell us his assailant's name, but all he could do was make fluttering motions with his hands.'

'What kind of fluttering motions?' asked Chaloner curiously. 'Show me.'

Obligingly, Dorcas flapped her fingers, but Elsie was dissatisfied with the performance and did it herself. Her movements were much more precise.

'Hadie signalled *exactly* like that?' asked Chaloner urgently. 'You are certain?'

Elsie nodded. 'Yes, why? Does it mean something to you?'

'If you have replicated these signals accurately—'

'Which I did,' stated Elsie confidently.

'Then Hadie was making letters with his fingers,' explained Chaloner. 'W, I and L.'

'What nonsense!' scoffed Drinkell. 'You cannot possibly draw conclusions from all that random wiggling. You are a charlatan!'

Chaloner was not about to explain that Hadie had deployed a system of communication that every Commonwealth spy had been taught, which Hadie would have known, because Newdick had already said that he had been employed by Cromwell's government to monitor dissidents. He was spared from devising an alternative reply by Lester.

'Tom is an authority on this sort of thing,' the captain declared loftily. 'And if he says Hadie spelled out WIL, then Hadie spelled out WIL.'

'Then what does it mean?' asked Drinkell, although it was clear he was still sceptical. 'That Hadie's killer was named Wil? Did he mean William?'

'Your first name is William,' said Farmer pointedly.

'It is,' acknowledged Drinkell coolly. 'However, I

imagine Hadie would have been more inclined to spell out a *surname*, given that time was of the essence, would he not? Williams, Williamson, Wilkins . . . the possibilities are endless.'

'Perhaps it refers to a place,' suggested Collins, sheepish because this was a clue he had missed when he had interviewed the women. He looked hard at Drinkell and then at Newdick. 'Willesden, perhaps. That is where your farm is located, is it not?'

'Hadie never visited it,' said Drinkell firmly. 'I extend invitations to very few people, and he was not among them.'

Collins shot him a disbelieving look, which triggered another quarrel between the four male poulters. While they bickered and the two women listened with raised eyebrows, Lester whispered in Chaloner's ear.

'Why would Hadie use finger signs on two people who would not understand them? It makes no sense.'

Chaloner had no answer, but when Farmer, Drinkell, Collins and Newdick continued to argue amongst themselves, he indicated that the women were to resume their tale.

'Hadie died,' replied Dorcas simply. 'Elsie hammered on the coffee-house door to raise the alarm, but the killer was gone. We looked for him, of course, but the task was hopeless.'

'What did you notice about him?' asked Chaloner.

'Nothing,' replied Dorcas. 'It was too dark.'

'But I watched him leap up after looming over his victim,' put in Elsie, 'and he did not move like a very tall man, if you understand what I mean.'

Strangely, Chaloner did. 'Is there anything else you can tell us?'

'He was wearing a cloak, despite the heat, and a high-crowned Puritan hat,' replied Elsie. 'But I had the sense that it was a disguise – that this man wanted any witnesses to think he was a religious fanatic, to throw us off his scent.'

'Do you know what I think?' asked Dorcas. 'That he was a higgler. Everyone knows that Collins hired Hadie to spy on them. Well, one decided that it was too risky to leave such a man alive, so he was dispatched.'

'That makes sense to me,' said Drinkell, overhearing and rejoining the discussion. He glared at Farmer. 'I told you it was a bad idea to let Collins employ a helpmeet. Just because Hadie was a spy during the Commonwealth does not mean he was any good at it.'

'Well, he told me he was,' said Collins, resenting the criticism. 'But Hill will not allow himself to be dispatched. He has promised to sit in the Sunne and the King's Head all day, listening for the agitators to start spouting their poison. Then he will pounce.'

'Only if he can stand,' said Drinkell acidly. 'And if he has been drinking all day . . . '

'Send him to Skiner's Coffee House instead,' suggested Elsie. 'He cannot get drunk in a place that sells no ale or wine. Dorcas and I will monitor the taverns instead.'

'No!' cried Farmer in horror. 'It is far too dangerous, and I refuse to sanction your involvement. You are women!'

'We are,' agreed Elsie mildly. 'But that does not mean we are incapable of listening for agitators, following them home, and reporting their whereabouts to Beadle Collins. Or to Mr Chaloner and Captain Lester, if you prefer.'

'And I suspect we will do it better than he did,' said Dorcas, nodding at Hadie. Then she glanced disparagingly at Chaloner and Lester. 'And perhaps better than them, too.'

We shall see about that, thought Chaloner indignantly.

He sailed out of Poulters' Hall, bristling with confidence and purpose, but was obliged to go back inside again when he realised that Lester was not at his heels. He found the captain leaning nonchalantly against a wall, chatting to Elsie.

'Stay,' suggested Chaloner, feeling it would do Lester good to spend time with someone who had so obviously caught his fancy.

'I am afraid I must go back to work, Salathiel,' she said, and smiled in a way that made Lester blush with pleasure. 'It is market day tomorrow, and I cannot leave Dorcas to do everything alone.'

'Christian names already,' remarked Chaloner, as he and Lester walked down Butcher Hall Lane together. 'That did not take long.'

Lester smiled beatifically. 'Elsie is a fine lady, and I think I shall court her. You can have Dorcas. Neither of them is married.'

Chaloner raised his eyebrows. 'How did you learn that in so short a space of time?'

Lester shrugged. 'I asked. We seamen do not beat around the bush when we want to know the lie of the land.'

'Well, leave me out of it, Sal. I have enough to do without my life being complicated by romance.'

'Nonsense,' declared Lester. 'Now, I appreciate that you feel the need for us to race away and hunt villains, but can we visit the Navy Office first? I would consider it a great kindness.'

Chaloner nodded, and when he spotted an empty hackney carriage, he jumped out to hail it – the Navy Office was near the Tower, and he had no intention of walking so far in the heat. They climbed in, and Lester began to hum, his spirits lifted by the encounter with a lady who seemed amenable to his attentions. Then the driver initiated a conversation about a coffin-shaped cloud he had seen in the sky above St Paul's Cathedral the previous week.

'It was blood-red and the lid was off, ready to receive a corpse,' the man elaborated darkly. 'Perhaps it signified the death of our city, because it was a very *big* casket. After all, we came close to losing London last year, while the pestilence raged. I lost twenty-one kinsmen, and dozens of friends.'

'I am sorry to hear it,' said Chaloner, and his thoughts turned, as they often did, to his two wives, both in their graves because of plague.

'Well, what can you expect from a year with three sixes in it?' sighed the driver. 'I recommend you go to church every Sunday and repent of your sins, because only then will you survive the calamity that is so fast approaching.'

'Goodness!' breathed Lester. 'You are a cheery soul.'

Chapter 4

The Navy Office was located on the east side of Seething Lane, near the junction with Crutched Friars and in the shadow of the Tower of London. It was in an enormous building, with a front courtyard, a rear garden, two hundred windows and innumerable rooms, fifty of which were large enough to accommodate a hearth.

Chaloner and Lester alighted from their hackney carriage, and walked into the lobby, where a porter was on duty to repel anyone who might make a nuisance of himself inside. This included sea-captains desperate for a ship, so Chaloner was forced to leave Lester kicking his heels in the garden while he went in search of Pepys by himself.

The building was as gracious within as it was outside. Handsome furniture, wood-panelled walls and elegant artwork abounded, although Chaloner barely noticed any of it. His attention was caught by the men who worked there, because there was an atmosphere of barely contained panic among them – they scurried along with their heads down and worried expressions plastered across their faces. None would stop to tell him why.

When he reached Pepys's office, he was irked to discover that the Clerk of the Acts had been to work and had gone home again, even though it was barely mid-morning.

'Perhaps I can help,' offered the young official whose desk was in the antechamber that led to Pepys's domain. 'I am his secretary, Will Hewer.'

Chaloner knew there was no point in begging favours from a minion, and had no intention of wasting his time by trying. 'Has something happened?' he asked instead, as several men hurtled past the door, their clattering footsteps signalling urgency and fear.

'We have just heard that the Dutch fleet is out in the Channel,' explained Hewer, 'whereas our own ships are still being provisioned, and will not be ready to leave port for days. Ergo, we are now under enormous pressure to speed matters up.'

'I should hope so,' said Chaloner, unimpressed to learn that 'enormous pressure' had not been applied sooner. 'The Dutch will not attack London, but they may well raid some coastal town instead, to do to us what Holmes did to Ter-Schelling.'

'I know that,' snapped Hewer. 'But how can we hurry when everything is against us? We have no money to buy supplies, the weather is always too rough to transport goods to ships at anchor, and we do not have crews to sail the victualling craft anyway, because the navy has snapped them all up.'

Chaloner was not surprised to learn that the government's inefficiency extended to the navy, as well as all the other areas in which it poked its grubby fingers. Cromwell would not have tolerated such a state of affairs, and Chaloner wished yet again that the Lord Protector had not died, and that the King and his worthless rabble were still living off their long-suffering kinsmen in France.

'When will Pepys be back?' he asked, changing the subject lest Hewer read the disgust on his face and reported it to the wrong people.

'Well, he has just ordered some new purple upholstery for his closet, so his mind will be on that for the foreseeable future,' replied Hewer. 'Come back next month.'

'I will see him tomorrow,' stated Chaloner, thinking that the navy's predicament was unlikely to improve if its shore officials were more interested in home furnishings than carrying out the duties for which they were paid.

'You are welcome to try,' sniffed Hewer. 'But do not be surprised if he is not here. And do not ask me where he lives, because it would be unethical to tell you. Besides, he will dock my pay if I do.'

Chaloner left before he said something he might later regret. He found Lester, who hurried towards him with hopeful eyes. Chaloner shook his head and the captain's shoulders slumped, although Chaloner thought it was absurd of him to have expected instant success. For some inexplicable reason, Lester had purchased a lobster while Chaloner had been busy inside, and he carried it under his arm.

'Perhaps you should go to Deptford again,' suggested Chaloner, racking his brain for something to distract him from his disappointment. 'The fleet is still in port, so talk to your fellow captains. One might put in a good word for you, which is a safer bet than Pepys anyway. Captain Harman, for example. He knows the Duke of York, does he not?'

And as the Duke of York was Lord High Admiral, he could allocate a ship to a deserving commander with no more than a snap of his fingers.

'They quarrelled,' said Lester glumly, shifting the lobster from one arm to the other. 'And the other captains cannot use up favours on me anyway, because they need them for themselves. Or rather for their ships.'

'What do you mean?'

'The only way to get your vessel properly rigged, armed and victualled is by bribing officials,' explained Lester. 'If you wait for them to do it without greasing their palms . . . well, you are likely to be sent to sea with no food, no ammunition and leaking like a sieve.'

'Then let us hope the Dutch never learn about this state of affairs,' muttered Chaloner, more disgusted than ever, 'or they may decide to invade London after all.'

'Where shall we go now?' asked Lester despondently. 'And do not say home, Tom, because I shall go mad if I have to stay indoors, brooding.'

'Pudding Lane then,' said Chaloner. 'To hunt killers, rabble-rousers and those who break the city's trading laws. Lord, Sal! I never thought *that* would be a sentence to pass my lips. My father would be appalled if he knew how low I have sunk. There are times when I am glad he is not alive to see it.'

'Your salary – no matter how you earn it – keeps his other children out of debtors' gaol,' said Lester tartly. 'Needs must in these difficult times, Tom, and he would have no right to frown on what you do.'

There had been 'difficult times' for almost as long as Chaloner could remember, so Lester's words were of little comfort. But dwelling on the matter would do no good, so he pushed it from his mind and set off for his next port of call.

*

69

According to Beadle Collins, the agitators who encouraged higgling operated mostly on Pudding Lane, Fish Street Hill and the alleys that ran between them. Fish Street Hill was the main road to the Bridge, so was always busy; it carried the salty scent of the river, overlain with a hefty dose of seafood. By contrast, Pudding Lane was smaller and narrower, and was said to be named for the 'puddings' – offal – that dropped from butchers' carts as they were transported to waste barges on the Thames. The road reeked of blood and rotting meat, but was quieter than its traffic-choked neighbour, and safer for pedestrians.

The biggest taverns in the area were the King's Head and the Sunne Inn, but there were many smaller ones as well, not to mention ale-shops, coffee houses and 'ordinaries' – establishments where cheap meals could be bought. Altogether, there were dozens of places in which agitators could foment unrest, and Chaloner found himself rather daunted by the challenge.

He decided to begin in the King's Head, an ancient but venerable building that was popular for its proximity to the Bridge and the main highways in and out of the city. It had one entrance on Fish Street Hill and another on Pudding Lane, and its rambling jumble of rooms, stables and courtyards spanned the entire distance between them. It attracted a wide range of customers; nobles and merchants tended to hire its private chambers, while traders and boatmen formed noisy throngs in its public ones.

'I shall not mind sitting in here for a while,' Lester confided, as they found a bench in a shadowy corner and settled down to monitor their surroundings. 'Elsie told me that when she and Dorcas finished work, they would come here to look for agitators, too.'

'They are already here,' said Chaloner. 'We must have taken longer than I thought at the Navy Office.'

'Where?' demanded Lester, looking around eagerly.

'By the door,' replied Chaloner. 'Disguised as apprentice-boys to avoid being mistaken for prostitutes.'

'No one would believe that!' exclaimed Lester, shocked. 'Not of them.'

'Two unaccompanied women in a tavern? Think again, Sal. No, do not wave and give them away! If they want to talk to you, they will come over. For all we know, they have already identified the culprits and are watching them, ready to report back to us.'

'They should not risk themselves,' muttered Lester worriedly. 'They are poulters, not spies. Female freemen are rare, but Farmer accepted them, because they are so talented. There was a lot of opposition from the Company bigots, of course, but Elsie and Dorcas can handle Newdick and his ilk.'

'You really did learn a lot about them in the few minutes you had together,' said Chaloner, thinking it must have been an interrogation worthy of any experienced spy.

Lester grinned. 'Elsie enjoyed talking to me, and I to her. But catching killers is hungry work. Shall we eat while we are here?'

Without waiting for a reply, he handed his lobster to the King's Head cook, while Chaloner was offered a choice of chicken stew or something called 'a dish of meat'. As he never ate bird, he ordered the meat, pleasantly surprised when it transpired to be quite palatable and contained nothing he could not identify. Lester's lobster returned boiled to perfection and garnished with anchovies and olives.

71

While they ate, they watched the other patrons, but there was no sign of anything untoward, other than an orange-seller who distracted people with her fruit while an accomplice picked their pockets. After a while, Chaloner cornered the landlord, Rob Cradock, and asked if he was aware that his tavern had been used by men who did not have the best interests of the city at heart. Cradock, a harried, anxious man, sighed heavily.

'I had no idea until one of my pot-boys came to tell me. We are busy in the evenings, when everyone wants ale to wash away the dust of the day, and it was then that these rogues chose to spout their poison.'

'Did you hear any of what they said?' asked Chaloner.

'I did, and it was hard to tell them to stop when it was clear that my public-room customers agreed with every word. Their speeches were about the unholy alliance between White Hall and influential Companies like the Goldsmiths, Mercers and Poulters – how they unite to oppress the common man with laws that favour the wealthy.'

'So what did you do?'

'I gave them free jugs of ale. While they drank, I told my musicians to play as loud as they could, and thus prevent the rogues from making themselves heard again. They have been back several times since. I send them packing, but they always return.'

'Are they here now?'

'No, and do not ask when they will appear next, because they come and go at random. Do not beg me to describe them either – they arrive after dark, and their hats shadow their faces. All I can tell you is that they truly believe what they bray, because you can hear the conviction in their voices.'

'Fanatics, then,' surmised Chaloner. 'What do they

preach, exactly? For the law to be broken? For your customers to indulge in violence and rebellion?'

'They urge folk to consider the liberties that have been lost – the right to sell goods where and when they please; the right to buy at reasonable prices, not ones set by rich City Companies; and the right not to be treated like dirt by a lot of arrogant barons.'

'They do not sound like rebels to me,' remarked Lester. 'More like champions of the downtrodden. No wonder your patrons listen to them. It is an appealing message.'

'Yes, if you are a pauper,' averred Cradock. 'But I am a freeman of the Company of Vintners, and I do not want a lot of free-traders coming along to steal my business. I would rather these rogues kept their seditious opinions to themselves. Of course, it is the Company of Poulters that suffers most from illicit hawkers.'

'Is it?' asked Lester. 'Why is that?'

'Because every country yokel has a few hens, and it is easy to shove eggs in a basket and sell them on a street corner. And the Poulters are not as powerful as some of the other Companies – they do not have the resources to catch every higgler who rears his ugly head.'

'They have a beadle who has been trying his best.'

'Collins?' scoffed Cradock. 'He is too old, and should make way for a younger man. Besides, how can he and a few hirelings monitor the whole city? It will take an army.'

'He seems to have managed well enough until these agitators came along,' Chaloner pointed out.

'He did,' acknowledged Cradock. 'But now the flood gates have opened, the poulters will *never* eradicate higgling. It is here to stay, and my only concern is that the same thing does not happen to inns and taverns.'

*

Pleasantly replete, Chaloner led Lester to the Sunne. Like the King's Head, it could be entered from Pudding Lane or Fish Street Hill, although its rooms and yards were smaller and shabbier than those of its grander neighbour. Lester claimed he was still hungry, and ordered a plum syllabub. This arrived in a massive basin, and was clearly intended to be shared by several people. Chaloner tried a spoonful, but it was unpalatably sweet and so heavily laced with cheap brandy that he declined to take more.

The landlord was Thomas Padnoll, a tall man with a yellow moustache. He was in a good mood, because a group of courtiers had hired one of his function rooms. They were enjoying a noisy dinner with several lively prostitutes. Thus Padnoll was not only being paid for the venue and the food, but a percentage of what the women would earn, too.

'It is White Hall's Poultry Department,' he explained to Chaloner and Lester when he came to refill their flagons. 'They are treating themselves to a feast, because the rest of the palace has decanted to Greenwich with the King, but they were left behind. Apparently, His Majesty wants them to organise a party in honour of the Pope.'

'An English-born pope,' interjected Chaloner quickly, suspecting the tale would have London's Protestant majority foaming at the mouth unless it was tempered with a few facts. 'One who is long dead.'

'There was an English pope?' asked Padnoll sceptically. 'That does not sound very likely. But I do not care what they do in White Hall, just as long as they come here when they want a break from all the pomp. Oh, they are leaving now – I had better go and make sure they do not forget to settle the bill.'

Chaloner watched the courtiers swagger towards the Pudding Lane exit, all drunken yells and noisy chatter. The women were draped around the most intoxicated ones, who were more likely to risk a quick romp in an alley. The arrogant Catline brought up the rear, looking like a brawler with his bruised nose. He was less inebriated than his cronies, and his mood was sullen, perhaps because his face still hurt from the carter's assault. Chaloner tried to make himself inconspicuous, but Catline saw him anyway.

'What are you doing here?' the courtier demanded unpleasantly. 'Hiding from your pompous Earl? His days are numbered now that Bristol is back, so take my advice and find yourself another master before the current one drags you to the scaffold with him.'

His braying remarks brought his friends tottering back to see what was going on. Chaloner knew them all by sight, but only one other by name: Jeffrey Crookey, who bore the peculiar title of Supernumerary Groom. It was an open secret at White Hall that Crookey had been hired to sniff out cheap supplies, so that his colleagues could pocket the difference. Chaloner recalled what the apprentices had said about him outside White Hall the previous day – that he bullied members of the Company of Poulters. Chaloner did not doubt it for an instant.

'Perhaps we can find him a place with us,' said Crookey in his soft and rather sinister voice, as he eyed the spy appraisingly. 'But he will have to prove himself worthy first. Play me at cards, Chaloner. If you win, I will make you my deputy; if I win you can tell us how your Earl thinks he might defeat Bristol.'

'Excellent idea!' crowed Catline. 'What do you say to lanterloo, Chaloner?'

'I say no thank you,' replied Chaloner shortly, sure they intended to cheat, and that even if he defeated them, Crookey did not have the authority to appoint him to a post in the Poultry Department anyway – not that he would accept one, of course.

'How about a round with rapiers, then?' asked Catline, fingering his sword. 'I hear you are good, but I doubt you are better than me.'

'I hardly think this is the place to find out,' said Chaloner, knowing who would be charged with public brawling if he agreed to meet the challenge. 'I understand you have been left in London to oversee preparations for the Adrian Masque. That is quite an insult – to be forced to labour while your friends have fun in Greenwich.'

Catline eyed him with dislike, and his hand tightened on his sword. Crookey gave a low, hissing laugh.

'The masque will make us famous, and it will be remembered for years to come, so we have no objection to ensuring that all goes according to plan. It is for the King, after all. Come, Catline. We have pressing business to attend today.'

Chaloner could not imagine what was 'pressing' about organising a debauched party, but was unwilling to prolong the discussion by saying so. He watched Crookey lead his colleagues out on to Pudding Lane. A few burst into song as they tottered away. Catline joined in, but Crookey did not, and Chaloner noticed his dark eyes were everywhere, seeing everything and missing nothing.

'Not a man to cross,' said Lester, echoing Chaloner's thoughts. 'A sly fellow, who would be more likely to stab you in the back than confront you like a man.'

'Yes,' agreed Chaloner. 'And I imagine he did business

with Bowles, given that one of the Poultry Department's responsibilities is to procure eggs for the King's table.'

Lester blinked. 'You think *he* knifed the grocer – and Hadie, given the identical wounds? Do you have any evidence?'

'None whatsoever,' replied Chaloner airily. 'Other than the fact that I do not like him.'

The Sunne was quieter once the White Hall contingent had left, and Chaloner was not the only one who was glad to see them go. The other patrons relaxed, and then began to mutter disparagingly about decadent courtiers. Padnoll came to sit with Chaloner and Lester again, revelling in the fact that he had just hosted such august guests, and caring not a whit that the rest of his customers did not share his high opinion of them.

'They are characters,' he said admiringly. 'Especially Mr Catline, who is the life and soul of any party.'

'Do they come here a lot?' fished Chaloner, always interested in the habits of men who posed a threat to his employer.

'Not often enough for me,' sighed Padnoll, and lowered his voice conspiratorially. 'They are friends with Lord Bristol, the man who has sworn to destroy that nasty old Earl of Clarendon. Bristol is great fun, whereas the Earl is a bore, and I shall dance for joy when his head is on a spike outside Westminster Hall.'

'Did they tell you what Bristol plans to do?' Chaloner was sorry his employer should be subject to such enmity from a man he had almost certainly never met.

'Just that he will strike so fast that the Earl will not know what hit him. Incidentally, you know that scurrilous pamphleteer – the Paladin? Well, he published a

77

broadsheet today, which claims that Bristol urinates in White Hall's potted plants. It is a wicked lie!'

Unfortunately, it was not, and Chaloner wondered who had spilled the beans, because even the most dim-witted courtier knew better than to provide the general populace with that sort of ammunition. He hoped the culprit was not his Earl, as Bristol was sure to find out, and then there would be repercussions.

He continued to ask questions, but Padnoll knew nothing tangible about Bristol's malicious intentions, and eventually the landlord turned the discussion to the 'papal ball'.

'The highlight will be the syllabub,' he enthused. 'Catline says it will be the best dish ever created.'

'A syllabub like this?' asked Lester, gesturing to his empty bowl. Chaloner had no idea how he had contrived to eat so much sugar and cream without being sick.

'Catline says it is a *new* recipe,' replied Padnoll with the delight of a man who loved to cook. 'One involving whipped egg yolks, which is very exciting, as the resulting flavour will be unique. But speaking of eggs, have you heard the latest omen? A hen laid one with a flaming cross branded into it, after which she spoke to a local mystic in Fish Yard.'

'And what did this miraculous bird have to say?' asked Chaloner warily.

'That all wrongs will soon be righted, and that a new age will dawn in which the righteous will inherit the Earth.'

'What, *again*?' groaned Lester. 'I have been regaled with promises of a looming Utopia for as long as I can remember, but not one has ever come to pass.'

'This one will,' averred Padnoll. 'Next Sunday, apparently

– the day after the papal ball. Well, at least the King can enjoy his syllabub before he loses his crown.'

'I am sure that will be a great comfort to him,' muttered Lester, although Chaloner was alarmed to hear that a specific day was being mooted. In his experience, that usually meant there were people who intended to help it along. 'Although I imagine he would rather things stayed as they are.'

'So would I,' averred Padnoll. 'I much prefer merry Cavaliers to grim old Puritans. Cromwell tried to close me down during the Commonwealth, because he said I promote wantonness and immorality. Well, of course I do! It is a lot more fun than endless praying.'

'I am surprised you claim to be a Royalist,' remarked Chaloner coolly. 'Because we have it on good authority that agitators come here to make anti-government speeches.'

'They did it *once*,' spat Padnoll crossly. 'I was away at the time, and I was livid when I found out. I told my staff to trounce anyone who tries it again.'

'It was not only once,' argued Chaloner. 'According to reliable sources, these agitators are regular visitors to your tavern.'

'Then your "reliable sources" are mistaken,' stated Padnoll firmly. 'I am loyal to the King, and I do not want him replaced by a lot of virtuous dullards. I assure you, no rebel will ever use *my* domain to spread his poisonous message.'

He stalked away, muttering about tidying the room that Catline and his cronies had hired. Through the open door, Chaloner could see food sticking to the ceiling and wine dripping down the walls, making him wonder if Padnoll would be quite so devoted to courtiers once he had finished cleaning up the mess they had made.

While Padnoll bawled for mops and brushes, Chaloner questioned the staff, and quickly ascertained that they did not share their employer's political sympathies; whenever he went out, they turned blind eyes to anyone who came to tell Londoners their rights.

'Not that we condone sedition,' said the cook, unconvincingly. 'But we believe that everyone should be allowed to say what they think.'

'Very democratic,' muttered Chaloner. 'Are these champions of liberty in here now?'

'No, and we do not expect them any time soon,' replied the cook. 'They were in last night, and they never visit the same place two days in a row.'

'Do you know anything about them? Their names? Where they live?'

The cook shook his head. 'But if you meet them, tell them to come here whenever Padnoll is out, and we will give them free ale. Speaking the truth is thirsty work.'

In the interests of thoroughness, Chaloner insisted on visiting every alehouse, 'ordinary' and inn on Pudding Lane, Fish Street Hill and the alleys between them. There were so many that it took him and Lester the rest of the day and most of the evening. To avoid standing out in their courtly clothes, they shoved their long-coats in an old sack bought from a miller, both glad to be down to shirtsleeves as the city continued to swelter.

'We must have been everywhere by now,' grumbled Lester as they emerged from a tiny alehouse in Fish Yard run by a crone named Widow Noest. 'Because if I drink any more, I shall explode.'

Chaloner leaned against a wall for a moment, wits reeling from the amount of beer he had swallowed in

80

their quest – so far fruitless – for information. He took a deep breath, surprised when all he could smell was the sweet scent of bread from a nearby bakery – he had been expecting the usual reek of urine and rotting rubbish.

The old city was full of tiny squares like Fish Yard. It was a fraction of the size of Wiseman's garden, and was surrounded on all sides by towering buildings – in an attempt to extend available living space, each upper floor was bigger than the one below, so that they leaned towards each other overhead, all but blotting out the sky. It had roughly twenty houses, most large enough to accommodate several hearths, and was unusually clean, with no piles of fermenting rubbish in the corners or chamber-pot deposits staining the walls.

'Elsie and Dorcas live here,' said Lester, glancing around hopefully as if expecting them to materialise. 'Perhaps we can call on them.'

'It must be nearly nine o'clock, Sal,' Chaloner pointed out. 'Far too late to visit respectable ladies.'

'That will be their house,' said Lester, pointing out one with gaily painted window shutters and potted plants decorating the doorstep. 'Are you sure it is too late to see them? Elsie did invite me to drop in at any time.'

Chaloner did not reply, because he had spotted a coffee house in the shadows, identifiable by the sign above its door portraying a long-spouted jug.

'That must be Skiner's, where Hadie was killed.'

With a weary sigh, Lester followed him towards it. Chaloner opened the door, and was assailed by the familiar scent of burned beans and pipe smoke. Like most coffee houses, Skiner's comprised a single room with long tables and benches, all positioned to facilitate the controversial discussions for which such establishments were famous.

Inside, fifteen or so men sat huddled over their coffee dishes. As one, they stopped talking and stared at the newcomers. Chaloner's first thought was that some treasonous debate had been in progress, but no one looked particularly alarmed or guilty, so he surmised it was just the appearance of two strangers at an unusual time that had startled them into silence.

The owner, Erasmus Skiner, was a plump man with a mop of golden curls, startlingly blue eyes and pockmarked skin. He chewed constantly on what Chaloner assumed was a wad of tobacco, and his accent revealed him to be a man from the north.

'What news?' he demanded, making it sound more like a challenge than a greeting.

'The Dutch fleet is out,' provided Lester helpfully. 'But ours is not.'

'We already know that,' said Skiner. 'But sit down and tell us about it anyway. You look like one of them sea-officers, so you might know more than the average man.'

'I do,' averred Lester, accepting a dish of scalding coffee, then helping himself to sugar nipped from the loaf on the table. Chaloner took the coffee but declined the sugar, in his customary silent but futile protest against the inhuman conditions of the labourers who toiled on the plantations where it was grown.

While Lester regaled Skiner and his regulars with an eye-witness account of the Four Days' Battle, Chaloner studied them covertly. They were a mixed bunch, ranging from well-dressed merchants to scruffy street traders. One was selling eggs from a basket at the back, so Chaloner went to talk to him.

'Want some?' the man asked; he was small and greasy, with the kind of face that could only belong to a felon. 'Fresh-laid today and very cheap. My name is John Bibie, and I am known for the fine quality of my eggs.'

'Do you ply your trade here regularly?' asked Chaloner conversationally.

Bibie's expression changed from amiable to suspicious. 'Why? Or will you call me a higgler, and forbid me to sell my wares to friends and neighbours? You do not come from the Company of Poulters, do you?'

Chaloner shook his head. 'But I have met one of its freemen – James Hadie.'

He did not mention that Hadie had been dead at the time.

'He was murdered on Tuesday,' mused Bibie. 'The first I knew about it was when Dorcas and Elsie sounded the alarm. They thought the killer might have come from in here, but he never did. We had the door locked.'

'Did you?' asked Chaloner curiously. 'Why? Because rebels were telling you about your right to trade as you please?'

'They are not rebels,' countered Bibie hotly. 'They are liberators. They urge us to throw off the shackles imposed by the rich, and they are right. Why should I not sell my wares when and where I like? The men from the Company of Poulters are bullies, and I hate the lot of them.'

'Do you hate them enough to kill one?'

Bibie eyed him beadily. 'I did not dispatch Hadie, if that is what you are asking. I was in here when he died, with a score of witnesses to prove it.'

'Then what about your "liberators"? Were they here when he was stabbed? Or did one slip outside and

83

dispatch someone whose remit was to put an end to their antics?'

'No, because everyone knows they were in the King's Head that night,' replied Bibie. 'And for your information, we locked the door because I was counting my day's earnings. There was a lot of it, as eggs are scarce these days and I can charge a premium.'

'Did you know Bowles the grocer?' asked Chaloner, beginning to be frustrated by the lack of progress. 'He was also murdered, probably by the same man who took Hadie's life.'

Bibie was clearly shocked. '*Bowles* was murdered? But I thought he had an apoplexy.'

'The King's personal surgeon says otherwise. So, can I assume from your reaction that you did know Bowles?'

Bibie nodded. 'He bought my eggs. He sold the ones he purchased from the Company of Poulters to his customers, but he got his personal supply from me. Mine are better quality, see, because my hens are free to roam and scratch outside. A lot of the Company's eggs come from farms where the birds are kept in barns – those have no flavour.'

Chaloner considered the information. If Bibie was telling the truth – and there was no reason to think otherwise – there was a problem in assuming that Hadie and Bowles were dispatched by the same assailant. Hadie had likely been killed for undertaking surveillance work for Beadle Collins, but Bowles had defied the Company by buying eggs from higglers. Ergo, on the surface of it, they appeared to be on different sides. Chaloner recalled the letters that Hadie had signalled as he lay dying – W, I and L – and asked Bibie if he knew what they might mean.

'No idea,' replied Bibie. 'But there are no Wills or Williams in this coffee house, so I suggest you look elsewhere. Now, I cannot hang around here all night. I got work to do.'

Chaloner watched him open the door and slink away into the darkness outside. He supposed he should report his higgling to Beadle Collins, but part of him felt Bibie had a point. Why should he not sell his wares to whomever he pleased? Moreover, Chaloner did not like the sound of Drinkell's vast hen-stuffed barns, and suspected Bibie's birds had a much better life. Besides, his job was to locate the agitators, not persecute the paupers who followed their recommendations.

By the time Chaloner rejoined the discussion at the main table, it had moved on from the war, and views were being aired about the end of the world. There was a general consensus that it would happen in the year with three sixes, but opinions varied as to what it would entail. Some believed that King Jesus would oust His Majesty from White Hall and take over the reins of government Himself, while others expected a more dramatic finale, involving war, famine, death and pestilence.

'Those are already here,' said a quietly spoken Welshman; he was perhaps sixty years old, with sombre eyes and an intelligent face. 'War with the Dutch, the recent plague, and now our crops wilt in the heat so that the harvest will fail and folk will starve.'

'King Jesus will put everything right when He comes in glory next Sunday week,' declared the man who sat next to him, a bulky fellow with brown hair and bushy side-whiskers; his robes indicated that he was a physician, but his words were those of a Fifth Monarchist. 'He will forbid sin, so the world will be a much nicer place to live.'

'He will have to do more than forbid it, Vernon,' said the Welshman soberly. 'Men have free will, and as long as they can choose, most will opt for the wrong path.'

'Not once King Jesus is here,' averred Vernon passionately. 'He will sweep away all that is old and corrupt, and replace it with goodness. No one will want to err after that, and we shall all live in Paradise.'

'You think this will happen in ten days?' asked Chaloner, yet again suspecting that a plot was afoot to bring it about, as was usually the case when specific dates were mooted.

Vernon gave a superior smile. 'It will, because Wogan's woman foresaw it.'

'She is not my "woman",' objected the Welshman uncomfortably, although his embarrassed blush suggested otherwise. 'She is just a friend.'

'Do not lie to us, you old dog!' jibed Skiner. 'Besides, Docility Gander is a great mystic, and you should be honoured that she has chosen you as her paramour.'

'I am not—' began Wogan, mortified.

Vernon cut across him as he turned back to Chaloner. 'Her hen laid an egg branded with a fiery cross yesterday, and then it spoke a message from the Lord of Hosts. It said that all wrongs will be righted two Sundays hence, and the just shall inherit the Earth.'

'She did say the chicken communicated with her,' acknowledged Wogan carefully. 'But I was not aware that it mentioned any particular timetable for the Second Coming.'

Vernon shrugged. 'Docility is not the only one with connections to God, so the Almighty must have passed that part of the message to some other worthy soul.'

'But why ten days?' pressed Chaloner, aware that if there was going to be some crisis engineered by fanatics, he needed to learn as much as he could in order to thwart it.

'Probably because that is when Satan in Rome will breathe his last,' replied Vernon.

'Satan in Rome?' echoed Lester, bemused. 'You mean the Pope? How do you know when he will die?'

'Because I read it in *The London Gazette*,' said Vernon. 'So it must be true.'

The London Gazette was the new biweekly government publication that had replaced the old *Newes* and *Intelligencer*. The updated title had not improved its content though, so Chaloner remained disappointed by the paucity of home news and horrified by the brazen misreporting of information from overseas. He would certainly not regard it as a bastion of truth, and his natural inclination was to take most of it with a good pinch of salt.

'There was an article noting the Pope's poor health,' he acknowledged, 'but nothing about him being on his deathbed.'

Vernon's eyes blazed. 'Well, the King is sure that the rogue is destined to die, because he is organising a great party in White Hall to celebrate.'

Chaloner supposed he should not be surprised by how the Adrian Masque would be interpreted by those with agendas of their own, but even so, he was horrified.

'Have any of you been encouraging higglers?' asked Lester in so blunt a non-sequitur that Chaloner stiffened in alarm.

'Some brave fellows *did* come to remind us of our rights,' replied Skiner warily. 'But before you castigate me, you should know that I am not in the habit of censoring what my patrons want to say. Any man can air his views in a coffee house – it is an ancient tradition.'

Actually, it was a very recent tradition, thought Chaloner, recalling that there had only been a handful of such places before the Restoration.

'You should not give the impression that you are a wild insurgent, Skiner,' said Wogan quietly. 'Not when all you do is listen.' He addressed Chaloner and Lester. 'Like most folk, including myself, everyone here is all talk and no action.'

The sheepish expressions – particularly Skiner's – suggested this was true, and that while they might wish they were bold radicals fighting for just causes, the truth was that they were no more than mealy-mouthed malcontents.

While Wogan had been speaking, a distant memory stirred in Chaloner's mind, of another man with a melodic Welsh accent holding forth to a group of determined men – men who had later signed the old King's death warrant. The occasion had been at the home of his uncle, and Chaloner had eavesdropped from under the stairs. With sudden appalled clarity, he recalled that *that* man had been named Wogan, too.

'Do not tell me you are *Thomas* Wogan,' he blurted, shocked.

The Welshman's eyes widened in shock. 'No, no – I am *Tam* Wogan,' he gulped, and stood abruptly. 'Now, if you will excuse me, nature calls. Your coffee has a peculiar effect on a man's bladder, Skiner.'

He made for the door, and although he tried to move casually, Chaloner could see the tension in his body. The spy waited a moment, then followed, leaving Vernon pontificating about what else would happen when King Jesus arrived to set up shop in White Hall.

Chaloner did not have far to look for Wogan. The Welshman had gone to the house opposite and was fumbling to set a key in its lock.

'I know who you are,' said Chaloner softly. 'I recognise you.'

Wogan spun around in fright, and his hand dropped to the knife in his belt, but something warned him that Chaloner would be no easy prey. He sagged in defeat, leaning against the wall for support. 'How?'

'My uncle,' replied Chaloner. 'Another Thomas. You were his friend.'

Wogan peered at him in the faint light from the lantern that hung above his door, then gave a sudden, startled smile. 'You are old Tom Chaloner's nephew! Yes! I can see him in your eyes. He was a character – always full of japes, which we needed in those gloomy times. I liked him very much.'

Chaloner's uncle had indeed been a 'character', which meant that everyone he had met tended to remember him, although not always very fondly.

'You are taking a risk,' Chaloner said wonderingly. 'You will suffer a traitor's death if the authorities catch you here. All the other regicides are either in their graves, in prison or hiding in another country.'

'I know,' sighed Wogan. 'I was arrested at the Restoration, too, but I managed to escape to Jersey and from there to Vevey in Switzerland. I should have stayed away, but I missed my country desperately. There is a word in Welsh – *hiraeth*. It means a sickness for the land. It is not something you English readily understand.'

'But this is not your land – it is London. You are insane to come here.'

'Perhaps,' sighed Wogan. 'But I am weary of living like a fugitive.'

'Does anyone else know who you are?'

'As far as I know, the only man to guess my identity is Vernon, but he is a friend and would never betray me. Moreover, my crime was more than seventeen years ago – no one remembers me now anyway.'

'I did,' Chaloner pointed out.

'But only because of your uncle,' argued Wogan. 'And no one else around here has regicides in the family. Besides, I have come to realise that beheading a monarch was a terrible mistake, and I am more sorry than I can say. I am a different person now, and all I want is to make amends for my offence with good works.'

'What good works?' asked Chaloner suspiciously.

'I live frugally so that I can use my money to assist those less fortunate than myself. I run a house for orphans, provide a nourishing broth for the homeless each day, buy medicines for the sick, and care for the sailors wounded in the Dutch war.'

'Even so, you cannot stay.' Chaloner felt the discovery put him in a horribly invidious position: to ignore it would make him guilty of treason himself, but to tell the authorities would condemn Wogan to a dreadful death. 'Your charitable deeds will count for nothing if you are found – and you will be.'

'I have had no trouble so far,' said Wogan, and gave a small, self-deprecating smile. 'To be honest, I suspect the authorities *do* know who I am, but they look the other way because they applaud what I do.'

'Perhaps they do, but it is only a matter of time before

90

one of them sees you as a way to curry favour with the King, and then you will be arrested.'

'No one will do that,' argued Wogan with what Chaloner thought was unwarranted confidence. 'There will be consequences if I am taken, not least of which is that the government will have to look after all these unfortunates itself.'

'The King will not care how popular you are with the poor,' warned Chaloner. 'Or what you do to improve their lot. He will just want you dead.'

'Then that is a chance I must take,' said Wogan with quiet dignity. 'Because I am *needed* here. And if I am caught . . . well, perhaps I deserve a traitor's fate. Even His Majesty cannot despise me as much as I despise myself.'

Chaloner supposed his courage was laudable, even if it was shockingly naive. He wondered what he would do in Wogan's situation. Resign himself to living in exile for the rest of his life, looking fearfully over his shoulder day and night? It was a dismal prospect, and he found himself beginning to understand why the regicide had decided it was time to stop running. He nodded a brisk farewell, and returned to the coffee house alone.

'I saw you talking to Bibie earlier,' said Skiner, coming to refill Chaloner's dish with his powerful brew before sitting back down. 'He lives in Pudding Lane, but his back door opens into Fish Yard. Wogan rents the attic. The place is a hovel, but Wogan refuses to leave it for nicer accommodation because it would cost more and thus take money from those he helps. He is a saint.'

'He is,' agreed Vernon, and then winked rather sala-ciously for a man who believed his sins would be weighed

91

in a few days' time. 'He rents the adjoining room for Docility. She is Farriner the baker's maid, but he does not provide lodgings, so Wogan does it instead.'

'She repays him by cooking broth for the homeless,' said Skiner. 'And he may be telling the truth about their relationship being chaste, because she is too busy communing with God for frolicking about. Did you hear what He told her about the Dutch – that we are in imminent danger of invasion?'

Everyone had opinions about that, so it was some time before Chaloner could bring the conversation around to higglers and the murders of Bowles and Hadie. When he did, he asked all the questions he could think of, but although everyone had all manner of theories about why they had died, no one could support them with actual evidence. Eventually he conceded defeat and stood to leave. Before he could open the door, it flew open, and a woman stood there, breathing hard. She was small, slim, and her auburn curls had escaped from under her hat to curl around her elfin face. She was prevented from being pretty by hard eyes and a thin-lipped mouth.

'John Vernon,' she shouted. 'You must come at once.'

'Is it King Jesus?' cried Vernon, surging to his feet with an expression of fierce joy. 'He has come to claim White Hall early?'

'No, it is Mr Hill,' replied the woman. 'The man hired by Beadle Collins to catch higglers. He has been stabbed, and folk are calling for a physician.'

Chaloner and Lester joined the procession that streamed out of the coffee house and hurried to Pudding Lane, where Hill had been found outside the Sunne tavern. As they went, Vernon informed them that the person who had made the announcement was none other than Docility Gander, the famous mystic, herself.

'And she *is* Wogan's woman, no matter what he claims, because she is devoted to him, and he to her.' The physician lowered his voice. 'Although even if she can communicate with miraculous chickens, I find it hard to like her. She is very opinionated.'

Chaloner nearly laughed, thinking this was rich coming from a man who propounded the wild views of the Fifth Monarchists. 'Is she?'

'I am surprised God chose her as a messenger, to be frank,' Vernon went on. 'He would have done better to pick me, because I am a respected member of the Pudding Lane community, which means folk listen to what I have to say.'

Chaloner watched Docility lead the way at a rapid clip to the Sunne, lantern lifted aloft. She oozed confidence and rectitude, and he was not surprised that her predictions had become the talk of the city.

They reached Pudding Lane, where a large crowd had gathered around a figure that lay on the ground. The victim was so still that Chaloner knew Vernon's skills would not be needed. Landlord Padnoll was among the gawpers, wringing his hands in dismay.

'This had nothing to do with me,' he informed anyone who would listen. 'I am as shocked as the next man by a corpse outside my tavern.'

'Well, *I* shall not weep for Hill,' spat one man, safe in the knowledge that darkness and a large hat rendered him anonymous. 'He aimed to report us all to the Company of Poulters for selling eggs. He will not be missed.'

A growl of agreement suggested that most of the

gawpers sided with the higglers. Vernon eased through them and Chaloner followed, wondering if the unfortunate Hill had been dispatched by the same person who had killed Bowles and Hadie. He tried to see the onlookers' faces as he went, aware that the culprit might well be among them, but it was far too dark, even with some folk holding lanterns.

'Who found him?' asked Vernon, kneeling next to the body to feel for a life-beat.

'I did,' came a familiar voice, and Bibie elbowed his way forward. 'But do not accuse *me* of dispatching him, because he was cold by the time I stumbled across his corpse.'

'Yes, he has been dead for hours,' acknowledged Vernon, standing up. 'So there is nothing I can do for him now. He is in God's hands. But why was he not discovered sooner?'

'Because he was hidden in the water butt,' explained Bibie, pointing to a great vat placed to catch the run-off from the tavern's roof, although it had not rained for so long that the keg was empty. 'I told Master Padnoll, and we pulled him out together.'

Vernon blinked. 'Why were you poking about in a barrel at this time of night?'

'I was looking for water,' replied Bibie tartly. 'Why do you think? I tripped in the dark, see, and smashed my last egg. I wanted to rinse it off my shirt before it set.'

Vernon's expression was openly sceptical, and Chaloner agreed. Surely Bibie would know the vat was empty after so many weeks of dry weather? Unless he was drunk, and not thinking clearly – Bibie certainly looked as though he had followed his visit to the coffee house with one to a tavern.

Chaloner crouched next to the body, noting that Hill had been a short man with the red nose and mottled complexion of the habitual drinker. He reeked of ale, suggesting he had disregarded the order to monitor the coffee houses for agitators, and had haunted the inns instead. Had he learned something about the killer that had sealed his fate? Or was the culprit simply taking no chances, so had dispatched him before he became a problem?

'Well?' murmured Lester in Chaloner's ear. 'Is this the killer's third victim?'

'There is very little blood, and the knife holes in the back of his coat are unusually small,' Chaloner whispered back. 'So, yes, I think so.'

They could do no more, and Chaloner was bone-weary. He asked a few questions of the onlookers, but no one could tell him anything remotely useful, so he and Lester began the trek back to Covent Garden. As they went, Chaloner told him about Wogan, knowing the captain could be trusted with the secret.

'He must be mad,' was Lester's blunt response. 'The King will show no mercy if he is caught – he will say that if Wogan really was sorry for what he did, he would have surrendered himself at the Restoration. Many regicides did, and some had their death sentences commuted.'

'But many died horribly, so I do not blame Wogan for being unwilling to risk it.' Chaloner raised his hands in a shrug. 'I thought lots of folk would recognise him, but regicides were influential men in the Commonwealth, far too important to hobnob with paupers. Perhaps Vernon really is the only one to guess his true identity.'

'Other than the government, if what he told you is true.'

'It may be – they might well look the other way if it is worth their while, and it does sound as if he is saving them lots of money. And there is the fact that they may not want to risk sparking trouble by staging another hideous execution.'

Lester turned his mind back to Chaloner's investigations, and when he spoke, he sounded disheartened. 'Despite our diligence today, the killer remains at large and we have failed to identify the agitators. Or do you think Skiner's customers are the culprits? I can see Vernon making feisty speeches, while Wogan transpires to be a violent radical.'

'Executing the old king was not considered radical at the time, and I think Wogan is telling the truth about his remorse. After all, who has not done something he later regrets?'

'I certainly have,' muttered Lester. 'I curse myself daily for not tossing Admiral Berkeley overboard the instant he gave his first stupid order. If I had, *Swiftsure* would still be mine, and I would not be pining for the sea. But what will you do about Wogan? Report him to Williamson?'

Joseph Williamson was the current Spymaster General, a man who was not nearly as good at his job as John Thurloe, who had run the intelligence services for Cromwell.

'I will see what Thurloe thinks,' replied Chaloner, more than happy to take the advice of a man he trusted more than any other. 'First thing in the morning.'

Chapter 5

Again, it was difficult to sleep in the stifling attic, so Chaloner was almost relieved that there was not much of the night left by the time he reached home and flopped into bed. He dozed on and off, waking often in a tangle of sheets, with questions about his enquiries buzzing around his head. By the time the market folk began their racket in the piazza below, he had a dull headache and his wits were sluggish.

He rolled up the soiled clothes he had worn the previous day, and put them out for the servants to launder. Then he donned a fresh white shirt, blue breeches and a grey long-coat, feeling obliged to dress reasonably smartly that day, because a message had arrived from the Earl the previous night, saying that Montagu had returned from Greenwich and would be available to answer questions about his dead wife.

He filled the bowl on the roof with water for the birds, although there was no sign of the kite. Then he took bread and a cup of weak ale from the kitchen, and went out into the garden. He tended his poultry, then settled on the bench to eat and ponder.

It was pleasant sitting in the shade of an old apple tree, and he could smell the honeysuckle growing up the wall behind him. Again, he wondered when the weather would break, and hoped it would be soon. The fruit in the orchard had dropped without ripening, the grass was crisp and brown underfoot, and the onions and lettuces in the vegetable plots had bolted from lack of water.

He began to plan his day. It would be about six o'clock by the time he had finished breakfast, which was too early to visit Thurloe, so he decided go to the Rainbow Coffee House first. Not only did he need the stimulation that Farr's poisonous brew would provide, but the place was a good source of gossip, and he wanted to know if the other patrons had anything to say about the agitators, the higgler murders, or Eleanor Montagu.

When he had finished at the Rainbow, he would visit Thurloe, then try the Navy Office again for Lester. Next, he would traverse the breadth of the city to White Hall, to speak to Montagu and report to the Earl. When he had finished at the palace, he would either act on any information Montagu was able to provide, or return to Poulters' Hall to ask questions about Hill.

He stood, brushed crumbs from his coat, and looked up to see Lester striding towards him. The captain looked smart and fresh, and was wearing his best blue coat. His hair had been brushed until it shone, and there was a powerful aroma of lavender about him.

'It keeps the moths away,' he explained defensively, seeing Chaloner wrinkle his nose. Then he looked anxious. 'Do you think it is too strong?'

'Not if you stay outside,' replied Chaloner. 'But why the finery? Do you plan on coming with me to White Hall later?'

'Actually, I thought I might call on Elsie and Dorcas, to see if they have heard any rumours about Hill's murder. I shall also ask if they learned anything useful at the King's Head last night.'

'I see,' said Chaloner, smothering a smile. 'But perhaps you had better not. I need to speak to them myself, and they may object to saying everything twice.'

'I shall chat to them of more pleasant matters, then,' determined Lester with a seraphic smile. 'They may be interested in a few tales of the sea.'

'They will be working,' predicted Chaloner. 'Friday is one of the days when poulters are permitted to sell eggs, and they have a living to make.'

'Then I shall offer to help.' Lester glanced at the basket of eggs Chaloner had collected from the coop. 'May I have those? Elsie told me yesterday that the heat is putting birds from the larger farms off their lay, which is why there is an ever-growing shortage of them. She will appreciate a few more to put on her stall.'

Chaloner indicated that he was to help himself. 'My birds dislike too much heat, but their laying has not been affected. Are you sure Elsie knows what she is talking about?'

Lester was indignant. 'Of course she does! It is her profession.'

Chaloner did not mind at all that Lester had other plans that day, as he much preferred working alone. They strode along the middle of the Strand together, ducking through the early-morning traffic, as neither was willing to walk at the side of the road lest they were doused with the contents of the chamber-pots that were being emptied out of every window.

They parted at the Rainbow, and Chaloner was amused to watch Lester break into a trot, so great was his impatience to reach the woman who had caught his fancy. Chaloner entered the coffee house's gloomy interior, coughing as the reek of burned beans wafted around him on a dense cloud of smoke.

'What news?' called Farr, then grimaced when he recognised Chaloner. 'Oh, it is you. Well, unless you know anything interesting about the King's syllabub or the Adrian Masque, you can sit down and shut up.'

Chaloner found a space between Stedman the printer and Speed, the purveyor of questionable books, who had set up shop at the back of the Rainbow. This was an arrangement that suited both parties, as Speed was assured of a steady stream of customers who browsed his collection while waiting for their coffee, and Farr was able to help men who needed a restorative beverage after seeing what kind of literature the book-seller had to offer.

'Actually, I do know something about the syllabub,' Chaloner said as Farr poured him a dish of coffee that was the colour and consistency of tar. 'The recipe includes egg yolks.'

It was such a worthless snippet that he was astonished when everyone was immediately agog, interrogating him for the next ten minutes until he was forced to admit that this was the full extent of his insider knowledge.

'You will have to bring us some,' said Stedman keenly. 'I would dearly love to taste it. After all, what is good enough for the King is certainly good enough for us.'

'Just do not let *them* know that their recipe is no longer a secret,' whispered Speed, and nodded towards the table near the back of the room. With horror, Chaloner saw it was occupied by half a dozen men from the Poultry

Department, including Catline and Crookey. 'They will not be pleased after guarding it so jealously these last few weeks.'

'Then they should not have shared it with a loose-tongued landlord,' retorted Chaloner, recalling that Padnoll of the Sunne had not hesitated for a second before blurting it out. 'But what are they doing here? The Rainbow is not usually frequented by courtiers.'

Which was one reason why he liked it, of course. However, if men from White Hall began to claim it as their own, he would have to find somewhere else to drink his coffee, because he was not about to spend his free time with courtiers. He was amazed by how much the possibility of losing the Rainbow dismayed him.

'They came to look at my books,' explained Speed. 'I have some that detail the lives of certain characters and events from the past, you see.'

'You mean like Pope Adrian?' asked Chaloner.

'Oh, I have nothing about him,' said Speed dismissively. 'He never did anything remotely scandalous. Well, other than being a papist.'

'They wanted to learn about some particularly lewd French nobles,' explained Farr. 'To gain new inspiration for entertaining the King in the future, apparently.'

Stedman, the devoted monarchist, nodded his approval, but everyone else was patently repelled by White Hall's determination to devise new debaucheries for themselves. A row broke out, and it was some time before the conversation turned to less contentious matters.

'Have you see the latest *London Gazette*?' asked Speed, poking it with a grimy forefinger. 'It contains nothing but a list of ships that have arrived in various ports.'

'Do not exaggerate,' chided Farr. 'It also described the

101

heinous actions of a few Dutch prisoners of war – they gave their word to do no mischief, but then tried to ignite a pile of faggots on a pier. Had they succeeded, the whole of Bristol might have burned.'

Stedman grinned. 'I was more interested in the bit about Holmes's Bonfire – how the enemy fled in terror when our brave admiral appeared.'

And they had been right to run, thought Chaloner. The merchant vessels were poorly armed and no match for warships. Staying to fight would have been suicidal and pointless.

'Have you heard that Eleanor Montagu is dead?' he asked, putting the question casually in the hope that no one would guess he had been charged to explore her demise.

'Yes, leaving her husband free to marry a younger woman,' said Stedman. 'Although I imagine he will leave a respectable interval before he drags her to the altar.'

'What can you tell me about Eleanor?' Chaloner fully expected someone to demand why he wanted to know, but the Rainbow's patrons loved to gossip, and did not care one jot why he had asked the question.

'Well, she loved reading,' began Speed. 'She bought lots of books from me.'

'Did she?' blurted Chaloner, wondering why a respectable lady should be interested in religious or political rants and highly explicit erotica.

'She bought everything I recommended, and had very catholic tastes,' elaborated Speed. 'Best yet, she always paid on time. I am very sorry she died.'

'You did not sell her the tome she was reading when she breathed her last, did you?' asked Chaloner. 'It was by John Downes the regicide.'

'But Downes is in the Tower,' said Stedman, frowning. 'So I cannot imagine he is in a position to write books.'

'Actually, he did produce one,' said Speed, and sniffed his disdain. 'It was a treatise on hen-keeping, and contained nothing remotely contentious, so you will not find it on my shelves.'

'Is not the fact that it was written by a traitor controversial enough?' asked Farr.

'No,' replied Speed firmly. 'Although I understand it raised some eyebrows in the poultry world. Its basic thesis is that it is possible to produce high-quality eggs while also keeping the birds happy. Apparently, the industry cares about the first, but not the second.'

'It sounds provocative to me,' said Stedman. 'As if Downes was accusing poulters of being cruel or unethical – of not looking after God's creatures as well as they might.'

'He was,' shrugged Speed. 'But my customers do not come to me for moralistic tirades – they want texts that are scandalous, lewd, radical or libellous. I scoured Downes' scribblings minutely in the hope of finding a snippet about his tempestuous past, but there was nothing. And unless you are interested in chickens, it was as dull as ditch-water.'

'Speaking of chickens, have you heard anything about agitators encouraging higglers?' asked Chaloner.

'No, but all higglers should be hanged,' declared Farr uncompromisingly. 'Why should I pay to belong to a City Company, while others do not bother but still prosper? It is not right, and all unlicensed traders should be wiped from the face of the Earth.'

'Eggs have grown scarce of late,' mused Stedman. 'I tried to buy some today, but there were none to be had. My poulter told me that the heat is responsible.'

103

'It is not affecting my flock,' said Chaloner. 'They are—'

'Did you hear that a great golden egg was seen hovering over St Paul's yesterday?' interrupted Farr, remembering something far more important than anything Chaloner might have to contribute.

'Over the cathedral? I thought that was a coffin-shaped cloud,' said Chaloner, recalling what the hackney driver had told him.

'That was another occasion,' explained Farr impatiently. 'But this egg is said to be a sign that all will be well after Sunday, when the world will change for the better.'

'What *again*?' groaned Speed. 'How many times have we heard this? I do not believe a word of it! The truth is that we shall all wake up on Monday morning to find that nothing has changed one iota. You mark my words.'

Time was passing, so Chaloner finished his coffee and made for the door. Unfortunately, Catline spotted him before he could open it, and called him over. Chaloner was tempted to ignore him, but suspected that would cause a scene, and he did not want to draw attention to the fact that he was acquainted with the more dissolute species of courtier.

'What are you doing here?' Catline asked, all sly eyes and indolent grace. 'Are you a fan of Speed's risqué books? Or is it his dubious political and religious essays that you enjoy? You should be careful. It is unwise for old Parliamentarians to study that sort of thing – you might be mistaken for a traitor.'

'Did you return to White Hall after leaving the Sunne

104

yesterday?' asked Chaloner, declining to be baited. He tried to see if any of them carried knives with long, thin blades, thinking they were exactly the kind of men to stab someone in the back and stuff his body in a water butt. Of course, he could not imagine what their motive would be for such an act.

'I do not recall,' replied Catline warily. 'Why?'

'No reason,' shrugged Chaloner. 'So, tell me, how well did you know Bowles the grocer?'

Catline's eyes narrowed. 'Why all these questions? And what gives you the right to ask them of us?'

'The authority of the Lord Chancellor,' replied Chaloner crisply. 'But feel free not to answer, although I should warn you that the last courtier who refused to cooperate with an official enquiry was stripped of all his titles by the King himself.'

It was a brazen lie, but not one that could easily be disproved, given that there was always someone at White Hall being sent away in disgrace. The claim had the desired effect, though, because Catline began to speak, albeit with ill grace.

'We barely knew Bowles,' he sniffed with a moue of distaste. 'We do not fraternise with tradesmen. They are beneath our dignity.'

'Then how do you buy your department's supplies?'

'I do it all,' said Crookey, who sat at the centre of the throng like a spider in its web; he gave a smile that was difficult to interpret. 'And perhaps I did business with Bowles, but perhaps I did not. I do not recall.'

He was lying, but Chaloner knew it would likely provoke a brawl if he said so, and he did not want to be banned from the Rainbow on Crookey's account.

'Did you know that your "secret" recipe for the Adrian

105

Masque syllabub is all over London this morning?' he asked, aiming to goad.

And if it was not common knowledge now, it would be by the end of the day, given that he himself had just spilled the details to Farr and the others.

Catline's smug arrogance slipped a little, although his shock was quickly masked. His cronies were less guarded, though, and stared at Chaloner with expressions of anger and dismay. Crookey merely looked exasperated.

'It was not a secret,' blustered Catline unconvincingly. 'Besides, we have not finalised the formula yet – there is still a lot of experimenting to do.'

'Then you had better buy eggs while you can,' said Chaloner with an amiable smile. 'They grow scarcer and more expensive by the day.'

Catline sneered at him. 'If our recipe calls for a thousand egg yolks, then that is what we shall have, no matter what the price. Nothing is too costly where the King is concerned.'

'I am sure you feel the same way about Clarendon,' said Crookey slyly.

'I doubt it,' sniggered a burly courtier named René Mezandier, who was Sergeant of the Poultry. As far as Chaloner could tell, this entailed nothing more arduous than strutting about with a sword on ceremonial occasions. 'No one could feel affection for that old goat. Bristol was right to challenge him last night.'

'Challenge him to what?' asked Chaloner, alarmed.

'A fight to the death,' smirked Mezandier. 'With pistols.'

'Do not tease him, Mezandier,' drawled Crookey, and grinned at Chaloner. 'Bristol is the driving force behind the masque, which will be the event of the decade, so he challenged Clarendon to devise an entertainment that the King will like even more.'

'Which Clarendon cannot do,' put in Mezandier with a snigger. 'Because not even his most loyal friends could describe *him* as fun. Bristol will win the contest handily.'

Chaloner supposed he would have to make sure that Bristol's dare did not conceal some deeper, darker purpose, one designed to see the Earl on the scaffold.

Chaloner's plan had been to visit Thurloe when he left the Rainbow, but a free hackney carriage happened to be passing, and as this was such a rare occurrence, he flagged it down and told the driver to take him to the Navy Office – riding there now would save him time walking there later. Moreover, Pepys often went to work at dawn, and might be more inclined to accept a visitor before he became too caught up in the daily grind.

He alighted, told the driver to wait, then ran quickly to Pepys's office, noting that the frantic scurrying he had seen the previous day was no longer in evidence. He supposed that either the crisis was over, or it was too early for most of the staff to be at their desks. Secretary Hewer was there, though, labouring over a stack of reports. He told Chaloner that Pepys was still occupied with his new upholstery and had not been seen since the previous morning.

'When do you expect him back?' Chaloner asked, fighting to control his exasperation.

'When he chooses to come in,' shrugged Hewer, and then hastily changed the subject, not liking the dangerous gleam in Chaloner's eye. 'Have you seen *The London Gazette*? It is afire with praise for what Holmes did in Ter-Schelling, but his "bonfire" was all luck and no planning.'

'I know,' said Chaloner shortly, tempted to confide that he had witnessed the incident, and so was in a better position to judge than most. But he held his tongue, unwilling as always to share information without good reason.

'He just *happened* to spot a Dutch fleet at anchor,' Hewer grumbled on, 'and it just *happened* to be poorly defended. There is no honour in what he did.'

'It dealt a blow to the enemy,' said Chaloner, wondering if Hewer aimed to trick him into saying something treasonous – to earn Pepys's gratitude by being able to order the arrest of a man who wanted a favour. 'And most such raids are down to luck.'

'But what he did will have consequences,' said Hewer crossly. 'He should not have burned that poor village, and his barbarism will return to haunt us in time.'

'The Dutch will want revenge,' acknowledged Chaloner cautiously, 'which is why our ships should be under the command of the best captains – like Salathiel Lester – who are most qualified to defend us.'

'I agree, and so does Pepys,' sighed Hewer. 'Unfortunately, the King has a lot of friends who clamour for a maritime adventure, and they take precedence over tarpaulins.'

'So the King would rather trust his country's safety to untried cronies than to officers who know what they are doing?' Chaloner already knew the answer to that question, so was not sure why he had bothered to ask.

Hewer shrugged. 'Lester can give him nothing but loyalty and good service, whereas courtiers will repay him in money and future favours. Did you not read the Paladin's pamphlet on this issue?'

He picked up a broadsheet from his desk and passed

it over. Chaloner recognised the distinctive red ink immediately. He scanned it quickly, and saw it was a damning
appraisal of the shameless nepotism that governed the
navy.

'Keep it,' said Hewer, when Chaloner started to hand
it back. 'Or give it to someone else to read, because
things will only change if there is—'

He stopped speaking and jumped to his feet when
there was a tap on the door and in walked a vigorous
man in his forties. The newcomer had a weathered,
homely face and a shock of curly brown hair that was
just beginning to be peppered with silver. Hewer gave a
delighted grin and hurried forward to grasp his hand.
Chaloner recognised him, too, although he had not seen
him in more than fifteen years.

Robert Blackborne had run Cromwell's navy, and had
done so with brilliant efficiency. There was no question
of experienced tarpaulins being pushed aside for
untrained gentlemen in his day, and every post had been
awarded on merit and ability. His fleets had sailed on
time, well provisioned, and with full complements of paid
crew. Needless to say, when Cromwell had fought the
Dutch, he had scored a quick and decisive victory.

'Young Tom Chaloner!' cried Blackborne, and beamed
as he took the spy's proffered hand. 'Although not so
young any more. Are you still fighting for Parliament?'

'No, of course not!' gulped Chaloner, acutely aware
that they were in a Royalist military headquarters. 'Are
you still employed here?'

Blackborne closed the door, so as not to be over-
heard by anyone walking along the corridor outside.
'I had hoped to continue serving my country after the
Restoration, but God had other plans for me.'

'It had nothing to do with God,' declared Hewer shortly. 'It was the King – he was afraid the fleet would follow your sensible orders, rather than his own stupid ones.'

'Young Will here is my nephew,' Blackborne told Chaloner with obvious pride. 'And if he keeps his incautious tongue in check, one day *he* will be Secretary of the Fleet.'

'So what do you do these days?' asked Chaloner, declining to comment.

'I work in the Customs Office, which is hardly the best use of my talents, but who am I to question the Almighty's will? However, my advice on navy matters is sought on a daily basis, which is why you find me here today. I am not paid for it, of course, but I am happy to be of use to King and country.'

Hewer snorted his disgust. 'We were just discussing the Paladin's broadsheet about the Royalist navy, Uncle. It is a—'

'You will never win promotion if you insist on speaking your mind, Will,' interrupted Blackborne sharply. 'No matter how justified. Put that pamphlet in your pocket, Chaloner, before some tattling Cavalier sees it, and we are all in trouble.'

Chaloner obliged, then shamelessly took the opportunity to lobby him on Lester's behalf. Blackborne shook his head with a weary sigh.

'I remember Lester from Cromwell's time. He is one of our most able mariners, but I doubt there is much Pepys can do to help him. You would do better approaching the King or the Duke of York – they are the ones who make the decisions these days.'

He turned the conversation to mutual friends before

Chaloner could ask how he was supposed to secure an audience with such august personages. Perhaps he *was* wasting his time with Pepys, but he had to help Lester somehow, and petitioning the Clerk of the Acts was the only realistic way he could think of doing it.

As uncle and nephew began to discuss a famous radical divine, Chaloner recalled that Blackborne had always demonstrated strong Puritan leanings. However, when Blackborne made a remark about the imminent end of the world, Chaloner wondered if he had embraced Fifth Monarchism since they had last met. He asked.

'Yes, I do believe King Jesus will soon appear in glory,' replied Blackborne. 'But not to live in White Hall. Londoners always think our Lord will come to their city, but it is very dirty and crowded. He may prefer somewhere nicer, like Hull or Swansea.'

Chaloner had no idea if he was serious, but time was passing, and his hackney carriage was waiting outside. He bowed and took his leave with a promise to meet another time for a more leisurely conversation.

In the hackney again, Chaloner held his arm over the lower half of his face in order to protect his lungs from the dust that was kicked up from hundreds of feet, wheels and hoofs. It had been hot before dawn, but now the sun had risen, the city wilted. He felt he was being boiled alive, despite the open windows, and sweat made the shirt stick to his back.

He alighted in Chancery Lane, and approached Lincoln's Inn, one of the four great legal foundations that licensed lawyers. A youthful porter wrote his name in a ledger, although Chaloner was careful to use an alias as always, not wanting anyone to know that Thurloe had been visited by the nephew of a regicide.

Inside its neat rectangle of imposing walls, Lincoln's Inn was a haven of peace and refinement. An air of hushed venerability hung over its ancient buildings, while lines of mature trees served to provide welcome shade from the sun. Better yet, the grounds smelled of scythed grass, warm earth and the roses in their well-watered flower beds, which was a pleasant change from the stench of sun-baked sewage outside.

He walked to Dial Court, a set of buildings named for the scientific instrument gracing the open space in the centre. Its designer claimed it would not only allow its owners to tell the time, but to predict the movements and alignments of the heavens, too. It had been severely damaged by a storm in the past, but that did not matter much, because the calculations required to use it were so complex that not even the combined intellect of Lincoln's Inn's residents could master them. Ergo, the dial was generally regarded as a curious but useless piece of garden furniture.

Chaloner climbed the stairs to Chamber XIII, breathing in deeply of the familiar, comforting scent of beeswax-polished panelling and old wood smoke. Thurloe lived on the third floor, which was hotter than the lower storeys, so the ex-Spymaster had left his door ajar in the hope of creating a through breeze with the open windows.

Chaloner tapped on the door and walked in, smiling at the man who sat at the table. John Thurloe was slightly built with shoulder-length brown hair and large, soulful blue eyes. Besides running Cromwell's extensive network of spies, he had also been sole Secretary of State, a heavy burden that he had carried with a vigour that belied his delicate appearance.

'Thomas!' he exclaimed, breaking into a rare smile. 'Are you here to inform me that Wogan the regicide is in London?'

Chaloner struggled to conceal his astonishment. Thurloe had been one of the most efficient Spymaster Generals in history, and his name alone had been enough to stop many would-be traitors in their tracks. The loyalty he commanded among his agents had survived the Restoration, and most continued to send him reports, even though he no longer dabbled in espionage. Thus he remained one of the best informed men in the city, far more so than the man who currently ran the intelligence services.

'How did you guess?' Chaloner asked.

Thurloe smiled. 'Because his friend Vernon visited me earlier, and he mentioned Wogan's alarm at being recognised by the kinsman of another regicide last night. It was not difficult to surmise who that might be.'

'You know Vernon?'

'He is a talented physician, and supplies me with all the latest tonics, although he is not a person whose company I find congenial.'

Thurloe thought he had a fragile constitution, and was always dosing himself with potions that promised improved health. Chaloner had never understood how a man possessed of such a brilliant mind could be so gullible when it came to quack cures.

'Vernon is a Fifth Monarchist. Are you sure it is wise to consort with such a person? Someone may think you share his views.'

'His Dragon Water is worth the risk,' said Thurloe

comfortably. 'Would you like a glass? It keeps the humours in balance and tastes of fruit and honey with a dash of pepper.'

Which was probably all it contained, thought Chaloner acidly, although it sounded a lot safer than some of the potions the ex-Spymaster swallowed in his quest to regain the vitality he had enjoyed as a youth.

'Wogan,' he prompted, unwilling to discuss Thurloe's worrisome devotion to exotic cure-alls. 'He is reckless to return to London. Does he not realise what will happen to him if – or rather *when* – he is caught?'

Thurloe raised his hands in a shrug. 'His return is a mystery to me, too, but the Welsh have a very strong sense of country. Regardless, he has done a lot of good in and around Pudding Lane.'

'But someone is bound to betray him, and then all the altruism in the world will not save him from a terrible death.'

'Do not be so sure. His generosity to wounded sailors alone is saving the government a fortune, and its ministers will overlook a great deal where money is concerned.'

'Money will not matter to the King, and nor will wounded sailors. He wants to avenge his father's execution too badly to care about anything else.'

'True, and Wogan *will* be in trouble if His Majesty ever learns he is here. But who will tell him? Not a cash-strapped government, certainly, or the many paupers he helps.'

'Wogan seems different from the angry firebrand I remember from my youth, but can we be sure that he no longer represents a threat to the Crown?'

'He understands our love-affair with republicanism is over, Tom, and I believe him when he says he wants to live a quiet life, doing good in the hope of redemption.'

'So you have met him since he came back?' asked Chaloner in alarm. 'I hope you did not entertain him here.'

'I was Spymaster General, Thomas,' said Thurloe tartly. 'I know how to deal safely with potential enemies of the state. We met in an anonymous coffee house, where he convinced me that he harbours no desire to meddle in politics again.'

Chaloner was not sure what to think, but he trusted Thurloe, and was willing to give Wogan the benefit of the doubt on his recommendation. For now, at least. 'Speaking of passionate old Parliamentarians, I just met Robert Blackborne.'

'Dear Robert,' said Thurloe fondly. 'He ran Cromwell's navy like a smooth clock, and the Royalists were wrong to dismiss him – we would have defeated the Dutch by now if he had been in charge. Our fleet is still not out, you know.'

Chaloner nodded. 'Blackborne is a Fifth Monarchist, too.'

Thurloe frowned. 'He always did believe the upheavals of the last two decades were a prelude to a new world order, although I was not aware that he followed any specific sect.'

'The latest prediction for a glorious Utopia is that it will begin on Sunday week – the day after the King and all his mistresses jump into a lake-sized syllabub at a masque designed to celebrate the death of the only English-born pope.'

'Goodness!' breathed Thurloe, shocked. 'His Majesty will offend Catholics and Protestants at a single stroke, which is an impressive achievement. Or do you think he aims to unite them all by presenting himself as a common enemy?'

Chaloner laughed as he turned to another subject. 'Do you recall that communication system you invented – making letters with fingers? All your spies were obliged to learn it.'

'Yes, why?'

'Because a man named James Hadie was stabbed on Tuesday night, and he died after making the signs for W, I and L. Did you know him?'

A deeply religious man, Thurloe closed his eyes and whispered a brief prayer for the dead man's soul. 'Yes, Hadie was one of my operatives, although I have not seen him in years. What did he mean by WIL?'

'I was hoping you might know.'

Thurloe shook his head. 'I doubt I can suggest anything that you have not already considered. The obvious answer is that he was spelling out the name of his killer.'

'I hope he was not trying to say that Spymaster Williamson was responsible,' said Chaloner uneasily. 'I do not want to conduct an enquiry that leads to *him* as the culprit.'

'No, it would not be politically expedient,' agreed Thurloe. 'However, there is no reason to jump to that conclusion. There must be thousands of people in the city with WIL in their names. So why are you looking into Hadie's death? I cannot imagine he was important enough to matter to your Earl.'

'No, but Bowles the grocer is, and Bowles, Hadie and a man named Hill – all members of the Company of Poulters – were killed with an unusually long, thin blade. I think there is a single culprit.'

Thurloe was thoughtful. 'There is another connection between Hadie and Bowles, too: Allhallows the Great on Thames Street. Hadie monitored that church for me when I was Spymaster – he watched the religious radicals who gathered there. Meanwhile, Bowles will be buried there this morning. Perhaps we should attend his funeral.'

'One of the poulters told me that Hadie spied there during the Commonwealth, but I did not know that Bowles was associated with the place, too. Was *he* a religious radical? He never came across as particularly fanatical to me.'

'I do not know, Tom. Incidentally, were you aware that Bowles was among those who were parodied in the Paladin's recent pamphlet about poulters?'

'Was he?' asked Chaloner, surprised. 'I should have read it more carefully.'

'The Paladin accused him of hypocrisy – of being a freeman of the Company of Poulters, but only following its rules when it suited him.'

'That is true,' said Chaloner. 'I met a man called Bibie, who claimed that Bowles bought Company eggs to sell in his shop, but the ones he ate himself came from higglers because they taste better. I wonder how the Paladin found out.'

'Common gossip, probably,' said Thurloe. 'Your Bibie does not sound very discreet. But the Paladin worries me, Tom. His work so far has been amusing, but there will come a time when laughter turns to outrage. Then there will be trouble.'

Chaloner pulled the broadsheet about the navy from his pocket. 'There may well be a backlash over this. Appointing inexperienced courtiers to defend our coasts is a dangerous practice, and the Paladin reminding people of it will do the government no favours.'

Thurloe winced. 'I wish I knew his identity. I would urge him to keep his opinions to himself, because he has

117

such a large following that he could ignite a riot with ease.'

'I am sure he has an informant in White Hall, because one of his diatribes exposed Bristol's habit of urinating in the potted plants. That is not widely known.'

'Well, it is now,' said Thurloe. 'And it will be used against White Hall at some stage, you can be certain of that.'

Chaloner helped himself to a piece of cake from the plate on the table. It was cut absurdly thin – Thurloe only ever picked at food, although the picking did go on all day – and it barely made a mouthful, so he took another. He declined to wash it down with a draught of Dragon Water, so Thurloe swallowed that himself.

'The time is ripe for another plot against the government,' said Thurloe, watching Chaloner take a third slice. 'We have not had one since April, and there are omens galore – talking birds, new stars, the unseasonably hot weather . . . '

'Coffin-shaped clouds and golden eggs above St Paul's, other eggs branded with fiery crosses,' added Chaloner. 'But other than the weather, most is pure fiction.'

'That does not matter, as your uncle taught me. He used to stand in the street and point excitedly at the sky. There was nothing to see, but it attracted a crowd, and within minutes people had claimed to have spotted all manner of fantastic phenomena. By the following day, every one of them was reported as fact in the newsbooks, coffee houses and taverns.'

'I remember,' said Chaloner. 'But I hope you do not want me to look into this sudden proliferation of omens. It would be like . . . like trying to prevent higglers from defying the Company of Poulters.'

Thurloe smiled, then stood. 'I would like to hear what you have learned about that matter, but it is too hot in here, so let us walk in the gardens before we attend Bowles' funeral – preferably before you eat me out of house and home.'

Chaloner looked at the empty plate. 'Next time, ask for larger slices.'

Lincoln's Inn's garden was indeed cooler than Thurloe's chambers, as ancient oaks, elms and beeches shaded the paths between the beds of roses and sweet-scented herbs. Thurloe stopped next to a patch of late-fruiting strawberries and bent to pick one. In the time he took to nibble it down to the stem, Chaloner managed to scoff ten others, and was sorry when the ex-Spymaster walked on.

'Do they not feed you at Clarendon House?' Thurloe asked pointedly. 'You are always alarmingly eager to gorge when you come here.'

'My post does not include board.' Chaloner eyed the plum trees. 'Just a salary.'

'Your Earl is wise. Other courtiers use food to conceal how much they really cost the public purse – their pay is modest, but the perks are enormous. Some claim hundreds of pounds in victuals, and feed not only themselves, but their entire households and extended families, too.'

'Not to mention free accommodation, fuel, furniture, artwork and servants.'

'It would never have happened under Cromwell,' averred Thurloe, although Chaloner was sure that wherever there was money, there would be people determined to get it, and Cromwell's Court would have been just as

119

susceptible to abuse as the current one. Of course, it had been a lot smaller, and so considerably less expensive to run.

'The King dispenses far too many sinecures,' he told Thurloe. 'Take the Poultry Department, for example. Its sole remit is to provide eggs and game for the royal table, which one clerk could manage – and probably *does* manage – with ease. But it employs a sergeant, two yeomen, four grooms, more than a dozen retainers, and Crookey.'

'Crookey?'

'The Supernumerary Groom, appointed to sniff out the cheapest supplies, so that he and his cronies can pocket whatever money is saved. And speaking of money, the stranglehold the Companies have on trade is being challenged all around Pudding Lane – malcontents urging folk to ignore the law and sell what they like.'

Thurloe grimaced. 'Personally, I sympathise, but it could lead to serious unrest if it spreads. You had better tell Williamson. I know he is busy with the Dutch war, but you do not want him accusing you of keeping him in the dark about brewing trouble at home.'

They walked in silence for a while, Chaloner eating a fallen apple he had picked up from the path. Eventually, he told Thurloe about the murders of Bowles, Hadie and Hill, although as he spoke, he realised he had learned very little since his investigation had started. Then, because Thurloe was a good listener, he told him about Eleanor Montagu, too, and the rumour – originating with Bristol – that her husband or Margaret Hay killed her.

'Montagu,' mused Thurloe. 'A pleasant man, but not a great one. Eleanor, on the other hand, was impressive.

She had firm ideas about right and wrong, and travelled to Virginia to claim her third husband's fortune with the aim of using it to fund her favourite causes.'

'What causes?' asked Chaloner uneasily, thinking the Earl had not mentioned those when he had ordered him to explore her death, and it would have been useful to know.

'She deplored hypocrisy and extremism. She was also vocal about our cavalier treatment of the natural world. For example, she tried to prevent new houses being built along Piccadilly, because it meant felling the trees where nightingales breed. I liked her, so I hope her life was not cut short by someone she antagonised.'

'So do I,' said Chaloner fervently. 'Especially if it transpires to be her husband or his new lady, because the Earl will not be very happy if I present him with that solution.'

'No,' acknowledged Thurloe, 'so let us pray that they are innocent. Now, I want you to do something for me. I had a letter from my old friend John Dixwell last week—'

'Dixwell?' cried Chaloner in alarm. 'The regicide? That is reckless! If messages from him to you are ever intercepted—'

'We take precautions,' said Thurloe impatiently. 'Besides, Dixwell wrote to me in the hope of preventing trouble, not igniting it. He is no longer a feisty radical.'

'If you say so,' muttered Chaloner, wondering if there were any regicides left who still stood by their former principles. 'He is not in London, is he? Like Wogan?'

'No, he is in Vevey, where he now lives. He wrote to tell me that in the last two years, eight of his fellow king-killers have died: four in prison, and four in Switzerland.'

121

'So what?' asked Chaloner, after Thurloe had listed them by name – all were men he had met at his uncle's house, although none stood out in his memory for any particular reason. 'Prisons are unhealthy places, while those who escaped live in constant fear of being assassinated – and unrelenting anxiety takes its toll. Besides, none of them were young.'

'According to Dixwell, these eight were particular friends,' Thurloe went on. 'Men who gathered around a leader: John Downes, who is currently incarcerated in the Tower.'

'Downes? Eleanor Montagu was reading his book when she died.'

'That was about poultry keeping,' said Thurloe dismissively. 'It can have nothing to do with her demise – or with the sudden spate of deaths among the surviving regicides.'

'Does Dixwell think Downes may be next?' asked Chaloner, not sure what to believe, but declining to argue.

'Downes is safe in the Tower – it is not like the prisons where the other four died, where security is lax. However, the most worrying part of Dixwell's message concerns two regicides who were *not* part of Downes' intimate coterie . . . '

'Which ones?' asked Chaloner uneasily.

'Edmund Ludlow and Nicholas Love. They were fanatical in their hatred of the monarchy, and Dixwell informs me that time has done nothing to temper their opinions.'

Chaloner recalled that they were among the least pleasant of his uncle's cronies, and he had always tried to be out if he knew they were coming to visit. 'Where are they now?'

'At the Restoration, they also fled to Vevey, where

122

Dixwell has been able to monitor them. However, they have recently disappeared and he fears they may be headed our way. He does not know what they intend, but warns me to be alert for trouble.'

Chaloner was concerned. 'Wogan said that *he* was in Vevey after the Restoration, and now he is here. Was he part of this group?'

'No, Wogan was always a loner – an outsider, even – never part of any clique. But being in Vevey means nothing, as most of our exiles fetch up there at some point, because it is one of the few places that turns a blind eye to political crimes.'

Chaloner had visited the town himself once, and had been astonished by the number of his fellow countrymen who lived there. Thurloe was right to remind him that it attracted radical expatriates.

'I do not like the notion of Ludlow and Love in London,' the ex-Spymaster went on. 'And eight regicides dead in such a short space of time is suspicious. It makes me wonder if they were dispatched to ensure their silence.'

'Their silence about what?' asked Chaloner, bemused.

'I do not know, which is why I need your help. I want you to find out.'

'But what can I do? The Earl is unlikely to sanction a trip to Switzerland – he needs me here now that Bristol is back.'

'You can visit Downes in the Tower and ask what *he* thinks is happening. I would do it myself, but it is not a place an ex-Spymaster should wander about in, for obvious reasons. Go tonight – the guards tend to be more relaxed in the evenings, so you will find it easier to bribe your way inside.'

123

'Very well,' said Chaloner, although he owned a passionate hatred of gaols, so Thurloe's request represented no small favour.

'But first, we shall talk to two of his other friends,' said Thurloe. 'Perhaps he confided in one, and you will be spared the task of speaking to Downes himself.'

'Not more regicides?' asked Chaloner uneasily.

Thurloe shook his head. 'Just a couple of religious fanatics. They are Thomas Glasse, the vicar of St Margaret's on Fish Street Hill, and John Simpson, the vicar of Allhallows. Simpson will be conducting Bowles' funeral today, so we shall corner him afterwards.'

'So Downes continues to associate with extremists?' asked Chaloner. 'Does he have a death wish? It is one thing to hold such opinions as a free man, but when you are locked in the Tower for executing a monarch . . . '

'There is nothing to say they discuss anything contentious these days,' said Thurloe. 'Assuming Downes is even allowed to see them, of course.'

'Regardless, are you sure it is wise to become involved?' asked Chaloner, certain it was not. 'The King will be delighted to learn that eight of his father's killers are dead, and if their ends *are* suspicious, the chances are that some faithful Royalist is responsible.'

'Murder is murder in any book, Thomas,' said Thurloe soberly. 'Besides, I have a feeling that there is more to this affair than the demise of a few elderly antimonarchists, and that by uncovering the truth, we shall be doing His Majesty a great service.'

The church of Allhallows, Thames Street, was located between two narrow alleys that led to the river. The road outside was always busy, but the church itself was oddly

124

quiet amid the bustle. Chaloner wondered if Thurloe had made a mistake, because it did not look as though a funeral was about to take place there. Then he saw a mourner slinking in through a side door in a way that was distinctly furtive.

'We should leave,' he said, afraid for Thurloe, who could not afford to be caught doing anything remotely contentious lest vengeful Royalists used it as an excuse to accuse him of treachery. 'There is something peculiar about this church.'

'When I was Spymaster, it was used as a rallying point for Fifth Monarchists,' said Thurloe. 'But I cannot imagine they are still here. Quickly now, or we shall be late.'

Reluctantly, Chaloner followed him inside. It was unusually dark because most of its windows had been boarded over. The doors were abnormally sturdy, and there were at least six that he could see, which was an extraordinary number for a building its size.

'I do not think I have ever seen a place more flagrantly equipped for illicit purposes,' he murmured. 'Precautions against eavesdroppers, multiple avenues of escape . . . and look at the door to the crypt – it is so thick that the Crown jewels would be safe down there!'

Thurloe smiled. 'That undercroft is alleged to be the most secure in the city. It was built by an infamous smuggler many years ago. Her name was Mary Lane, and her ghost is said to haunt it to this day.'

They walked towards the chancel, where roughly thirty people had gathered. It was a surprisingly meagre turnout for such a popular man, and Chaloner wondered if others had taken one look at Allhallows and opted to give the funeral a miss. He recognised five of the mourners – Master Farmer and Drinkell from the Company of Poulters; Robert Blackborne, whom he had met in the Navy Office; Vernon from Skiner's Coffee House; and Wogan's woman Docility Gander.

'Are you sure the Fifth Monarchists no longer use this place?' Chaloner whispered to Thurloe. 'Because Vernon is one, and so is Blackborne.'

Thurloe shrugged. 'Perhaps it *is* still their headquarters. I wonder if Bowles counted himself among them. I never heard anything to suggest it, but . . . Of course, Fifth Monarchism is not illegal.'

'No,' acknowledged Chaloner. 'Just dangerously radical and verging on the insane.'

At that moment, the vestry door opened and the coffin was carried out by six of Bowles' apprentices. Leading them was a red-faced, angry-looking man who eschewed the current dictates for clerical dress, and wore what appeared to be his gardening clothes. When he spoke, his voice was shockingly loud, and he declined to follow the funeral service in *The Book of Common Prayer*, electing instead to use one he had devised himself. In it, he seemed to be giving the Almighty an ultimatum: accept this man's soul or else.

'He is bold,' murmured Chaloner, listening in astonishment as the congregation was informed that Bowles would not be in the ground for very long, because King Jesus would need the coffin for burying White Hall's many sinners. 'Priests have been defrocked for less, and this is not some rural parish where the bishop will never know – it is in the centre of England's biggest city.'

'That is John Simpson,' Thurloe whispered back. 'Downes' friend. I had no idea *he* was a Fifth Monarchist. Clearly, I was wrong – they *do* still meet here.'

126

The service gained momentum, with Simpson bellowing that Bowles would rise in glory in nine days' time, ready to provide eggs and spices for King Jesus's victory feast. Several mourners made for the door, reluctant to listen to such controversial opinions. Master Farmer and Drinkell were among them, so Chaloner hurried out too, intending to ask more questions about Bowles, but he had underestimated their desire to be away, and they had gone by the time he reached the street.

When he rejoined Thurloe inside, Simpson had finished his tirade, and was leading the funeral procession into the churchyard. Once at the graveside, he lobbed a huge clod of soil on to the coffin as it was being lowered, causing it to tip and sway dangerously.

'There you go, Bowles,' he declared, wiping his hands on his breeches before turning to the bewildered onlookers. 'Now, who brought the ale? We shall have it in the church, because I am not standing out here in the blazing sun.'

Thurloe and the others followed him back inside, but Chaloner went to talk to Bowles' apprentices, who stood in an unhappy huddle around the grave, watching the verger fill it in.

'Why did you choose to bury him here?' he asked, thinking the grocer deserved better.

'Because it was his parish,' one lad replied miserably. 'We wanted the curate to perform the ceremony, but Simpson insisted on doing it himself. I am not sure Mr Bowles would have liked it.'

'No,' agreed Chaloner, thinking there had been nothing to admire, other than perhaps its brevity. 'Was Bowles a Fifth Monarchist?'

'Certainly not,' replied the apprentice stiffly. 'But this was his church, and he loved it. He refused to let lunatic preachers drive him away.'

'Have you read the Paladin's broadsheet about poulters?' asked Chaloner. 'Your master was accused of breaking Company rules to suit himself.'

'He did buy eggs from higglers on occasion,' admitted the lad reluctantly. 'But only to help them earn a living. It was an act of charity, not greed. He was a good man.'

'Yes, he was,' agreed Chaloner, and gave him a shilling to toast Bowles' memory in a tavern – Allhallows was no place for impressionable youths. They scampered away without a backward glance, patently relieved to be away from the dark church and its peculiar incumbent.

Back inside Allhallows again, Chaloner sank into the shadows to watch who was talking to whom. Thurloe was in conversation with Blackborne, while Simpson held forth to a group of people who wore classic Puritan garb – black coats and tall hats, and nary a button or a buckle to be seen. They included Vernon, so Chaloner assumed they were all Fifth Monarchists.

Nearby, perched on a chest tomb eating an apple, was a pert little man wearing a coat of rich burgundy, topped by a gloriously cavalier hat with waving feathers and large silver brooch. He had a slyly mischievous visage, like the gargoyles in St Paul's.

'Glasse!' Simpson bawled at him, drawing winces from all those who valued their ears. 'What did you think of my funeral service? I pared out all that flowery nonsense forced on us by a decadent Church.'

Glasse, thought Chaloner, was the other friend of Downes who might be able to answer questions about the eight dead regicides. Thurloe had said he was a vicar, although the man looked unlike any priest Chaloner had ever met, with the possible exception of Simpson. It was not just Glasse's handsome attire that made him so distinctly unclerical, but the expression of sly malice on his face.

'You call that paring?' he sneered at Simpson. 'It looked more like slashing to me, and unless you want the bishop to come a-calling, you should be more discreet.'

'Pah!' roared Simpson. 'King Jesus has no truck with silken tongues, and will appreciate a man who does not beat around the bush. Come Sunday week, all mealy-mouthed prelates will be rotting in hell, while preachers like me will rule in glory.'

'We are all looking forward to Judgement Day, Simpson,' said Vernon placatingly. 'But Glasse is right: there is no need to risk arrest in the interim by acting like a fiery radical.'

'But I *am* a fiery radical,' declared Simpson indignantly. 'I have never pretended to be anything else, unlike some I could name – your friend Wogan, for a start. He professes to be a passionately religious man, but does he attend my daily services? No! He is a wicked sinner, who slinks off to the cathedral to listen to the moderates.'

'Wogan is a saint with all his good works,' countered Vernon indignantly. 'And King Jesus knows it. You, on the other hand, do nothing remotely charitable.'

'Actually, Simpson and I work *very* hard,' argued Glasse, hopping down from the tomb in a way that made him look even more like a malevolent sprite. 'It is not easy being a vicar, you know. There is always someone clamouring for prayers or spiritual guidance, and they tend to object if you send them packing.'

129

'We will not have to endure pesky parishioners for much longer, Glasse,' yelled Simpson. 'King Jesus will soon raise us to God's right hand, where we will be ready to advise Him on the best way to govern. Do you not agree?'

The last question was directed at Chaloner, who was disconcerted, because he had imagined he was invisible in the shadows. Suddenly, the whole group was staring at him, waiting for an answer.

'I imagine it depends on what you do when this heavenly horde appears,' said Chaloner, seeing a chance for an impromptu interrogation. 'What are your roles exactly?'

'Oh, this and that,' bellowed Simpson. 'You will have to wait and see, like everyone else. Is there any more ale, Vernon, or have you finished it all?'

The physician objected to the implication that he was responsible for the empty barrel when Simpson himself was the main culprit, and sensing a spat in the offing, most of the Fifth Monarchists retreated to the nave, where they stood talking in low voices. Even if they had not been dressed like Puritans, Chaloner would have known them to be religious extremists by their unsmiling faces, hostile eyes, and lips pinched in permanent disapproval.

Meanwhile, Vernon continued to inform Simpson and Glasse that King Jesus would be unlikely to appoint heavy drinkers to posts of authority in the Kingdom of God, so they might want to be more abstemious.

'Do not lecture *me* on matters of religion,' boomed Simpson, outraged. 'I am a far better Christian than you.'

'If that were true, you would follow our Lord's instruction to help the poor,' flashed Vernon. 'But all you care about is yourself – your *own* place in the Kingdom of Glory.'

'And if *you* were a true believer, you would not keep a great hoard of treasure in your cellar,' Simpson shot back. 'You would trust King Jesus to provide for your future.'

'What hoard is this?' asked Glasse with keen interest.

'I do trust King Jesus,' said Vernon stiffly. 'But I am also aware that God helps those who help themselves. Besides, setting funds aside for my dotage will relieve God of the responsibility, so He can concentrate on other people.'

'Lord!' muttered Chaloner, astounded that anyone could hold such bizarre beliefs. He decided to ask his questions quickly so he could leave, disliking the shadowy church and its rabid occupants. He began with a bald statement of fact. 'I understand that you two are friends with the regicide John Downes.'

'We knew him once, but we have not been in touch for years,' said Glasse, eyeing him warily. 'He is in the Tower – a place where visitors are not permitted.'

'I tried to go there a couple of times,' blared Simpson. 'But the guards turned me away because I am a Fifth Monarchist. Bigots! I cannot abide intolerance.'

Chaloner struggled not to laugh. 'Is Downes a Fifth Monarchist?'

'No, sadly for him,' hollered Simpson. 'I hope he sees the light before next Sunday, though, or he will forfeit his place among us saints.'

'I understand he had eight other friends who shared his political beliefs, but all are now dead. Did you know any of them?'

'No,' replied Glasse shortly. 'We became acquainted

131

with him because his sister lived next door to me, but he never introduced us to any of his cronies. We always avoided political discussions with the man because he is such a bore on the subject.'

'He is a bore when he starts droning on about poultry, too,' hollered Simpson. 'In fact, on reflection, he is a tedious fellow all round. I have not missed him since his incarceration.'

Chaloner was not sure what to think. Was Thurloe mistaken in thinking the two vicars had been close to Downes? Or were they lying, because only fools acknowledged a relationship with convicted enemies of the state? Yet Simpson did not seem to be the kind of man to let prudence rule his tongue . . .

'He was generous with the ale, though,' recalled Glasse, smiling suddenly. 'I never had to buy my own when he was around.'

'You will not have to buy it in nine days either.' Simpson grinned in happy anticipation. 'King Jesus will make sure we get it for free – as much as we want.'

'You seem very sure that things are about to change,' fished Chaloner. 'Why?'

'Because of Wogan's woman,' explained Glasse, pointing to where Docility Gander had gone to kneel at the altar, eyes raised heavenwards. 'She has visions, and God told her in person that the long years of waiting are almost over.'

'Hey, Docility!' bellowed Simpson, his voice reverberating all around the church and making several mourners jump in alarm. 'Come here.'

Scowling, Docility stalked towards him. 'Why do you interrupt when I am in conversation with the Lord? It is rude.'

'He forgives *me* anything,' yelled Simpson with conviction. 'But tell this man here how we know the world will change on Sunday week.'

'Because God said it would,' replied Docility loftily. 'He spoke to me through a hen, which had just laid an egg branded with a cross of fire.'

'That must have been uncomfortable for her,' muttered Chaloner, then wished he had held his tongue, aware that it was rash to mock the beliefs of fanatics, especially when they outnumbered him by a good two dozen to one. Fortunately, Simpson and Glasse were more interested in what Docility had to say and had not heard him.

'God sent an angel to me just this morning,' she declared piously. 'The one called Daniel, I believe. Anyway, he said that all is going according to plan, and Jesus is almost ready to descend from heaven. And when that happens, the faithful can sit back and enjoy the carnage.'

'Enjoy the carnage?' echoed Chaloner, startled. 'That does not sound like something an angel would say.'

'Of course there will be carnage,' said Docility impatiently. 'How else will God get rid of the wicked? And—'

'Docility!' Everyone turned to see Wogan hurrying towards them. 'There you are! I have been worried. Where have you been?'

'First I went to Mr Bowles' funeral, and then I was listening to God,' replied Docility grandly. 'Why?'

'Oh,' said Wogan, as Fifth Monarchists clustered around her, eager to hear what the Almighty had had to impart this time. 'But our beggars want their soup. We cannot keep them waiting when they are hungry.'

All puffed up importance, Docility sailed out, gratified when the Fifth Monarchists surged after her, clamouring questions. Vernon, Glasse and Simpson followed. Simpson's expression was one of fierce hope, while Vernon was openly chagrined that God should have chosen her as a mouthpiece when he himself was available. Glasse was more difficult to read, so Chaloner could not tell what he thought about Pudding Lane's resident prophet.

'I wish she would not excite them so,' said Wogan worriedly, watching them leave. 'They are fanatics, and I have never been easy in such company.'

This was rich, coming from a regicide, thought Chaloner. 'She does not seem to mind the attention.'

'She loves it, but I fear for her safety. No one knows better than me how dangerous it is to hold extreme ideas. I have tried to reason with her – and with Simpson's disciples, too – but no one will listen to me.'

'*You* should be wary of associating with them, too,' warned Chaloner. 'I imagine the intelligence services have them under surveillance, and one of their agents might recognise you. Besides, these Fifth Monarchists do not seem entirely sane to me.'

Wogan gave a wry smile. 'There is no "entirely" about it – they are all as mad as March hares. But perhaps we shall not have to endure their eccentricities for too much longer. If Docility is mistaken about Sunday week, they will likely leave the city in disgust, and if she is right, lunatic sects will be the least of our worries.'

'Do *you* believe something will happen then?' asked Chaloner, wondering if the Welshman would join in if it did. He was a regicide, after all, and might forget his claims of contrition if presented with a chance to oust another king.

'Not really,' sighed Wogan. 'I would like a more just

134

society, of course, but I know it will never happen. The truth is that we are stuck with what we have.'

Unhappily, as there was an awful lot wrong with the current regime, Chaloner conceded that Wogan was right.

The post-funeral gathering was breaking up, so Chaloner went to find Thurloe, who was still talking to Blackborne. When the ex-Spymaster said it was time to be on his way, Blackborne led him and Chaloner through a door that was concealed behind a tomb, which opened on to a quiet alley. The fact that he knew about it suggested he was very familiar with the building, and Chaloner wondered why. From attending meetings led by the fanatical Simpson? He determined to find out there and then, although he would have to be subtle about it, as Thurloe would object to an old friend being too bluntly interrogated.

'I wonder the Church tolerates Simpson,' he began, as the three of them stood on Thames Street together. 'He makes no pretence at following its edicts, and other vicars have been ejected from their livings for far less serious infractions.'

Blackborne had an explanation. 'It is because Allhallows is haunted, and no other cleric is willing to take it on. Did you not notice its uneasy atmosphere?'

'I noticed it was dim and gloomy,' retorted Chaloner. 'If the boards were taken off the windows, it would feel a lot more welcoming.'

'Mary Lane the smuggler,' Blackborne went on in a low voice, and glanced around, as if he imagined she might suddenly appear. 'She is buried in the crypt here, but her spirit is said to roam the church, looking for brandy.'

Chaloner laughed, but then saw Blackborne was serious. 'Perhaps she will rest more easily after next Sunday week, when King Jesus is in charge,' he suggested facetiously.

Blackborne regarded him lugubriously. 'I seriously doubt God will oblige us with a countdown when He comes to reign, so we cannot possibly predict when He will arrive. However, I do believe the Second Coming is an inevitability, so if you have any sense, you will live a godly life in order to be ready for it.'

'Do you say this as a Fifth Monarchist?' fished Chaloner. 'And as a member of Simpson's—'

'I say it as a Christian,' interrupted Blackborne crisply, before bowing to Thurloe and walking away.

'Why did he come today?' Chaloner asked of Thurloe, watching him walk away. 'Did he know Bowles?'

'Yes, they met years ago, when Blackborne commissioned him to supply the navy's eggs and spices. They had been friends ever since.'

'I do not suppose you questioned him about Bowles' murder, did you?'

'I did. He told me that Bowles was a good man, and he has no idea why anyone would want to hurt him.'

'Bowles' apprentices say he was no Fifth Monarchist either. Did Blackborne agree?'

Thurloe nodded. 'Bowles attended this church, but did not accept Simpson's radical theology. However, Blackborne warned me not to forget that Bowles was a businessman.'

Chaloner frowned. 'Meaning what? That he was less than scrupulous?'

'Bowles was as honest as the day is long. No, Blackborne was reminding me that not all merchants are upstanding citizens, and that the world of commerce is a murky one.

But how did you fare with Simpson and Glasse? I had intended to help you, but you looked to be managing well enough alone.'

'They denied a close relationship with Downes, and said he was dull.'

Thurloe frowned. 'They were as thick as thieves when I was Spymaster. Perhaps they decided the friendship was too dangerous once he was charged with treason. You can ask Downes himself when you visit him in the Tower later.' ·

'Yes,' said Chaloner, although the notion of setting foot inside such a place was so unsettling that he knew he needed more time to steel himself for the ordeal. He would do it tomorrow instead. He turned to another matter. 'I do not care what Blackborne says about the ghost of Mary Lane, I still find it astonishing that Simpson and his ilk are so brazen in expounding their beliefs. It is almost as if they are daring the authorities to arrest them.'

Thurloe shrugged. 'People were guarded immediately after the Restoration, unsure of what the future might hold. But now we *know* what we have: a dissolute king and a morally bankrupt Court. Is it any surprise that the fanatics feel justified in braying their opinions to anyone who will listen?'

'So it is White Hall's fault that all these lunatics are making their presence felt?'

'The palace certainly bears some of the blame. When the monarch declines to exercise moderation, how can he expect it of his people?'

Chaloner had spent far more time in Allhallows than he had intended, and he still had to report to the Earl, speak to Montagu and visit Poulters' Hall. It was unfortunate that Master Farmer and Drinkell fled Bowles' funeral early, as nabbing them there would have saved him one port of call.

It was just after noon, and most people were eating their dinner, which meant there were several hackney carriages for hire on Thames Street. Chaloner hailed one, dropped Thurloe at Lincoln's Inn, then continued to White Hall alone.

He arrived sweating and dusty, so he stopped at the fountain in the Great Court to wash his face. The water was warm and smelly, and did nothing to refresh him. Two of the King's favourites were paddling about on the shady side, so he lingered to eavesdrop – there was no harm in monitoring the Earl's enemies when an opportunity arose.

'Bristol challenged him outright,' chortled the debauched and corrupt Will Chiffinch, whose job it was to provide a steady stream of prostitutes for the King. Londoners called him the Pimpmaster General.

'What did the old goat say?' asked Lady Castlemaine, the King's oldest and most powerful mistress. The 'old goat' was Clarendon, whom she hated with a passion – he had tried to end her relationship with His Majesty by urging him to keep his marriage vows.

'That he had better things to do than organise asinine japes,' replied Chiffinch, and sniggered again. 'Which did nothing to endear him to the King, of course. But speaking of japes, I understand that preparations are well under way for the Adrian Masque. I cannot wait to see what the Poultry Department has done to the Banqueting House.'

'And *I* cannot wait to dive in the syllabub,' crooned

138

the lady. 'My costume is ready. I am going as Adrian's whore – I am sure he had one, because all popes do.'

Chaloner was horrified, knowing Catholics all over the country would be offended by her antics. Part of him began to hope that there *would* be an uprising to depose the King and his useless monkeys, because it would be no more than they deserved. But the saner part of his mind reminded him that there had already been too much bloodshed over the last three decades, and it was his duty to prevent more.

Even so, he could not resist a small act of petty spite. He climbed up the fountain and adjusted the nozzle on one of the spouts, directing it towards the gossiping pair like a hose. While they screeched their shock at the sudden drenching, he slipped away before they could see who was responsible.

The Earl was in his office, all the windows open in an attempt to catch a breeze. They faced west, so the heat was overwhelming – too much even for the Earl, who hated the cold and usually basked in the sun like a lizard. His plump face was a mask of unhappiness, and his gouty leg was propped on a stool in front of him.

'Bristol is going to tell the King that I have refused to arrange a saturnalia for him,' he told Chaloner miserably. 'His Majesty will see it as an insult, even though none was intended, and I shall fall even further from his favour. Bristol knows exactly how to harm me most.'

'Then stay away from him,' advised Chaloner in the hope – albeit frail – that Bristol would tire of the game if his victim refused to play.

'Then he will declare himself the winner, and I shall be in even deeper water. No, Chaloner, all I can do is meet him on his own terms and hope to best him. I cannot deliver a wild romp – I would not know where to begin – but I am sure I can devise something else the King will enjoy. A chess tournament, perhaps. Or a literary event.'

Then God help everyone at Clarendon House, thought Chaloner, knowing the Earl would be laughed out of Court if he tried to equate one of those with the delights of an orgy. 'I will try to think of something to blunt Bristol's horns, sir.'

'Well, think fast then,' said the Earl wretchedly, 'because time is not on our side. Have you heard the rumours that say everything will change on Sunday week? Well, Bristol is telling everyone that it is because *I* shall no longer be here to ruin everyone's fun.'

'He will not be here either, if the predictions are true,' said Chaloner. 'The Kingdom of God is expected to oust everyone in White Hall, not just you.'

'That is not very reassuring, Chaloner,' said the Earl lugubriously. 'But is it just the usual discontented rumbling, or is there some actual plot afoot?'

'I am doing my best to find out.'

'Good. Now, what have you done about Eleanor? Bristol is making much of the fact that Margaret Hay has not left Montagu's side since Eleanor died, and I cannot afford to let his poisonous tongue destroy one of my few remaining allies.'

'Wiseman will examine the body tomorrow, and I will talk to Montagu today.'

The Earl winced. 'I was wrong when I wrote to tell you he was back – he changed his mind at the last minute, and will not return to the city until tomorrow. You will have to settle for asking questions among those who were not invited to Greenwich.'

'I have already done that,' said Chaloner. 'It was—'

'Then do it again,' snapped the Earl. 'Particularly the men of the Poultry Department. They are firmly in Bristol's camp, and I have never liked them. Now, what have you learned about Bowles?'

'I have just come from his funeral. His parish church is a nest of religious radicals, and he broke the trading rules set by the Company of Poulters. It is possible that one of these things led to his murder.'

The Earl was disappointed. 'So Bowles' killer is still free, you have found nothing to exonerate Montagu, and Bristol grows more dangerous with every passing hour.' He gave a shuddering sigh. 'I have a bad feeling that even your dubious skills will be unequal to thwarting my enemies this time.'

Chaloner sincerely hoped he was wrong.

Unwilling to antagonise the Earl by flouting a direct order, Chaloner walked to the irregularly shaped area of cobblestones known as Scotland Yard. The Buttery, Pantry and Poultry departments were all located here, as well as the Great Bakehouse, the coal yard, the wood store and the charcoal house.

The Poultry Department occupied rooms in three different buildings, none of which were next to each other, which Chaloner imagined must be inconvenient for the clerk who did all the work. The biggest section was the underground chambers where game and eggs were stored. These were not as cool as they might have been, and seemed to be populated by half the flies in London. Chaloner backed out fast, wrinkling his nose at the ripe stench of decay from the hanging game.

The second part of the Poultry Department's domain

141

was a tiny room at the top of a teetering medieval warehouse, which had been allocated to the clerk, a small, harried man named John Munger. It was wickedly hot, and Munger had stripped down to his nether-garments to pore over his ledgers. Wasps had made a nest above the window, and the office was thick with them.

'How can you bear it?' gasped Chaloner, flapping them away from his face.

Munger placed a piece of paper over his inkwell, which was immediately covered by insects desperately trying to get at the scented substance beneath. 'A couple of months ago, I had a lovely room overlooking the river, but when Crookey was appointed, I was forced to surrender it to him, because he is more important than me. Now I am here instead.'

His face was a mask of bitterness, which was good news for Chaloner, as men who felt they had been slighted were more likely to be indiscreet.

'Yet I am sure you do more work than anyone else,' he said sympathetically, leaning against a wall and trying to ignore the wasps. 'Palace clerks always do.'

Munger nodded vehemently. 'And I am especially overwhelmed at the moment, because our department is responsible for organising the Adrian Masque. All the victuals must be medieval, which means a lot of eggs and table birds.'

'And there is the syllabub,' said Chaloner encouragingly. 'I understand it is to be the centrepiece of the entire affair, made to a secret recipe.'

'That is secret no longer,' spat Munger in disgust. 'Some slack-tongued fool let it slip and now the whole city knows. But the syllabub *will* be impressive. The recipe calls for a thousand egg yolks and enough cream to fill the fountain in the Great Court.'

Chaloner blinked. 'You plan to serve it in that? But it is filthy!'

Munger made an impatient gesture. 'I am trying to convey an idea of its size. It will actually be presented in a special vat, which will stand in the centre of the Banqueting House. The King and selected favourites will jump in it at the end of the night – to splash about and eat at the same time.'

'Is that not rather unwholesome?' asked Chaloner, thinking that people who had been dancing, drinking and enjoying themselves all evening were unlikely to be very fragrant when they got in, and *he* would certainly not fancy eating something that had been used as a bath by a lot of sweaty bodies.

'No one will care by that time,' replied Munger, truthfully enough. 'Of course, the eggs and cream will have to be bought at the very last minute, or the heat will spoil them. Eggs are especially dangerous, because they can cause egg fever.'

'I have never heard of egg fever,' said Chaloner, although he was aware that they were ranging rather far away from the subject of Eleanor Montagu.

'Some eggs produce a poison when left too long,' lectured Munger, delighted to talk to someone who listened, 'which is particularly deadly because it has no taste or smell. Unlike cream – everyone knows when that has turned, because it stinks.'

'So do eggs,' argued Chaloner.

'Only when they are bad,' said Munger. 'But there is a stage before they rot when there is no unpleasant odour, yet they contain a toxin that can bring a man very low.'

143

'I keep hearing that eggs are scarce because of the hot weather. Are you sure there will be a thousand to buy when you need them?'

Munger sniffed. 'Crookey may be a selfish, office-stealing bastard, but he is good at sourcing victuals. He will not let us down. Do you know why he was appointed?'

Chaloner nodded. 'To find the cheapest supplies – not to save money for the public purse, but so you and his colleagues can pocket the difference.'

'Not me!' flashed Munger, bitter again. 'I am tossed the occasional shilling, but the others take the lion's share. He has already made them very wealthy. Of course, I am not sure how much of Crookey's activities are legal.'

'You mean he gets his wares from higglers?'

Munger was dismissive. 'Higglers sell a few dozen eggs at a time, but White Hall requires hundreds every day. Ergo, higglers cannot possibly meet our demands. No, Crookey definitely gets them from poulters. And from Bowles, when he was alive.'

Chaloner frowned, and wondered if Crookey had killed Bowles, perhaps because the grocer wanted to charge him too much. He decided to bear it in mind when he next spoke to the Supernumerary Groom.

'So, how *do* you think he has been breaking the law?' he asked.

'Well, before Montagu appointed him, our department was losing money hand over fist, but now we are always in the black. However, some of the wares he acquires are suspiciously cheap – *impossibly* cheap, even. It is all rather too good to be true.'

'Do you have proof of any wrongdoing?'

Munger sniffed. 'He is too clever to leave anything incriminating for me to find. Meanwhile, every week sees him win ever better contracts from his suppliers, and more money pours into his cronies' pockets. Everyone is delighted with Crookey.'

'Except you,' said Chaloner quietly.

Munger smiled wanly. 'Except me, although I shall deny saying so if you ever repeat our conversation. He is too dangerous a man for me to cross.'

Eventually, Chaloner brought the discussion around to Eleanor, but Munger had never met her or Margaret Hay. He had plenty to say about Montagu, though.

'Other than making Crookey a Supernumerary Groom, he is a decent soul. His servants adore him, and he is popular with nearly all his fellow courtiers.'

'Lord Bristol does not like him,' Chaloner pointed out, 'or he would not have started the rumours regarding Eleanor's allegedly suspicious death.'

Munger gave a disgusted snort. 'Bristol would like him well enough if he broke off his friendship with Clarendon. Perhaps Montagu should, because he deserves better than to be dragged into a vicious quarrel that is none of his making.'

'You think Bristol has the right to dictate who Montagu should befriend?'

'Not in an ideal world,' replied Munger. 'But this is White Hall, and Montagu needs to be more careful than most because he made the mistake of siding with Parliament during the wars. It was a stupid and dangerous choice that will haunt him for the rest of his life.'

On that note, Chaloner took his leave.

The rooms occupied by the rest of the Poultry Department were far more pleasant than Munger's. They were airy, well lit, overlooked the river, and were decorated almost as sumptuously as the King's. There was evidently a meeting in progress when Chaloner arrived, because the entire cabal was there, other than its hapless clerk. They lounged on comfortable benches or chairs, and everyone had a cup of cool wine in his hand.

'Bugger off,' growled the loutish René Mezandier, coming to his feet and dropping his hand to the sword at his side. 'We are discussing sensitive business and, as Sergeant of the Poultry, it is my duty to oust you – by force if necessary.'

'You hold important meetings without your clerk?' asked Chaloner, feigning astonishment. 'Whose remit it is to take notes and record what is decided?'

'We do not bother with all that nonsense,' declared Mezandier. 'What is written is permanent, and we prefer there to be no account of our—'

'Thank you, Mezandier,' interrupted Catline briskly, and unfolded himself from his chair. 'I am sure Chaloner is not interested in our affairs.'

Chaloner was very interested, given that they sounded brazenly corrupt, but he forced himself to stick to the business at hand. 'I came to ask you about Eleanor Montagu.'

'We did not really know her,' replied Catline. 'She spent most of her time away from Court, which meant our encounters with her were rare and brief.'

'Margaret Hay will be different, though,' put in Mezandier. 'She is in White Hall all the time, and we shall certainly socialise with her when she marries Montagu.'

'*If* she marries Montagu,' said Crookey, who had chosen to sit in the dimmest corner of the room. Just like a spider, thought Chaloner, shunning the light to

146

spin his webs in the shadows. He recalled thinking exactly the same when he had seen Crookey the last time. 'Perhaps he will choose someone else.'

'I suppose you are exploring Eleanor's death,' said Catline, and exchanged a sly grin with his cronies. 'Doubtless your Earl thinks Montagu will be grateful if you uncover the truth. However, you should bear in mind that Montagu may not want the matter probed.'

'So you think he killed her?' pounced Chaloner. 'Why?'

Catline raised an eyebrow. 'Well, she was in Virginia until recently, minding her third husband's estates. Then she came home to a spouse who was used to being without her . . . '

'And who already has his eye on someone else,' put in Mezandier.

'It was Lord Bristol who pointed out that not all men will be happy to see the return of an aged and somewhat eccentric wife,' Catline went on. 'And it is an interesting point, although we accuse no one, of course.'

'Well, we should, because of course Montagu killed her,' said Mezandier, evidently a man who believed in speaking his mind. 'Perhaps he did it because she was always trying to do what was right. There is no room for that sort of thing in White Hall.'

'So I see,' said Chaloner, looking around pointedly at the overly lavish surroundings, almost certainly funded by dishonest practices.

'She was unhinged,' Mezandier went on. 'The bookseller at the Rainbow said she bought all manner of controversial texts from him. It is hardly the kind of behaviour one expects of a courtier.'

'Perhaps she should have jumped in a syllabub instead then,' muttered Chaloner.

147

'Everyone laughed at her foibles,' said Crookey, 'and it hurt her husband's standing among his peers. He probably felt he had no choice but to dispatch her.'

'Does he know you think him capable of murder?' Chaloner asked, and glanced at Crookey. 'Surely you owe him some loyalty for appointing you as Supernumerary Groom?'

'I owe him nothing,' flashed Crookey. 'And I prefer to throw in my lot with Bristol – a man who is *not* under Clarendon's tedious sway.'

'And who is not accused of dispatching an embarrassing spouse,' added Catline. 'Because Eleanor *was* embarrassing. For example, the day before she died, I saw her reading a common broadsheet. She gave it to me when she had finished, and I still have it.'

He pulled it from his pocket and handed it over. It was the Paladin's denunciation of the egg industry – the same issue that Chaloner had read on the Strand a few days earlier.

'The Paladin has written another piece on poulters since then,' said Mezandier, chuckling as he went to rummage for it among the muddle of papers on the table. 'Here it is. Clearly, the man hates them, because this one verges on the libellous. Doubtless, Eleanor would have embarrassed her husband by studying this one, too, had she not been dead. Such behaviour is hardly genteel in a woman.'

Personally, Chaloner saw nothing 'embarrassing' about Eleanor – or any other person of either sex – perusing the Paladin's remarks. As far as he was concerned, the more people who knew what Drinkell was doing with his vast flocks of barn-confined hens the better. Then he remembered that the Paladin had also written about

148

Bristol's nasty habit of urinating in White Hall's potted plants, which suggested a familiarity with the palace or one of its residents.

With a sudden sense of disquiet, it occurred to him that Eleanor might have been the anonymous pamphleteer herself. She was educated and intelligent, and she would have had the funds to publish her rants and make sure they were circulated around the city. It was not an activity usually enjoyed by high-ranking noblewomen, but he was beginning to appreciate that Eleanor had been anything but ordinary.

He glanced at the Poultry men, wondering if they had reached the same conclusion. He hoped not, because then Bristol would use it as a stick to beat not only Montagu, but anyone associated with him, especially the Earl.

Of course, if Chaloner's suspicions were right, then a lot of people would want revenge on Eleanor, given how many of them had been ridiculed by the Paladin's pen, especially the lunatic religious sects. So did it mean Eleanor *had* been murdered? Unfortunately, he would not have his answer to that question until the following afternoon, when Wiseman would tell him once and for all if there was anything to investigate.

Chapter 6

Chaloner was relieved to be away from White Hall with its undercurrents of treachery, spite and greed. There were no hackney carriages available, so he began to walk to Poulters' Hall, wilting in the fiery heat of mid afternoon. He stopped to eat at the Hercules' Pillars tavern on Fleet Street, which was famous for its enormous portions of meat. It was too hot for such heavy fare, so he ordered a 'Cheddar tart', although this transpired to be a large pastry case filled with molten cheese, which was just as rich as the roasts devoured by everyone else.

While he ate, he studied the broadsheets that Catline and Mezandier had given him. Mezandier was right to say the second verged on the libellous, because it was considerably more outspoken than the first, and castigated large-scale egg producers with a ferocity that was vicious and unbridled. It also contained a reference to Downes' book, which convinced Chaloner even further that his reasoning about the pamphleteer's identity was correct.

He pondered the subject matter – essentially that poulters with a few dozen free-ranging hens were beginning to be replaced by massive concerns that kept birds in crowded and unsanitary conditions, and that nothing mattered more to these large-scale farmers than making money. He recalled how Drinkell had boasted about the size and profitability of his enterprise, suggesting that the Paladin's allegations might well be true.

Chaloner knew nothing about how eggs were supplied to cities. However, Munger had said that White Hall alone used hundreds every day, so it was clear that small producers would struggle to meet London's demand – a demand that would increase exponentially as the population expanded again after the plague. Ergo, there was obviously a pressing need for them to be produced on an industrial scale, so that shortages would not put prices beyond the reach of all but the wealthiest buyers. But, as the Paladin so eloquently pointed out, there was a cost to mass production in terms of the quality of the eggs and the welfare of the birds.

Feeling queasy from the amount of fat he had just consumed, Chaloner walked the rest of the way to Poulters' Hall, arriving hot, dusty and sticky with sweat. He almost turned back, loath to set foot in such an august establishment while he was less than sartorial, but then supposed that everyone else would be no better. He was shown into the main hall by an apprentice, then left to wait while the boy fetched Master Farmer. He sat on a bench, enjoying the relative cool after the heat outside.

'Do you have news about poor Hill?' asked Farmer, hurrying into the hall and wringing his hands in agitation. 'We understand you were in the area when he was stabbed, so I hope you are here to say the culprit is caught.'

The Master was accompanied by his deputy, Drinkell,

151

who looked suave and elegant in a well-cut long-coat, his face glowing with good health. By contrast, Farmer was a man under strain, with unkempt hair, unshaven cheeks and dark rings under his eyes.

Chaloner shook his head apologetically. 'The killer was long gone by the time I arrived – which I can say for certain because a physician said that Hill had been in the water butt for hours before his body was discovered.'

'Three of our members murdered, and higglers on every street corner,' said Farmer in despair. 'And now even a White Hall investigator is confounded.'

'I am not confounded,' objected Chaloner indignantly. 'I just need more time.'

'But we do not have more time to give you!' cried Farmer, distraught. 'We are under attack from all sides: agitators urge higglers to undercut our prices; the Paladin pens vicious attacks on our new farming methods; and the hot weather puts hens off their lay. How can we compete with higglers when they have eggs to sell and we have none?'

Chaloner frowned. 'So the higglers' hens are producing, but yours are not? Why is that? Because there is truth in the Paladin's claims that the Company mistreats its birds?'

'I resent that accusation,' snarled Drinkell. 'All three thousand of my hens are perfectly content. They just dislike the heat.'

'If I were not a rational man, I would say we have been cursed,' said Farmer miserably, 'because I cannot see any other explanation for all this bad luck. As the public face of the Company, I am under immense pressure to pretend that all is well. But it is not!'

'Pressure,' mused Chaloner. 'I understand that Crookey

from White Hall visited you recently. Does he bully you into supplying him with eggs at unreasonably low prices?'

It was Drinkell who replied. 'Of course not! Crookey did come, but it was rabbits he wanted, not eggs – for the Adrian Masque. Apparently, medieval popes liked rabbit.'

'I am to provide ten dozen of them,' whispered Farmer, his unsteady voice telling Chaloner that the order was large enough to be daunting.

'So where *does* Crookey get the palace's eggs?' pressed Chaloner. 'Not from higglers, because he would need to deal with too many of them to make it practical. And not from Bowles now that he is dead.'

'He probably deals directly with some country estate,' replied Farmer wretchedly. 'It is against Company rules to import them into the city without a licence from us, but . . . well, who am I to challenge a man who has the ear of the King?'

Drinkell's contemptuous glance suggested that *he* would not allow anyone to ride roughshod over his Company's rights and privileges, no matter whose ear they had.

At that moment, Chaloner became aware that someone was listening in on the discussion, having crawled through the door and crept under one of the benches. He strode forward and hauled the eavesdropper out by the scruff of his neck. It was Collins, who blushed with mortification at being caught. Farmer gaped at the beadle in astonishment, while Drinkell laughed aloud.

'I dropped a coin,' blustered Collins unconvincingly. 'I was looking for it.'

'I am pleased to see you, as it happens,' said Chaloner, releasing him. 'I have some more questions.'

'About Hill, I suppose,' sighed Collins unhappily. 'I

153

thought he would catch these agitators. He said he could, and I paid him a lot of money – from my own purse.'

'Where were you last night?' asked Chaloner. 'Or rather early evening, as that seems to have been when Hill was stabbed, according to Vernon the physician.'

Collins winced. 'In the King's Head, looking for the agitators. But, as I said before, they always seem to know where I am, so while I waited in the tavern, they brayed their seditious messages in Allhallows the Great.'

'They used a church?' asked Chaloner, surprised to hear that Simpson supported other forms of popular dissent as well as the religious kind, because he did not seem like a man who cared about anyone else's opinions. 'Have they done that before?'

Collins shook his head. 'Perhaps they heard it is not just me who aims to catch them now, so they changed their haunts accordingly.'

Chaloner supposed that was possible. 'I saw you two in Allhallows yesterday,' he said to Farmer and Drinkell. 'At Bowles' funeral. I do not suppose you identified anyone there who might bear a grudge against your Company?'

'All I noticed was that it was a very peculiar ceremony,' said Drinkell with a moue of distaste. 'We left halfway through lest the government's spies assumed it was a meeting of radicals and arrested everyone.'

'So when you challenge that vicar about allowing the agitators to use his pulpit, you might want to be on your guard,' advised Farmer. 'Did you see the great sword he wore on his belt? And him a man of the cloth!'

'It was just a knife,' said Chaloner, not acknowledging that it *was* a very big one. He turned back to Collins. 'Have you discovered anything about Hill's murder?'

154

Collins shook his head sheepishly. 'I told him to stay in the coffee houses, but he elected to visit the alehouses instead. As far as I can tell, his last stop was Widow Noest's place in Fish Yard, but no one saw him leave and no one saw him killed.'

He looked dejected, and Chaloner felt sorry for him, aware that Drinkell would use his lack of progress as another excuse to replace him, and what would happen to him then? He was unlikely to find a new job at his age, and Chaloner could not see the Company supporting him in his dotage, especially once someone like Drinkell was at the helm.

'But I have drawn new conclusions about the agitators,' the beadle went on, struggling to pull himself together. 'Namely that they speak with such eloquence that they must be *professional* speakers. They are not common rabble-rousers, as I first supposed.'

'Have you told the Spymaster this?' asked Chaloner. 'He should know that the brewing unrest might be driven by experienced troublemakers.'

'We do not want *him* involved, thank you very much,' said Drinkell firmly, and shot Chaloner an unpleasant look. 'It is bad enough having the Lord Chancellor's man peering over our shoulders.'

'I understand your reservations,' said Chaloner, aware that no one in his right mind would willingly attract Williamson's attention. 'But—'

'I do not like him,' interrupted Drinkell. 'He may not be as terrifying as old Thurloe, but I still do not think it is a good idea to put ourselves in his sights on the basis of old Collins's dubious assumptions.'

'He does not frighten me,' blustered Farmer unconvincingly, and lowered his voice. 'But his helpmeet

Swaddell . . . well, he calls himself a clerk, but we all know that his real business is murder. I do not think I have ever encountered a more sinister individual.'

Chaloner decided not to tell them that Swaddell had recently become his kinsman by marriage. He had hoped the happy couple would go to live with her family on the Isle of Man, thus sparing London Swaddell's dark presence, but they had settled in Westminster instead, where Swaddell continued to work for the intelligence services.

'I am afraid Williamson must be told,' said Chaloner firmly. 'Preferably today, because he will be irked if you fail to report something that later becomes a problem.'

'You do it, then,' said Farmer, ignoring Drinkell's irritable scowl that his opinion was going to be ignored. 'Because I refuse to order any of my own people into a place where they might encounter that horrible assassin.'

'But first, Chaloner, you are coming to my farm,' announced Drinkell, somewhat out of the blue. 'Your remark about my hens being unhappy has offended me, and I want to show you that nothing is further from the truth. Then you can tell everyone at White Hall that the Paladin is a filthy liar, and thus clear my name of these vile accusations.'

'You mean the farm in Willesden?' asked Chaloner, recalling the place being mentioned when they were discussing the letters W, I and L that Hadie had spelled out as he lay dying. 'But that must be at least eight miles away. I do not have time to go all the way out there.'

'It is *not* eight miles – and not in Willesden either,' scoffed Drinkell impatiently. 'It is much closer than that. Now, prepare yourself for a pleasant excursion, because we leave in ten minutes.'

*

The farm transpired to be just east of the tiny hamlet of Harlesden, and while it was technically not as far as the larger settlement of Willesden to the north, it was still a good seven and a half miles from the city. When he realised he had been blatantly deceived, Chaloner was tempted to stop the carriage and walk home, but the day was so hot that a lengthy trek on foot was distinctly unappealing. Crossly, he stayed where he was.

The coach was Drinkell's personal one, which revealed him to be a very wealthy individual, as these were expensive to buy and to run. The liveried driver was able to coax the horses along at an impressive lick, because the prolonged dry spell had baked the roads rock hard, making the going unusually easy.

The vehicle was uncomfortably crowded, though, as Drinkell had crammed in a number of his apprentices as well as Newdick, Elsie, Dorcas and Lester. The boys and Newdick were going to refill the storage silos, while the women were included because Drinkell aimed to pick their brains about improving his birds' productivity. They were to be paid for their expert opinions with free eggs, to augment their own supplies when they next went to market. And Lester had invited himself along, because he fancied a jaunt with Elsie.

A couple of the boys rode on the roof, but the rest had jammed themselves inside, so that ten people were packed into a space that was designed for six. The unsavoury Newdick was opposite Chaloner, reeking of sweat and bird droppings, and the spy did not know how Dorcas and Elsie, who were on either side of the man, could bear to be so close. Chaloner himself was sandwiched between Drinkell and a grubby child with a runny nose.

'Seven and a half miles is not close,' he grumbled again, deeply resenting the lost time when he had so much else to do. 'Even travelling at this pace, we will be gone for hours.'

'You will be home by sunset,' promised Drinkell impatiently. 'And it certainly *is* close. You cannot have poultry farms too near a city because of the smell. Our Company has had rules about that since time immemorial.'

'We shall *all* be home by sunset,' put in Newdick. 'The feast to celebrate Holmes's Bonfire is tonight, and we cannot be late for that – it will be the highlight of the Company's year.'

Chaloner recalled all the food he had seen in the cellar the previous day, and conceded that Drinkell was unlikely to risk missing such an occasion, so perhaps the visit would not take as long as he feared. He looked at Elsie and Dorcas.

'I have been told that the heat is putting Drinkell's hens off their lay, so what makes you think he will have any eggs to give you?'

'He has three thousand birds,' shrugged Dorcas. 'Some will produce, even if the majority do not, so we will not go home empty-handed. Of course, our own chickens do not seem to mind the hot weather.'

'Perhaps it is because they live in a pleasantly shaded wood,' suggested Elsie, 'and our flock is small – just four dozen birds. Still, our customers will be grateful for whatever extra Mr Drinkell can provide.'

The farm was located on a narrow track east of the main Harlesden–Willesden road, and occupied much less land than Chaloner would have expected, given the scale of the operation – almost certainly less than two acres. At

158

one end was a house for the manager, which had all its windows boarded over, perhaps to exclude the powerful reek of chicken manure. The rest of the compound comprised outhouses for storage, a silo for grain, and half a dozen large, low-roofed barns where the birds were kept. All were surrounded by a fence to deter predators and trespassers.

'It stinks!' exclaimed Lester in distaste as they rolled to a standstill. 'Good God! How can you bear it?'

'Now you understand why we cannot be too near the city,' said Drinkell. 'I would not like to live downwind of this myself, and I am used to it.'

'And the noise,' cried Lester, as Drinkell led the way towards the nearest barn and hundreds of avian voices grew louder. 'I can barely hear myself think.'

'Stay close,' ordered Drinkell, shouting to make himself heard. 'I am protective of my charges, and I cannot have you wandering off and disturbing them. The birds in the other buildings are unused to visitors, so I shall only show you one of them.'

He opened the door, and Chaloner was not surprised that the chickens had stopped laying, because the shed was like a furnace. Hens panted and spread their wings in an effort to cool down, and the area around their water trough was a frantic mêlée of thirsty birds. Surreptitiously, Newdick toed a couple of dead ones behind a pile of filthy straw.

'You can see that they are happy,' said Drinkell, gesturing around him. 'They have perches to roost on, plenty of nest-boxes, and we feed them twice a day.'

But Chaloner was appalled, and could tell from the expressions on Dorcas and Elsie's faces that they were, too.

'This is downright cruel,' he declared, making no effort to conceal his revulsion. 'It is far too hot and crowded – and they cannot get out.'

'They do not *want* to go out,' countered Drinkell indignantly. 'They feel safe in here, and none are willing to stray too far from their food bins.'

'Yet I think they would benefit from some fresh air, Mr Drinkell,' said Dorcas, more inclined to be diplomatic. 'And as there are only about two hundred hens in here, but you own three thousand, it means the birds in the remaining five barns must be a lot more densely packed. It is not—'

'Each bird has exactly as much space as she needs,' said Drinkell authoritatively. 'I have investigated the issue thoroughly, and my farm is based on sound scientific principles.'

Dorcas did not look convinced, but Newdick whisked her and Elsie away to his house, to write down their views on which feeds were best for improving the hens' frequency of laying. Lester followed, leaving Chaloner alone with Drinkell.

'This is the only practical way of meeting the city's needs,' explained Drinkell earnestly, seeing Chaloner still had serious reservations, 'and my innovations will be adopted by all poulters in time. They will *have* to, if they want to stay in business.'

'I sincerely hope you are wrong,' muttered Chaloner fervently.

Drinkell looked mystified. 'I rarely bring anyone here, lest it unsettles the birds, but those few I have invited have praised my system without reservation. I am astonished that you are not equally impressed – I thought the visit would alleviate your concerns, not exacerbate them.'

Chaloner found it difficult to believe that anyone seeing the farm would consider it a laudable enterprise. Moreover, he was stunned that a poulter, who was supposed to know what he was doing, should think the birds were happy in their cramped and airless furnace. He stepped outside the barn in relief, and glanced around, noting that the soil was so poor it would not support a hundred free-ranging hens, let alone three thousand, should they ever be set free to forage. He supposed Drinkell had been innovative in transforming a patch of scrubland into something that made him wealthy, but at what cost to the hens?

'You are overly sensitive,' Drinkell went on when Chaloner made no reply. 'My work has won widespread acclaim among my more enlightened colleagues, and I even count nobility among my admirers – the wife of an earl, no less.'

'Not Eleanor Montagu?' asked Chaloner warily.

Drinkell gaped in surprise. 'How did you know? Did she tell you?'

'Not exactly.' Chaloner was tempted to say that she had not approved at all, and had gone home and written two vitriolic pamphlets about it. Drinkell's reaction suggested *he* had not made the connection between the Paladin and his guest, though, and Chaloner was not about to enlighten him. However, Drinkell's ignorance about the Paladin's identity meant that if Eleanor *had* died by foul means, then he had not dispatched her for writing disparaging remarks about his nasty enterprise.

'I should get back to the city,' Chaloner said, eager to be away from the sweltering farm and its hapless inhabitants. 'I cannot solve your higgling problem out here.'

'I doubt you will solve it there, either,' said Drinkell

cuttingly. 'And if you had any sense, you would leave it to Newdick. It is inappropriate for outsiders to meddle in Company affairs.'

'So you have said before,' said Chaloner flatly. 'Several times.'

The journey home was even less pleasant than the outward one, because although some of the apprentices had elected to walk, Elsie and Dorcas had been given five hundred eggs. These could not go on the roof, because they were fragile, which meant that every passenger was obliged to cradle a box on his or her knees. The only person who seemed content with the arrangement was Lester, because Elsie was squashed up against him.

'Your hens have done well for birds that are off their lay, Drinkell,' remarked Lester, indicating the crates. 'Perhaps they do not mind the heat as much as you think. Tom's do not seem to be affected and nor are Dorcas's.'

This sparked a debate among the poulters, which lasted all the way home. When the coach finally rolled to a standstill, everyone unravelled themselves carefully, and Lester disappeared to help the women with their eggs. By this time, the sun was low in the sky, and Chaloner felt too hot, tired and dirty to resume his enquiries, so he accepted an invitation to stay for the feast instead. A nagging voice at the back of his mind reminded him that he was supposed to visit Downes in the Tower, but the regicide was not going anywhere, so he decided to leave it until the following day.

Since that morning, the hall had been transformed. Candles were lit, and the tables covered with fine white linen cloths. To give the feast a nautical feel, ropes hung from the rafters to represent rigging, and a large piece of sailcloth had been hoisted over the dais.

Already, members were filing in to take their places – freemen at one end of the hall, apprentices at the other. As a guest of Drinkell, Chaloner was allocated a place on the dais between him and Master Farmer, although he would far rather have been with Lester, Elsie and Dorcas in the main body of the hall. The two women had managed a hasty change of clothes, and wore dresses with gathered skirts and tight-fitting bodices. Expensive but discreet necklaces glittered at their throats, reminding him that they were respectable merchants in their own right.

The other diners were predominantly men, who flocked in noisily, calling greetings to friends and colleagues. By the time everyone was seated, the benches were packed so tightly that Chaloner wondered how some of them would be able to move enough to eat.

Farmer gave a welcome speech that was full of half-finished sentences and non sequiturs, after which the chaplain, sensing his audience's increasing restlessness, stood, intoned a two-word grace, and sat down again. There was a cheer as the victuals began to arrive.

Chaloner supposed he should not be surprised that most of the food was avian in origin – a vast amount of it, ranging from turkeys, geese and ducks to tiny song-birds. Belatedly it occurred to him that accepting an invitation from the Company of Poulters was probably not a very good idea for a man who never ate anything with feathers.

'So many birds,' he remarked unhappily, aware that some were so small that it could hardly have been worth the effort of preparing them for the table.

163

'I counted forty-one different kinds in the kitchen earlier,' said Farmer proudly, and rubbed his hands in gluttonous anticipation. 'Besides the usual fowl, we have woodcock, egrets, thrushes, sparrows, snipe, knots, plover, larks, herons, doves, cranes and buntings.'

'And a wren,' put in Drinkell. 'Would you like it?'

'No, thank you,' replied Chaloner, struggling not to sound ungracious. 'But you said there would be eggs?'

'Unfortunately, we only have fifty to share between us all,' replied Farmer, waving his hand around the hall, where at least three hundred people waited to be served.

Chaloner regarded him askance. 'But I saw piles of them in your pantry yesterday.'

'All sold in the markets today,' explained Farmer. 'London has a voracious appetite for them, especially now, when they are scarce because of the heat.'

'Then what about the ones that Drinkell gave to Dorcas and Elsie?'

'Those will be raw,' said Farmer. 'So I would not recommend sending for a couple if I were you. But what did you think of Drinkell's enterprise?'

'I was sickened and horrified,' replied Chaloner, uncharacteristically blunt because, thirsty after the trek to the country, he had downed two large cups of wine that had gone straight to his head and obliterated his sense of discretion. He glared accusingly at Drinkell, but the man was deep in conversation with the guest on his other side and did not hear.

'His methods are the way of the future, I am afraid,' sighed Farmer. 'It does not matter what you – or I, for that matter – think. London demands so many eggs that operations like Drinkell's are the only way to meet the demand at prices folk can afford. Hah! Here is a radish. Perhaps you would like that instead?'

The moment the food had arrived, all conversation had ceased in the body of the hall, so the only thing to be heard now was the crunching of tiny bones and the clatter of knives on pewter plates. Even Farmer and Drinkell were disinclined to talk much when there were rare and unusual species to devour. Chaloner's fastidiousness left him with a piece of ham, two apples and the solitary radish, which no one else seemed to want.

'And now we shall have some music,' declared Farmer, when every table was littered with skeletons, claws and beaks, and the poulters sat back with sighs of contentment. The wine flowed, and a babble of lively conversation rose again.

Chaloner loved music. It calmed him when he was uneasy, cheered him when he was despondent, and cleared his mind when he needed to think. With delight, he saw Collins carry in a consort of viols. Several freemen stepped forward to play, Dorcas and Elsie among them, although Dorcas was by far the most talented. When she offered Chaloner a turn, he accepted eagerly, and joined in a number of popular jigs. He had already noticed she was pretty, but her skill with a particularly difficult flying spiccato made him consider her anew, and he thought that if he was in the market for an amour, he would certainly ask *her* to visit the Foxhill Pleasure Gardens with him.

Eventually, some of the audience began to sing – not necessarily the same tunes as the viols – so she suggested they repair to an adjoining chamber, where they could play without being obliged to compete with three hundred bawling voices. No one noticed them leave, and Chaloner spent the rest of the evening happily losing himself in a selection of challenging works by Lawes and Charpentier.

When Dorcas finally indicated that it was time to stop, Chaloner was surprised to see that most of the revellers had gone home and the servants were busy cleaning up. A few apprentices slumped drunkenly across the tables, while several knots of men discussed business here and there in low, intense voices. One included Farmer, and Chaloner heard the word 'higgler' spoken with a good deal of agitation. Meanwhile, Lester had declined to leave before Elsie, but full of food and bored by the virtuosic turn the viol players had taken, he had fallen asleep while he waited. Chaloner shook him awake.

The captain jumped to his feet in dismay, looking around wildly, but relaxed when he saw the object of his desire was still there.

'You and I must see the ladies safely home,' he told Chaloner. 'You can talk to Dorcas, who is very pleasant, but I want Elsie to myself.'

It was not far from Poulters' Hall to Pudding Lane, but Lester hailed a hackney anyway, aiming to impress. On the journey, Chaloner quizzed the two women about their Company and its officers, but learned nothing that he had not already determined for himself – that Beadle Collins did his best but was no longer young; that Farmer was pleasant but too weak to be an effective Master; and that Drinkell was determined to succeed him.

The coach dropped them in Pudding Lane, and Elsie led them down an alley to the house she shared with Dorcas in Fish Yard, where Lester took an age to bid her goodnight. Left with Dorcas, Chaloner held forth enthusiastically about the evening's music, but soon realised he was doing all the talking. Unwilling to come across as a bore, he flailed about for something else to discuss with her.

'Did you discover anything about Hadie's killer when you were in the King's Head last night?' he asked, although it occurred to him even as he spoke that this was not most people's idea of sophisticated late-night conversation.

'Well, we found an eye-witness to the murder,' replied Dorcas, and gave a small smile that showed she was rather proud of it. 'A woman named Alice Spencer, who was nearer than Elsie and me when Hadie was cut down. She is a prostitute, and was waiting for potential customers to emerge from Skiner's.'

Chaloner was astonished, as no one else had mentioned a witness. He glanced across to the coffee house. Its door was closed and the window shutters secured for the night.

'What did she see?' he asked keenly.

'Not the killer's face, unfortunately. She had been loitering for some time, so she saw the culprit arrive and stand in the doorway next to Widow Noest's alehouse. She assumed he was a common cutpurse hoping for easy prey, and was irked, lest he interfered with her own business. Then Hadie arrived.'

'And?'

'Alice said the moment Hadie saw Elsie and me, he hailed us. I cannot prove it, but I think he had identified the agitators – or he knew something about them that he wanted to share. As freemen, Elsie and I had a vested interest in anything he discovered, so it makes sense that he opted to pass that information to us.'

'I suppose it does,' acknowledged Chaloner.

'Then the killer made his move. Alice said it was an

167

attack of unbelievable speed – over and done before she could open her mouth to shout a warning. She also said that the killer moved with such determination that it was obvious this was no random assault – Hadie was clearly his intended victim.'

'Where does Alice live?' asked Chaloner, eager to speak to her himself.

'Wherever she can find a bed,' replied Dorcas. 'But she will never talk to you. She only confided in Elsie and me because she recognised us as kindred spirits – women struggling to make our way in a world of men.'

'I would like to try anyway, because—'

'No,' interrupted Dorcas with finality. 'We cannot risk the killer finding out there is a witness to his crime, because it may put Alice in danger.'

She refused to be convinced otherwise, so Chaloner reluctantly conceded defeat. 'Could she describe the killer?'

'Only to say that he was of average height and build, and that he wore a cloak and a hat, which she thought was odd for such a hot night. It occurs to me that a stranger would not have bothered with a disguise, which may mean he is local.'

As far as Chaloner was concerned, this observation did not help very much, given how many people lived or worked in and around Pudding Lane, although he was impressed by her logic in making it. 'Did she say anything else?'

'Just one thing: that Hadie whispered something to shock his assailant.' Dorcas grimaced. 'Elsie and I saw the killer grab him and give him a shake. I assumed he was a robber looking for valuables, but Alice's testimony proves me wrong. Elsie had the right of it – the rogue *was* trying to make Hadie speak.'

'Did Alice hear what Hadie whispered?'

'Something about a letter. As I said, I think Hadie had learned something about the agitators – their names or something to expose them. Alice's mention of a missive leads me to surmise that he wrote everything down and sent it to someone he trusted.'

'But either this message was never delivered, or his confidant has declined to act on it,' finished Chaloner. 'I wonder if he kept a copy. Did anyone search his house?'

'I went with Collins this morning, but someone had been there before us – Hadie was an untidy man, but his home was as neat as a new pin. If you want to see it yourself, ask Master Farmer for the key.'

Chaloner decided he would, because he had a lot more experience at locating sly hiding places than most people, and might succeed where others had failed. Dorcas could tell him no more, but at that point Lester indicated that he was ready to go home. Chaloner bowed a farewell to the two women, wishing he did not have quite so far to walk on a night that was so sticky and airless.

He and Lester were halfway down Pudding Lane when a shadow hurtled from an alley towards them, wielding a dagger. Chaloner reacted instinctively, turning to deflect the blow that was aimed at his chest and drawing his sword in one swift, smooth movement. The attacker faltered when he saw his victim armed, so Chaloner took the opportunity to swipe out himself, and had the satisfaction of feeling the flat of his sword connect with an arm. The assailant howled with pain, and his blade clattered to the ground. Then he fled.

Chaloner gave chase, pursuing him down a lane that led into Fish Street Hill, but when he emerged, the knifeman was nowhere to be seen. He closed his eyes and listened intently for footsteps, but there was nothing. He hurried back along the alley, supposing he must have run past the culprit in the darkness, but that was deserted, too. He reached Lester, who had retrieved their attacker's dagger, and was examining it in the light that spilled from a nearby window.

'It is very long and thin,' he said, handing it to Chaloner. 'More like a spike than a knife. I would have opted for something larger in his position.'

'So would I,' said Chaloner, peering at it. 'But I suspect this is the weapon that killed Hadie, Hill and Bowles – all three had wounds that will likely match it. Did you notice anything that might help us identify him?'

'He was shorter than me, but thinner than you. Just average, in other words.'

'Like the man who killed Hadie, then,' said Chaloner, thinking of the description the prostitute had given Dorcas. 'Along with the fact that he was also wearing a hat and cloak, despite the heat. If someone wants us dead, it means that we are coming near the truth. That is good news.'

'If you say so,' said Lester, unconvinced.

Chapter 7

Although it was well into the small hours by the time Chaloner arrived home, he still woke before dawn. He felt woolly-headed, and there was a nagging headache behind his eyes from too much wine and too little sleep. He tried to nod off again, but the market traders were making a terrible racket, so he rose and went to look out of the window at them.

The lamp-lit piazza was a hive of activity, with at least two dozen carts and barrows arriving with fresh produce from the country. He noted several new faces among the vendors, which included at least two with eggs. He surmised that they were higglers, taking the opportunity afforded by the Company of Poulters' loss of control to make some illicit cash.

He washed and shaved, then donned a dark-blue long-coat, black breeches and a fresh shirt. He was about to leave when his eye was drawn to his viols. He remembered the music from the night before, and the pleasure it had given him. He sat to bow a scale, closing his eyes to savour the richness of the sound, and was about to launch into a lively piece by Ferrabosco when he heard an irritable hammering on the ceiling below. He stopped with a sigh, supposing Lester had a right to object, given the earliness of the hour.

He trotted downstairs, where he discovered that Lester was not the only one who wanted a lie-in. None of the servants were up, taking advantage of the fact that Wiseman was away in Greenwich and so not in a position to object.

A survey of the eggs in the pantry told him that the weather was having no impact on his own hens, and they were laying just as well now as they had been before the heatwave had started. He boiled three eggs and put them in his pocket, then went into the garden. It was growing light, so he opened the coop and watched his flock pour out in a feathery torrent. Then he spent the next half hour removing soiled bedding, filling feeders and water bowls, and checking each bird for illness or injury. When he had finished, he sat on a bench to eat his breakfast and think.

The previous night's assault told him that someone feared he was making progress on the murders of Bowles, Hadie and Hill. It also suggested that the attacker was the killer himself, and that Chaloner now had the blade used on the other victims. He took it from his pocket and inspected it. It was a simple thing – a plain metal hilt with a long, thin blade. It was worn but well-honed, and he suspected its owner would be sorry to lose it. He replaced it in his pocket and began to plan his day.

First, he had to speak to Downes, despite the fact that the thought of the Tower filled him with dread. However, Thurloe expected it of him, so he would have to grit his teeth and get on with it. If he learned nothing there, he would speak to Downes' friends again – Vicar Simpson of Allhallows and Vicar Glasse of St Margaret's. Perhaps one would be more inclined to talk if cornered away from the other. While he was there, he would find out why Simpson had allowed his church to be used by the agitators.

After that, he decided to visit Wogan. As a regicide himself, the Welshman might have some insights into why eight of his fellows were dead, and why two more of them might be heading towards London.

In the afternoon, he would go to the charnel house, where he hoped Wiseman would determine once and for all that Eleanor had died of natural causes. Then he would make sure that everyone at White Hall knew it, proving that Bristol's accusations were baseless and stemmed solely from spite.

He also needed to tell Williamson that professional rabble-rousers were at large in and around Pudding Lane – the Spymaster probably already knew, but it would be wise to make sure – and speak to Pepys about a ship for Lester.

And, if there was time after all that, he would turn his attention to the agitators, assailed with the uncomfortable sense that they might be building towards something a lot more serious than breaking a few trade laws. Londoners had a lot of grievances – the heatwave, the egg shortage, White Hall's profligacy – and uprisings were easy to spark when a city was full of dissatisfied people. Thus the agitators needed to be stopped, and his best chance of doing that lay in the hope that Hadie had made a copy of the letter Alice had heard him mention to his killer – a letter that might reveal whatever he had learned. Ergo, a search of Hadie's house was in order, and he should do it as soon as practicable.

Chaloner finished the boiled eggs, wiped his hands on his breeches and set off.

His route to the Tower took him through the market, which was already busy with customers despite the early hour. As he passed the egg-sellers, he saw he was wrong to assume they were both common higglers. One was just a country man, hawking three dozen eggs alongside produce from his garden, but the other was clearly wealthy. His wares were displayed on a purpose-built stand, and contained nothing but eggs – rows of them, graded by size and colour. Below them, his name was painted on a board: Daniel Norton of Enfield.

'Have you heard the news?' he asked excitedly, when Chaloner paused next to his stall. 'Our fleet is out, and is patrolling the Channel to protect us from the Dutch.'

'Good,' said Chaloner, hoping it was true. 'I have not seen you before. Are you—'

'You had better not say we have no right to trade here,' interrupted the second higgler belligerently. He was slightly built with pale eyes and a beak of a nose. His clothes verged on the gaudy – a rich chestnut with plenty of red, green and white. Like a pheasant, thought Chaloner. 'Because we do. Why should the Company of Poulters dictate our lives? I would not join their ranks, even if I could afford the membership fees.'

'Well, I *am* one of their freemen,' said Norton. 'However, that should not prevent me from selling my eggs where and when I like, so I stand with Pheasant here.'

'Pheasant?' blurted Chaloner, wondering if the name was a joke.

'We both have land in Enfield,' Norton went on, 'and

we usually sell our eggs up there, but the Company cannot meet London's demand at the moment, and we would be fools not to step in and help. I have sold half my wares already, and the sun is barely up.'

'Did someone recommend that you come here?' fished Chaloner.

'Not in person,' replied Pheasant. 'But my brother heard a man in Pudding Lane say that if we all stand together, there will be too many of us for the Company of Poulters to crush. He was right – we higglers are an army now!'

'Will your brother know where I might find this man?'

'I wish he did because I should like to shake his hand – I have made a fortune here this last week – but no one knows who he is or where he lives.'

Chaloner started to leave, but then turned back. 'One last question: is the hot weather putting your hens off their lay?'

'No, of course not,' said Norton, startled. 'And nor will it, as long as they have access to shade and water.'

Chaloner walked away, his mind full of questions. He believed Norton's answer about hens and the weather, because it matched his own experiences, so why was there a dearth of eggs? Was it because major producers like Drinkell kept their birds in the wrong conditions? Yet Drinkell was not stupid – his goal was to make money, and if the intensive system he had devised meant a fall in productivity, he would not persist with it. Moreover, Elsie and Dorcas had done well out of eggs from him the previous day.

Could the agitators be controlling how many eggs came into the city, to create a demand that would allow higglers to profit? It was certainly one way to take money

175

from the rich and give it to the poor, but how could such a feat be accomplished? The poulters were unlikely to stand idly by while their livelihoods were destroyed, and would notice anyone preventing their wares from reaching the markets. With a sigh, he conceded that he had no idea what was happening at all.

He had just reached the Strand when he heard his name called. It was Lester, dressed in his best hat, coat and breeches. The captain beamed happily.

'I cannot traipse around with you today, Tom, because Elsie has invited me to see her family farm in Wapping. However, I shall not forget about your enquiries, so while I am there, I shall learn all about the poultry business on your behalf.'

'Do not interrogate her,' advised Chaloner, pleased Lester had found a way to shake off his despondency over *Swiftsure*. 'She will not like it, so just enjoy yourself.'

'I can do both,' said Lester airily.

Despite the early hour, the streets were busy as Chaloner walked to the Tower. It was already sweltering, and there was not so much as a whisper of a breeze. Even the pigeons seemed enervated, and either sat listlessly or tried to snatch drinks from the public conduits, which were thick with people gathering water for the day's cooking, washing and cleaning.

The talk on the streets was mostly about omens, and he was astonished to hear the tale of the egg with the flaming cross on so many lips. There was also mention of Jesus's face in an omelette. Several people claimed to have seen it, because it had been on display in St Paul's Cathedral. Unfortunately, not long after an eager queue had formed, a dog was said to have raced in and eaten it, which sounded suspiciously convenient to Chaloner.

He reached the Tower, but was informed by a yeoman that no visitors would be allowed in that morning, because Sir Gilbert Talbot, Master of the Jewel House, had ordered a detailed inspection of the entire castle, which meant all the guards were too busy.

'Does the Master of the Jewel House have the authority to demand that sort of exercise?' asked Chaloner, sure it was the Constable's prerogative.

'The Constable has gone to Dover, and left Talbot in charge until he returns,' explained the yeoman. 'And Talbot aims to make his mark. I cannot let you in, sir. You must come back this afternoon.'

Grumpily, as it had been a long trek, Chaloner took his leave. The Navy Office was nearby, so he decided to see if Pepys was in. He arrived to find the building deserted apart from a porter, who told him that the fleet had sailed the previous evening, so the shore staff were having a well-earned lie-in. No one was expected to show up before noon.

'You can rest easy in your bed tonight, sir,' the man declared gaily. 'The Dutch will not invade us now.'

Out in the street again, Chaloner recalled being told at some point in his enquiry – probably by Beadle Collins – that Hadie had lived in Canning Street by the Sign of the Bull. It was only around the corner, so he decided to search the place now and save himself the bother later. He had no key, so he picked the lock on the front door instead.

It was immediately obvious that Dorcas was right: someone had indeed searched the house before her, as he was sure that she and Collins had not poked about inside the chimney or prised up loose floorboards. He began his own search, working carefully and methodically in the hope that he would find something the others had missed, but all he discovered was a week-old message from a notary, saying that Hadie's last will and testament had been drawn up and was lodged with his executor. Chaloner peered at the lawyer's signature, wondering if Hadie had given *him* the letter, but it was illegible – which meant that not only was he untraceable, but he could not be asked the name of the executor either.

Still, the message revealed one thing: that Hadie had been in fear of his life for at least three days before he had been killed.

Chaloner arrived at St Margaret's to find that Glasse had just finished Morning Prayer and was standing in the porch, greeting his parishioners as they filed out. His clerical robes did nothing to detract from his resemblance to a denizen of hell. A number of congregants tried to sidle past without stopping, and Chaloner saw why when it became clear that even small children and beggars were expected to put a donation on his collection plate.

'I want more than that, Wogan,' he shouted when the regicide dropped a few small coins in the dish and kept moving. 'I need money and you are a wealthy man.'

'Yes,' acknowledged Wogan, pausing reluctantly. 'But I use my fortune to help the poor. What happens to yours, because I see no evidence of charity?'

'I do God's work,' argued Glasse indignantly, and rattled the plate again. 'Come on – your orphans, sailors and widows will not miss a shilling. Give.'

Scowling, Wogan dropped another handful of change into the dish and strode away before Glasse could demand more. Chaloner intercepted the regicide by the lich-gate.

'So what *does* Glasse do with the money he extorts from his parishioners?' he asked.

Wogan looked old and tired. There were lines of strain around his eyes and mouth, and his complexion was sallow. Chaloner wondered if he was ill, and had returned to London to make amends for his past while he was still in a position to do so. Or was it just the stress of being wanted for treason that robbed him of his health?

'He uses it to play cards,' replied the Welshman shortly. 'And I would rather give my money to those who deserve it, not to pay his debts.'

'A Fifth Monarchist who gambles?' asked Chaloner doubtfully.

'Hypocrisy is just as common among extremists as it is in the established Church,' said Wogan acidly.

'Speaking of extremists, I am surprised to see you here. Simpson said you prefer the moderates in the cathedral to the Fifth Monarchists' tirades.'

'I do,' said Wogan, 'but I overslept this morning, so had to make do with Glasse's offering instead.' He gave a sudden smile. 'Incidentally, I understand you and I have a mutual acquaintance. I have known and admired John Thurloe for many years.'

Chaloner lowered his voice, although no one was close enough to hear. 'He told me that eight of your fellow regicides have died within the last two years, which is a lot in so short a span of time. Do you know anything about it?'

Wogan blinked his astonishment. 'Me? Why would I?'

'Because they were your friends.'

Wogan looked exasperated. 'Chaloner, *dozens* of men were involved in the old king's execution! Besides the fifty-nine who signed the death warrant, there were

179

another forty who played other roles, and God knows how many more who egged them on. I never met most of them, and by no stretch of the imagination could they all be called "friends".'

'But have you heard anything about the deaths of these eight?' persisted Chaloner.

Annoyance flared in Wogan's eyes. 'Will I *never* be free of this filthy business? How many more times must I say it? I broke with such men years ago, and know nothing of what they are up to now.'

'You broke with *all* of them?' asked Chaloner sceptically. 'But you told me that you liked my uncle. Are you claiming that you shunned him, too?'

Wogan sighed irritably. 'I *did* like him – he was a bright spark in an otherwise grim and colourless world. But when Cromwell decided to turn the Commonwealth into a Protectorate, with himself as de facto monarch, I withdrew to Wales. It marked the end of my association with politicians, your uncle included.'

'So you do not care that so many old regicides have died recently?'

'Only insofar as I care about the fate of any Christian soul. But what makes you think that something untoward happened to them? None would have been young, and living with what we did takes its toll.'

Chaloner was unwilling to let the matter drop. 'These eight men were particular friends – a group led by John Downes, who is incarcerated in the Tower.'

Wogan grimaced. 'I knew Downes, but I had no idea he had formed a cabal. However, there were factions and cliques galore in those wild times, as men fought to impose their own brand of politics on everyone else. It was part of what drove me away in the end – we had killed a king, but the regime we replaced him with was just as flawed.'

'Thurloe said that Glasse and Simpson are Downes' friends, too. Neither are regicides, but they are certainly radicals. Would it be fair to say that Downes gravitates towards such people?'

Wogan raised his eyebrows. 'As far as I recall, Downes is a quiet, thoughtful, devout man, and I am astonished to hear he associates with the likes of Simpson and Glasse – one is barely sane, while the other seems more devil's familiar than man of God. Indeed, I wonder the Church does not defrock them.'

'Perhaps you should write to the bishop and suggest it.'

'I try to avoid drawing attention to myself with the authorities for obvious reasons. Hah! Here is Docility, coming to see what is keeping me.'

'Have you heard the latest omen?' she demanded without preamble. 'A dragon soared over St Paul's Cathedral an hour ago – a big green one with red eyebrows.'

'Goodness!' said Chaloner, struggling not to laugh. 'Red eyebrows, eh? Whoever saw them must have been very close.'

'I was,' said Docility coolly. 'The tale will be all over London by sunset, and everyone will know it is true. And its meaning is obvious, of course: that the old, corrupt, dirty order will be blasted away, and a new, shiny one will emerge.'

Chaloner wondered how she had drawn that conclusion from what she claimed to have seen, but then reminded himself that mystics always interpreted their visions to suit their own agendas, and reason rarely came into it.

'You should be careful, Wogan,' he warned, when she went to report her news to Glasse. 'Your association with a woman who makes claims about new world orders may lead people to assume you are here to foment rebellion again.'

'But I am not!' cried Wogan, alarmed. 'I told you – I am finished with that sort of thing, and all I want is to live a quiet, anonymous life, helping the needy.'

'Then perhaps you should find yourself another lady.'

Wogan's expression was anguished. 'But she has been good to me – she found me lodgings in Pudding Lane, and helped me establish our orphanage and home for wounded seamen. I cannot abandon her after all she has done. It would not be right.'

'Perhaps not,' acknowledged Chaloner. 'But it would be wise.'

When Wogan had retrieved Docility and taken her home, Chaloner approached the church. Glasse was in the vestry, counting the money he had extracted from his parishioners. His eyes lit up when he saw Chaloner, and he held out the plate.

'A shilling will buy you a prayer,' he said. 'You look as if you need one.'

'No doubt,' said Chaloner. 'But I am here to ask you about Downes the regicide again, not to buy indulgences.'

Glasse scowled. 'There is no need to make my offer sound sordid. Catholics do it all the time, so why should a poor Fifth Monarchist not adopt the practice? But what about Downes? As I told you yesterday, I have not seen him in years.'

'Then what about letters?' persisted Chaloner. 'I know he considers you a friend, so it stands to reason that he writes—'

'No,' stated Glasse firmly. 'I pray for him – when I remember – but that is the sole extent of our association now.'

But there was a sly cant to his eyes that made Chaloner suspect he was not telling the truth. However, he saw he would prise no more from him without some sort of leverage, so he went to see if he might have better luck with Simpson.

The vicar of Allhallows was also just finishing his morning devotions, although, unlike Glasse, he had not bothered to don religious vestments, and wore a tall hat, bucket-topped boots and a dirty leather jerkin. His congregation comprised two elderly widows who were almost certainly deaf, because Chaloner was sure they would not have sat smiling and nodding through a brazenly explicit sermon on sodomy otherwise.

'If you are here to criticise my choice of subjects for a homily, you can piss off,' Simpson bellowed, all bristling defiance as he shoved Chaloner out through the door and locked it behind them.

Chaloner determined to ask his questions and leave as quickly as possible, because the vicar was clearly mad, and he had no desire to spend any longer than necessary in such company. 'I understand you lent your church to agitators,' he began. 'They stood in your pulpit and encouraged higglers to—'

'I never did!' snarled Simpson. 'I forgot to lock it *once*, and when I got back it was to find that someone had been in without my permission. It was an outrage, and when I discover their names, I shall rip out their hearts.'

'I see,' said Chaloner. 'Do you often forget to secure your domain, then?'

'No, because there are too many light fingers in this damned city. All thievery will stop next Sunday, though, because King Jesus will not put up with that sort of thing.'

'So you expect me to believe that someone just happened to notice your church was unlocked, and decided to use it to preach sedition to a conveniently available mob?' asked Chaloner archly. 'Even you must see that does not sound very likely.'

'Likely or not, it is what happened,' roared Simpson, and Chaloner took another step back to avoid being drenched in spit. 'And next week, King Jesus will turn you into sausages for casting aspersions on his favourite helpmeet.'

'Your friend Downes is—'

'He is *not* my friend!' screeched Simpson, so loudly that it startled the pigeons roosting on the roof. 'A moderate man like me does not associate with radicals.'

Chaloner laughed. 'You think Fifth Monarchism is moderate?'

'Fifth Monarchism is what will happen in eight days, fool!' barked Simpson, but then a crafty expression suffused his face. 'Or perhaps it will not. Do not repent of your sins, and steal and lie to your heart's content. God will not mind.'

'So, you want me damned on the Day of Judgement,' mused Chaloner. 'Why? So that your own sins will pale by comparison?'

'I have no sins,' declared the vicar with utter conviction. 'All I have to do is keep being holy until next Sunday, which is when I shall be installed at God's right hand.'

'I thought that was Jesus's place. But no matter – just tell me about Downes.'

184

'There is nothing to say,' bawled Simpson. 'I have not seen him in years, although I cannot say that I have missed him. He is a dull fellow with a feeble mind, quite unable to equal my brilliant intellect.'

'Are you aware that eight regicides have died in the last two years?' asked Chaloner, although he felt he was wasting his time and that Simpson should be in Bedlam.

'No, why would I?' yelled Simpson. 'The only one I ever met was Downes, although that fellow Wogan bears an uncanny likeness to one of the others . . . Are you here to ask me to pray for their souls?'

'I suppose it would not hurt,' said Chaloner. 'Will you keep your church locked from now on, to prevent these agitators from coming back and using it again?'

'I *always* keep it locked,' snapped Simpson. 'Other than the time I forgot.'

As there were no hackneys available, and Chaloner did not fancy walking all the way to Westminster, he took a boat from the Dowgate Stairs. He shared it with two fishmongers and a bookseller, who were full of news about the 'sacred omelette'. Each knew a man, who knew another man, who had seen it in person. Chaloner was reminded of his uncle's penchant for inventing lies to see how fast they would spread.

It was not a pleasant jaunt, as there was no shade in the boat, and the water reflected the sun to the point where it was all but blinding. The boatman's eyes were red and puffy, and his arms were burned to the colour of old oak. He spoke not a word the whole way, and Chaloner sensed that his work had become a miserable trial.

At the Westminster Stairs, a number of black-robed

185

clerks surged forward, demanding to be taken downstream. Climbing out, Chaloner felt that perhaps his own occupation was not so bad after all, as he could not imagine much worse than rowing up and down the river all day, ferrying self-important passengers. Then he thought of Drinkell's farm, and reflected that he would not like to be a poulter either. All told, he supposed he should count his blessings, even if he was tied to an earl who did not like him and who might fall from grace at any moment.

The Palace of Westminster comprised a jumble of buildings, added to and adapted by every king since the Normans. It was home to the law courts, the Houses of Parliament, and the older administrative departments such as the Exchequer. It was populated by lawyers, clerks and politicians, rather than courtiers, so was a quieter, more sober place than neighbouring White Hall.

Williamson's lair was in New Palace Yard and boasted a fine view of the traitors' heads impaled on spikes outside Westminster Hall opposite. There were more skulls than there had been when Chaloner had last visited, some very fresh, and he wondered anew whether it was wise to investigate the eight deceased regicides. It was entirely possible that their deaths had been ordered by the very man Chaloner was about to visit.

The offices of the Spymaster comprised a large chamber on the ground floor for the clerks who decoded and read the reports from his spies, and rooms on the floor above for him and his senior staff. Williamson's office was sumptuous, although Chaloner suspected it had been furnished with property confiscated from those accused of treason – the artwork was peculiarly eclectic, while the rugs on the floor were of excellent quality, but

186

did not match. In pride of place were busts of great historical figures, although it did not escape Chaloner's notice that all were either despots or warmongers.

When he arrived, the Spymaster was sitting at a desk that was piled high with papers. He was a tall, aloof individual, who was disliked by his staff and not very popular with his government colleagues. Chaloner considered him to be inefficient, untrustworthy and disagreeable. Williamson scowled when he saw him at the door.

'Oh, you have deigned to put in an appearance, have you?' he said unpleasantly. 'You took your time.'

Chaloner was bemused, as he was under no obligation to visit the Spymaster, and was not aware that he had been expected. 'Why would you—'

'Holmes's Bonfire!' snapped Williamson. 'You sent me a written account, but it was tediously factual, so I expected you to provide me with the more colourful details in person. The audacity of the raid was astounding! What if those merchant ships had come out to fight? We might have lost his entire squadron. Holmes is a dangerous fool!'

'But there is one advantage to his exploits,' shrugged Chaloner. 'News of them takes people's attention away from other things, such as the King's plan to jump in a gigantic yolk-rich syllabub at a time when eggs are scarce and expensive.'

'There is that,' conceded Williamson. 'I do not know whose idea it was to hold a papal masque, but it is sure to cause trouble. Personally, I suspect Bristol. Or the Poultry Department. I am not sure what to make of Catline, while Crookey is downright sinister.'

Coming from the Spymaster, who dealt with all

187

manner of unsavoury individuals and who was hardly a bastion of guilelessness himself, this was damning indeed.

'Speaking of sinister,' Williamson went on coolly, 'I wish you had not corrupted my clerk. Swaddell is not the man he was since marrying into your family.'

Although Swaddell held the title of clerk, everyone knew he was really an assassin, as evidenced by the discussion at Poulters' Hall the previous day, and Williamson used the man's murderous skills liberally. However, if Swaddell had been 'corrupted', Chaloner felt *he* was certainly not responsible.

'I did all I could to prevent the match,' he said truthfully. 'But he was determined to wed my cousin, and she was equally keen to secure him, so that was that.'

'He has changed,' Williamson hissed, 'and not for the better. He refuses the bribes that allow the wheels of government to turn, and has become infuriatingly honest. But worse yet, he demands proof of guilt before agreeing to execute anyone.'

'How very tiresome for you,' said Chaloner, supposing this was Ursula's influence.

'It *is* a nuisance,' agreed Williamson fervently. 'None of my other agents are as good as him at dispatching enemies of the state without leaving fingers pointing in the wrong direction.'

Chaloner tried to change the subject before he was made privy to some other government policy he would rather not know about, but Williamson was on a roll.

'Catline asked us to hunt down and dispatch a carter who punched him during a fracas on the Strand,' he continued. 'He offered a handsome reward for the favour, but Swaddell refused to oblige, maintaining that a common assault should not warrant a cut throat. He—'

'Are you aware that agitators in and around Pudding Lane have been encouraging higglers?' interrupted Chaloner hastily, afraid the Spymaster might ask him to murder the hapless carter instead.

'Yes,' replied Williamson shortly. 'Why?'

'Because a lot of folk are listening to them, and it is only a matter of time before there is some serious trouble.'

Williamson's expression turned angry. 'So these agitators advocate flouting trade rules, but their real aim is to provoke civil unrest?'

'Possibly – or to strike at the Companies, which have a stranglehold on so much that happens in the city. Regardless, you should investigate.'

'You do it,' said Williamson, ignoring the fact that he had no right to give Chaloner orders. 'And if you do discover dangerous radicals at large, I shall arrange for them to be quietly eliminated.'

Chaloner would deal with the matter in his own way, without recourse to sly murder, although he was not rash enough to tell Williamson so. 'Have you heard that a number of regicides have died recently?' he asked instead.

'Yes, but I cannot say I am sorry – they should have been executed years ago. Why? Are you looking into it?'

'That would be impractical,' hedged Chaloner. 'They either died in Switzerland or in distant prisons. Do you know anything about the circumstances of their deaths?'

'I have more important matters to concern me than the fates of a few traitors. Such as Eleanor Montagu. Her death bothers me, because she was perfectly well the day before.'

'How do you know?' asked Chaloner warily.

'Because she visited my wife and me at home. We all share a passion for moths, you see, and she often came to chat about them. I was fond of her.'

Chaloner was astonished to hear it, as Eleanor sounded too decent a lady to have pursued a friendship with the Spymaster. However, he did know that Williamson liked moths – or rather, he liked pinning their little bodies inside purpose-built drawers – so it was possible that a common interest had put them in each other's company.

'I cannot escape the feeling that something untoward happened to her,' the Spymaster went on. 'Your Earl told me that he has ordered you to explore the matter, but if you share your findings with me, too, I will arrange for Lester to be given a ship.'

'You can do that?' asked Chaloner sceptically.

'If I so choose. Do you accept my terms?'

Chaloner nodded. 'Have you read the broadsheets by the Paladin?'

Williamson blinked at the apparent change of subjects. 'Of course. I rather like his work, and he must be a Royalist, because he has attacked a lot of our enemies.'

'Which enemies? The Company of Poulters? The navy?'

Williamson regarded him lugubriously. 'Of course not! I mean the religious maniacs like those lunatic Fifth Monarchists.'

'I think the Paladin was Eleanor Montagu,' said Chaloner bluntly.

Williamson stared at him, then burst out laughing, although it was not a pleasant sound. 'You are insane! For a start, the Paladin's latest broadsheet – another one about the Fifth Monarchists – was published today. Eleanor cannot have done it, because she is dead.'

'Perhaps it was at the printing house,' suggested Chaloner. 'These things take time to produce, and she was alive on Monday – five days ago. She may have set it in motion then.'

'Well, you are wrong,' stated Williamson, then smiled. 'The Paladin has done us yet another favour, because Fifth Monarchists are the worst of all the radicals. They include men like Robert Blackborne, whose words of wisdom the Navy Office cannot seem to manage without. How dare they beg his advice! The man is a damned Parliamentarian!'

'Yes,' acknowledged Chaloner. 'But one who knows how to run a fleet.'

'Trust you to defend a fellow Roundhead,' sneered Williamson. 'Next, you will be saying that he is right to think that King Jesus is coming to live in White Hall.'

'Next Sunday, according to popular rumour,' said Chaloner, unruffled by his ire.

Williamson scowled. 'I cannot abide Fifth Monarchists. I had a letter from one only yesterday, informing me that the Archangel Gabriel will take over my responsibilities as Spymaster after I am cast into the devil's darkest pit.'

Chaloner felt like telling him that if he was worried about such a fate, he should take a leaf from Wogan's book and start living a more ethical life. Williamson took a breath to calm himself and continued in a more moderate tone of voice.

'So forget the Paladin and those dead regicides, and concentrate on Eleanor and the Pudding Lane agitators. Swaddell will help you.'

'I do not need help, thank you,' said Chaloner firmly, feeling that even if he did, he would not want it to come from Swaddell.

'Perhaps not, but he is of scant use to me as long as he persists with this annoying integrity,' said Williamson. 'I shall be glad to get rid of him for a while, to be frank.'

Chaloner was none too pleased when Williamson summoned Swaddell at once, and ordered him to stay at Chaloner's side until the investigations into the murders and the Pudding Lane unrest were complete. The assassin beamed his delight with the assignment, revealing his sharp little teeth and red tongue.

'Anything for a kinsman,' he told Chaloner as they left the Spymaster's lair, relishing their new and official connection. 'What first?'

'The charnel house,' replied Chaloner, hoping to put him off, although he should have known better than to expect an assassin to baulk at visiting such a place. Swaddell's grin widened, and he skipped after Chaloner almost merrily.

He was famous for dressing entirely in black, except for the spotless white falling band – a kind of decorative bib – that lay across his chest. However, that day he had donned a russet long-coat with a yellow hat. It did not render him any less sinister, but Ursula's hand had definitely been at work. As they walked the short distance to the place where Wiseman waited with his saws and knives, Swaddell waxed lyrical on the pleasures of married life.

'I never thought it would happen to me,' he confided. 'To have won a pretty young bride who loves me . . . well, it continues to be beyond my comprehension.'

'And mine,' said Chaloner, who still failed to understand what his cousin saw in a man who was twenty years her senior, singularly unattractive, and wholly devoid of social graces. He only hoped they would not make each other unhappy, because a miserable Swaddell was likely to be even more dangerous.

'I am in heaven,' sighed Swaddell, smiling beatifically. 'More content than I have ever been in my life. Of course, she is a regicide's daughter, which may hinder my career, but you are the nephew of one, and it does not seem to have spoiled your rise from common spy to valued henchman of the Earl of Clarendon.'

'I was an intelligencer, not a spy,' corrected Chaloner stiffly. 'And the Earl does not value me – other than the times when he wants me to protect him from his various enemies.'

'Yes, you and I might have to do something about Lord Bristol,' said Swaddell, absently fingering the dagger at his belt. 'Because otherwise, your Earl will be dead before the year is out. Bristol means business this time.'

'Leave it to me,' gulped Chaloner, unwilling to be faced with a slyly murdered noble, because the chances were that everyone would assume *he* was responsible. 'We should discuss Eleanor Montagu while we walk. What can you tell me about her?'

'Williamson liked her,' obliged Swaddell. 'He and his wife often entertained her in their home, both before and after she went to Virginia to inspect her third husband's plantations. She inherited a fortune from him – one that now belongs to Montagu.'

Chaloner was uneasy. 'Are you saying that Montagu dispatched her for money? The rumour Bristol started claims it was to make way for a younger wife.'

'I should have known *he* was behind that nasty gossip,'

said Swaddell in distaste. 'He did not like her, because she once berated him for kicking a peacock – all White Hall heard, and she made him look like a beast. However, *Montagu* would never have hurt her, because they were genuinely fond of each other.'

'It was you who pointed out that he will inherit all her worldly goods.'

'He will, but that does not mean he killed her for them. Why would he? He has plenty of money of his own.'

'What about Margaret Hay, set to become Wife Number Five? Could she have done it?'

'I do not see Montagu taking up with a murderer. If you ask me, we should concentrate on Bristol as the culprit. If nothing else, your Earl will approve.'

'He will,' acknowledged Chaloner. 'But I think we should follow less dangerous lines of enquiry first. Can you think of anyone else who disliked her?'

Swaddell considered. 'She could be curt to those she deemed to be cruel or unethical, but, other than Bristol, I cannot recall anyone who drew her particular displeasure. However, I can tell you that she was always a Royalist – unlike Montagu, who was a Parliamentarian until the Restoration, when he promptly changed his allegiance.'

'I think Eleanor wrote the broadsheets by the Paladin,' said Chaloner, hoping surprise at the claim would prevent Swaddell from remembering that he had done the same himself.

'You may be right,' mused Swaddell, after listening to Chaloner's reasoning on the matter. 'We shall certainly bear it in mind. Now, what about these agitators?'

Chaloner related all he had learned about the higglers and the murders of Bowles, Hadie and Hill. Then, he told him about his third enquiry – the regicides – on the grounds that the assassin would stick to him like glue from now on, so would find out about it anyway. Again, Swaddell listened without interruption.

'You are wise to be concerned,' he said when Chaloner had finished. His expression was dark and angry. 'Four of these men died in prison, and as I did not eliminate them, it means someone is stepping on my toes. I want to know who.'

'It may be Williamson,' warned Chaloner. 'Or a friend of the King. After all, what better way to win His Majesty's favour than by murdering the men who killed his father?'

Swaddell huffed his disagreement. 'Most of his monkeys do not have the courage or the intelligence for such bravado. They would rather please him with lake-sized syllabubs.'

The Westminster charnel house had grown much more upmarket since Chaloner had first visited it. It had originally been sandwiched between a granary and a ramshackle warehouse in a grimy back alley, but tending the dead was a lucrative business in a city where disease, accidents and violence were rife, and its owner, Mr Kersey, had made a handsome profit from it. He had earned enough to buy all the surrounding buildings, and had turned the biggest into a museum to house some of the more interesting artefacts that had come his way. The rest he had demolished, and in their place was a pleasant courtyard with benches.

The deceased had also benefited, and the smelly, low-ceilinged mortuary had been replaced by a cool basement with whitewashed walls and a new stone floor. It was full of tables, and each 'guest' was respectfully covered with a fresh grey blanket. As the weather was hot, there were more bodies than usual, because Londoners slaked their thirst with disease-laden water, drowned trying to cool themselves in rivers or ponds, or were killed in heat-aggravated brawls.

Kersey himself was a dapper little man with two wives and a mistress. He had once confessed to murdering his predecessor, although it was difficult to believe ill of a man who so genuinely cared about the dead and those who mourned them – Chaloner had always been impressed that paupers were given the same polite consideration as nobles. However, Kersey had seen the worst of the plague, and was appalled when the King and his Court had fled, leaving the city to cope on its own. He had sworn never to forgive them.

When Chaloner and Swaddell arrived, he was entertaining Wiseman in his office, serving the surgeon excellent red wine in crystal goblets. There was also a plate of smoked beef and pickled onions, although Chaloner felt there was something inappropriate about eating uncooked meat in a place where dead people were stored. No such squeamishness afflicted Wiseman, who had finished one platter and was on his second.

'I was telling Kersey all the news from Greenwich,' said Wiseman, addressing Chaloner and ignoring Swaddell. He did not like the assassin, but dared not insult him openly, so usually settled for pretending he was not there. 'I have only just returned.'

'Yet again, His Majesty deserts his people in their hour of need,' said Kersey with a moue of disgust.

'He cannot do much about the weather,' Wiseman pointed out reasonably.

'No,' acknowledged Kersey. 'But he could stay around

to make sure his subjects have clean water and wholesome food. I have seen three fatal cases of egg fever today alone.'

'The Clerk of the Poultry Department – Munger – mentioned egg fever,' recalled Chaloner. 'He said you get it when you eat rotten eggs.'

'Not *rotten* eggs,' argued Wiseman pedantically. 'If they were rotten, there would be no problem – those reek, so everyone knows not to touch them. However, the ones carrying egg fever look and smell normal, yet they can be deadly.'

'The heat means that many eggs are not stored in a cool enough place,' put in Kersey. 'Moreover, they have become scarce *and* expensive, which means folk are unwilling to waste them – they eat them when they should not.'

'Is that what happened to Eleanor?' asked Chaloner, aware that wealthy households would be just as vulnerable as poor ones, because servants were trained to be thrifty.

'Shall we find out?' asked Wiseman, brushing fragments of meat from his long-coat.

'So what *is* the latest news from Greenwich?' asked Swaddell, as he led the way down to the basement. This was kept dark, as the dead had no need for illumination, and his torch cast eerie, wavering shadows on the walls.

At first, Wiseman pretended not to have heard, but a glance at the assassin's face, made more sinister still by the unsteady lamplight, forced him to reconsider the wisdom of an affront.

'Well, Sir William Morice went to fill a pail from his cistern, but he found all the water had turned to blood. Needless to say, there is much speculation as to what it means.'

'It means that Morice mistook what he "saw",' said Kersey with a disparaging sniff. 'Water does not turn to blood.'

'Perhaps some red mineral leached out of the stone-work,' suggested Chaloner.

'Or someone had his throat slit down there,' put in Swaddell with unseemly relish. 'A little blood goes a very long way, as I can attest from personal experience.'

The others regarded him uneasily before the surgeon continued with his gossip. 'Well, none of these explanations occurred to the Court, and there is a general consensus that it is a bad omen. The King has decided not to return to White Hall until the day of the Adrian Masque, and he will leave again the minute it is over.'

'No surprise there,' muttered Kersey. 'It is what we have come to expect – a clean pair of heels every time our city comes under threat. Well, I hope he drowns in his syllabub!'

'Where is Eleanor?' asked Chaloner hastily, aware that it was rash to engage in such talk while a government assassin was listening.

Kersey went to the nearest table and removed a blanket to reveal an elderly lady with grey hair and a kindly face. Eleanor Montagu had been a beauty in her prime, and there was still something of the elegant younger woman in her long neck and slender hips.

'She was a good person,' murmured Wiseman, staring down at her. 'So let us hope she died the death she deserved – quietly, in her sleep.'

He began work, watched with keen interest by Kersey and Swaddell, although Chaloner stayed well back. He had never liked witnessing what Wiseman did to the dead in the name of justice.

'No wounds,' reported the surgeon. 'And no obvious disease. I would have said she was in excellent health, despite her age. There is a little blood in her ear, but . . . good God!'

Chaloner returned to the table to see that Wiseman had inserted a long probe into the side of Eleanor's head, and was waggling it about. He looked away quickly.

'I should not be able to do this,' said Wiseman to Swaddell, who had craned forward for a closer look. 'Bones should stop me, but someone has driven a long thin spike through her ear and into her brain.'

'Is that possible?' asked Chaloner doubtfully. 'It would require a lot of precision, and she was unlikely to have sat meekly while a killer came along and lined himself up.'

'I imagine a soporific was administered first,' said Wiseman. 'Then, when she drowsed, the culprit grabbed his blade and something heavy . . . ' He mimicked a hammering motion with one hand while holding the blade with the other. 'In short, Lord Bristol is right: she *was* murdered, poor soul.'

'Probably with a stiletto,' supplied Swaddell, who knew all about knives. 'Those are popular in the Italian states, because they are small and easy to conceal.'

'You mean something like this?' asked Chaloner, pulling out the one that someone had tried to deploy on him and Lester the previous night.

'Exactly like that,' said Swaddell, inspecting it carefully. 'An assassin's blade, although not one I favour myself.'

'If Bowles was still above ground,' put in Wiseman, 'I would compare Eleanor's wound to his. Even so, I suspect that your stiletto – or one very similar – is the weapon that claimed both their lives.'

199

'And Hadie and Hill's,' said Chaloner. 'Their injuries were identical to Bowles', too.'

'What a curious set of victims,' mused Wiseman. 'A lady, a wealthy merchant, and a lowly pair from Poulters' Hall. But why do you have this weapon?'

'It was dropped when someone tried to stab me with it.'

'Then it was fortunate you were on your guard,' averred Wiseman. 'A tiny thing like that could slide between a man's ribs before he knew it, and who would rent my attic then?'

By the time Wiseman had finished, Chaloner felt the need for a restorative cup of wine, so Kersey led him, Wiseman and Swaddell to his office, where he fussed around his guests with crystal goblets and finger-sized bites of food, although Chaloner did not feel much like eating.

'Do you have time for this, Kersey?' asked Swaddell. 'You must be very busy.'

'We are,' acknowledged Kersey. 'And although we do not see many plague cases these days, there are still far more than are reported in the Mortality Bills. But I employ three assistants now, which is why I am free to drink wine with my friends.'

Swaddell and Wiseman looked flattered that they should be described as such, reminding Chaloner that both were men whom others tended to shun. Then it occurred to him that he might be considered in much the same light, because several people had accused him of being sinister and dangerous in the past. It was not a pleasant insight.

'Tell me more about Eleanor,' he ordered, aiming to

200

pump the surgeon for information and leave. He had wasted days anticipating a verdict of natural causes, which meant that now he had to visit the scene of the murder as a matter of urgency.

'There is little more to tell,' shrugged Wiseman. 'I smelled poppy syrup – and wine –in her stomach, which means she was probably insensible when her attacker struck. I imagine she experienced a momentary flash of pain, then nothing. There was virtually no blood, and I doubt she struggled.'

'When she arrived here, her maid told me that she was found in bed with a book on her chest,' supplied Kersey. 'It was assumed that she had dozed off with the tome in her hands and died as she slept.'

'She must have been on her side while the killer hammered his weapon into her ear,' mused Chaloner, 'after which he rolled her on to her back, and arranged the book so as to make her death appear natural. He wanted his crime concealed.'

'He wanted Bowles' murder concealed, too,' said Wiseman. 'The parish constable did not notice the wounds, and it was left to me to point them out. What about the other two – Hadie and Hill?'

'Hadie was stabbed in front of witnesses,' replied Chaloner. 'Ergo, there was no point in trying to disguise what had happened to him. And Hill was stuffed inside a water butt, so again, his death was very obviously due to foul play.'

'It is a pity you did not nab him when he came for you last night,' said Wiseman, 'because no one should feel safe while he remains at large. Did you see his face?'

'No,' sighed Chaloner. 'And all I can say is that he was of medium height and build, and he knew his way around the Pudding Lane area. He was also very fast on his feet.'

At that moment there was a tap on the door, and one of Kersey's assistants appeared, to inform his employer that Sir Gilbert Talbot had arrived with their latest guest.

'Talbot is Master of the Jewel House,' explained Kersey, standing up. 'He has charge of the Tower while the Constable is away, and he takes his responsibilities very seriously. The Constable never accompanies the bodies he sends me.'

'Has an important prisoner died, then?' asked Wiseman, and his eyes took on an acquisitive gleam. 'Or better yet, a lowly one, who will come to Chyrurgeons' Hall and help me introduce future surgeons to the delights of dissection?'

'It is John Downes the regicide,' replied Kersey. 'A controversial figure whom we shall bury quietly in an unmarked grave. The government will not want his final resting place to be used as a rallying point for discontented Roundheads.'

'Downes?' blurted Chaloner in horror. 'But I was going to visit him when we finished here! I tried this morning, but the yeomen would not let me in.'

'Pity,' said Swaddell, a little accusingly. 'He might have provided answers to some of our questions, but now we shall have to find other avenues of investigation.'

With disgust, Chaloner saw he should have visited the Tower when Thurloe had first told him to, and dreaded to imagine what the ex-Spymaster would say when he heard the news.

'According to the message Talbot sent me earlier,' Kersey went on, 'Downes was found lifeless in his cell this morning. Natural causes, apparently.'

202

'No,' said Chaloner, shaking his head. 'Nine dead regicides – all friends – in so short a space of time is suspicious.' He turned to Wiseman. 'I need you to look at him.'

Wiseman returned to the basement to begin his grisly work, while Kersey went to complete the formalities with Talbot. Chaloner accompanied Kersey, Swaddell slithering along at their heels like a dark shadow. The way the assassin moved made all the hair stand up on the back of Chaloner's neck, and he thought that while Swaddell might now be kin, he would never forget what the man did for the government or feel completely comfortable in his presence.

Talbot was a small, fussy man in his sixties. He was honest, prudent and meticulous, which made him the perfect choice for minding the Crown jewels. He pored and frowned over the documents transferring the dead prisoner to Kersey's care, and refused to sign anything until he was completely satisfied that all was in order.

'You have to be careful with king-killers,' he explained to Chaloner. 'They are either revered and treated like martyrs, or they are at risk of being dug up and desecrated. But the problem is yours now, Kersey.'

'When was he found?' asked Chaloner. 'Exactly.'

'When the guards took him his breakfast,' replied Talbot. 'Why?'

'Was this before or after the inspection you ordered?'

Talbot's eyebrows almost disappeared into his hair. 'Was it *you* who tried to talk your way past my yeoman earlier?' He went on before Chaloner could reply. 'But even if we had let you in, you would have been too late to speak to Downes. He died in the night.'

'How do you know?'

'Because he was lying on his side, curled up like a baby. The rascal slipped away in his sleep – unlike the king he murdered, I doubt *he* knew he was about to meet his Maker.'

'Did he have any visitors yesterday? Or were any unusual foods or gifts sent that—'

'Of course not,' snapped Talbot. 'We pride ourselves on security at the Tower. Besides, I want our traitors alive to reflect on their misdeeds. Divine judgement is all very well, but one never gets to watch it happen, and I like to ensure that these rogues pay for their crimes in *this* world before heading to the next.'

'So there was nothing—'

'Yesterday was a normal day for Downes,' interrupted Talbot shortly. 'He read, scribbled letters that will never be delivered – we do not allow it – ate his meals and slept. I assure you, no one comes to a bad end in the Tower unless we arrange it ourselves.'

'That is reassuring to hear,' murmured Chaloner. 'Where are the letters?'

'I burned them, because he was denied the privilege of writing to kith and kin. The rest of his belongings are in the box that accompanies his corpse. Kersey will give them to his family.'

'When was he last seen alive?' asked Swaddell.

'When he was taken his supper at about six o'clock last night. He told the guard that he planned to spend the evening reading, and seemed in reasonable spirits.'

By the time Chaloner and Swaddell returned to the mortuary, Wiseman had Downes on a table and was hard at work. While they waited for his verdict, they examined the dead man's possessions. They were pitifully meagre

– just some clothes, a few religious books and a sketch of a woman, presumably his wife. There were no papers of any kind, suggesting that Talbot had been assiduous in making sure his prisoner did not communicate with the outside world, even after death.

Eventually, Wiseman called Chaloner over, and began his report by saying that Downes had been in good health for a man of his age, and surprisingly well-nourished, given where he had lived.

'But he *was* murdered,' he said soberly. 'You were right to be suspicious. Of course, any other surgeon would have missed the signs, but you appointed *me* to—'

'How?' interrupted Chaloner urgently.

Wiseman turned Downes' head. 'I might have missed this if I had not conducted such a thorough assessment of Eleanor Montagu. See here – blood in the ear. She and your regicide were killed identically. When I open him up, I expect to find poppy syrup in his stomach, too. You are looking for a single culprit.'

'Bowles, Hadie, Hill, Eleanor Montagu and now Downes,' mused Swaddell. 'Five victims claimed with a stiletto, but what a peculiar selection. The first three are connected through the Company of Poulters, but the last two? It makes no sense.'

'*Thirteen* victims,' corrected Chaloner. 'I have a feeling that Downes' death is linked to those of his eight regicide friends.'

'Then we had better find the culprit,' said Swaddell soberly. 'Before he adds anyone else to his tally.'

'Perhaps losing his dagger will slow him down,' said Chaloner, turning the weapon over in his hands.

'No – he will have another,' predicted Swaddell with the confidence of a man who knew what he was talking about. 'Now, what shall we do first? Visit the Tower to see about Downes? Or White Hall to see about Eleanor Montagu?'

'I will take the Tower,' said Chaloner. 'You go to White Hall.'

But Swaddell shook his head. 'I would rather we stayed together, Tom. I shall feel safer with you at my side, and I am sure you will appreciate having me at yours.'

Chaloner was not sure which was worse: a killer watching him from the shadows, or Swaddell at his elbow. For the second time that day, all the hair rose on the back of his neck.

Chapter 8

Chaloner and Swaddell left the charnel house and walked towards White Hall – Swaddell had decided they should start with Eleanor, because the Earl and Williamson would expect it of them, and Chaloner could not find it in himself to push for a visit to the Tower that day. When they reached the palace, the plan was to see if Montagu had returned. If not, they would ride to Greenwich, as both wanted to observe his reaction when informed that his wife had not died of natural causes.

'Downes' book on poultry is what connects Eleanor to him,' said Chaloner. 'And through him, to the other eight regicides.'

Swaddell was not so sure. 'Perhaps the killer put it there to mislead us.'

Chaloner shook his head. 'He did all he could to conceal his crime, so why would he leave a tome that would result in raised eyebrows? Eleanor *was* interested in poultry, but this particular book has drawn attention to her death, which cannot be what he intended.'

Swaddell sniffed. 'If you say so.'

'The other victims have links to poultry, too,' Chaloner

went on. 'Bowles, Hadie and Hill were members of the Company of Poulters; Bowles died surrounded by smashed eggs; Hadie and Hill were charged to catch higglers; and Eleanor visited Drinkell's farm and I am sure she then wrote two scathing pamphlets about it.'

Swaddell frowned, still uncertain. 'And Downes' eight regicide friends? We received reports of their deaths from our spies, and I studied them all myself. None mentioned anything suspicious – and certainly nothing about eggs or hens.'

'Well, Bowles, Eleanor and Downes himself were adjudged to have died of natural causes until Wiseman discovered otherwise,' Chaloner pointed out. 'Unless a surgeon happened to look at the bodies, who would ever find the truth?'

'So how are the other eight king-killers connected to poultry?' pressed Swaddell. 'Were they members of the Company?'

'At least two of them were not,' admitted Chaloner. 'They were professional soldiers – I remember them in my uncle's house, braying about artillery.'

'Which means your theory is fatally flawed. You—'

'I *know* I am right,' insisted Chaloner. 'The evidence will be there – we just need to find it. And do not forget Eleanor's pamphlets. Those denounced not only the poultry industry, but radicals as well – and few folk are more radical than a regicide.'

'I have been pondering your Paladin theory, and I think you are wrong to accuse Eleanor, because some of the broadsheets appeared after she died. And do not explain it as a printing delay, because any sane publisher would abandon such a contentious project the moment he learned his client was no longer in a position to stop him.'

'The publisher!' exclaimed Chaloner. 'Broadsheets always carry the printer's name, so we shall pay him a visit and *he* will tell us the Paladin's identity.'

Swaddell shot him an arch glance. 'If it were that easy, the intelligence services would have done it already. However, the fellow is careful to leave nothing to give him away, so all our attempts to trace the Paladin by that route have failed.'

'Then I will ask Stedman at the Rainbow,' persisted Chaloner. 'He is a printer, so perhaps he will recognise the work of a colleague.'

'Be my guest,' shrugged Swaddell. 'But I wager anything you choose that you will be wasting your time. You will be wasting your time if you pursue your belief that Eleanor is the Paladin, too, so I recommend you abandon it before it leads us astray.'

Chaloner was disinclined to argue when he knew neither would yield without more evidence to convince him, so he moved to another matter. 'The stiletto man sounds like a professional assassin to me, because it cannot have been easy to conceal quite so many murders. Do you know anyone with those skills?'

Swaddell considered the question carefully. 'No,' he said eventually. 'There *was* a man whose weapon of choice was a long, thin blade, but I was obliged to eliminate him last year, when he took the lives of three of our agents.'

'Are you sure he is dead?' asked Chaloner, disliking this reminder that Swaddell could and did kill without compunction.

'Oh, yes,' said Swaddell, a nasty gleam in his eye. 'You do not recover from a slit throat, especially one that cut right down to the bone. I know my business, Tom.'

'There is no one else?'

'Not that I am aware. However, the weapon is unusual, so maybe the culprit is new to our shores.'

'I do not see why a stranger would murder those particular victims,' countered Chaloner. 'Unless he is just a paid assassin, following someone else's orders.'

Swaddell gave a wry smile. 'Perhaps Lord Bristol hired him. That would be a pleasing solution to present to your Earl.'

'It would,' agreed Chaloner. 'Unfortunately, I do not see Bristol's hand in this. He would not waste his time with regicides and poulters.'

Swaddell inclined his head in reluctant agreement. 'So we speak to Montagu and his household, and ask if they know why Eleanor was singled out by this killer. Then what?'

'I want to question Glasse and Simpson again. Perhaps they will be more forthcoming once they learn that Downes was murdered.'

'Question them about what? Why he wrote a book on chickens?'

'It would be a start. However, I am sure they know more than they are telling about Downes and his regicide friends. I also want to see the room where Eleanor died. Perhaps the culprit left some clue that was missed when her death was thought to be natural.'

Swaddell glanced up at the sky. 'That should keep us busy for the rest of the day.'

'And tomorrow, we will visit Downes' cell in the Tower. He—'

'Not me,' interrupted Swaddell. 'I have promised to take Ursula to see *The Mayd's Tragedy*. I love that play – most of the characters end up stabbed.'

'Perfect entertainment for you, then,' said Chaloner.

*

White Hall was unusually quiet, with the King and most of his Court still in Greenwich, and had a dusty, abandoned feel. The Great Court's fountain, where Chaloner had recently hosed down two of the King's favourites, had been turned off, and was already bone dry.

Chaloner and Swaddell started to walk towards the building where Montagu lived, keeping to the shade to avoid the glaring sun. Halfway around, they met a plump, motherly woman named Barbara Chiffinch. She was married to the 'Pimpmaster General', but was as unlike him as it was possible to be. She had been kind to Chaloner when he had first arrived in London, and they had been friends ever since.

'Montagu arrived back an hour ago,' she said when Chaloner asked if she had seen him. 'He has his own duties as Lord Chamberlain to attend, plus some of the Lord Steward's. He could not afford to linger too long in Greenwich.'

'He did not return because he has just lost his wife?' asked Chaloner pointedly. 'And the company of rowdy courtiers is unsuitable for a grieving man?'

'I imagine that was a factor, too,' said Barbara quietly. 'He was fond of Eleanor. Of course, they did not see each other very often. Perhaps that is why their marriage was so famously free of discord.'

'I see my wife every day, and I shall never tire of it,' Swaddell informed her smugly. 'I am devoted to her happiness, and cannot imagine us ever spending a night apart.'

'Crikey!' muttered Chaloner, hoping Ursula felt likewise, or that alone was going to drive a wedge between them.

'Then you are fortunate indeed,' said Barbara, and

211

changed the subject so abruptly that Chaloner was convinced she was thinking the same. 'I am sure the heat grows worse with every day that passes. Have you ever known a summer like it?'

'Yes – the one last year,' replied Swaddell. 'That was just as bad.'

'No, this year is worse,' argued Barbara. 'The common folk believe it is a sign of disasters to come. My maid, for example, thinks the Dutch will burn London in revenge for what Holmes did to Ter-Schelling. And there have been other omens, of course.'

'Casket-shaped clouds, hens laying eggs marked with crosses,' recited Chaloner with a weary sigh. 'Dragons flying over the cathedral, Jesus in an omelette.'

'I have not heard about those,' said Barbara. 'I was thinking about the new star in the north sky, and the fact that the Pope lies on his deathbed.'

'Oh yes, the Holy Father,' said Swaddell. 'Apparently he has taken to sleeping with a coffin in his bedchamber to remind him that he will soon meet his Maker, and he now bitterly regrets his brazen nepotism – giving all the best posts in his administration to his brother and nephews.'

'If he does die, I hope the King has the sense to cancel the Adrian Masque,' said Chaloner worriedly. 'Otherwise it will look as though he is celebrating the current pontiff's demise, not the one who died five hundred years ago.'

'Unfortunately, it is too late to call it off now,' said Barbara. 'Too much preparation has gone into it, and a fortune already spent. The Poultry Department has done the lion's share of the work, but every White Hall servant and courtier is involved to some degree.'

'We know about the syllabub,' said Chaloner. 'It calls

for a thousand eggs at a time when most Londoners cannot buy them for love nor money.'

'The syllabub is nothing compared to what else is happening,' said Barbara. 'Even I have been pressed into sewing a "medieval" tapestry, and my services are rarely sought out for japes. Come to the Banqueting House with me now, and I shall show you.'

Because it was the largest building in White Hall, the King's favourites had taken to using the Banqueting House for all their revels, so it was a theatre, ballroom and dining hall far more than it was used to receive foreign dignitaries in stately pomp, which had been its original purpose.

Since His Majesty had left for Greenwich, it had been transformed again, and Chaloner and Swaddell gazed around in astonishment. There were religious murals on the walls, tiny chapels and oratories made from wood painted to look like stone, and a very passable copy of the famous baldachin by Bernini – the great bronze canopy that loomed over the high altar in St Peter's Basilica. Clearly, it had not occurred to the organisers that Bernini was still alive, so could not have crafted anything for Pope Adrian the Fourth half a millennium before.

'Heavens!' breathed Swaddell. 'It really does look like a papal palace. Not that I have ever been in one, of course.'

'Just imagine what it will be like when the Court is here in fancy dress,' said Barbara. 'The Poultry Department has even hired canons from the cathedral to chat to each other in Latin, to provide a more authentic atmosphere.'

'I hope they do not intend to put the syllabub in that,'

213

said Chaloner, pointing to a spectacular replica of the Lateran Palace's baptismal font.

The original was a beautiful creation of green basalt, carved with bas-reliefs of various scenes from the Bible. The one in the Banqueting House had been crafted from plaster, then rubbed with dye until it was the right colour. It was much bigger than the one in Rome, making Chaloner certain that it was going to feature in some outrageously irreligious lark that would amuse the King and scandalise his subjects.

'I fear that is exactly what they have in mind,' said Barbara unhappily. 'And even if they demur, Bristol will not.'

'But Bristol is Catholic,' Chaloner pointed out. 'He would not mock an item of such great significance to his faith.'

'I disagree – he will do anything to snag His Majesty's attention at the moment,' argued Barbara. 'He needs to re-establish himself as the Court's leading debauchee, because he lost his place in the pecking order while he was in exile. Besides, he can always repent any impious behaviour at Confession and all will be forgiven.'

Chaloner looked at the font, and wondered how to sabotage it before it became the focus of a national scandal, although he would be sorry to damage such a splendid work of art.

'I have been asked to investigate the death of Eleanor Montagu,' he told Barbara, as she, he and Swaddell walked back outside together. 'Did you know her?'

'I liked her very much.' Barbara's expression was troubled. 'I hope you are not about to tell me that the rumours are true – that someone really did make an end of her.'

'They are true,' said Swaddell. 'And we are exploring a

number of possibilities. One is that her husband did it in order to marry a younger woman – namely Margaret Hay.'

Barbara was shocked and angry. 'Margaret and Eleanor were friends – like mother and daughter. The tales about Margaret and Montagu cavorting behind Eleanor's back are vicious, unfounded lies devised by the dreadful Bristol.'

'Yet Margaret and Montagu are always in each other's company,' Swaddell pointed out. 'I have seen them together myself – a lot more than I ever saw Montagu with his wife.'

'That is because Eleanor so rarely came to White Hall,' explained Barbara. 'She disliked all the noise and debauchery, so she rented a house in the city instead. She preferred the company of quiet friends to that of rowdy courtiers. And of birds, of course.'

'Birds?' queried Swaddell, startled.

'She loved them,' said Barbara. 'And she aimed to use the money she had acquired in Virginia to their advantage – to found an infirmary for injured ones, and to work with poulters to design farms that would increase egg production while being kind to the hens.'

'That explains why she had Downes' book,' said Chaloner to Swaddell.

'She adored reading,' acknowledged Barbara. 'I saw her with tomes on all manner of diverse subjects – a history of the navy, the breeding habits of moths, the lives of various fanatical clerics . . . '

'She bought some of them from the Rainbow Coffee House,' said Chaloner, recalling what Speed had told him. He glanced at Swaddell. 'Books that provided her with the kind of information that the Paladin would have found useful.'

'Eleanor Montagu was *not* the Paladin,' snapped Swaddell irritably.

Barbara gaped at Chaloner. 'You think *she* wrote those scandalous broadsheets?' Then she reconsidered. 'Actually, it is possible. She had firm opinions on all the subjects the Paladin likes to write about, and was not afraid to voice them.'

'Two of the tirades were directed against the Company of Poulters,' said Chaloner. 'And you just said she liked birds . . . '

Barbara nodded. 'She once told me that there is nothing to stop a poulter from going to a marsh and killing every heron, bittern, duck, teal, plover and goose in sight. She thought the trade should be regulated, before these lovely creatures disappear for ever.'

'It *is* regulated,' argued Swaddell. 'There are rules about which species can be taken.'

'Yes, but these rules are set by the Company of Poulters, whose members do the killing,' said Barbara. 'And Eleanor told me that they only relate to who has the right to take which birds – they do not restrict the scale of the slaughter. Breeding seasons are taken into account, but not much else.'

'So she might have fallen out with the men who rely on bird-killing to make a living,' mused Swaddell. 'Interesting.'

'We had better talk to her husband about it,' said Chaloner.

Because he was responsible for the smooth running of the royal household, the Lord Chamberlain had been furnished with some very handsome accommodation, comprising a withdrawing room, bedchambers, numerous

216

closets and a private dining room, which was a lot of space for one man. His domain was located in the heart of the palace, in the section known as the Privy Gallery Range.

He was sitting at a table in one of his reception rooms when Chaloner and Swaddell arrived, a tall, long-faced man with sad eyes, heavy black eyebrows and a prominent chin. There was an air of quiet nobility about him, and he came to his feet when visitors were shown in, a courtesy that few of his rank usually afforded those of lesser standing.

'Chaloner,' he said pleasantly. 'Clarendon mentioned that you might call. And Swaddell, too. Does this mean that Spymaster Williamson will also help me end these foul rumours about my wife?'

'Which rumours, sir?' asked Chaloner guilelessly. 'Specifically?'

Montagu shot him a bemused look. 'The ones about her death being unnatural, of course. She was in her eighth decade, and had not long returned from a gruelling journey to New England. I am heartbroken, of course, but there is nothing untoward about her passing.'

'Wiseman declared her in excellent health,' countered Chaloner. 'But she—'

'Wait,' said Montagu, raising a hand to stop him. 'Let us not discuss this standing like soldiers to attention. You both look hot and dusty, so allow me to pour you a rose-petal sherbet. You will find it most refreshing.'

Chaloner and Swaddell exchanged wary glances. It was unheard of for nobles to offer expensive treats to minions, let alone serve it themselves. Was Montagu's hospitality genuine, or was he trying to disarm them in the hope of forestalling awkward questions? They sat at Montagu's invitation, although neither touched the sherbet.

'The Earl values you very highly,' Montagu informed Chaloner with a smile. 'He assures me that you will bring this unfortunate business to a satisfactory end.'

'I will look for the truth, sir,' said Chaloner carefully, wondering if this was Montagu's way of hinting that he aimed to control whatever was concluded.

'Mr Williamson has never praised you, though,' Montagu told Swaddell. 'But he is a man of few words, and I am sure you are equally well regarded.'

'Less well regarded now than I was,' sighed Swaddell. 'A year ago, I virtually lived in his pocket, but I have scant time for him these days, because I am married.'

'Goodness!' breathed Montagu, and Chaloner saw him wondering what sort of woman would be brave enough to wed such a man. The Lord Chamberlain cleared his throat uncomfortably. 'But to business, gentlemen. You may have heard that my marriage to Eleanor was unhappy, but that is a lie. We were actually very fond of each other.'

'Before we go any further, I should tell you that we come bearing bad news, sir,' said Chaloner. 'Your wife *was* murdered. Someone killed her by piercing her brain with a long, thin blade – a method of execution specifically designed to conceal the crime.'

Montagu gaped at him, and the blood drained from his face. 'No,' he managed to gasp eventually. 'You are wrong. Eleanor was . . . she . . . '

'It was discovered by Surgeon Wiseman,' said Chaloner. 'If you know him, you will appreciate that he is unlikely to be wrong.'

Montagu scrubbed at his face with unsteady hands. 'Did she suffer?' he whispered.

Chaloner watched him intently, thinking that if he had ordered her death, he was putting on a very convincing display of shock.

'Wiseman believes she was insensible at the time,' he replied. 'So, no.'

'Thank God!' breathed Montagu. 'But who could have done such a terrible thing?'

'We thought you might have some ideas, sir,' said Swaddell.

'Me?' gulped Montagu. 'But I have no notion who . . . She was an old lady, for God's sake! Who harms the elderly? It makes no sense!'

'You cannot think of anyone who disliked her?' pressed Swaddell. 'Or who might strike at you through her?'

Montagu swallowed hard. 'You mean Bristol, who deplores my friendship with the Earl. But if he killed Eleanor, why draw attention to the fact by telling everyone that she was murdered, especially as you say considerable trouble was taken to disguise the fact?'

'Then what about some other courtier?' asked Chaloner.

'No! She was a kindly soul – intelligent and with a keen sense of justice.'

'Quite,' said Chaloner. 'Not everyone at White Hall appreciates those qualities, particularly if it means them being exposed for wrongdoing or ineptitude.'

'I cannot think of anyone other than Bristol,' said Montagu miserably. 'There was a peacock-kicking incident, you see, and she used her clever tongue to shame him.'

'When was this?'

'Oh, years ago, although no one who was there will ever forget the way she castigated him. However, she was rarely in White Hall – she found it noisy and louche – so I doubt their paths crossed very often, if at all. Yet there is one thing . . . She brought a large sum of money home from Virginia.'

'We know,' said Chaloner. 'Williamson mentioned it.'

'She kept it in her nether-garments,' Montagu went on. 'I urged her to lodge it with a banker, but she was happier having it to hand. However, it seems to have disappeared.'

'You mean stolen?' asked Chaloner. 'By her killer?'

Montagu raised his hands to indicate he did not know. 'She kept it in her bodice during the day and under her pillow at night. When her body was found, there was no sign of it. It is possible that she put it somewhere else that night, although I am doubtful – the servants and I searched high and low for it with no success.'

'Would you like us to look?' asked Chaloner; he and Swaddell were far more likely to uncover cunning hiding places than Montagu and his people.

'Would you?' asked Montagu gratefully. 'She rented a mansion on Gracious Street, so I will tell her footman to take you there today.'

'Who else knew about the money?' asked Swaddell.

'No one, other than me, Margaret and her retainers. Oh, and she mentioned it to the Company of Poulters, because she wanted to use some of it to establish a haven for hens.'

'A haven for hens?' echoed Swaddell warily.

'A place where they have access to trees and grass, spacious coops, nice food, clean straw, that sort of thing.' Montagu pondered. 'The Poultry Department here knew, too, because they happened to be there while she was explaining her plans to me.'

'So it was essentially public knowledge that she had a fortune to hand,' said Swaddell heavily. 'Do you think this is why she was killed?'

'It is possible, which is why I am telling you about it.'

'Then we shall bear it in mind,' said Chaloner, although he was sure the killer had taken Eleanor's life – and those of his other victims – for reasons other than money. 'Did she ever visit the Tower? Or talk about a regicide named Downes?'

Montagu gaped at him. 'Of course not! What peculiar questions! She may have enjoyed some unusual pastimes, but hobnobbing with rebels was not among them.'

'What unusual pastimes?' asked Swaddell.

Montagu took a deep breath to calm himself. 'Other than bird welfare, she also liked moths, and even wrote a short treatise about them, although under a male pseud-onym, naturally. It would have been improper for her to publish under her own name.'

'Why?' asked Swaddell, frowning his bemusement.

'Because she is a woman,' replied Montagu, as if the answer were obvious. 'The only lady who breaks that rule is the Duchess of Newcastle, and she is certifiably mad.'

'Did your wife ever publish her views on religious or political affairs?' asked Chaloner.

'Good Lord, no!' cried Montagu, shocked. 'How could you even think such a thing? She was a respectable lady.'

Chaloner raised his hands in a shrug. 'She read a wide range of controversial books, and she was intelligent. The question is not so outlandish.'

'I admit she liked radical tomes,' conceded Montagu, struggling to regain his equanimity. 'But reading them is not the same as writing them. She also enjoyed hearing

221

dissidents speak, but that did not mean she went out and had a rant herself.'

'She did *what?*' blurted Swaddell.

Montagu grimaced, irked with himself for letting something slip that he would rather have kept to himself. 'She attended gatherings of fanatics on occasion. I warned her that it might be dangerous, but she said they made her laugh.'

'Then you were right to warn her,' averred Chaloner. 'Such people do not appreciate being viewed as a source of entertainment, and what she did was dangerous.'

'She did not let them *see* she was amused,' argued Montagu crossly. 'She was not a fool. She always made them believe she was listening with rapt attention.'

'What did she think of the Paladin?' asked Chaloner, ignoring Swaddell's soft sigh of exasperation. 'He and she seem to have a lot in common.'

'We never discussed him,' replied Montagu stiffly, 'although I imagine she thought he had some interesting ideas. I hear he published a new tract today. It is about Fifth Monarchists again, and if half of what he says is true, then they all belong in Bedlam.'

Chaloner watched him intently. 'And you are *sure* she never mentioned him to you, sir? Or perhaps wrote pamphlets herself – under a pseudonym, of course. As you say, she was not the Duchess of Newcastle, happy to publish under her own name.'

Montagu was so angry that he spoke through clenched teeth. 'You malign her by asking all these questions, and if you want evidence of her innocence, then here it is: first, the Paladin wrote about Bristol and the potted plants, but Eleanor was too rarely in White Hall to know such things.'

'She was there enough to berate him for kicking a peacock,' Chaloner pointed out.

Montagu ignored him. 'Second, she would never flout convention by writing for the masses. And third, she has been dead since Tuesday, so how could she publish a broadsheet today?'

'Told you so, Tom,' murmured Swaddell.

'Please believe me,' Montagu went on tightly. 'If you pursue this idea, thinking it has a bearing on her death, you will never catch the person who . . . Clarendon promised me you would restore the honour of my house, not besmirch it further. I hope he was not wrong.'

It transpired that when Eleanor died, Montagu had arranged for all her servants to work for him until they could find alternative employment, unwilling to see them starve. He told Chaloner and Swaddell that she would have expected it of him, because she had been a compassionate and caring mistress herself. Chaloner wanted to speak to them, so Montagu sent a page to assemble them all in the dining room.

While they were waiting for the page to return, the door opened and a woman glided in. Montagu introduced her as Margaret Hay, although Chaloner knew this, because she had been the lady in Montagu's coach when it had left for Greenwich a few days earlier. She was much younger than Eleanor, and wore a dress of pale blue silk, cut to show off her lithe figure. Montagu blurted the news that his wife had not died a natural death, causing Margaret to whimper her distress.

'But who would do such an awful thing?' she whispered, once she had been escorted to a chair to regain her composure. 'She was never at Court.'

223

The implication being, Chaloner thought with wry amusement, that the only people Margaret could conceive as killers were the residents of White Hall.

'Do you know how she spent her last few days?' he asked her.

'Reading, mostly. Oh, and there was an excursion to an egg farm. It upset her terribly, and she came home railing about cruel practices.'

'Did she indeed?' asked Chaloner, recalling Drinkell's claim that she had been impressed. Clearly, she had kept her true opinion to herself until she could share it with someone she trusted. And why? So that Drinkell would not suspect her when the Paladin got to work, because despite Montagu's passionate denials, Chaloner remained certain that she and the anonymous pamphleteer were one and the same.

'Where were you when she died?' asked Swaddell baldly.

'It is all right,' said Margaret, when Montagu leapt angrily to his feet to defend her. 'I understand why the question must be put. After all, there is gossip all over the palace that she was dispatched so that I could marry you.'

'Which you will, after a respectable interval,' said Montagu tightly. 'But that does not give these men the right to—'

'Stop, Edward,' interrupted Margaret quietly. 'We both want the truth about Eleanor, and they will not find it if we obstruct them by standing on our dignity. We have nothing to hide, so why not answer their questions?'

'Very well,' said Montagu, albeit with ill grace. 'We were both here in White Hall on Tuesday evening, with dozens of witnesses to prove it. Eleanor was in Gracious

224

Street. She was never in the palace when the King was here, because she considered him lewd.'

'Along with most of London,' muttered Chaloner.

'She was like a mother to me,' Margaret went on, and there was a catch in her voice as she spoke. 'I already miss her more than I can say.'

Not long afterwards, the page appeared to say that Eleanor's retainers were assembled and waiting. Montagu reached the dining room first, and proceeded to assure everyone that they had nothing to worry about, which Chaloner thought was premature, given that he and Swaddell had yet to ascertain exactly what had happened and who might have been complicit. Montagu went on to announce that Eleanor had been murdered, which resulted in a great clamour of shock and dismay. Some of the younger ones began to weep, while one maid swooned and had to be helped to a chair.

'Does anyone recall what she ate and drank that night?' asked Chaloner, once the hubbub had died down and he judged them ready to answer his questions.

'Just her usual cup of wine,' replied the maid, a middle-aged, drab little woman named Sybil. 'It had been in the cellar, so I set it to warm on the doorstep. She hated cold wine.'

'Why there?' asked Chaloner, frowning. 'Why not somewhere inside the house?'

'Because she said wine tasted better when it had been touched by the sun.'

'Did you leave it unattended?' asked Chaloner, thinking of the soporific that Wiseman had found in Eleanor's stomach.

Sybil swallowed uncomfortably. 'Briefly, but I swear it

was wholesome when I took it to her. I would have noticed otherwise. So would she.'

Chaloner was not so sure about that, given that some very nasty substances were virtually undetectable by taste or smell. Poppy syrup was one of them, and while Wiseman had declared it present in Eleanor's innards, he was an experienced anatomist, trained to identify dangerous substances in corpses. However, it was unlikely that Eleanor and Sybil would have acquired such a skill. Indeed, it was obvious that Eleanor had not, or she would have refused the soporific when it had been slipped to her.

'Do you know of any association between your mistress and a regicide in the Tower called Downes?' he asked.

'Yes, she was reading his book before she died,' replied Sybil shakily. 'It was called *The Chicken and her Egges*, and she told me that it was fascinating.'

'Was there any other connection?' asked Chaloner. 'For example, did she write to Downes or receive letters from him? Did they have any mutual friends?'

'No!' gulped Sybil, aghast. 'She would not have associated with a man who connived to behead the King's father. She was a good Royalist all her life.'

'Just like me,' put in Montagu, apparently having forgotten that he had been one of Cromwell's major-generals until he had been forced to resign for intransigence.

'Tell us what happened the day she died, Sibyl,' ordered Swaddell.

'She was in White Hall all morning with the Queen,' replied the maid, 'but she returned to Gracious Street when she heard the King was going to host a party. She disliked those, because they always turned debauched. Then she decided to go to church.'

226

'On a Tuesday?' asked Swaddell dubiously.

Sybil nodded. 'In Allhallows the Great. Its priest is very outspoken, and she loved listening to him, because he makes such outlandish claims. I sat next to her, and sensed her suppressed mirth all the way through his sermon.'

'Allhallows the Great?' asked Chaloner, his mind beginning to reel at the connections that were emerging. 'She went to hear Vicar Simpson?'

'Yes, the Fifth Monarchist. He announced that King Jesus will be installed in White Hall a week tomorrow, and that those of us who currently live here will rot in hell.'

'Your wife chose risky ways to spend her time,' said Swaddell to Montagu. 'Why did you allow it?'

'Because she was an independent spirit who would not have appreciated the interference of a fourth husband after three others who gave her free rein,' replied Montagu shortly. 'Besides, she had been enjoying the rants of fanatics for years with no problem.'

Swaddell glanced at Chaloner. 'Perhaps she sniggered at one dissident too many, so he made sure she would never do it again.'

'But she was always discreet,' objected Sybil. 'These radical preachers never knew what she really thought of them.'

'Do not be so sure,' said Chaloner. 'They may be fanatics, but that does not mean they are stupid. The truth is that they are very good at sniffing out pretenders and spies, because their lives depend on it.'

And here was another connection between Downes and Eleanor, he thought but did not say: Eleanor had laughed at Downes' friend. He decided to visit Simpson

227

as soon as he and Swaddell had searched Eleanor's house, and demand the truth about the vicar's relationship with the regicide once and for all.

'What happened when you left the church?' Swaddell was asking. 'Were you followed? Did anyone approach you?'

'No, nothing. It was a sultry evening, so we strolled slowly, enjoying ourselves. When we got home, Rye the footman locked the doors and closed the windows, and everyone retired to their quarters. I took my lady the wine I had left to warm and went to bed myself.'

'Wait a moment,' said Chaloner, raising his hand. 'The wine was on the doorstep the whole time you were at church? You said it was only there briefly.'

Sybil flushed guiltily. 'It *was* briefly – less than two hours.'

'And during those two hours, her killer dosed it with a soporific,' said Swaddell in disgust. 'The potion that kept her asleep while he crept into her chamber with his long, sharp blade. In other words, you helped him to kill her.'

Sybil was horrified. 'But I always left it there! She *wanted* me to.' She appealed to Montagu. 'You know she did, sir.'

White-faced, Montagu nodded mute agreement. Swaddell fixed Sybil accusingly with his beady black eyes, so she burst into tears, although Chaloner saw no need to make the hapless woman feel worse than she did already.

'If the wine had been unavailable, her killer would have found another way to do it,' he said tiredly. 'I doubt you made any difference to the outcome.'

'I found her body . . . the next morning,' wept Sybil,

speaking with difficulty. 'She was lying . . . exactly as I left her the night before. The book was on her chest . . . I assumed she had fallen asleep . . . while she was reading it.'

'She probably did,' muttered Swaddell, 'thanks to whatever was in that wine.'

'But why bother with a soporific?' asked Montagu, shaking his head in incomprehension. 'Why not just poison her outright? Surely, it would have been safer for the killer than breaking in with a blade?'

'I imagine he wanted to be sure of success, and poison is notoriously unreliable,' explained Swaddell. 'What if she had neglected to swallow it, or someone else had taken it instead? Knives are always preferable, believe me.'

While everyone regarded the assassin uncomfortably, Chaloner turned his attention to the footman. Rye was a slight man with the kind of sullen expression that said he thought the world owed him something – something that had not been forthcoming, hence his air of simmering resentment. He had bitten his nails to the quick, and some of them had bled.

'How did the killer get in if you had locked the house up?'

'My lady liked her window open,' he explained, 'even though everyone knows that night air is toxic. I always shut it with all the others, but she unlatched it again every time.'

'That is true,' nodded Margaret. 'She believed that a well-ventilated room was good for the lungs, and none of us could convince her otherwise.'

'I understand she had a fortune in her possession,' said Swaddell, looking intently at each servant in turn. 'From New England.'

229

'Yes, but we cannot find it,' said Rye. 'She kept it in her dress during the day, and under the pillow at night, but it was in neither place when Sybil found her body. It was in a bag with a crest on the front, and comprised solid gold coins. She showed it to us once.'

'You searched for it immediately?' asked Swaddell keenly.

'Of course not,' replied Sybil unhappily. 'First, I howled the alarm, so that everyone came running. Then we felt for a life-beat and tried to restore her to life by holding her hands and calling to her. It was only after all that that Rye remembered the gold. He was the only one brave enough to . . .'

'I was respectful, sir, I promise,' Rye assured Montagu. 'When it was not where we expected it to be, we searched the whole room, but it was not there either.'

No one had any more to add, so Chaloner and Swaddell made their farewells, leaving Margaret to comfort Montagu and the disconsolate staff – other than Rye, who was ordered to take them to Eleanor's house. He obliged with bad grace, afraid of missing his dinner.

'Eleanor's people made it easy for the killer,' spat Swaddell, once they were away from White Hall. 'She was reckless to trust such a rabble.'

'You cannot lay the blame on them,' said Chaloner wearily. 'Not with a culprit as determined as this one. I hope we do catch him, though, because Eleanor sounded like a decent lady.'

'She did,' acknowledged Swaddell. 'Which is why I am disgusted with her useless retainers. I should dispatch the lot of them for their disgraceful negligence.'

'Leave them alone,' ordered Chaloner hastily, afraid he might actually do it.

230

Swaddell pretended not to hear, and instead began to reflect on what they had learned. 'It is a peculiar business, is it not, with links to the Company of Poulters, regicides and religious zealots? Solving her murder may be easier said than done.'

Chaloner had a bad feeling that he might be right.

Gracious Street was a wide thoroughfare with its own supply of fresh running water. This flowed into a conduit that resembled a miniature castle, which had been built by a lord mayor some two hundred years before. The road merged into Fish Street Hill at its southern end, and had the bustling Leadenhall Market at its northern extremity. Despite being more elegant than the neighbouring streets, it still could not avoid the all-pervasive stink of the city – rotting fish, spoiled milk and festering rubbish. It was enough to make Swaddell remark that unless the weather broke soon, London would suffocate in its own filth.

Eleanor Montagu had rented a pleasant house with windows facing the street, and Rye pointed out the one which had been open that fateful night. Chaloner shook his head in disgust when he saw the leafy tree growing outside, which not only provided a convenient ladder, but would also have concealed the killer as he had climbed up it. He imagined the culprit scarcely crediting his luck.

'Do you think the killer could be Simpson?' whispered Swaddell, watching Rye unlock the door. 'For going to his church and giggling during his sermon? I can certainly see *him* clambering trees to stab elderly women in their sleep.'

'He has an alibi in Sybil and Eleanor herself,' Chaloner

whispered back. 'Whoever put the soporific in the wine did so while they were listening to Simpson's rant, because that was when Sybil left it unattended. Ergo, he cannot have done it. There *is* a connection between him and Eleanor, but it is not him being her killer.'

'What is it, then?'

'Downes,' replied Chaloner. 'Eleanor was reading his book, and Simpson was his friend. I have questioned Simpson twice now with no success, so let us hope he will be more forthcoming with you.'

People were, generally speaking, given the assassin's deadly reputation.

'It will be too late to tackle Simpson by the time we have finished here,' predicted Swaddell. 'We should not have spent so much time with Montagu and his household. And I am not doing it tomorrow. It is Sunday.'

Chaloner was reluctant to delay the encounter. 'I am sure we can fit it in before you take Ursula to the theatre.'

Swaddell's expression was haughty. 'I shall be in church then, and Holy Communion in our parish tends to be a lengthy affair. And do not suggest slipping out before the rite has finished, because that would be impious.'

Chaloner regarded him askance. 'Since when did you become a God-fearing man?'

'Since I got married.' Swaddell shrugged. 'I never had much time for religion before – in my profession, it is better to stay away from it, lest it makes you feel guilty all the time – but Ursula likes me to go. Now I rather enjoy it. We sit at the back and hold hands. The vicar complained at first, but I persuaded him to let us be.'

'He objected to you holding hands?'

'To me being in his church at all. He claims the altar

candles always flicker when I am there, and that it is my fault that he keeps dropping the Host.'

Chaloner said nothing. Swaddell's priest was not the only one who thought the assassin was an agent of the devil.

'So while I am being devout with my wife,' Swaddell continued, speaking the last two words with unbridled relish, 'you can be a heathen and work on the Sabbath. We shall resume our enquiries together on Monday.'

Chaloner was glad to be free of Swaddell for a day, although there was no point in tackling Simpson without the assassin to provide some suitable menace, so that part of the investigation would have to wait. But there were plenty of other leads to follow – searching Downes' cell, asking questions in White Hall about Eleanor, and visiting the Rainbow to see if Stedman could tell him the name of the Paladin's printer.

'Are you coming in or not?' called Rye irritably from the door. 'Lord Montagu will accuse me of skiving in a tavern if you keep me here too long, so hurry up.'

Chaloner and Swaddell entered a house that was elegantly furnished and smelled of lavender. It was a light, airy place, and every room held shelves of books.

'Why did your mistress choose to live on this side of the city?' asked Swaddell, opening a bureau and beginning to rummage through its contents. 'It is a long way from White Hall.'

'Exactly,' replied Rye. 'She considered courtiers to be selfish rakes, and wanted as much distance from them as possible. She knew, see.'

'Knew what?' asked Swaddell warily.

'That their time in power is almost done. God has given them six years to prove they can govern justly, but they slide deeper into iniquity with every passing day. The common folk chafe under their corrupt authority, but they do not care – they are only interested in being debauched and greedy.'

'Those are not sentiments I would expect to hear from a servant of the Lord Chamberlain,' said Swaddell mildly.

Rye's expression was defiant, and Chaloner saw he was indeed a resentful man who felt the world owed him something. 'You asked, so I told you. My mistress was a wise lady – she saw the omens, she heard the rumours, and she listened to the right people. She understood what is coming in six days.'

'You mean eight days,' said Chaloner. 'Next Sunday.'

Rye smirked. 'Word is that King Jesus is so eager to install justice that He has decided to come early. He will arrive on Friday now.'

Chaloner regarded him thoughtfully. 'So Lady Montagu had a Fifth Monarchist among her retainers. Did she know?'

Rye drew himself up to his full height. 'Of course she did. Who do you think told her when we were having our meetings, so she could come and join us? And she did *not* go to laugh. She wanted to listen to the truth about everything.'

'*She* was a Fifth Monarchist?' breathed Swaddell, shocked.

Rye grimaced. 'We invited her to join us, but she said she had too many questions and doubts. Unlike most of her ilk, she had a brain and she used it.'

Before they could ask him more, he stalked away to sit on the front steps until they had finished. Since he left a lot to be desired in a servant, Chaloner surmised that she had hired Rye as a way to gain access to gatherings she would otherwise have missed. And he knew exactly why she had gone to such lengths to monitor the Fifth Monarchists: she had recognised that they posed a serious threat, and, like the resourceful woman she was, she had made her concerns public through the Paladin.

He and Swaddell began a systematic search of the house, which was not easy, because Eleanor had owned dozens of display trays containing moths, any one of which might have held some vital clue. There were also enough books to fill a library, and mounds of papers and broadsheets, although not one was by the infamous pamphleteer.

'It means I am right,' said Swaddell with satisfaction. 'Eleanor may well have applauded what the Paladin wrote, but they are two different people. If she had been him, she would have had piles of his rants sitting around – all writers keep multiple copies of their own works, because they like bestowing them on friends and family.'

'On the contrary, their total absence *proves* she was him,' argued Chaloner. 'Clearly, someone has removed them all, specifically to conceal what she did.'

'Well, we can debate it later,' said Swaddell, his tone of voice telling Chaloner that he remained unconvinced. 'But look – here is the book she was reading when she died.'

'*The Chicken and her Egges*,' said Chaloner, giving it a cursory glance. 'By Downes. We already knew that. So what?'

Swaddell showed him the title page. 'But we did *not* know that Downes gave her this particular copy himself. You see? He has inscribed it for her: "To my lady Montagu, a strong backbone in the battle against wicked-nesse." An odd thing to write, but . . . '

235

Chaloner inspected the book more carefully. It was handsomely bound, but the pages were worn, and someone had scribbled copious and untidy notes in the margins. He knew Eleanor had not done it, because there were plenty of examples of her neat writing around the house. He could only surmise that the messy scrawl belonged to the regicide.

'My uncle wrote a pamphlet once,' he said thoughtfully. 'But he was unhappy with it, and later produced a second edition with revisions.' He indicated the book. 'These annotations suggest to me that Downes hoped to do the same, and that this was his working copy. Perhaps he hoped that Eleanor would oversee its re-publication for him.'

'Why would she do that?' asked Swaddell sceptically. 'Other than the inscription, there is nothing to suggest they had any connection to each other.'

'"A strong backbone",' mused Chaloner, and examined the book's spine before exclaiming his triumph. 'Hah! There is something shoved inside it! The dedication was Downes' way of telling her where to look.'

With Swaddell watching intently, he took his smallest knife and poked until a small roll of paper dropped out. Swaddell snatched it up, then growled his disappointment.

'It is encoded. I cannot make head nor tail of it.'

Nor could Chaloner, although it would be a poor cipher if its message was immediately apparent to anyone who happened across it. 'I doubt she found this – if she had, I do not see her replacing it in the book. She would either have destroyed it or hidden it somewhere else.'

'Do you think this is why the two of them were murdered?' asked Swaddell. 'The killer guessed what Downes had done, so took steps to silence them both?'

Chaloner nodded as answers piled into his mind. 'Eleanor was easy to dispatch, so he did it first. Then he turned to the more difficult task of gaining access to the Tower. Downes must have been terrified when he learned Eleanor was dead.' He winced, angry at himself. 'If I had gone to see him when I was first told, he might still be alive.'

'Or you would be lying next to him in the charnel house with a stiletto in your ear,' countered Swaddell, and tapped the message with his finger. 'I suggest we keep this to ourselves until we have worked out what it means.'

Chaloner agreed, although if he could not break the code himself that night, he would ask Thurloe to do it in the morning. But Swaddell did not need to know that.

'Finished yet?' came an impatient voice from the door; Chaloner had heard Rye coming, so the note had been secreted in his pocket long before the footman appeared.

'We still need to look upstairs,' replied Swaddell. 'We shall start in her bedchamber.'

Rye sighed his irritation, and stamped up the stairs to fling open the door of a room that was almost pitch black because all the shutters had been closed. He opened them at Chaloner's request, then stood tapping his foot to express his impatience. By tacit agreement, Chaloner and Swaddell took far longer than they would otherwise have done to search for the gold, both disliking the way Rye was trying to rush them. But eventually, they had to concede defeat: Eleanor's money was not in the house, suggesting that the killer had taken it along with her life.

Chaloner stood for a moment by the bed, which Rye said had not been touched since his mistress's body had been removed. The covers were rumpled, and a pillow pushed to one side to reveal a hollow, which was clearly where she had kept the gold while she slept. There were a few very faint blood smears that Chaloner assumed were from the wound in Eleanor's ear.

'We told you it had gone,' said Rye, watching them with unconcealed dislike. 'You have wasted your afternoon and made me miss a meal. King Jesus will have something to say about *that* on Friday.'

By the time they left Gracious Street, night was fast approaching. Alert for trouble, Chaloner kept his hand on the hilt of his sword, while Swaddell held a dagger in either fist. They reached the Strand, where the assassin suggested dining in an 'ordinary' before they went their separate ways. Chaloner agreed because it was safer than expecting something to be available at home. He ordered a mutton pie, but the pastry was hard and tasteless, which the cook explained was due to a lack of eggs.

'I got three dozen on Monday, but the weather has been so hot . . . well, I dare not risk using them lest they give everyone egg fever,' he confided. 'My brother made that mistake, and when three of his customers died, the Company of Bakers revoked his licence. Now all he can do is sell his wares on the sly in Covent Garden.'

Chaloner made a mental note to warn Wiseman's servants against buying baked goods from there. As he was still hungry, he ordered a marrow pudding, and ate it while Swaddell picked fastidiously at a boiled pigeon.

'Ursula and I had better find you a wife soon, Tom,' said Swaddell, watching him eat. 'You need someone to look after you, or you will be condemned to eating that sort of muck for the rest of your life.'

Chaloner pointed through the open window to the

238

house opposite, where a faint white cross was still visible on the door. 'I could not bear to lose a third one to plague. Besides, I am finished with affairs of the heart. They are too complicated and take up too much time.'

'Perhaps you should wed one of your hens, then,' quipped Swaddell, and chortled.

'Perhaps I should,' muttered Chaloner, thinking it would be safer, easier and a lot less fraught with anxiety.

Then Swaddell turned serious again. 'I do not think Eleanor was killed for her money, Tom. It was an added bonus for the killer, but that was not why he struck. He dispatched her for whatever is in the note you carry in your pocket.'

Chaloner agreed. He pushed away the empty bowl, bade Swaddell goodnight, and hurried home to begin work on decoding it at once.

Chapter 9

Despite working into the small hours, Chaloner failed to decipher Downes' message, and eventually gave up and went to sleep. It was another sweltering night, although he was exhausted enough not to care. He dropped off at once and slept surprisingly well until the market clatter woke him. He lay in bed for a while, thinking about Downes' communiqué, and frustrated that the regicide had made it so difficult to translate. He appreciated the need for caution, but how could Downes have expected Eleanor to understand it when it had defeated him, an intelligencer with many years of experience?

He went to the kitchen, where he scrubbed himself down vigorously with cold water and shaved with his sharpest blade, although he did not attempt to leave the thin moustache and chin patch – the T-beard – that was currently in fashion, as that required a good mirror, which he did not have. Then he donned a fresh, well-laced shirt, loose brown breeches and white hose. He did not bother with a coat, but buckled his sword around his waist and secreted his usual arsenal of knives and daggers about his person.

When the servants heard someone moving about in their domain, they reluctantly rolled out of their beds and came to see what was happening. They comprised a footman who was missing a leg, a cook who was minus an arm, and a groom who had lost an eye. Chaloner had always wondered if Wiseman had been responsible, and whether the absent items were displayed in the glass jars that festooned his laboratory on the floor above. He had never asked, lest he did not like the answer.

'We went to listen to Simpson in Allhallows the Great last night,' the footman told Chaloner conversationally, as he poured himself some breakfast ale. 'My God! That man knows how to preach a sermon!'

'You went to church on a Saturday?' asked Chaloner sceptically, aware that the trio usually preferred to visit taverns in their time off.

'Oh, yes,' replied the footman. 'Simpson did not really talk about religion, see.'

'It was more about the Companies,' elaborated the groom. 'How they set high prices that us common folk cannot afford, but stop free traders from selling stuff cheaper.'

'He said they are a blight on fair commerce,' the footman went on. 'Which they are.'

Chaloner recalled what Beadle Collins had told him: that the agitators had used Allhallows to bray an identical message on the night that Hill had been killed. When questioned about it, Simpson claimed he had forgotten to lock the door and the agitators had marched in without his permission. Was that true, or was Simpson one of the orators? Or had the feisty Fifth Monarchist noted the agitators' popularity, and decided to hijack their message for himself, perhaps in the hope of winning

241

more converts to his sect? Chaloner supposed he would have to find out.

'Well, King Jesus will put an end to that sort of thing when He takes over White Hall on Friday,' said the groom sagely. 'According to Simpson, He will do it as soon as He has had His breakfast.'

'Simpson is a Fifth Monarchist, see,' put in the cook, and raised a hand to prevent Chaloner from speaking. 'Yes, yes – we know they are lunatics with their tales of old kingdoms falling to new ones, but I hope something spectacular *does* happen on Friday, because I should like to witness the Second Coming.'

'So would I,' said the footman keenly. 'Of course, King Jesus will find Himself very busy at first, because there is a lot for Him to put right. For example, eggs were plentiful a month ago, but you cannot get them for love nor money now. He certainly needs to sort that out.'

'Not that *we* need worry about eggs,' said the cook, and smiled at Chaloner. 'Your hens do their duty, so we are never short. We shall sell a few in church later. We have plenty, and we can charge a fortune now that they are scarce. Supply and demand, see.'

'That would make you a higgler,' warned Chaloner. 'And you would be breaking three of the Company of Poulters' laws – doing business on a Sunday, setting your own prices, and trading in an illegal location.'

'We do not care about that,' retorted the cook. 'We just want to make some easy cash.'

'But do not even think of demanding a share,' put in the footman quickly. 'Not when we looked after them birds the whole time you were off enjoying yourself in Holland. Consider it payment for services already rendered. Agreed?'

242

'We went to the Sunne on Pudding Lane after the sermon,' put in the groom, before Chaloner could say whether he agreed or not. 'The whole place was alive with tales of omens proving that the Kingdom of God is nigh.'

'One was that Simpson had a vision of Christ arriving at White Hall in a burning chariot,' elaborated the groom, 'while a swan told his friend Vicar Glasse to expect the Second Coming this week.'

'A talking swan?' Chaloner managed to interject. 'Was Glasse drunk?'

'He claimed not,' shrugged the groom. 'Although he seemed very unsteady on his pins to me, and he was—'

'You should be wary of listening to preachers like Simpson,' interrupted Chaloner warningly. 'Wiseman is the King's surgeon – he cannot employ servants who want the monarchy gone, and if anyone finds out what you have been doing, he will have to dismiss you to protect himself.'

'It will not matter once King Jesus has ousted all the Cavaliers,' shrugged the groom. 'But do not worry – we will not let Mr Wiseman suffer the fate that awaits all the other courtiers. He is not really one of them anyway – he just pretends to be, so he can earn the money to pay our wages.'

The truth was that Wiseman loved being at Court, and certainly did not work solely to support three servants who were insolent, lazy and rebellious. Chaloner started to say so, but the cook forestalled him by handing over a broadsheet.

'This started circulating late last night. It is by the Paladin, whose pieces are a lot more interesting than the dull old *London Gazette* – that rag only lists which ships have arrived in which ports. Who cares about that?'

'Not me,' declared the footman. 'And nor do I care about the Dutch war. We should either defeat the butter-eaters or forget about them.'

Unwilling to listen to their unpalatable views any longer, Chaloner told them to tend his poultry, feeling that if they were going to sell the eggs and keep the money, they should continue to earn it. Then he took the broadsheet up to his rooms, aiming to read it in peace and break his fast with a slice of cold oatmeal at the same time.

The Paladin had evidently tired of satirising religious radicals, courtiers and the poultry industry, and had turned his attention to the war. According to him, Admiral Holmes had done much harm by burning a defenceless Dutch village, and the enemy would avenge themselves tenfold. He also pointed out that the conflict was costing a fortune in ships and supplies, yet it would not be the rich who would foot the bill, but everyone else.

Its appearance forced Chaloner to reconsider his conviction that Eleanor was the Paladin, because even the most loyal of publishers was unlikely to keep churning out her work quite so long after her death. And yet the solution had made so much sense . . . He studied the page closely, looking for clues regarding the writer or the printer, but there was nothing. Conceding defeat, he crumpled it into a ball, and began to plan his day.

He wanted to start with Simpson and Glasse, to demand answers about Downes, what was in the offing for Friday, and whether Simpson was one of the agitators, but he knew it would be a waste of time without Swaddell to provide the necessary touch of menace. Reluctantly, he conceded that they would have to wait until the following morning. Therefore, his first task was to visit the Rainbow to see if Stedman knew which of his colleagues was willing to publish controversial leaflets.

Next, he would have to tell Thurloe about Downes and ask him to decode the message, since he was unable to do it himself. After that, he would visit the Tower, and find out how the regicide had come to be murdered in a place that was meant to be secure. He also needed to go to church, lest his absence was noted and he was branded a dissenter.

He left his rooms and was walking down the stairs when Lester emerged from his lodgings below to intercept him. Chaloner shook his head apologetically when asked if he had managed to corner Pepys.

'But Williamson has promised to secure you a ship if I find out what happened to Eleanor Montagu. I am not sure he can be trusted, but I will hold him to it if I can.'

Lester managed a smile. 'Well, time does not hang quite so heavily now that I have Elsie to spend it with. She is a remarkable lady, and I grow increasingly fond of her. We shall go to Foxhall Gardens today. Will you come? Dorcas is tired of playing chaperone.'

'I wish I could,' said Chaloner, thinking it would be infinitely preferable to confessing his negligence to Thurloe and visiting the Tower. 'But I need to work on my enquiries.'

'You do not want my help, do you?' asked Lester, and sighed his relief when Chaloner shook his head. 'Good! I should hate to disappoint Elsie.'

Afraid he might not have time if he left it until later, Chaloner started by attending to his devotions in the

Covent Garden church. He walked across the piazza in the early morning sunshine, relishing the peace on the one day when trading there was strictly forbidden. Bells rang all over the city, but fell silent one by one as the first services of the day began. Realising he was late, he broke into a trot, and arrived just as the vicar was intoning the opening prayer.

Usually, he waited until his name was recorded in the parish ledger, then slipped away when no one was looking. Unfortunately, Morning Prayer was less well attended than the later Holy Communion, which meant he could not escape without being noticed – and leaving early was a worse crime than not going in the first place.

He sat at the back, and used the time to scribble a report for Williamson, outlining what he had learned about Eleanor so far. He wrote it in code, hoping that by the time the Spymaster had managed to decipher it, there would be something more substantial to add. Then he fretted and fidgeted through the rest of the rite, his mind on all he needed to do.

It was over eventually, and after paying a chorister to deliver his report to the Spymaster, he set off to the Rainbow, pleased to see Stedman already there. However, he was disappointed to learn that Swaddell had been right: London's printing fraternity had no idea who had been publishing the Paladin's work, despite every one of them professing to be keen to find out.

'Are you sure you have no suspects, Stedman?' he pressed, exasperated. 'I do not ask to see anyone in trouble, but to help me solve the murder of a good lady.'

'If I did, I would tell you,' promised Stedman, 'because I do not like the way the Paladin has turned on the government of late. But I have discussed the

246

matter *ad nauseam* with my colleagues, and we are all mystified.'

Full of frustration, Chaloner crossed Fleet Street and hurried to Lincoln's Inn, only to be informed that Thurloe was in the chapel. He knew better than to interrupt the devotions of a pious man, and stood uncertainly in Chancery Lane, wondering what to do next. Then he saw an empty hackney carriage. It was too good an opportunity to miss, so he told the driver to take him to the Navy Office. Williamson had agreed to help Lester, it was true, but Chaloner wanted a second string to his bow lest he himself failed to solve the mystery surrounding Eleanor's death or the Spymaster decided to renege on their agreement.

Despite the fact that it was a Sunday, he arrived to find sea-officers bustling in and out of the building, and secretaries scurrying urgently about their business. He went to Pepys's room, and was disappointed but not surprised to be informed that the Clerk of the Acts was not there.

'He is still busy with his closet,' Hewer explained, evidently finding nothing amiss with the fact that Pepys seemed more concerned with his soft furnishings than the threat of an enemy invasion. 'You should have come yesterday. He was here most of the day.'

'Will he be in later?'

Hewer shook his head. 'He is summoned to White Hall by the King, to explain why the fleet has not yet sailed.'

Chaloner frowned. 'But yesterday, the porter here told me that it had.'

Hewer lowered his voice. 'Not only is it still in port,

but it is nowhere near ready to leave. His Majesty is furious, and has summoned all our senior officials to tell him what is going on. He came back from Greenwich specially, and all his courtiers with him.'

'Good,' said Chaloner, thinking it would give him an opportunity to quiz more of them about Eleanor, should there be no answers in the coded message from Downes.

'Did you hear that it rained fish in Kent last week?' asked Hewer unhappily. 'Such an event usually presages ill fortune at sea, which has put everyone here in a pother.'

Chaloner turned at a sudden rattle of running footsteps in the hall outside. 'Is that why this place is so hectic today? From fear of an omen, not because our navy is unable to protect us should the United Provinces decide to attack?'

'We are used to worrying about the Dutch,' said Hewer wryly. 'But a predicted naval disaster is new and alarming.'

Somewhat disgusted, Chaloner turned to leave, but had not taken many steps along the corridor before bumping into Hewer's uncle. Robert Blackborne exuded a sense of calm efficiency, and Chaloner noticed how many officials nodded and bowed to him as he passed, clearly comforted to see him there.

'Still trying to petition Pepys?' Blackborne asked. 'I admire your tenacity for a cause that I have already told you is hopeless.'

'Lester is worth the trouble. He is an excellent captain, and our country needs him.'

'Of that I have no doubt. However, he will never win another ship after losing *Swiftsure*. I imagine it was all Admiral Berkeley's fault, but it is Lester who will bear the blame. After all, we cannot malign a dead "hero" – or, worse yet, risk people thinking that one of His Majesty's appointments was a mistake.'

'Fortunately, Lester now has a powerful supporter,' said Chaloner, hoping that Williamson would keep his word, given that Pepys was probably going to be a lost cause.

Blackborne raised his eyebrows. 'Then I shall be interested to see how he fares, because it will take a man of enormous influence to help the likes of Lester.'

Chaloner sincerely hoped that the Spymaster had not misjudged the authority he thought he held, because he would be irked if he found Eleanor's killer only to be informed that Williamson could not keep his end of the bargain. He flailed around for other ways to help his friend back to sea.

'Will money work instead?' he asked. 'The so-called gentlemen who are promoted over tarpaulins must offer more than just being fun at parties.'

'Oh, very likely,' agreed Blackborne. 'But unless you happen to have a spare palace or country estate, bribery is not an option that is open to you. Of course, it may not matter soon, if the rumours about the Kingdom of God transpire to be true.'

Chaloner regarded him thoughtfully. 'So you believe the Fifth Monarchists' predictions now? At Bowles' funeral, you seemed unconvinced.'

Blackborne gave an enigmatic smile. 'Who are we to know the Almighty's mind? He will come when the time is right, and no mere human can know when that may be.'

'If your co-religionists are plotting something for Friday, it will fail,' warned Chaloner. 'You must urge them to stop while they still have their heads.'

'I have no sway over them,' said Blackborne. 'Whatever makes you think I might?'

'In past attempts to oust the King,' Chaloner went on,

249

'there were rumours of troops, gunpowder, fireballs and cannon, which at least gave the rebels a fighting chance of victory. But this time, there seems to be nothing but hope. Wishful thinking will not win your friends what they want, so please urge them to—'

'King Jesus does not need earthly weapons and armies,' interrupted Blackborne serenely. 'He has the power of heaven at his disposal.'

Chaloner was beginning to be exasperated. 'So what is going to happen, exactly?'

Blackborne continued to beam seraphically. 'Read the Book of Revelation, Chaloner. After the last battle, the wicked shall be cast into a bottomless pit, while the righteous shall take their places with the saints in the New Jerusalem.'

'Will this be on Friday?' pressed Chaloner, thinking that sometimes, when he spoke to people with extreme religious opinions, he was forced to wonder if they were entirely sane.

'Who knows?' shrugged Blackborne. 'All I can say is that it would behove us all to greet the Lord with pure hearts and clean consciences.'

Outside, Chaloner's hackney carriage had been snapped up by another customer, forcing him to walk back to Lincoln's Inn. The streets were busy, but as it was the Sabbath, people tended to stroll rather than rush. Bells rang in nearly every church, ranging from the tuneful peals of six or eight in the wealthier churches, to the tinny clanks of those with only one.

He strode briskly, aware that time was passing. The sun was already hot, and there was not a cloud in the sky. His feet kicked up puffs of dust as he went, and so did everyone else's, including horses, so by the time he arrived in Chancery Lane, his clean white shirt was covered in a coating of brown grime.

He was tense and nervous, unsettled by the gossip he had overheard as he had walked – some about the Paladin's latest broadsheet, but most about omens. The single dragon over St Paul's Cathedral was now an entire flock of them; it had rained whales in Kent rather than fish; and Vicar Glasse had been approached by an arch-angel, not a talking swan. It was taken as a given that something important was poised to take place, and almost everyone expected it to be on Friday.

Chaloner aimed for Dial Court, but was intercepted by an elderly man wearing a woollen cap to disguise the fact that his ears had been chopped off. It was William Prynne, one of the Inn's benchers, and perhaps the most rabid pamphleteer the country had ever known. Prynne had views about everything, from bishops to dancing, and was not afraid to express them. He had railed against the government until he had been appointed Keeper of Records, after which he had become the King's most ardent supporter.

'The devil has acquired himself a pen,' Prynne snarled, reaching out a claw-like hand to prevent Chaloner from walking past without stopping. 'I have a challenger, a miserable sinner who is the most inbred, depraved, vane, wanton, proud, profane—'

'You mean the Paladin?' interrupted Chaloner, not surprised that Prynne was jealous, given that his rival's prose was a lot easier to read, and witty rather than just plain nasty.

Prynne looked ready to explode with outrage. 'Yes, and now he has turned his spleen on *me*! A broadsheet mocking my opinions was slipped under my door this very morning, so fresh that the ink was still sticky when I picked it up.'

Chaloner grimaced. Here was yet more evidence that Eleanor could not be the author, because antagonising the odious Prynne was something no sane printer would risk unless he had a very powerful *living* patron. Without such protection, Prynne was likely to avenge himself on the culprit as only he knew how. Chaloner wondered who else the Paladin might be, and had a bad feeling that he might be ordered to find out if the pamphleteer continued to attack the government.

'Do you have any idea who wrote it?' he asked, although not with much hope of a sensible answer. He was not disappointed.

'Satan!' hissed Prynne venomously. 'And it was spewed from the printing presses of hell. There is no other explanation, because no London publisher would dare produce such foul and pestilential fabrications.'

'What did the Paladin write about you?'

'Nothing I would repeat, because it was lies,' snapped Prynne, then proceeded to do exactly what he declared he would not. 'I was called a trumpeter of windy nonsense, whose words are offensive and nonsensical. And he said I do not know what I am talking about.'

'Goodness!' murmured Chaloner. 'The audacity of the fellow!'

'Quite,' snarled Prynne. 'It is the Paladin who knows nothing! In one of his ignominious and depraved tirades, he claimed that Jamestown's main church is made of brick. Well, I happen to know it is crafted from wood, because I saw it with my own eyes. I travelled there before the wars, you see.'

Chaloner supposed that Eleanor would not have made such a mistake – she had not long returned from Virginia, so would know what materials had been used to construct its biggest place of worship. Even so, the faint gleam of a solution began to glow at the back of his mind, born from a knowledge of his own time in the New World. He politely, but firmly, extricated himself from Prynne's clutches and went on his way.

Thurloe was not in his chambers, but walking under the ancient oaks in the garden. Sunlight filtered through the leaves, which were beginning to crisp in the unrelenting heat, and the paths underfoot were littered with ones that had fallen early.

When Thurloe saw Chaloner, his eyes turned cold and hard. 'You did not visit Downes,' he said tightly. 'And now he is dead.'

'Yes,' acknowledged Chaloner with a weary sigh. He slumped on a bench and indicated that Thurloe was to sit next to him. 'I tried to go yesterday morning, but I was not allowed inside because of some castle-wide inspection.'

'He would have been dead by then anyway,' said Thurloe curtly, perching on the edge of the seat with obvious reluctance. 'You should have found time on Friday, as I asked. Poor Downes! I am now more certain than ever that the other eight regicides were murdered.'

'Probably,' agreed Chaloner. 'But I do not see how we will prove it.'

He told Thurloe all he had learned since they had last met. Thurloe listened without interruption, and by the time he had finished, Chaloner was relieved to see he no longer looked quite so deadly. He handed over the message he had found in Eleanor's house.

'I hope you can decode it, because it is beyond me.'

Thurloe studied it intently. 'It is a very sophisticated cipher, which tells us two things: first, it seems that Downes had great respect for Eleanor's intelligence, and second, that it contains some very dangerous information.'

'So you can work out what is in it?'

'Clearly, I must,' replied Thurloe shortly, slipping it into his pocket, 'because I refuse to imperil anyone else by begging their help with it.'

'No one knows it exists except Swaddell and me,' said Chaloner, aiming to assuage his concerns. 'And he can be trusted to stay quiet.'

'Yes, but you just told me that Eleanor was unlikely to have known this message was in her book,' retorted Thurloe acerbically, 'yet I suspect it saw her killed anyway, while you have already been attacked once. We must both be on our guard. Swaddell, too.'

'Yes,' acknowledged Chaloner tiredly. 'We must.'

Thurloe tapped the pocket containing the missive. 'I have a feeling that this will explain how all the murders are woven together – the nine regicides, Eleanor, Hadie, Bowles and Hill. As so often happens, disparate enquiries are merging into one.'

Chaloner was less certain, but was unwilling to argue as long as Thurloe was still irked with him. He was silent for a while, pondering the spider's web of connections and associations that was beginning to emerge.

'When this matter is resolved,' he said eventually, 'I am going to leave London. The Earl cannot fend Bristol off for ever, and there is only so much more I can do to protect him. When he falls – which he will – I shall be tainted by association. No one will hire me again.'

'Oh, there will always be work for a man with your

talents,' said Thurloe, although Chaloner was not entirely sure it was meant as a compliment. 'But sitting here is doing neither of us any good. It is time we went to the Tower and searched Downes' cell.'

'You cannot come,' blurted Chaloner in alarm. 'That would endanger both of us.'

Thurloe sighed irritably. 'Then I shall wait outside. I have Downes' letter to keep me occupied, so I shall not be wasting my time.'

It was patently obvious that he did not trust Chaloner to go there unless he took him himself. Full of chagrin, Chaloner indicated that Thurloe was to lead the way outside.

As they passed the porter's lodge, they saw a visitor in the process of getting directions to Thurloe's chambers. It was Wogan, who had donned a badly fitting ginger wig and a lawyer's ancient gown. Vernon was with him, wearing the robe that marked him as a physician and a huge hat that hid his face. Chaloner had never seen more miserable attempts at disguises, and was furious with them both.

'*You* should not be here,' he hissed, grabbing the Welshman's arm and hustling him out into Chancery Lane. Vernon started to jump to his friend's defence, but stopped abruptly when he saw a knife appear in Chaloner's hand. 'Thurloe cannot be seen entertaining fugitives from justice – especially one wanted for a crime like yours.'

'I know,' said Wogan apologetically. 'But I have information for him that—'

'Then send him a letter,' interrupted Chaloner angrily.

'And how would he know it came from me?' demanded

Wogan, irked in his turn. 'I can hardly sign it with my name – for both our sakes. Besides, Vernon and I have been careful: we took a tortuous route to ensure we were not followed here and we are both unknown at Lincoln's Inn.'

'Yet Chaloner is right,' Vernon told him tightly. 'You and I should *not* be here. This errand does nothing to benefit us, and I think we should let events unfold as they will.'

'But I must speak to someone about what we know,' said Wogan desperately. 'How else will I atone for . . . I *must* prevent more bloodshed. If I had the courage, I would approach Spymaster Williamson, but I am not ready to die just yet, and Thurloe is good at getting what I find out into the right hands.'

'It is all right, Tom,' said Thurloe, indicating that Chaloner was to release the regicide's arm. 'What did you want to tell me, Wogan?'

The Welshman drew him into a doorway, so they would not be overheard by anyone passing by. Chaloner followed and so did Vernon, which made for a tight squeeze, and probably looked very strange to anyone who happened to notice them.

'When I first returned to London,' began Wogan, 'you demanded to know my intentions, and I explained how I aim to make amends for my role in the old King's execution. To prove it, I promised to keep you informed of anything I heard that might affect the peace of our city.'

'You did,' acknowledged Thurloe. 'And you have provided several helpful snippets since, all of which have been passed to Williamson.'

'That incompetent scoundrel,' growled Vernon. 'He is a—'

'Now I have more to impart,' interrupted Wogan, cutting across his friend's grumbles. 'I have already reported the rumours about a Kingdom of God scheduled for Sunday, but now there is talk that it will happen on Friday instead.'

'We already know that,' said Chaloner coolly. 'And so does most of London.'

Wogan continued to address Thurloe. 'You probably think the Fifth Monarchists are behind it, but all they do is sit and wait. They long for the Second Coming with all their hearts, but none plot to bring it about. As far as they are concerned, it is in God's hands.'

'I doubt Vicar Simpson agrees,' said Chaloner tartly. 'He is under the impression that King Jesus wants his help.'

'And that is why we came to see you, Thurloe,' said Wogan, continuing to ignore Chaloner. 'The government's likely reaction to the news will be to arrest every Fifth Monarchist they can find, but if they do, they will imprison a lot of innocent people.'

'Are you saying that there will be no trouble on Friday?' asked Thurloe sceptically. 'That the rumours are nothing but wishful thinking?'

'No,' replied Wogan. 'I suspect something *is* in the offing, but whatever it is has nothing to do with Simpson and his misguided horde. In my opinion, someone is using them as a shield to hide behind.'

'Who?' demanded Chaloner. 'And what is your evidence? Do you know of any movements of troops? Places where weapons are being stored?'

'If I did, I would have reported it already,' snapped Wogan, resenting Chaloner's intrusive questions when he was trying to confide in Thurloe. He turned back to the ex-Spymaster. 'I was going to suggest we work together to find out what is brewing and who is responsible.'

'In that case,' said Thurloe briskly, 'you can come with us to the Tower to see what might be learned about the murder of John Downes.'

Wogan gaped at him. 'Downes is dead?'

'*He* cannot go to the Tower!' cried Vernon at the same time. 'They may not let him out again. He thinks no one will recognise him after so many years, but Chaloner did, and it is possible that some vigilant yeoman might, too.'

'That is true,' said Chaloner, loath to enter such a place in company with a man who was wanted for crimes against the state.

But Thurloe remained implacable. 'Two pairs of eyes are better than one, and we must do our absolute best with this search, because I am certain that solving the murders of Downes and his friends will help us understand what is behind all this bubbling unrest.'

Wogan shook his head as he considered what he was being told. 'I seriously doubt Downes was murdered, Thurloe. His guards are unlikely to have looked the other way while *he* dabbled in insurrection. You are mistaken.'

'I do not say he played an active role,' said Thurloe. 'However, I suspect he knew something about it, and I am hoping that he left a clue behind to tell us what it was. Now, shall we go?'

One of Lincoln's Inn's porters, whom Chaloner was sure could not have been more than twelve, ran to summon them a hackney carriage, because Thurloe was not about to walk anywhere in a heatwave. While they waited, Chaloner reflected on the plague, which had killed so many people that it was no longer unusual to see children doing the work of adults.

While Vernon tried desperately to dissuade Wogan from entering the city's most formidable prison, Chaloner pulled Thurloe back into the porter's lodge on the pretext that it would be cooler.

'Are you sure it is wise to involve Wogan?' he whispered. 'At best, we collaborate with a king-killer, and at worst . . . well, you do not need me to spell that out for you.'

'No, I do not,' agreed Thurloe tartly. 'However, he is observant, and I would rather you did not search Downes' cell alone – it is too important to risk mistakes being made. I know you are sceptical, but I really do believe that solving Downes' death will provide the key to understanding what is going on.'

Unhappily, Chaloner saw that Thurloe's trust in him had been so damaged by his failure to visit the Tower when he had first been asked that Wogan was his way of ensuring that he did not fall short a second time – monitoring Chaloner in a place where he himself dared not tread.

'There *is* a common factor in all these deaths,' he acknowledged, wondering how to win back the ex-Spymaster's good opinion. 'However, I think it is eggs.'

'Explain,' ordered Thurloe curiously.

'Downes wrote a book about egg production, which he gave to Eleanor with the ciphered message; Bowles was surrounded by smashed ones when he died; Hadie and Hill were killed while investigating higglers; and Bowles, Hadie and Hill were members of the Company that regulates the egg trade.'

'But what about the other eight regicides? They have

no links to eggs, and you cannot dismiss their deaths as serendipity, because it is suspicious that Downes was killed so soon after the rest of them.'

'Perhaps we should look more closely at *him*, then,' said Chaloner, nodding to where Wogan listened patiently to Vernon's agitated tirade. 'The tenth regicide in our mystery.'

'He is trying to redeem himself, not commit more crimes,' said Thurloe. 'Besides, I *know* I am right about the dead regicides being the key. Indeed, I have rarely been more sure of anything in my life.'

Chaloner regarded him through narrowed eyes, sensing he was holding something back. 'You said on Friday that you were alerted to the first eight deaths by another king-killer – Dixwell. What else did his letter tell you?'

Thurloe smiled wryly. 'Sometimes, you are too clever for your own good, Thomas, and one day it will see you in trouble. But you are right: Dixwell reminded me that two of the eight – Hardresse Waller and Gilbert Millington – had a reputation for devising intricate but clever plots to neutralise their enemies.'

'Neutralise? You mean kill?'

'Not usually, although I understand one or two might have involved fatalities. So, this pair would cook up some ingenious scheme and then tell Downes, who would arrange for it to be implemented by the other six.'

'So you think Waller and Millington conceived some plan that precipitated all this?' asked Chaloner doubtfully. 'How, when they were in prison?'

'They were both in Jersey, where they were almost certainly allowed to meet. Both were brash, angry men, who would not have been content to sit around waiting to die of old age – they would have tried one last time to oust the monarchy.'

'Even if they did come up with a plot, Downes and the rest were not in a position to put it into action.'

'I disagree. Four of the cabal were in Switzerland, so *were* free to do whatever was required. However, Dixwell said they were the first to be killed . . . '

'So Millington and Waller's scheme – if it ever existed – died before it was born. I still do not understand why you think this business is so important.'

'I cannot explain it any better than I have,' said Thurloe irritably. 'It is a hunch, and I have learned to trust those. Besides, I have not forgotten what else Dixwell told me, even if you have – that two of the most dangerous regicides of all are probably heading this way.'

'Ludlow and Love,' recalled Chaloner. 'But you cannot be sure that they are part of this business, especially as you say they were not part of Downes' original clique. It may just be chance that they have chosen to move now.' He glanced at Wogan again. 'Just as it is chance that *he* is here. Assuming his contrition is genuine, of course.'

'I think it is,' said Thurloe. 'For a start, he has spent a lot of his own money on helping the poor. If he was lying about his desire to make amends, he would have promised the Earth and then done nothing about it.'

'I shall reserve judgement until I know more about him.'

'Good,' said Thurloe, nodding his approval. 'That means I have trained you well.'

At that moment, the boy arrived with the hackney carriage. Vernon disappeared to visit patients, leaving Wogan, Thurloe and Chaloner to clamber in without him. The three of them travelled in silence until they reached St Paul's, where the sight of the majestic old cathedral, rising so solid and proud above the huddle of houses around its feet, brought a smile to Wogan's tired face.

'There is something that will never change,' he said fondly. 'She will stand sentinel over London long after we are dead and gone.'

'Have you not heard of Christopher Wren?' asked Chaloner archly. 'He would demolish it tomorrow if he could, and replace it with something modern.'

'That will never happen,' said Wogan confidently. 'The people would not allow it.'

'And what will King Jesus allow?' fished Chaloner.

Wogan shrugged. 'Just because I do not want to see Fifth Monarchists needlessly slaughtered does not mean I am intimately acquainted with all their odd beliefs.'

'Yet Vernon seems to be your closest friend, and he is as fanatical as any of them.'

Wogan nodded. 'I love him like a brother, but his conviction that the Second Coming will be on Friday . . . well, it is nonsense, as far as I am concerned.'

'So you do not believe a new world order will unfold in five days' time?'

'Of course not. Oh, there may be a bit of trouble in some parts of the city, and doubtless a few die-hard rebels will race in to take advantage of it, but they will not succeed in changing anything. Besides, as I have told you already, I think we should stop yearning for the impossible, and learn to appreciate what we have.'

'Amen,' said Thurloe. 'It is time for peace and stability.'

It might be time, thought Chaloner, but that did not mean they were going to get it. There had been dozens of uprisings since the Restoration, but the King had learned nothing from any of them. He would be told about the possibility of a crisis for Friday, but it would not stop him from jumping in a syllabub with his mistresses, and as long as he remained so dedicated to his dissolute lifestyle, there would be people who wanted to get rid of him.

'Here we are at the Tower,' said Thurloe, as the carriage rolled to a standstill. 'St Olave's Church is nearby, so I shall wait for you there. Find me when you have finished.'

Chaloner had hated prisons ever since he had been incarcerated in a particularly unpleasant one in France on a charge of espionage. Thus it took considerable courage to walk up to the Tower's main gate and ask to inspect Downes' cell. Naturally, the yeoman on duty refused, and then, just as naturally, changed his mind when Chaloner slipped him a shilling.

The fortress was busy, because Londoners were permitted inside on Sundays to see the Jewel House and the royal menagerie. Their numbers were swollen by the friends and family of the Tower's many inmates, who were there to beg for visits or to deliver food.

'We never let anyone see Downes,' said the yeoman, when Chaloner asked how many people had called on the prisoner over the last few weeks. 'He was not eligible for that sort of privilege.'

'How much would it cost to see Sir Robert Tichborne?' asked Wogan, referring to another regicide currently languishing within. He lowered his voice to a silky whisper. 'Bearing in mind that we are *very* wealthy men.'

The guard looked around quickly to make sure no one

else was within earshot. 'I am sure arrangements can be made. When would you like to come?'

'Not today,' said Wogan, and when the man had gone to fetch them a guide, muttered to a deeply unimpressed Chaloner, 'There! Anyone can get in with a heavy enough purse, so we may never know how many visitors Downes actually enjoyed.'

'Sir Gilbert Talbot wants to escort you to Downes' cell himself,' said the guard, returning a few minutes later. 'He just needs a moment to affix his wig, so he told me to show you the King's animals while you wait.'

The royal menagerie was the eclectic collection of creatures that the Crown had been sent as gifts by foreign heads of state. There was a threadbare lion with teeth rotted black from the sweetmeats it was fed, an ape with a penchant for cheese, a camel that could spit with impressive accuracy, and a wide variety of birds.

'I hate seeing things caged,' confided Wogan to Chaloner, as they inspected an aviary that contained an assortment of colourful waterfowl and, for some unaccountable reason, a pigeon. 'If I am ever captured, I would rather suffer a traitors' death than be locked in here for years on end.'

'So would I,' agreed Chaloner with a shudder, although he thought that in Wogan's case, he might not be given a choice.

'You dislike prisons, too?' Wogan studied him intently. 'Yes, you have turned quite pale. Courage, my friend. Stay close to me, and we shall brace each other for the ordeal.'

At that moment, Talbot bustled up, resplendent in a hairpiece of golden curls that reached his waist. He recognised Chaloner from their meeting at the charnel house, and professed himself horrified that a prisoner should have been killed on his watch. As he was almost frantic to cooperate with any enquiry into the matter, Chaloner took the opportunity to ask him some questions.

'Did Downes have any visitors the day he died?'

Talbot produced a ledger from his pocket, and ran a short, thick finger down the entries until he found Downes' name. 'He had just two this year. We do not usually allow regicides the pleasure of outside company, but exceptions were made for these.'

'They were rich, I suppose,' said Wogan pointedly.

While Talbot spluttered an indignant denial, Chaloner read the first name.

'Lady Montagu?' he blurted. 'A week before he died?'

Talbot was glad to be talking about something other than bribery. 'I allowed her in because of her rank – I am not a fellow to refuse the requests of noblewomen. She was escorted by her footman, a slippery fellow named Rye, whom I did not like.'

Rye had not mentioned this, thought Chaloner. 'Did she explain why she wanted to see Downes?'

Talbot nodded. 'He had written a book about poultry, and she was eager to discuss it with him. Naturally, I stayed the whole time, and so did Rye. She and Downes talked for hours, and by the time she left, it was clear they felt they had become friends.'

'What did they talk about exactly?'

'How to maintain high standards of welfare for egg-producing chickens, and the importance of breeding from healthy stock. Nothing else – I would not have permitted them to discuss anything controversial.' Talbot grimaced at the memory. 'It was all rather tedious actually, but they enjoyed it. I had never seen Downes so animated.'

'Did he give her anything before she left?'

'She asked if she could borrow his personal copy of *The Chicken and her Egges*, as she had been unable to source one herself, but he said he wanted to keep it for a day or two, to make notes on their conversation. He promised to send it to her when he had finished. And he did – I delivered it to her house myself.'

So, thought Chaloner, the meeting had convinced Downes that Eleanor could be trusted, and he had composed a coded message that he had expected her to be able to decipher. It was unfortunate for him that she had been killed before she had realised what he wanted her to do.

'And Father Tyme,' said Wogan, reading the second entry in the ledger, which revealed that someone had visited Downes on the day he had died. 'Who is he?'

Talbot peered at the ledger. 'It says here that he is a cleric. He is not one of our regulars, but we always allow clergy access to the inmates, even regicides. It would be unchristian to deny them spiritual comfort.'

'Right,' said Chaloner, wondering how Talbot could be so gullible. Father Tyme indeed! 'Did you remain with *him* while he was with Downes?'

Talbot was shocked by the idea. 'Of course not! Even a traitor's relationship with God is private, and I would never presume to eavesdrop on those.'

'Clearly, this "Father Tyme" did not visit Downes to comfort him, but to end his life,' said Chaloner heavily. 'Did you meet him?'

Talbot was white-faced and growing frightened. 'Very briefly. But he *looked* like a vicar. He wore black clothes

266

and a cheap wig, and he exuded an air of piety. I had no reason to think he was not who he claimed, and if you cannot trust a priest, who can you trust?'

It was not Chaloner's place to castigate him for his ineptitude, so he asked what kind of man Downes had been.

'Quiet and undemanding,' replied Talbot wretchedly. 'Until the last few weeks, when he learned that a number of his friends had died, some in prison and others abroad. Then he became agitated. He wrote letters and bribed the guards to send them for him. Naturally, they took the money, then brought the missives to me. I burned the lot.'

'Did you read any first?' asked Chaloner hopefully.

'A few,' admitted Talbot. 'And I am sure they contained secret messages, so I did him a favour by destroying them. They were to dangerous men – relatives of Cromwell, still-powerful Parliamentarians like Robert Blackborne, and even old Spymaster Thurloe. Downes would have been executed if the government had seen them.'

'So what did he write exactly?' asked Wogan, while Chaloner tried to conceal his alarm at hearing Thurloe's name spoken in such a place.

Talbot caught the urgency in Wogan's voice, but gave an apologetic shrug. 'On the surface, it was just a lot of twaddle about poultry. However, the stilted phrasing suggested that this was not the real message being conveyed, as did pinholes under some of the words. He was definitely trying to communicate something, but I do not know what.'

'Is there anything else you can tell us?' asked Chaloner, wondering if Downes – and perhaps Eleanor, Bowles, Hadie and Hill, too – might still be alive if Talbot had not taken it upon himself to act as censor.

'Well, the day before he died, he donated a bird to the royal menagerie. I assumed he was trying to curry favour with the King, in the hope that the conditions of his incarceration might be relaxed. It happens to everyone in the end – they all baulk against our restrictions eventually, and itch to have more than they deserve.'

'How did he buy a bird when he was locked in here?' asked Wogan sceptically.

'He gave me the money and I did it,' replied Talbot. 'He specified a chicken, but they are expensive these days, so I got him a pigeon instead. He said to tell the King what he had done, and to call the bird Eghfeva.'

Chaloner frowned. 'Why?'

'It is the name of a medieval saint, apparently. The guards had been gossiping to him about the Adrian Masque, so obscure historical figures must have been on his mind.'

Chaloner was sure the name was significant, but other than its similarity to 'egg fever', he was not sure how or why. Could it be a clue to decoding the cipher that had been sent to Eleanor? He wracked his brains, but failed to see how a single word could be the key to unlocking a multi-sentence message. Moreover, sending the key to the King and the message to Eleanor did not seem a very reliable way to proceed, especially as several people had told him that Eleanor had avoided His Majesty's company whenever she could, because she considered him lewd.

He asked to see Downes' cell, so Talbot conducted him and Wogan there at once, leading the way along dank passages until they reached the place where the regicide had spent his final years. Chaloner grew shorter of breath with every step he took, and his legs were unsteady. He itched to turn around and run. Then Wogan rested a reassuring hand on his shoulder. It helped, and he was grateful for it.

Despite the seriousness of his crime, Downes had been kept in relative comfort. His cell was a reasonable size, and his family had been permitted to send him enough money to buy reading material and decent food. Even so, it was a prison, and Chaloner longed to be away from it. Again, he was glad of Wogan's calm presence at his side.

While the Welshman continued to ply Talbot with questions about every aspect of Downes and his imprisonment, Chaloner began to search the cell, although he knew it would not take long because most of the dead man's possessions had been sent to the charnel house for his kinsfolk to collect. The only things left were the prison's basic furniture and a few books that had been deemed too tatty for his relatives to want. Talbot watched nervously, afraid something would be discovered to see him in more trouble.

Chaloner inspected the table, bed and chairs for hiding places, then checked each book for concealed messages or meaningful annotations. There was nothing, so he turned his attention to the walls, immediately noticing a tell-tale pile of dust under the window. Sure enough, part of the sill was loose. He removed it to reveal a hollowed-out space beneath.

'I did not know he had done that!' gasped Talbot, horrified. 'I swear!'

'It does not matter,' shrugged Chaloner. 'It is empty anyway.'

It was certainly empty now, because the roll of paper

that had been there was safely tucked up his sleeve. The discovery had Wogan going down on his hands and knees to hunt for other secret hidey-holes, although it was not long before he conceded defeat.

By then, Talbot was as eager for the visitors to leave as Chaloner was to go, so it was not many moments before they were back in the street outside. Chaloner took several deep breaths to flush the stench of the Tower from his nostrils.

'That was a waste of time,' said Wogan despondently, as he and Chaloner began to walk to St Olave's. 'I thought I might be able to help in there, but I was useless.'

'It was a futile exercise from the start,' said Chaloner, declining to share his discovery with the regicide until he knew more about it. 'Did you prise anything else from Talbot? I could not hear all your conversation.'

'Just an admission that his guards do not always record visitors' names in the ledger, because not all of them can write. He took them to task about it once he had learned that Downes was murdered, and it transpires that *four* people were allowed to see him of late, not just Lady Montagu and Father Tyme.'

'Did he get their names?'

'He said they were family members who bribed their way inside.' Wogan glanced at the sky to gauge the time. 'Some of the yeomen will come off duty soon. Shall I waylay a few, and see if free ale will buy us more information about it?'

Chaloner doubted it would do more than confirm what they already knew, but was happy to let him try. He left him to it, and continued to St Olave's alone. Thurloe was in the nave, head bent as he worked on the cipher.

'Where is Wogan?' the ex-Spymaster demanded. 'I hope you did not leave him behind.'

'Questioning the guards,' explained Chaloner. 'What does the cipher say?'

'Unfortunately, it is even more complex than I anticipated. Downes was obviously terrified by what he was doing – for himself and the recipient – and was so desperate to keep the information from the wrong hands that I fear he may have overestimated Eleanor's ability to decode it. But what did you discover?'

Chaloner pulled the roll of paper from his sleeve. Again, it was in cipher, but this time it was a simple one, with letters moved one place to the right, so that A became B, C became D and so on. Thurloe translated it in his head and summarised it.

'He writes that if we are reading this, he will be dead. He apologises most abjectly for bringing about the death of Eleanor Montagu, who died ignorant of what he had asked her to do.' Thurloe glanced up. 'Well, this certainly proves that she was an unwitting agent.'

'I doubt her husband will find much comfort in that.'

'He goes on to say that Millington and Waller once devised a good way of ousting one regime and installing another, but that it was so insidious that Downes and the other six in their cabal vowed never to deploy it.'

'Does he say what it entailed?'

'No, although he claims he lodged an account of it with me. He never did!'

'I suspect he tried, but Talbot destroyed it before it could be sent. I am not sure whether to be angry or relieved: we might have had answers if Talbot had been less assiduous, but I am glad there are no documents implicating you in this business.'

271

Thurloe turned his attention back to the message. 'He finishes by asking the reader to pray for his soul, and to make sure that His Majesty knows that he made him a gift of a chicken for the royal menagerie. He gave her a name . . . it sounds like one of the ancient martyrs associated with Ely Cathedral.'

'Yes, Eghfeva,' replied Chaloner and added pointedly, 'It has the word "egg" in it.'

'So it does,' acknowledged Thurloe, and shook his head in puzzlement. 'Why did he bother? He must have known the King would not care about being presented with a bird – assuming he was even told, of course. Even if Talbot passed the message to the palace, I cannot see the royal clerks bothering His Majesty with it.'

'Downes should have bought him a prostitute instead,' muttered Chaloner. 'That would have been far more likely to snag his attention.'

'And it cannot have a bearing on the cipher he sent to Eleanor,' Thurloe went on. 'If it did, he would have given this chicken to her, not the Tower's menagerie.'

'Talbot decided a chicken was too expensive, so he bought a pigeon instead,' put in Chaloner. 'I saw it in an aviary with the ibises and pelicans.'

Thurloe stood abruptly. 'Let us return to my chambers and work on the first cipher together. Once we crack it, perhaps we shall have all the answers we need.'

They left the church, and hurried towards Thames Street, where Thurloe thought they could hire a hackney carriage. He was wrong, so they were obliged to walk all the way, which did not please him.

En route, they saw several men emerge from the Rose tavern, an upmarket establishment famous for its fine food. Chaloner recognised several members of the Company of Poulters. Master Farmer led the way, all fluttering hands and anxiety. His deputy, Drinkell, was behind him, smug and confident, with Newdick slinking at their heels. There were others, too, sleek and wealthy, suggesting that business was good in the poultry world, despite the current shortage of eggs.

'Do you have news about the higglers?' Farmer demanded when he saw Chaloner. 'I am at my wits' end with the wretches.'

'Not yet,' replied Chaloner. 'Did you ever meet a man named John Downes?'

'You mean the regicide?' asked Farmer uneasily. 'Yes, but only *before* he was declared a traitor and thrown in the Tower. He was interested in poultry, you see, so he often attended our meetings.'

'He was a member of your Company?'

'Not during *my* tenure as Master,' blustered Farmer. 'You will have to track down my predecessors for that sort of—'

'Yes, he was,' interrupted Drinkell, and raised his hands when Farmer regarded him in alarm. 'It will be in the records, Master, so there is no point in lying. Besides, those were different times – Downes was deemed a hero then for ridding us of a tyrant. We did nothing wrong by admitting him to our ranks.' He turned to Chaloner. 'Why do you want to know?'

'Because he was murdered with the same – or a very similar – weapon to the one that dispatched Bowles, Hadie and Hill.' Chaloner did not mention Eleanor, because he knew it would lead to a barrage of questions that he was not prepared to answer.

Farmer was appalled. 'You mean these deaths are

273

politically motivated? Lord! We are confronting forces even more deadly than we feared!'

'What nonsense,' spat Drinkell contemptuously. 'Bowles might have known Downes, because they were equal in wealth and status, but Hadie and Hill were paupers. Why do you think they agreed to hunt higglers? It was not for the glory, but for pay, and you will waste your time if you start seeing grand plots where there are none.'

'Yes, that is true,' said Farmer in relief. 'But please keep us informed, Chaloner. The higglers increase daily, and our members clamour ever more loudly for justice.'

He hurried away, and his colleagues followed, although the unsavoury Newdick lingered a moment to gloat over Chaloner's lack of progress.

'Let me know when you concede defeat,' he said tauntingly. 'And then *I* will step in to save the day.'

Chaloner grabbed his arm before he could follow his colleagues. 'Are you aware that the Paladin has written another scathing indictment of the egg industry? It includes a description of a large farm – probably the one you run for Drinkell.'

Newdick freed himself with rather more force than was necessary, causing Chaloner to stagger. 'Impossible! The Paladin has never been to our domain. However, I shall make enquiries, and when I find the rogue, you will have another murder to investigate.'

Chaloner raised his eyebrows. 'Well, given that no one else has threatened to dispatch the pamphleteer, that case will not be difficult to solve, will it?'

Newdick sneered. 'He has more enemies than stars in the sky, including religious sects, courtiers and the navy. Should I ever decide to put an end to his scurrilous scribblings, you will never prove my guilt – not with so many other parties eager to see him dead, too.'

He strutted away, leaving behind the distinctive odour of chicken muck.

Chapter 10

Although Chaloner and Thurloe spent the rest of the day working on the cipher, they met with no success. When the sun began to set, Chaloner threw up his hands in defeat, and without looking up Thurloe waved a hand, telling him to go home. Chaloner needed no second bidding. He left at once, glancing back to see the ex-Spymaster deeply engrossed, his face set and determined.

Outside, the heat was oppressive. He stopped at an ordinary to eat a beef pastry, washed down with copious quantities of cool ale, then returned to his rooms, where he fell asleep at once. He only woke when the market vendors began their clatter, telling him it was dawn on Monday, and time to resume his enquiries.

The day promised to be yet another hot one, so again he dispensed with wearing a coat for the more comfortable option of shirtsleeves. Then he sat at his table and wrote another report for Williamson, sure the Spymaster would be glad to learn that Eleanor was innocent of plotting, although the relief would doubtless be tempered by indignation that a regicide had dared to use her for his own ends.

He went downstairs, asked the footman to deliver it, and strolled into the garden to tend his hens. He wondered again why the Company of Poulters had no eggs, when the heat had not affected his own flock. True, they had plenty of shade, grassy areas in which to forage, and unlimited access to food and water, so did that mean professional poulters failed to provide these basic amenities? Drinkell was remiss in that respect, but surely the others would know better?

While he broke his fast with boiled eggs and a lump of bread, he pondered his enquiries – or rather, his single enquiry, given that they all seemed to have merged into one. He ran through the probable sequence of events in his mind.

First, Downes and eight other regicides had formed a cabal. Two of their number, Millington and Waller, had liked to devise elaborate plots to 'neutralise' those who stood against them. At the Restoration, all had either escaped to Switzerland or had been caught and imprisoned. Four years later, they had started to die, ostensibly of natural causes, so their fellows were unlikely to have been concerned at first. Millington and Waller were victims seven and eight, and had breathed their last in a Jersey gaol within a few weeks of each other. By then, Downes had realised that an executioner was at work.

The terms of his imprisonment prevented him from communicating with the outside world, although that had not stopped him from frantically penning letters to men he trusted. None had been delivered, so he had pinned his hopes on Eleanor Montagu, an intelligent lady with views on compassionate farming that matched his own. He had not been able to confide in her immediately, because Talbot and her footman had been there,

277

so he had sent her a coded report instead. She had failed to find it before the killer, guessing what Downes had done, had dispatched her, too. Three days later, Downes had fallen prey to the sly stiletto himself, almost certainly wielded by the man who had signed his name in Talbot's ledger as 'Father Tyme'.

The regicides and Eleanor were not his only victims. Bowles and Hadie had been stabbed within a few hours of each other. Dying, Hadie had managed to finger-sign three letters to Elsie and Dorcas. Chaloner wished Hadie had had time for more, because on their own, they were useless. He may have written an account of his findings, but as this had failed to materialise, Chaloner supposed it had either been found and destroyed by the killer, or its recipient had elected to ignore it. Either way, it was unavailable.

Hadie's place investigating the higglers had been taken by Hill, who was murdered himself within two days. Elsie and Dorcas had expressed scant faith in Hill's abilities, so it seemed likely that he had been dispatched as a precaution, rather than because he had uncovered anything important.

The killer had attacked Chaloner, too, almost certainly for the same reason, but had not tried again after his attempt had failed. Perhaps he was unused to victims who fought back, and was unwilling to risk a second encounter. Or perhaps he knew that Chaloner was on the wrong track entirely, so posed no particular threat.

As far as Chaloner could see, the only way forward was to decipher Downes' message to Eleanor. Perhaps it would describe the plot that Waller and Millington had contrived, and all would become clear.

He was about to leave for Lincoln's Inn when a note

arrived. It was from the ex-Spymaster himself, and reported that although he had laboured all night, he had failed to break the code. He planned to sleep for a few hours, then try again. Frustrated, Chaloner pushed Downes' letter from his mind and began to make other plans for the day instead.

First, he should report to the Earl, although he had little to tell him about Eleanor, and he had done nothing at all about Bristol's machinations. While he was at White Hall, he would visit Montagu again. The nobleman had denied his wife knowing Downes. However, now there was proof that she had, Chaloner needed him and her household to tell him the truth – or at least to reassess what they knew about her last few days in light of her visit to the Tower to chat to a regicide.

Then he would go to the Rainbow, where he had agreed to meet Swaddell, and together they would see what they could prise from Simpson and Glasse. He hoped the menacing presence of the assassin would work its magic, and one of the pair would break, because he was sure they were hiding something.

His route to White Hall took him across Covent Garden's piazza, and he stopped when he saw a commotion by the stall of one of the higglers he had spoken to a few days before – the poorer of the two, aptly named Pheasant. The other traders clustered around him, shaking their heads and muttering. Chaloner asked what had happened.

'Tell him, Pheasant,' urged a fruiterer. 'You can trust him. I know for a fact that he has nothing to do with the Company of Poulters, because his cook told me.'

'Daniel Norton died last night,' explained Pheasant

279

miserably. 'You met him, sir – he was selling eggs with me here, and we chatted about higgling together.'

'How did he die?' asked Chaloner, an uneasy feeling in the pit of his stomach.

'We thought it was an apoplexy at first,' said Pheasant. 'But he was my friend, so I prepared him for the grave myself. As I washed him, I saw he had been stabbed in the back. There was almost no blood, which is why no one noticed until . . . '

'I am sorry,' said Chaloner gently. 'Where did it happen?'

'At his home in Enfield,' replied Pheasant, and tears spilled. 'Not content with murdering him, the bastard went to his sheds and smashed all his eggs.'

Just like Bowles, thought Chaloner, while the other traders murmured their disbelief at such a craven act.

'Norton is not the only higgler to die this week,' Pheasant went on. 'I heard two passed away over in Smithfield, and another by Aldgate. It is suspicious, and I reckon the Company of Poulters has something to do with it. Someone should demand answers.'

'I will,' said Chaloner quickly, afraid that Pheasant would try, and suffer the same fate as his friend.

'You?' asked Pheasant warily. 'Why would you help us?'

'Because I work for the Lord Chancellor, and he will want the matter investigated,' replied Chaloner loftily, although he was sure the Earl would not care one way or the other.

'All right, then,' conceded Pheasant. 'Will you tell us what you discover?'

Chaloner nodded. 'Meanwhile, go back to selling your eggs in Enfield. If someone really is killing higglers, you do not want to be next.'

'Very well,' agreed Pheasant reluctantly. 'Although it is hard to walk away from such easy money. The Company of Poulters has virtually no eggs at all, so we higglers are the only ones who can meet London's demand. We can charge twenty times what we could get a month ago.'

'It is because of White Hall,' said the fruiterer darkly. 'The King is holding an Egg Masque, see, and is buying up crates of them to throw at a statue of the Pope.'

'Goodness!' muttered Chaloner, amazed anew at how quickly facts became distorted once they began circulating around the city.

'And to put in his syllabub, so he can swim about with his whores,' added Pheasant. 'Well, I hope he drowns!'

Chaloner hurried to White Hall and trotted up the stairs to the Earl's offices, hoping his employer had not decided to stay in the cool of Clarendon House for the day, because he could not afford to waste time racing from pillar to post. He was in luck: the Earl's antechamber was busy with clerks and servants, most still rubbing sleep from their eyes. There was an atmosphere of urgency and unease.

'He dares not stay home now that Bristol is back,' whispered Secretary Wren, who was impeccably dressed as always, but sweating profusely in his finery. 'He needs to be here, to counter all the rumours that keep starting about him.'

'What rumours?' asked Chaloner uneasily.

'Old gossip about the sale of Dunkirk mostly,' replied Wren. 'Perhaps our Earl did accept a bribe from the French to keep the price low, but anyone in his position would have done the same, Bristol included. It is the way things work in politics.'

'People will tire of this talk soon,' said Chaloner, although with more hope than conviction. Bristol was clever to resurrect the Dunkirk story, as nothing deprived a man of friends faster than an accusation of corruption – even the most loyal allies were loath to associate with someone embroiled in a fiscal scandal.

'Then Bristol will find something else to harm him,' predicted Wren gloomily. 'Our Earl's star has never been lower, while Bristol's soars. He has the King's ear again, and he vomits a constant stream of poison into it. Of course, our Earl is his own worst enemy.'

'Why? What has he done now?'

'Last night, he offended the King's favourites by calling the Adrian Masque "stupid and provocative". He seems physically incapable of keeping his opinions to himself. You are not going to see him dressed like that, are you? He will think you mean to insult him.'

He lent Chaloner his own coat, which was too small, along with a ridiculously elaborate hat that boasted enough feathers to stuff a mattress. Chaloner felt foolish and overdressed, although Wren nodded his approval.

'That is better. You do not want to aggravate him unnecessarily, because he is in a fearful temper. He was displeased when there were no eggs for breakfast, but he exploded with rage when he learned that Bristol's cook is awash with them.'

'So, not only do eggs feature in several murders and the King's controversial syllabub,' mused Chaloner, 'but now they are a cause of dissent in White Hall.'

'The Poultry Department says they are rarer than diamonds and worth their weight in gold. I cannot imagine how they will make this special syllabub, which calls for a thousand of them. And even if they do

282

manage to get enough, it will cost the public purse a fortune.'

'They will have to leave them out,' shrugged Chaloner. 'Syllabub is not supposed to contain them anyway.'

'Unfortunately, they promised the King a new recipe, and Catline is determined not to disappoint. Did you know that syllabub is His Majesty's favourite food?'

'No, but if Catline intends to produce it at the end of the masque, no one will know whether it is a new recipe or not – they will all be too drunk to tell. And the flavour will be irrelevant once people have gone bathing in it.'

Wren grimaced his distaste. 'The Earl begged the King to postpone the occasion until eggs become plentiful again, but Bristol mocked him for his prudence, calling him a dull old killjoy. Bristol will *have* to make sure it goes ahead on Wednesday now, because otherwise it will appear as if the Earl has prevailed.'

'On *Wednesday*?' echoed Chaloner, startled. 'I thought it was on Saturday.'

'Catline brought it forward – something to do with hams needing to be eaten early because of the heat. That suits the King, because it means only two days to wait before he can jaunt back to Greenwich, where he says the weather is cooler.'

'Greenwich cannot be that different from—'

'Apparently, he can barely contain his excitement,' interrupted Wren, not interested in listening when there was gossip to share. 'If the masque is the success that everyone anticipates, then Bristol will be firmly back in favour, and our Earl will be doomed for certain. Incidentally, did you know that Bristol and Catline were childhood friends?'

Chaloner shook his head. 'But it does not surprise me. They are of an ilk.'

'Catline has known Crookey for years, too, and I am told that he and Bristol united to *force* Montagu to make Crookey a Supernumerary Groom. The appointment has benefited them both: Catline has grown rich on Crookey's ability to sniff out cheap supplies, while Bristol's efforts to entertain the King will never be thwarted by a lack of suitable victuals.'

'Is Montagu so easily malleable, then?'

'Well, he is no match for the combined might of Catline and Bristol, certainly. And as for Crookey, perhaps you should investigate how he gets all these inexpensive foods, because I doubt it is legal.'

'I did ask him, but he was not very forthcoming,' said Chaloner. 'Clearly, I should try again when I have a bit more time.'

As it happened, Chaloner need not have worried about his informal appearance, because the Earl wore nothing but voluminous drawers and a shirt that was unlaced to his navel. It was an unusual sight, because his employer was cognisant of his dignity and was rarely anything less than perfectly attired, even in bed.

'I hate the heat,' he said miserably. 'I hate the cold, too. And the damp. Perhaps I have lost the ability to live in the country of my birth, because I was healthier and happier when the King and I were in penniless exile together in France.'

'Where there were no rich foods or unlimited wine,' muttered Chaloner, sure that some of the Earl's discomforts could be alleviated if he lost some weight.

'I like your coat and hat,' said the Earl, eyeing him up and down approvingly. 'That style must be in fashion, because I saw Wren wearing something very similar earlier. But tell me what you have discovered about Eleanor. I hope you have some good news.'

The Earl was not very good at keeping secrets, so Chaloner did not tell him that her death was connected to a plot involving regicides, or that Thurloe was helping him to investigate. Instead, he gave an account of how the killer had rendered her helpless with a soporific and then climbed through her bedroom window with a long, sharp knife.

The Earl shuddered. 'How terrible! I assume you have informed Montagu?'

Chaloner nodded. 'He has no idea who might have done it.'

'Bristol!' spat the Earl venomously. 'He murdered her to strike at me, because Montagu and I are friends. He aims to destroy all those who love me, so I shall be left alone and unsupported. Did you know that he threatened to expose the dear Dean of St Paul's as a lecher unless the poor fellow had no further contact with me?'

'And is the Dean a lecher?' asked Chaloner.

'Well, yes, but no one has ever objected before, and Bristol is not exactly chaste himself. The man is a damned hypocrite, but when I said so, he accused me of defending inappropriate behaviour among the clergy.'

Chaloner was not surprised that Bristol had twisted the Earl's accusation to his own advantage, given his reputation for quick rejoinders. 'Perhaps it would be better not to bandy words with him, sir.'

'But it is hard to say nothing while he defames me.' The Earl heaved a self-pitying sigh, and changed the subject. 'Have you heard that there is sickness in the Buttery? Seventeen men are laid low, and two are dead.

Wiseman says they ate heat-spoiled food, and for once all the other royal *medici* agree with him.'

Chaloner recalled the rank stench of decay in the Poultry Department's cellars, and supposed the Buttery would face similar problems with wares that went off in hot weather.

'Of course, food is not nearly as nice now there are no eggs for pastry and pies,' the Earl went on. 'You keep poultry, do you not? Are your birds affected by the heat?'

'No, so I will ask one of Wiseman's servants to bring you some of their eggs later.'

A rare smile of gratitude came Chaloner's way. 'How kind. Thank you.'

Montagu was alone in his apartments when Chaloner arrived. The Lord Chamberlain looked as though he had aged ten years since Chaloner had last seen him: his face was grey, there were dark pouches under his eyes, and he had dispensed with his wig to reveal an oily, hairless pate that did nothing to improve his appearance. He had not donned clean clothes in days, and the room smelled of stale sweat.

'Have you come with news about my wife?' he asked hoarsely, sitting back and tossing aside the pen with which he had been writing. 'You have found her murderer?'

Chaloner sat opposite him. 'Not yet, sir, but I know why she was killed.'

Montagu struggled to moisten dry lips. 'I suppose you still think she is the Paladin, even though half a dozen new pamphlets have appeared since her death.'

'Publishing them posthumously is a clever way to prevent anyone from accusing her of it,' said Chaloner, standing quickly when he sensed someone slip into the room behind him, but it was only Margaret Hay. He sat again. 'However, it is time to stop.'

'Eleanor was *not* the Paladin,' Margaret said firmly, going to Montagu and placing a supportive hand on his shoulder. 'You and Bristol are mistaken.'

'Bristol thinks it, too?' asked Chaloner, now certain of the veracity of the solution that had been forming in the back of his mind ever since his conversation with Prynne in Lincoln's Inn.

Margaret grimaced. 'Because he says she once saw him defiling White Hall's potted plants and made her displeasure known. But everyone at White Hall knows he does it, so he cannot claim that being caught by her is proof of her guilt. Nor can you.'

'No,' acknowledged Chaloner. 'But there is other evidence to incriminate her – and to incriminate you, too.'

Montagu and Margaret eyed each other nervously. 'What do you mean?' she blustered. 'We have done nothing to—'

'She was passionately interested in every subject the Paladin wrote about, so it is strange that not one of his broadsheets was in her house,' interrupted Chaloner. 'And the reason for that is because, after she died, you removed them all.'

'You found none because they were beneath her dignity to hoard,' argued Margaret. 'Even if she had taken one home to read, she would have thrown it away the moment she had finished with it.'

'Unfortunately for you, you neglected to remove the many reference books that allowed the pamphlets to be written,' Chaloner went on. 'Tomes on the navy, the poultry business, various religious sects, the Dutch war . . . they were all there on her shelves.'

287

'But I have books on those topics, too,' blustered Montagu. 'It means nothing.'

'Where are yours, then?' demanded Chaloner, and continued with his analysis when the nobleman was unable to answer. 'I suspect you ordered her servants to destroy every copy of the Paladin's work, and in return for their cooperation, you agreed to employ them here until they can find permanent posts elsewhere.'

'You misconstrue an act of kindness,' argued Margaret. 'Edward is a good man who cannot bear to think of people losing their livelihoods. *That* is why they are here.'

'And they are very grateful to him,' said Chaloner quietly. 'Grateful enough to keep his wife's secret. But there is one final clue that led me to draw—'

'But there cannot be!' cried Margaret, flustered. 'We were very careful to hide—' She stopped in horror when she realised she had effectively blurted an admission. 'Oh.'

'It is all right, Margaret,' sighed Montagu tiredly, and looked at Chaloner with defeated eyes. 'What is the last clue?'

'All the Paladin's work is minutely analysed by a jealous competitor,' explained Chaloner. 'Namely William Prynne, the King's Keeper of Records. You may know him.'

Montagu shuddered in distaste. 'An unpleasant fellow. Eleanor's publications were nothing like his brutal tirades. He could not be amusing to save his life.'

'Prynne said that one of her pamphlets mentioned a brick church in Jamestown, which he claimed was a mistake because it is really made of wood. However, he visited it before the wars, but when I was there during the Commonwealth, there was talk of rebuilding it. Your

288

wife was not long returned from Virginia – she saw the new one.'

Margaret gaped at him. 'Ships sail back and forth from New England on a weekly basis, so lots of people will have seen this church. Your "clue" is nothing of the kind.'

'People go, but few come back,' argued Chaloner. 'Most stay to make new lives there. And the ones who do return tend not to have the money to print controversial pamphlets. Distributing free copies all over London must be expensive.'

'But . . . ' objected Montagu, then could think of nothing more to say.

'Moreover, there is a marked difference between the broadsheets published before her death and those that came after,' Chaloner went on. 'The early ones targeted religious lunatics and groups that defy the government. There was also one accusing the poultry industry of putting profit before hen welfare.'

'But . . . ' began Montagu a second time before faltering into silence again.

'The more recent ones deal with far more contentious subjects,' Chaloner went on. 'The Dutch war, the navy's shortcomings . . . There was also a second assault on poulters that was much more vitriolic than the first, exposing them as cruel and unscrupulous.'

'So?' asked Margaret warily.

'So you published tracts she had no intention of making public – ones she wrote for her personal satisfaction alone. Some of the things you printed are treasonous, while others are vindictive. I do not believe she intended those to see the light of day.'

'I told you so,' said Montagu to Margaret crossly.

'Especially the one about Prynne. Eleanor disliked him, but she would never have wanted to hurt his feelings.'

'But we were running out of material,' objected Margaret defensively. 'And we could not write more ourselves, because neither of us is witty enough. What choice did we have?'

Montagu's face was full of anguish. 'So my wife was killed because someone guessed she was the Paladin?'

'No,' said Chaloner, and told them about Eleanor's meeting with Downes and how he had later tried to enlist her help. They listened with mounting horror.

'She was used by a *regicide*?' cried Montagu, aghast.

'She never found his message, so no,' replied Chaloner. 'Now, I know I have asked you this before, but please think again: did she ever mention him? Visiting the Tower is not something you do every day, so I am sure she would have talked about it to her friends.'

'She told me that she had met a man who agreed with her views on poultry farming,' replied Margaret. 'She had been appalled by an excursion to one place, and wrote those two tracts about it. She published the witty one before she died, and, as you have surmised, Edward and I issued the second, which was brutally vicious and not funny at all . . .'

'Did she say any more about Downes or their encounter?'

'She never mentioned him by name, and she certainly did not say that he was in the Tower,' replied Margaret. 'However, she did tell me that she had never met anyone with such a detailed knowledge of the subject.'

Chaloner continued to ask questions, but they could tell him nothing else, other than that they had questioned the servants again about the missing money, and the general consensus was that the killer must have been delighted to win such an unexpected bonus for his bloody work. Eventually, Chaloner stood to leave.

Montagu eyed him uneasily. 'Now what? Will you tell everyone what she did?'

'Of course not,' replied Chaloner indignantly. 'But please do not publish any more broadsheets. London is volatile, and they may cause trouble.'

'I am afraid it is too late to stop the one about Catline, Crookey and their friends,' said Montagu apologetically. 'That is being distributed as we speak.'

Chaloner regarded him uneasily. 'Is it very caustic?'

'Oh, yes,' said Montagu with a gleam in his eye. 'But do not feel sorry for them. It serves the rogues right for throwing in their lot with the dreadful Bristol.'

'Bristol,' mused Chaloner. 'Will you let me write one last rant under the Paladin's name? I promise there will be nothing in it to divulge your wife's identity. On the contrary, I will make sure fingers point in other directions entirely.'

'Well then,' said Montagu with a conspiratorial grin. 'How can we refuse?'

As Chaloner was leaving White Hall, he met a dozen men from the Poultry Department swaggering through the Great Gate. All were sleek and smug, as if already revelling in the success of their masque and the kudos it would bring them. The flamboyant Catline led the way, while the sinister Crookey brought up the rear, talking to the loutish Mezandier.

Chaloner would have loved to challenge Crookey about his suspiciously inexpensive supplies, but he could not allow himself to become side-tracked that day. He promised himself the pleasure of exposing the man's dishonesty the moment he had some free time. He attempted to walk past them without stopping, but Catline had other ideas.

'Was it you?' he demanded, waving a broadsheet. 'Are you responsible for this libellous nonsense?'

'What libellous nonsense?' asked Chaloner, although he could see the familiar red ink.

Catline shoved the pamphlet in his hand, and Chaloner scanned what transpired to be a blistering attack on Catline and his colleagues, denouncing them for taking large salaries and perks, but doing nothing in return except organise debauched japes. It was so venomous that he was certain Eleanor had never intended for it to be read by anyone else, let alone the entire city, and would have been appalled by what her husband and friend had done.

'The Paladin must be a courtier,' spat Mezandier, watching him. 'How else would he know what we do? He was delightful when he mocked religious dissenters, but now he has turned his spleen on men of quality—'

'Well, he is not me,' said Chaloner firmly. 'I was not even in the country when his first work appeared. And before you suggest it, my Earl is not responsible either.'

'No,' acknowledged Catline spitefully. 'He is not witty enough. But he knows men who are: Matthew Wren, for example.'

'Wren is far too busy for idle nonsense,' said Chaloner. 'And nor is he cruel.'

'True.' Mezandier scowled at him. 'So who did write it, then?'

Chaloner raised his eyebrows. 'How should I know? However, I can tell you that it was not Eleanor Montagu

– not unless she can write from beyond the grave. Bristol owes her family an apology.'

'Montagu told us she had been murdered,' said Catline. 'And that you have vowed to bring her killer to justice.' He smirked. 'That was rash, Chaloner. You may find the culprit is a friend of your Earl – like Montagu himself.'

'But if Montagu is innocent, there are plenty of other suspects to choose from,' said Crookey slyly. 'Eleanor had some very peculiar opinions, so she offended a lot of people.'

'She certainly offended me,' growled Mezandier. 'Once, she told everyone that I should be in Bedlam, just because I like watching the public hangings outside Newgate.'

Chaloner was not surprised to hear that the loutish Sergeant enjoyed that sort of entertainment. He changed the subject. 'It is common knowledge that she brought a fortune from Virginia, and kept it on her person—'

'I was not aware of it,' interrupted Mezandier, which Chaloner knew was a lie, because Montagu had already told him that the whole Poultry Department had over-heard Eleanor talking about her plans for the money. He treated the claim to the contempt it deserved by ignoring it.

'Her killer stole it,' he went on, 'so anyone with a sudden windfall will be interrogated by Spymaster Williamson. He will chew his way through a great many innocents before he reaches the real culprit, of course, but that cannot be helped.'

He was gratified to see them blanch – everyone but Crookey, who stared back at him with an expression that was impossible to read.

'But we have all received large bonuses of late,' objected Mezandier, alarmed. 'It is because Crookey is good at sourcing cheap supplies, not because we are thieves.'

Chaloner found himself turning to Crookey, although he knew he should leave the matter for another day. 'Where do these "cheap supplies" come from?'

'You have asked me that before,' said Crookey icily. 'And my answer now is the same as it was then: it is none of your business.'

'No, but it will be Williamson's,' blustered Chaloner, although the threat was wasted on Crookey, who looked as if he could not care less. 'Especially if you have been breaking the law.'

'Breaking the law?' drawled Crookey, and smirked. 'You had better watch your tongue, because I do not take kindly to accusations that cannot be proved – which yours cannot, because there *is* no evidence. Now, get out of my way. I have important matters to attend.'

'Important matters like organising masques that will further alienate the King from his people?' asked Chaloner coolly, aware that Crookey had not actually denied the allegation, only stated that no one would catch him.

Catline laughed jeeringly. 'His *people*? Who gives a damn what they think?'

'You will not say that if they march here to—'

'They will never attack White Hall!' scoffed Mezandier. 'They dare not, lest they damage it for King Jesus on Friday. Pah! What nonsense these commoners believe!'

'I heard you brought the date of the masque forward, Catline,' said Chaloner, wondering if it was significant that it would still take place before the so-called Second

294

Coming. 'Was it really because your hams are rotting in the heat?'

'Not rotting,' countered Catline curtly. 'Just maturing more quickly than we anticipated. However, that will not matter to you, because you are not invited.'

He swaggered away, his cronies trailing at his heels.

Chapter 11

It was late morning by the time Chaloner reached the Rainbow. He considered collecting Swaddell and hurrying about their enquiries at once, but then decided a dose of Farr's best might sharpen his wits, as the heat was making him sluggish. He arrived to find the assassin sitting with Lester, which was odd: they tolerated each other, but Lester was uncomfortable with what Swaddell did for a living, while Swaddell found Lester worryingly jovial.

'There you are at last, Tom,' said Swaddell rather accusingly, 'Much later than we originally agreed.'

'I have been working,' retorted Chaloner, and added pointedly, 'Did you have a nice relaxing day in Foxhall Gardens with your wife yesterday?'

The barb missed its mark completely, because Swaddell beamed at him without the merest hint of shame. 'Oh, yes! We ate oranges and drank tea, although neither of us liked the tea. It will never be as popular as coffee.'

'I think I might soon have a wife, too,' put in Lester conversationally. 'Elsie has captured my heart just as securely as the Dutch laid hold of *Swiftsure*.'

'Does this mean you no longer want to go back to sea?' asked Chaloner, liking the notion of being free of his pact with Williamson.

'Oh, I still long to rejoin the fleet,' said Lester. 'Ideally, I shall do it in a fortnight, after Elsie and I are wed.'

'Does she know you have these plans for her?' Chaloner sincerely hoped his friend was not about to learn that love could be painful.

'I do not want to rush things,' said Lester. 'We only met on Thursday, after all, so I shall give her one more day before putting the question.'

'Pounce now,' advised Swaddell, evidently considering himself an expert on such matters given his recent success. 'You do not want her to slip through your fingers. I did not hold back for a minute once I decided to make Ursula my own.'

While they discussed tactics for securing female prey, Chaloner accepted the coffee that Farr poured for him, but declined the apple cake that arrived with it – made without eggs, it was half its usual height and had the consistency of rubber. Lester produced bread and cheese from the bag he carried over his shoulder, and while they shared it, Chaloner told them all he had learned since they had last met. However, he refrained from mentioning the letter from the spine of Downes' book, unwilling for Lester to be burdened with the knowledge of it; Swaddell gave a small nod of approval for his caution. Chaloner finished by saying that Crookey topped his list of murder suspects.

'A good choice,' said Lester. 'I did not take to him either.'

'It is based on more than his unappealing personality,' objected Chaloner. 'His White Hall duties connect him to all the murder victims: to Bowles, who supplied him with produce; to Hadie and Hill who were investigating the sellers of illicit eggs that he probably purchased; and to Eleanor through Court functions.'

'But not to Downes or the other regicides,' Swaddell pointed out.

Chaloner made no reply, thinking that just because a link was not immediately apparent did not mean it was not there.

'Elsie is busy today,' said Lester in the silence that followed. 'So I am available to help you until sunset. After that, I shall take her to an ordinary to eat sprats.'

'That might be dangerous,' warned Swaddell. 'Helping us, I mean, not eating sprats.'

'So is fighting the Dutch,' retorted Lester. 'Although at sea at least you can spot the enemy and take appropriate action. On land, it is difficult to tell between friend and foe.'

'Trust no one except me and Tom,' advised Swaddell. 'Then you cannot go far wrong.'

But Chaloner did not want Lester involved, feeling he was unsuited for dabbling in such murky waters. Unfortunately, the captain was determined to make himself useful, so Chaloner suggested that he monitor Pudding Lane for the agitators. Lester was instructed not to approach them if they appeared, but to follow them discreetly and find out where they lived. The captain tipped his hat in salute and hurried away.

'You do recall that the agitators are never active during the day, do you not?' asked Swaddell, watching him go. 'They save their poisonous messages for the safety of night and darkness. Poor Lester will be wasting his time.'

'Yes,' acknowledged Chaloner. 'Which will keep him

298

safe. I should not like Elsie to lose the man who aims to marry her.'

Swaddell nudged him in the ribs. 'Apparently, Dorcas is looking for a husband, too. She is a pretty lady, and you both share a fondness for music and birds. You can run a poultry farm together, and escape the turbulent politics of White Hall.'

'Crikey!' breathed Chaloner, astonished that Swaddell should have his future so neatly mapped out with a woman he barely knew.

'Did you decode Downes' cipher?' asked Swaddell, returning to business.

'No, but someone else is working on it now.'

'Thurloe,' surmised Swaddell, and gave a reassuring smile when Chaloner regarded him in alarm. 'Do not worry, Tom, no one will learn of his involvement from me. It will be better for everyone that way.'

How odd, reflected Chaloner, that one of the two men he now trusted most in the world was a Royalist assassin who was more sinister than anyone he had ever met. He did not always like Swaddell, and there was no question that he was dangerous, but he knew, without the shadow of a doubt, that the assassin would rather die than betray him or blab about their enquiries.

When Chaloner and Swaddell arrived in Pudding Lane, they saw a number of people hurrying into Fish Yard. Their interest piqued, they followed, and saw that free food was being distributed from Bibie's house, where Wogan and Docility rented rooms. The regicide was handing out bread dunked in a meat broth, Vernon was on hand to provide medical attention for anyone who was sick, while Docility stood on a box and informed everyone that an angel had just assured her that God's chosen would soon reap fabulous rewards.

'God's chosen?' mused Swaddell. 'And who are they, exactly?'

'Well, not you,' she flashed, very bravely, given that the assassin had reverted to his trademark black that day, and looked decidedly deadly. 'Only those deemed worthy will be saved.'

Chaloner regarded her sceptically. 'Where did you meet this heavenly being? What did he look like? Did you see his face?'

'He came to me in a dream,' replied Docility serenely. 'So do not claim he was a human imposter. Besides, there have been plenty of omens to support his promises – a pyramid of fire in the sky over Southampton, a storm in Kent with hailstones as big as turkey eggs, brooks running red with blood . . . '

'What do you think, Tom?' asked Swaddell worriedly, as she strutted away bursting with a sense of her own importance. 'Is she telling the truth? Or are these visions the result of an over-active imagination?'

'It does not matter which – the point is that *she* believes them, and by the end of the day, so will most of London. So, we have just four days before something catastrophic will happen. It is not long to find answers when we have no idea where to look.'

'All the more reason for a word with Glasse and Simpson, then,' said Swaddell. 'If they know anything – about the festering trouble or the murders – I shall prise it from them.'

'Good,' said Chaloner, although he hoped they would yield up their secrets before the assassin became too inventive with his knives.

300

Swaddell nodded to where Wogan was busy with a ladle. 'We have been monitoring him for weeks, but our spies say he really does feed the poor and care for wounded seamen.'

Chaloner regarded him askance. 'So Williamson knows that a regicide is at large, but lets him roam free? I cannot see the King being very pleased about that.'

'Possibly not, but Wogan is saving the government a fortune, so we have been instructed to turn a blind eye to his presence. As long as he behaves, of course – if he attempts anything seditious . . . '

'Instructed by whom?' asked Chaloner. 'And does the King know about this decision?'

'Members of the Privy Council,' replied Swaddell. 'And I have no idea if they discussed it with His Majesty first. We are far too lowly to be told such things.'

Chaloner looked back at Wogan. 'He does not seem poised to cause trouble. Even so, I wish he would leave. Politicians are fickle and may change their minds about him – and another bloody execution will do nothing for peace and reconciliation.'

At that point, Wogan called for Docility to help him clean the pots. She went reluctantly, clearly thinking such menial labour was beneath her. As no one was in immediate need of medical advice, Vernon came to speak to Chaloner and Swaddell.

'I give my time to help the poor, but Wogan buys all their medicines,' he said, watching the regicide admiringly. 'The man is a saint, and never baulks at the cost. Of course, not even the best and most expensive remedies have saved those hedonists at White Hall. Have you heard about them?'

'Heard what?' asked Chaloner uneasily.

'That seventeen rogues from the Buttery Department have fallen prey to a sickness sent by God to punish sinners. Two have died already.'

'Oh, that,' said Chaloner. 'According to Surgeon Wiseman, it was caused by heat-tainted food. It can happen anywhere.'

'It was *God*, and no one can prove otherwise,' declared Vernon, eyes blazing. 'The Almighty struck that villain Bibie down, too.'

'Bibie is dead?' blurted Chaloner, shocked.

He recalled the last time he had seen the higgler: when Bibie had discovered Hill's body hidden in the water butt. Had he been killed for raising the alarm more quickly than the killer intended? Or had he found a vital clue at the same time, and been dispatched to ensure his silence? Chaloner wondered if Wiseman would have time to look at the body.

'He died last night, but no one will mourn him, because he was a thief and a drunkard,' declared Vernon viciously. 'Well, Wogan will be sorry, because he is soft-hearted, but the rest of us are glad to see him gone.'

'That makes five higglers – that we know of – who have died in the last two days,' said Chaloner. 'One was killed in Enfield, two in Smithfield and another near Aldgate.'

Vernon sniffed. 'Not five – six. Widow Noest died yesterday, too. She ran an alehouse, but her illicit egg-selling was much more lucrative. Incidentally, I saw you talking to Robert Blackborne the other day. I would stay away from him if I were you. The man is a zealot, and such people are dangerous.'

'You mean zealous in his religious beliefs?' asked Chaloner, thinking of pots calling kettles black. 'Or in his politics?'

'Religion *is* politics,' averred Vernon fiercely. 'Like me, he is a Fifth Monarchist, but he is passionately radical. The government is right not to let him have control of the navy.'

He would have added more, but a woman came to beg his help with a sick child. He nodded a farewell to Chaloner and Swaddell, and went to oblige.

'If *he* considers Blackborne too extreme,' muttered Swaddell, 'then Blackborne must be halfway to lunacy. I had better tell Williamson, and recommend that he warns the navy. I know for a fact that they rely heavily on him.'

'You might want to see what Blackborne thinks of Vernon before besmirching his reputation,' warned Chaloner. 'There are two sides to every story.'

'There are,' acknowledged Swaddell. 'But I have never really been comfortable with Blackborne's continuing influence in military affairs. When all is said and done, he is a committed Parliamentarian, no matter what he claims to the contrary.'

Chaloner and Swaddell were about to go in search of Simpson and Glasse when Wogan emerged from his lodgings, raising his hand to say he wanted a word. It took him a long time to reach them, because so many people wanted to thank him for their food.

'I found the guards who took Father Tyme to see Downes,' he reported, when he had eventually shaken off his admirers. 'But they transpired to be singularly unobservant, and could tell me nothing about him, other than that he looked like a cleric.'

Chaloner was not surprised, but tracking them down was something that had needed to be done anyway, and he was grateful to Wogan for saving him the bother. He said so.

The regicide sniffed. 'You have better manners than Thurloe. I went to see him an hour ago, but he barely looked at me when I told him the results of my labours. He was working on some cipher or other, and clearly resented my interruption.'

'I thought I told you not to visit Lincoln's Inn,' said Chaloner sharply, while a distant part of his mind noted the news with disappointment – sleep had not stimulated the breakthrough the ex-Spymaster had hoped for. 'It may put Thurloe in danger.'

'There was no risk, because I went in disguise,' replied Wogan, curt in his turn. 'I saw the business with those dead regicides had upset him, so I thought he might appreciate some new intelligence. I was trying to help.'

Chaloner relented, reminding himself that Wogan *had* risked his life by going to the Tower and questioning the yeomen, and it was ungracious to find fault with his efforts.

'Then come with us to speak to Simpson and Glasse,' he said, seeing an advantage to descending in force on the unsavoury duo. 'They claim to know nothing, but I am sure they are lying.'

'I doubt we will get any meaningful answers from that mad pair,' said Wogan doubtfully. 'Besides, even if they are embroiled in something untoward, they will never tell us about it. Like all fanatics, they are too convinced of their own rectitude.'

'Just like you, then,' retorted Swaddell tartly. 'Your deeply held convictions saw a king relieved of his head.'

'Yes,' said Wogan wearily. 'And I shall regret it until my dying day.'

*

As St Margaret's was closer than Allhallows, they decided to see if Glasse was at home first. The plan was for Swaddell to ask the questions with appropriate menace, while Chaloner and Wogan loomed in the hope of intimidating their victim even further.

They arrived to find Glasse in his vestry, poring over a pile of money. His scowl suggested that he did not have as much as he hoped, so he kept re-counting it to see if the final figure would improve. He tensed when he saw Wogan and Chaloner, but it was the sight of Swaddell that caused him to sweep the coins into his purse and bolt for the door. He would have escaped, but Chaloner had anticipated such a move, and was ready to block his way.

'What do you want?' the vicar gulped. 'I have done nothing wrong!'

'Why did you run, then?' asked Wogan.

Glasse tipped his head towards Swaddell. 'Because *he* looks dangerous.'

'I *am* dangerous,' hissed Swaddell, drawing one of his sharp little knives. 'But only to liars, so think very carefully before you speak. If I detect a single untruth, you will die.'

'I am a man of God,' blustered Glasse, struggling to conceal his fear. 'You cannot treat me like a—'

'You were friends with Downes the regicide,' interrupted Swaddell. 'We know he was entangled in something deadly, so what did he tell you about it?'

Glasse pointed at Chaloner, who stood by the door to prevent another bid for freedom. 'I have already told him: I know nothing about what Downes does these days, because I have not spoken to him in years. Besides, we do not need plots – from him or anyone else – when King Jesus is poised to come in glory.'

305

'Tell us what you know about that,' ordered Swaddell, and began to hone his blade on the wall, eyes glittering. 'Has Christ requested any human help?'

'I assume He will use angels and the like,' gulped Glasse, and swallowed hard as he added, 'Although there are rumours that some folk aim to offer Him their services anyway.'

'What kind of services?'

'I have no idea – I am just a lowly foot soldier. You will have to ask a general.'

'Then who are the generals?' asked Swaddell, testing the sharpness of the blade with his thumb.

Glasse flinched. 'Simpson might be one.'

'There, now that was not so difficult, was it?' said Swaddell, with a smile that made Glasse whimper in terror. 'So, back to Downes. I know you have more to tell us, but before you reply, bear in mind that he was murdered, along with eight of his fellows.'

Glasse paled. 'He was *murdered*? God's blood! I know he lived in fear of assassins, but I thought he would be safe inside the Tower.'

'So you *did* communicate with him,' pounced Chaloner, unable to remain silent any longer. 'How else would you know he was afraid?'

Glasse was furious with himself for the slip. 'I may have visited him once or twice when he was first arrested, but not recently, because I have been too busy with my flock.'

'Busy with their purses,' muttered Wogan. 'To fund your gambling debts.' He turned to Swaddell. 'You are wasting your time with this scoundrel. No self-respecting conspirator would involve him in a plot because he is too untrustworthy.'

'He is unreliable,' agreed Swaddell. 'But you are wrong to think him innocent of treachery.' He swung his beady glare back to his victim. 'Now, you had better tell us exactly what you know about Downes, or you will learn first-hand whether the dead will rise on Judgement Day, because you will be among them.'

Rattled, Glasse began to gabble. 'A few months ago, I learned that he and some of his cabal had devised a certain scheme—'

'Do not lie,' objected Wogan angrily. 'Downes was in the Tower. He cannot possibly have communicated with anyone else.'

'Guards can be bribed,' Glasse shot back. 'They—'

'He aims to lead you astray, Swaddell,' interrupted Wogan, eyeing Glasse contemptuously. 'Not even the most lax of wardens will overlook a lot of regicides conspiring together.'

'I agree – he is not being fully honest with us,' said Swaddell, regarding Glasse with such menace that the vicar gulped audibly. 'So, now we shall have the *whole* truth, if you please.'

Glasse shrieked in terror when the assassin swooped towards him and in one smooth, swift movement grabbed his head and pressed the blade to his throat.

'No, Swaddell!' cried Wogan in horror. 'Not in a church!'

He darted forward and wrenched the assassin away so vigorously that Swaddell fell into Chaloner, causing them both to lose their footing. Glasse seized the opportunity to shoot through the door.

'Oh, Lord!' breathed Wogan, watching sheepishly as Chaloner and Swaddell picked themselves up from the floor. 'I should not have been so vigorous, but I thought you were about to . . . Come on! We can still catch him.'

'No, we cannot,' said Swaddell, giving Wogan a look of such malevolence that the regicide blanched. 'There are too many alleys for him to have escaped down, and tracking him will be impossible. So you had better hope that Simpson is more forthcoming, or I am going to hold you personally responsible.'

Wogan swallowed hard, then tried to downplay the incident. 'I doubt he had much more to tell us anyway. He is too self-serving to be given a meaningful role in any brewing mischief, so you would have been wasting your time by questioning him further.'

'Well, we will never know now, will we,' said Swaddell acidly.

'I was trying to save you from committing a mortal sin,' objected Wogan defensively. 'Murder serves no purpose other than to diminish the perpetrator.'

'I have never found that to be true in the past,' said Swaddell, tight-lipped with suppressed fury.

Wogan shot him an uneasy look. 'Well, perhaps the fright he has had here will be enough to drive him from the city. The way you played with that nasty little knife would certainly make *me* think twice about breaking the law if I were a budding rebel.'

'Then let us hope you are right,' said Chaloner shortly, every bit as irked with the regicide as Swaddell.

As usual, Allhallows Church appeared to be deserted, its locked doors and boarded-over windows serving to give it an abandoned, desolate feel. However, Chaloner glimpsed a flicker of lamplight through a crack in one door, so he knew someone was within. He knocked, politely at first, then with increasing irritation when there was no reply.

'Now what?' asked Wogan. 'We cannot smash a window to get in, because they are all blocked up.'

Chaloner walked to the back of the church, where he would not be visible to passers-by. He climbed on a tomb outside the biggest window, took his stoutest knife, and levered away one of the planks. Then he removed a second and a third, until he had made a gap large enough to squeeze through.

Once inside, he heard voices in the vestry at the far end of the building. As Swaddell and Wogan clambered in after him, he motioned them to silence, then led the way up the nave until he was close enough to see what was going on.

Simpson stood with a group of ten or so men who looked so obviously like conspirators that Chaloner was unable to suppress a snort of amusement. All were cloaked and hooded against recognition, even though they were inside a secure building. Most were armed, but with swords so ancient that he was sure they were relics from the previous century. They were all nervous, and spoke in urgent whispers, other than Simpson who seemed incapable of anything less than a bellow.

'There is mischief afoot here,' whispered Wogan, evidently not averse to stating the obvious.

Chaloner eased deeper into the shadows. 'Someone else is about to join them – I can hear him tapping at the vestry door.'

'A *secret* tapping.' Swaddell cocked his head to listen. 'Three long and three short, to let them know he is a friend.'

'Try again,' hollered Simpson to whoever was outside. 'I missed the first bit, and you cannot be too careful these days.'

Chaloner heard Swaddell snigger softly as the sequence was repeated, after which the vicar unbolted the door and hauled the newcomer inside. It was Glasse, who had donned a thick red cloak to disguise himself, although it must have aroused the suspicions of anyone who saw him, given the heat of the day. He carried a cudgel so old that splinters flaked off it as he moved.

'They know,' he gasped. 'They nearly killed me, and will be looking for Simpson next. They are probably at his house as I speak.'

'Well, they will not find me there,' bawled Simpson, 'because I am here. Incidentally, I heard today that a man called Hadie has been killed. Is that the fellow you lied to, Glasse – he wanted information about higglers, but you fed him a lot of nonsense in exchange for his money?'

'Yes, I met him while he was serving soup to beggars with Wogan,' replied Glasse. 'I cannot abide do-gooders, so if he is dead, then I am glad of it.'

'Glasse is a monster!' breathed Wogan, shocked. 'I was wrong to dismiss him as too selfish to play a leading role in any treachery – clearly, he is ruthless enough for anything. But I will prise the truth from him, never fear. He will not escape from us a second time.'

Before Swaddell or Chaloner could stop him, he stormed into the vestry. Assassin and spy exchanged an alarmed glance – none of the conspirators were very well armed, but there were an awful lot of them, and Wogan was rash to have broken cover so precipitously. Knowing they would be discovered now anyway, they hastened to stand at his side.

310

'I have heard enough!' Wogan informed the startled radicals, and pointed an accusing finger at Glasse. 'You are guilty of treason. I want answers to my questions, after which you will all be placed under arrest.'

'Will we indeed?' breathed Glasse in astonishment. 'And how will you detain us, exactly, when we outnumber you four to one?'

'Enough quibbling,' blustered Wogan, and Chaloner saw him reach the uncomfortable realisation that he had made a mistake by blundering in. 'We want to know what terrible thing you plan to do on Friday. It is—'

'Terrible thing?' bellowed Simpson. 'The Second Coming is not terrible! King Jesus will descend in glory so the Fifth Monarchy can be installed, and we shall all live in Paradise for ever. Well, some of us will. Unbelievers are destined for a different fate.'

'They will burn in hell,' put in one of his cronies, and Chaloner saw with a start that the speaker was Eleanor's footman, Rye. 'Because they will not be deemed worthy to enjoy the Kingdom of God.'

'I said *enough*!' roared Wogan. 'Tell us—'

He faltered when Glasse hurtled forward, the rotten cudgel exchanged for a knife. Chaloner yelled a warning, but too late, and could only watch as the blade flashed. Wogan cried out in agony and crumpled to the floor.

Chaloner gaped his disbelief at the speed of Glasse's assault. Then all was pandemonium as weapons were drawn, and he and Swaddell found themselves fighting for their lives. Simpson was in the vanguard, slashing wildly and inexpertly, howling about the army of God. Glasse scuttled behind a tomb to keep himself safe until the fighting was over.

*

311

The mêlée was chaotic and deadly, especially as the vestry was not really large enough for a lot of flailing weapons. Some of the conspirators were inexperienced but determined, while others had clearly learned to fight during the civil wars and were good at it. Chaloner tried to wound rather than kill – he was in a church, after all – but Swaddell had no such compunction, and soon one Fifth Monarchist lay dead and two more bore mortal injuries.

Then Swaddell was overwhelmed by sheer force of numbers. Chaloner battled on until someone yelled that the assassin would be executed unless he surrendered. He glanced across to see Glasse with a dagger pressed to Swaddell's throat, and knew the threat was real. His sword clattered to the floor, after which the malevolent little cleric came to search both prisoners for weapons, which he did with annoying efficiency.

'You should not have yielded, Tom,' whispered Swaddell when Glasse had finished. 'Now we will both die.'

Chaloner stared at Wogan, who lay where he had fallen. The man had killed a king, but had tried to redeem himself, and he deserved better than to be dispatched by the very man whose throat he had just saved from Swaddell's blade.

Meanwhile, Simpson and his disciples began a panicky discussion about what to do with captives they had never expected to take. Seeing Rye among them caused several facts to come together in Chaloner's mind.

'We must kill them,' the footman was snarling at his cronies. 'Alive, they pose too great a danger. I will do it.'

'You are already a liar and a thief,' said Chaloner contemptuously, as Rye stepped towards him, dagger at the ready. 'But will you answer to King Jesus for murder, too?'

Rye faltered and licked his lips uneasily. '*I* do not lie and steal.'

'Then why did you fail to mention that you went with Eleanor Montagu to visit Downes in the Tower?'

'Because she had paid me for my silence,' snapped Rye. 'Keeping a confidence is not lying. On the contrary, it shows me to be loyal and trustworthy.'

'Then what about theft? Because it was *you* who took the money from her bedroom.'

Chaloner could tell by Rye's horrified expression that he had hit upon the truth. The footman swallowed hard, and struggled to bluster his way out of the situation, especially when he saw the other Fifth Monarchists begin to regard him uncertainly.

'Do not listen to Chaloner,' he ordered sharply. 'He is just trying to drive a wedge between us.'

'There were faint smears of blood under her pillow,' Chaloner went on, and nodded to the footman's painfully bitten nails. 'I assumed it was hers, but it came from your raw fingers as you groped about under her body. It was an impressive sleight of hand, because none of the other servants saw you shove the coin-bag up your sleeve.'

Rye sneered at him. 'Why would I steal from a lady who was good to me?'

'To secure yourself a comfortable future. You thought you would lose your job after her death – you did not anticipate that Montagu would keep you on – so you took precautions.'

'Montagu did not help us out of kindness, but to make sure we told no one about her connection to the Paladin,'

313

argued Rye, as if he thought this justified his crime. 'It was no more than a business arrangement.'

'Perhaps corpse-robbing was not the worst of your crimes,' Chaloner pressed on. 'Maybe you murdered her, too.'

'These are grave charges,' put in Glasse slyly before Rye could defend himself. 'And the only way to save your soul is by donating all your ill-gotten gains to the Church. Give this money to me.'

'But I do not have anything,' Rye bleated unconvincingly. 'Chaloner is making it up, and I am going to kill him for it.'

'So one Fifth Monarchist wants us executed, while another stabbed Wogan without a flicker of remorse,' said Chaloner in disgust. 'I cannot see King Jesus being very impressed with you lot.'

'No,' agreed Swaddell, and glared at the assembled horde. 'So which one of you stabbed Downes, Eleanor Montagu and the rest? Clearly, no low crime is beneath you, despite your claims to be God-fearing people.'

'We had nothing to do with those,' objected Glasse indignantly. 'And I only killed Wogan because he was making nasty accusations. Rather like you, in fact.' He turned to Rye. 'Make an end of them before we waste any more time.'

Rye stepped forward purposefully, but Simpson intercepted him. 'No!' he bawled. 'Chaloner is right: we cannot meet King Jesus with blood on our hands. Besides, I have just remembered that we have a nice safe crypt here in Allhallows. We shall lock them in there to keep them from under our feet.'

Rye tried to push past him. 'King Jesus will understand why we—'

'I said no!' snapped Simpson, shoving him back. 'The crypt is a much better solution. They can howl and scream as much as they like down there, but no one will hear. And anyone who does will think it is Mary Lane's ghost.'

Chaloner had noticed the thick cellar door during Bowles' funeral, and recalled what Thurloe had said: that the crypt had been built to hide contraband and was the most secure vault in the city. Muttering furiously under his breath about foolhardy decisions, Rye went to open its door. Chaloner baulked when he saw steep stone steps leading down into an impenetrable blackness. It looked like the entrance to a dungeon.

'I am not going down there,' he said, pulling away when Simpson grabbed his arm.

'Oh, yes, you are,' countered Rye sourly. 'Or I will stab your friend.'

Chaloner resisted anyway, but it was hopeless and, inch by inch, he was propelled towards the door. By contrast, Swaddell stalked through of his own volition, head held high and eyes promising vengeance the moment he got free: he even had the aplomb to help himself to a lamp as he went. With one final heave, Chaloner was shoved in after him.

'Wait!' Chaloner shouted desperately, and flailed around for something to keep them there. 'Just answer some questions. Simpson – are you the one who has been making fiery speeches in the taverns and coffee houses around Pudding Lane?'

'Why would I do that when I have a nice pulpit to use?' bellowed Simpson.

'Then tell me about Downes,' yelped Chaloner as the door started to close. 'Have you seen or heard from him recently?'

'I told you – I do not consort with radicals,' boomed Simpson, and the door closed even further.

'I know where Rye hid Eleanor's gold,' yelled Chaloner frantically, willing to say anything to avoid being shut inside. 'I will take you to it if you let us out.'

'Do you?' murmured Swaddell in surprise.

'No,' Chaloner whispered back unsteadily. 'But it will not be too difficult to find, now we know who filched it.'

'I am not a thief,' Rye was bleating to his cronies. 'Truly, I am not!'

'You will only be locked up for four days,' roared Simpson, ignoring the footman. 'So do not worry. King Jesus will let you out on Friday.'

'Thursday,' corrected Glasse. 'Wogan's woman had another vision last night, and an angel told her that the Kingdom of God is coming on *Thursday*.'

'You cannot leave us down here all that time,' shouted Chaloner, wrapping his fingers around the edge of the door to prevent Rye from closing it. 'We might die, and as you pointed out, you cannot greet King Jesus with blood on your hands.'

'You will not die,' bawled Simpson. 'There is a well for water, and as eggs are growing scarce, we put a few aside to celebrate the start of the Fifth Monarchy – they are next to Mary Lane's tomb. Do not scoff them all, though, as I shall want some to offer King Jesus. He may be partial to eggs.'

Chaloner might have laughed if the situation had not been so desperate. Then the door was ripped from his hands, and a hollow boom reverberated all through the crypt as it slammed shut. He fumbled to tug it open again, but a lock clicked into place, after which there was only silence and darkness. He could not hear the

316

Fifth Monarchists on the other side of it, although he imagined they were there, almost certainly still arguing amongst themselves.

'I had better light the lamp,' said Swaddell, and Chaloner did not think he would ever be so grateful to hear the assassin's voice. 'And do not worry, Tom. We will escape, because I am not staying down here until Thursday.'

'I have a bad feeling that might be easier said than done,' said Chaloner bleakly. 'We are in a cellar built by smugglers to keep their contraband safe – breaking out is not going to be as simple as you think.'

Chapter 12

The crypt had seemed pleasantly cool when Chaloner
and Swaddell had first been shut in it, but they soon
began to feel its chill, especially as both were dressed for
the sultry weather outside. They lit the lamp with the
tinderbox Swaddell always carried, and began to explore.

'I hate underground places,' Chaloner muttered,
trying to control the agitated hammering of his heart as
he and Swaddell ventured deeper into the musty, low-
ceilinged vault. 'Prisons, dungeons and the like.'

'But this is none of those things,' said Swaddell. 'It is
a repository for the dead.'

Chaloner regarded him askance. 'Is that supposed to
make me feel better?'

'Yes,' shrugged Swaddell. 'Because those ancient
smugglers will certainly have designed this place with
more than one exit – just like the church upstairs has
several doors. Do not worry, Tom – we shall be free in
a few minutes.'

The crypt ran the length and breadth of the church
above, so was roughly rectangular. It had thick stone
walls and a barrel-vaulted roof, although the floor was

beaten earth. It was full of broken masonry, bits of wood and sundry other rubbish, along with several large tombs, the grandest of which belonged to the infamous Mary Lane.

Unfortunately, Swaddell had been mistaken to expect multiple ways in and out, because a thorough search revealed that there was only one: the door through which they had entered. It was made of age-hardened oak, very thick, and its lock was only accessible from the church side – clearly, the smugglers had never anticipated being obliged to secure it from within – which meant that Chaloner could not pick the lock. Moreover, the door opened inwards, which made kicking it down impossible. Chaloner tried anyway.

'I am sorry about Wogan,' said Swaddell, making no move to help, because he knew it was futile. 'I was furious when he let Glasse escape, but he did not deserve to die.'

'No,' said Chaloner, thinking that Thurloe would be saddened by the end of a man who had risked all to atone for his crime. He took a break from his assault on the door and sat next to Swaddell. 'Given that Glasse dispatched his victim with such chilling indifference, do you think he is the stiletto killer? Or could it be Rye?'

'Glasse,' said Swaddell promptly. 'There is something deeply unsettling about him, and he is greed-driven. Perhaps Wogan's quick death was a blessing, because Glasse is certainly treacherous enough to betray him to the King for money.'

'Glasse, Rye, Simpson, Blackborne and Crookey,' listed Chaloner. 'Those are my chief suspects. Glasse, Rye and Simpson are part of some brewing rebellion – and it is possible that Simpson is one of the Pudding Lane agitators; Blackborne is a Fifth Monarchist and I think he resents being ousted

319

from the navy; and Crookey is basically a professional criminal.'

'My money is on Glasse, because we actually *saw* him commit murder with a blade. Not Simpson, though – unlike Glasse, he really does believe some great religious event is imminent, and he will not risk his place in Paradise by killing.'

Chaloner stood and began kicking the door again, unable to sit still and do nothing. When he was eventually forced to admit defeat, he explored the crypt a second time, reassessing walls, floor and ceiling for possible weaknesses. There was nothing, although he found the eggs Simpson had mentioned – several hundred of them in crates. He was hungry, but could not bring himself to eat one raw.

'We cannot stay here,' he said agitatedly when he returned to Swaddell. 'God only knows what Simpson and his lunatics are planning, but we cannot let them do it.'

'First, they promised the Kingdom of God on Sunday, then Friday and now Thursday,' mused Swaddell. 'Why does it keep changing? It cannot be because *we* are edging closer to the truth, because we are nowhere near to understanding what is going on.'

'No, but they do not know that, and I suspect they are afraid that we – or someone else – will stop it before it can start. That is why so many people have been killed – to prevent clues from leaking out.' Chaloner sat down, but immediately stood again, restless and anxious. 'I am going to find a weapon in case someone comes back to gloat.'

'I have already looked. The only thing remotely suitable is Mary Lane's mace.'

'Her what?'

'There is a wooden sculpture on her tomb of a figure clutching a mace. Perhaps she thought she might have to fend off dead customs officials on her journey into eternity.'

'Then maybe we should open her tomb and see what else she took with her.'

Swaddell regarded him askance. 'That would be desecration, and her spirit is said to haunt this place.' He shrugged. 'Not that I believe in such things, of course.'

'Good,' said Chaloner, 'because it is obviously a tale put about by Simpson and his cronies to make sure no one comes down here. Come on – I will need help with the lid.'

The tomb was a huge stone chest with the occupant's effigy lying on top of it. Chaloner glanced at the face, and saw some childish prankster had been at it with charcoal, because he was sure the original artist would not have given Mary Lane a T-beard. The lid slid aside with such ease that it had clearly seen regular use. They peered inside and saw not a mouldering coffin, but neat piles of paper.

'Lord!' muttered Swaddell. 'No wonder her angry ghost is up and about – her body has been ousted from its final resting place. Mine would be peeved, too.'

Chaloner grabbed a handful of pages. 'Broadsheets,' he said, glancing at them. 'Telling people what to do when King Jesus arrives.'

Swaddell gave a short bark of laughter. 'And there are two sets – one for sinners and one for saints. The arrogance of these radicals, thinking they can decide who is which!'

Chaloner was thoughtful. 'If they intend to impose

their Fifth Monarchy by force, this would be an ideal place to store guns, yet there is nothing.' He stared at Swaddell. 'I think Wogan was right when he told Thurloe they are innocent. It seems to me that they honestly believe that Jesus will usher them into White Hall without a shot being fired.'

'Simpson had a weapon,' Swaddell pointed out. 'So did Glasse and Rye.'

'They had ancient swords, knives and cudgels – none had a firearm. And yet something deadly *is* unfolding. I sense it with every fibre of my being.'

Swaddell raised his hands to say he had no answers, and peered into the tomb. 'There is today's *London Gazette*, which proves someone was ferreting about in here this morning. Perhaps they will return to rummage some more, and we can use the opportunity to escape.'

He settled down to peruse the newssheet, although Chaloner did not know how he could be so stoical when he himself shook with tension. From time to time, the assassin read interesting snippets aloud – peace talks in Poland, the Dutch reaction to Holmes's Bonfire, and a mortality bill that listed forty-two plague deaths for that week, which was six fewer than the previous one.

'There is more about how those paroled Hollandish prisoners tried to set Bristol alight, too,' he said. 'Bristol is like London, all cramped wooden houses. Had the rogues succeeded, the whole city would have burned down.'

Chaloner was about to reply when the lamp ran out of fuel.

It was impossible to tell how much time was passing, because the crypt was, quite literally, as silent as the grave. Chaloner, too tense to sit still, stumbled around in the

322

dark until he eventually discovered an air vent beneath the altar above. If he put his ear to it, he could just make out the chime of Allhallows' new mechanical clock, which struck the hour.

'Ten rings,' he said into the blackness. 'We have been down here for hours.'

'You woke me up to tell me that?' came the assassin's irritable voice. 'Just try to rest, Tom. We cannot do anything else, so marshal your strength with a nap.'

But Chaloner had no intention of sleeping in such a place, and was listening and alert when the clock struck six the following morning – Tuesday.

'My wife will wonder what you have done to me,' said Swaddell, making him jump by speaking very close to his shoulder. 'She thinks you deliberately court danger, and is frightened for me when she knows I am in your company.'

'Goodness!' muttered Chaloner, feeling he must lead a precarious life indeed if Ursula thought it was riskier than an unpopular assassin's.

'She will go to Williamson for news, but raising the alarm with him will do us no good, because I never told him our plans. Did you confide in anyone? The Earl? Wiseman?'

Chaloner shook his head, forgetting that Swaddell could not see him. 'And Lester will never guess where we are, because we kept him in ignorance for his own safety.'

Thurloe might be concerned, he thought, but he would never consider looking in the crypt of Allhallows. And at that point, it occurred to him that if the Fifth Monarchists' plans went awry, and the whole cabal was killed or forced to flee, he and Swaddell might never be found. The possibility made him feel queasy.

'Perhaps we should eat some eggs,' said Swaddell, and Chaloner heard him groping towards the place where they were stored. 'Hunger gnaws, and starving will do us no good.'

'Not raw,' said Chaloner, the notion of something slippery and cold slithering down his throat filling him with revulsion.

'True,' acknowledged Swaddell. 'Although I might change my mind if we are still down here when Judgement Day has been and gone.'

Chaloner paced restlessly. 'I do not understand how you can be so calm.'

'I learned long ago not to rail against matters that I cannot control. Yes, I could pace and wear myself out like you, but I prefer to preserve my strength, ready to fight those who put me here, should the opportunity arise. It is not—'

He stopped abruptly at a sound from the door, and Chaloner heard a metallic rattle when the assassin grabbed the lamp to use as a weapon. Chaloner groped for Mary Lane's mace as light flooded down the stairs, bright and painful after the darkness. Through watering eyes, he saw someone silhouetted there.

'Tom?' came Lester's wary voice. 'Are you there? Swaddell?'

'Sal!' cried Chaloner, before bounding up the stairs as fast as his legs would carry him and making for the nearest door that led outside.

'Is Simpson with you?' asked Swaddell of Lester, watching Chaloner disappear. He showed his own relief with a brief nod of thanks, but his own ascent of the steps was considerably more dignified. 'Or Glasse?'

'Neither.' Lester held his lantern high as he looked

around. 'So this is where Mary Lane lies, is it? All navy men know her, because she was basically a pirate. Heavens! Is that crates of *eggs*? We could make a fortune selling those in Covent Garden.'

'Perhaps we should use them to buy you a ship, then,' quipped Swaddell.

Standing in the scrubby graveyard, face raised towards the sun, Chaloner thought the stinking, dusty London air was the sweetest he had ever breathed. He inhaled deeply, aware that the city was already busy, even though it was not yet seven o'clock. Bells rang to announce Morning Prayer, and there was a low, deep rumble as thousands of feet, hoofs and wheels went about their daily business.

'How did you know where to find us?' he asked when Lester came to join him; Swaddell remained in the church, looking for clues regarding the Fifth Monarchists' plans.

Lester leaned against a buttress to reply, arms folded. 'You told me to look for those agitators, so I did. I was in Skiner's coffee house when I overheard Glasse say something about imprisoning two "nuisances" who he thought should have been executed—'

'When was this?' asked Chaloner urgently, thinking if Glasse was still there, he could have him in Newgate within the hour for the murder of Wogan.

'Dusk last night,' replied Lester. 'He was with a dozen radical types, and all were downing coffee like water, to soothe their nerves.'

'Did you approach them?'

'Of course not – you told me not to.'

'I did,' acknowledged Chaloner, aware that Lester, as a navy man, tended to follow orders to the letter. 'So, how did you—'

'I left to meet Elsie shortly afterwards, but when I got home at dawn and discovered that you had been out all night, I was worried, lest you and Swaddell were Glasse's nuisances. I hastened back to Elsie, and she suggested questioning Skiner's other patrons. From them, we learned that you were last seen entering this church.'

'I see,' said Chaloner, not sure whether to be thankful or suspicious that Elsie had discovered their whereabouts with what sounded like almost indolent ease. He sincerely hoped she was not involved in the plot, or Lester was going to be heartbroken.

The lady in question arrived at that point with Dorcas. 'Simpson has gone,' she reported. 'The butcher's boy saw him leave last night on a cart with all his belongings. I peeked through the window, and his house is bare. He does not intend to come back.'

'But according to his neighbours,' put in Dorcas, 'he believes he will soon be allocated a handsome suite in White Hall, so I doubt he has gone far.'

While Swaddell scribbled a note to Williamson, asking for troops to track the conspirators down, Chaloner forced himself back inside the church. Further evidence that its vicar had decanted permanently was in the vestry, which was stripped of anything remotely portable – Simpson might believe the Kingdom of God was at hand, but that did not mean he intended to enter it without worldly accoutrements.

'Wogan's body is not here,' said Swaddell, watching him look around. 'However, there is a fresh grave in the churchyard, so I suspect they buried him under cover of darkness. But come – we should search Simpson's house for ourselves. Perhaps he left something that will tell us what he plans to do.'

Unfortunately, Dorcas and Elsie were right to say that the vicar had stripped the place bare, and all that remained was a bed that had been too heavy to move.

'We should see if Glasse has fled, too,' said Chaloner, conceding defeat.

On Thames Street, he picked the lock on Glasse's front door, not caring that the neighbours immediately bustled up to see what was happening. He entered to see that the avaricious little cleric had been far more thorough in moving out than Simpson: his home was even missing light fitments, window latches and the decorative tiles around the hearth.

Glasse had left one thing behind, though: Rye was in the parlour with his skull caved in. An empty bag lay next to the body, emblazoned with the Montagu crest, telling Chaloner that Eleanor's fortune was now in the vicar's acquisitive hands.

'Vernon is here!' Swaddell shouted urgently from the back garden. 'Tom, help me! He is still alive.'

The physician had survived only because he owned an unusually thick cranium, although blood had flowed from his scalp so copiously that Chaloner was not surprised that his assailant had believed him to be dead. Dorcas fetched a cloth to clean the wound, while Chaloner and Swaddell helped the injured man to sit up.

'He came out of nowhere,' Vernon croaked, as he slowly recovered his senses. 'Glasse, I mean. One minute I was alone, and the next . . . '

'Why were you here in the first place?' asked Swaddell.

'I was looking for Wogan. He was not there to give his paupers their supper last night, and I was worried.

The last time I saw him was when you two hauled him off to visit Simpson and Glasse, so they seemed the obvious people to ask where he might be. There was no reply at Simpson's house, so I came here instead.'

Swaddell told him Wogan was dead, and the physician went so white that Chaloner was afraid he might swoon. Elsie fetched wine, which restored some colour to his face, although not much. When he spoke again, his voice shook with emotion.

'He will rise in glory on Thursday, so I know I should not mourn, but it is hard to think of a friend coming to such an end.' He struggled to his feet, pushing away the hands that tried to help him, and tottered into the house. He stopped when he saw Rye on the floor.

'Glasse attacked him, too,' explained Chaloner, 'which I know for a fact because Glasse had an ancient cudgel with him yesterday, and there are flakes of rotten wood embedded in Rye's head. Furthermore, Glasse disguised himself in a scarlet cloak after escaping from us, and there is a red thread caught under one of Rye's fingernails.'

'They fought, then,' surmised Swaddell. 'Probably over Eleanor's money.'

'Glasse kills and steals on the eve of the Second Coming?' breathed Vernon, shocked. 'But he is a priest! What is he thinking?'

'He is hedging his bets,' shrugged Chaloner. 'He might claim to be a Fifth Monarchist, but he does not really accept your theology. He is too venal.'

'So did Glasse kill Bowles and the others, too?' asked Lester. 'The case is solved?'

'He currently tops my list of suspects,' said Swaddell. 'Although that does not mean we should forget about the others – and that includes Rye, because being dead does not mean he is innocent.' He glanced at Vernon. 'What will you do now?'

'Find Glasse,' replied Vernon grimly. 'I know all his usual haunts, and if he is still in the city, I shall catch him. He needs to answer for his crimes.'

'If you happen across him, send word to me and I will arrange his arrest,' ordered Swaddell, although Chaloner thought the physician was wasting his time and Glasse would be long gone from the city. 'Tom and I have other work to do.'

Leaving Vernon to his quest, Swaddell and Chaloner walked out into the street, where the neighbours were delighted to learn that their parish priest was unlikely to return.

'Now we might get a *proper* one,' said an elderly widow with relish. 'Not one of them radicals. I am tired of all their unseemly ranting.'

'*He* will be miles away,' said Chaloner to Swaddell. 'But Dorcas is right to think that Simpson and the others will not have gone far – not when they expect to be installed in White Hall the day after tomorrow.'

'Then why did they bother to vanish?' demanded Swaddell. 'It cannot be because they are worried about us giving them away – they think we are safely locked up until it no longer matters.'

'Such people always go into hiding on the eve of a plot,' explained Chaloner. 'It makes it more difficult for the authorities to round them up and put an end to their scheme before it can start. They will have a "safe house" somewhere, but we will only find that if one of them tells us where it is. And as they have all disappeared . . . '

Swaddell nodded at a group of soldiers who were marching towards them. 'Here come the troops I begged from Williamson. I appreciate that hunting for these rebels may be futile, but we have to try anyway.'

'Perhaps Blackborne will have some ideas about where to look,' mused Chaloner. 'He is a Fifth Monarchist, after all. I will tackle him as soon as I have seen Thurloe.'

'Very well,' said Swaddell. 'I will stay here and organise the search.'

Chaloner sprinted to Lincoln's Inn, partly because time was fast running out – it was already noon – but mostly because he felt the need to stretch his legs after being locked up for so many hours. As he went, he took note of the atmosphere around him.

There was certainly an air of expectation, but it was happy rather than fearful or angry. Some folk sang, while others called cheerful greetings to those they passed. A number of people were cleaning the fronts of their houses, and there seemed to be fewer piles of rubbish around than usual. He felt despair wash over him. His instincts clamoured at him to thwart whatever was being plotted, but then what? Disappointment might incite the very trouble he aimed to prevent.

When he reached Fleet Street, he saw Wiseman's mistress, Temperance North, emerge from Hercules' Pillars Alley, where her exclusive 'gentlemen's club' was located. She was in her personal carriage. Behind her were three hackneys loaded with prostitutes and two wagons containing their belongings. The driver made no effort to stop, so Chaloner jumped on the running board and leaned through the window to talk to her as the coach trundled along.

'We are going to Slough,' she explained. 'We cannot stay here – it is too dangerous.'

Chaloner was surprised to see her frightened, because she was usually a lot more sanguine about London's political and social upheavals than he was. 'You think it is worse than all the other times?'

Temperance grimaced. 'Yes, because there is a fervent belief that everything is about to be wonderful, and when nothing changes, the mood will turn sour. We do not want to be blamed for the postponement of Paradise.'

'Why would you be?' asked Chaloner, bemused.

'Because the fanatics will bray that the Kingdom of God will never come as long as we are here to encourage licentiousness, so we have decided to lie low for a while. It will only be for a few days, because the city will always revert to what it is – a haven for those who prefer fun to dull religious dogma.'

'Have you heard any rumours about what this Utopia might entail?'

'The general consensus is that King Jesus will install Himself in White Hall at dawn on Thursday.'

'Are you sure His arrival is scheduled for dawn?'

'No, but daybreak is always associated with new beginnings, and Christ is not going to come skulking along at night, when everyone is asleep, is He?'

'What else have you heard?'

'Just a lot of omens that "prove" something really will happen this time. Also the Pope is dying, and as many consider him to be the antichrist, the year with three sixes seems to be the right time for him to breathe his last.'

'So mostly the kind of talk that comes from Fifth Monarchists?'

Temperance nodded. 'They are vicious Puritan killjoys whose idea of heaven is a dictatorship where everyone is only allowed to do what *they* deem appropriate.'

331

'True.' Chaloner prepared to jump off the carriage before he was carried too far out of his way, but Temperance was still talking.

'When he heard the Pope had taken a turn for the worse, the King wanted to postpone the masque as a mark of respect, but Bristol urged against it. He said His Majesty should be able to do whatever he likes, and to hell with what anyone else thinks. It is bad advice.'

'It is, but if the King had been a sensible man, he would have stopped such an outrageous event from being organised in the first place.'

'The syllabub is the spark that will set everything alight,' predicted Temperance. 'It wastes eggs when they cannot be bought for love nor money. The poor will resent it.'

'Eggs,' said Chaloner worriedly. '*Everything* seems to revolve around eggs.'

Chaloner reached Lincoln's Inn and ran up the stairs to Chamber XIII, where he discovered Thurloe sitting at his table surrounded by discarded pieces of paper, every one of them thickly covered in inky scribbles.

'Wogan is dead,' said Chaloner bluntly. 'I am sorry. I know you liked him.'

Thurloe sat back, closed his eyes and whispered a prayer for Wogan's soul. Then he listened while Chaloner told him all that had happened since they had last met.

'Poor Wogan,' he said quietly when Chaloner had finished. 'I admired his efforts to redeem himself, and it cannot have been easy to live here, knowing what would happen if he was caught. May he rest in peace.'

'Until Thursday,' said Chaloner, seeing bread, cheese and ale on the window sill, and going to help himself.

'When the Kingdom of God arrives, and he might rise in glory.'

'Watch yourself, Thomas,' warned Thurloe sharply. 'You sail very close to the edge of blasphemy.'

'Surely *you* do not believe that Jesus is on the verge of taking over White Hall?'

'I believe in the Second Coming – it is a basic tenet of my Christian faith. However, I do not imagine it will happen the day after tomorrow, just because a few radicals hope so.'

Chaloner nodded to the chaos of papers on the ex-Spymaster's desk. 'Have you decoded Downes' letter yet?'

Thurloe stared down at it. 'I am *sure* it holds the key to all we need to know – and will explain why the nine regicides were murdered.' He watched Chaloner finish the bread and start on some slivers of cake. 'So who are your remaining suspects for all this trouble?'

'I have three,' replied Chaloner. 'Glasse, Crookey and Blackborne.'

'Not Blackborne,' said Thurloe at once. 'I know he is a Fifth Monarchist, but he is no rebel.'

Chaloner ignored the remark. 'We discounted Simpson as a culprit, because the killer is ruthless but Simpson argued for clemency when Glasse and Rye wanted to murder us.'

'That seems a reasonable assumption.'

'I am inclined to discount Rye, too, on the grounds that the culprit is passionate in his convictions, but Rye is just a common felon, following Fifth Monarchism to see what he can get out of it. If he truly believed the Kingdom of God was at hand, he would not have filched his employer's money. Swaddell disagrees, though.'

333

'I am inclined to agree with you.' Thurloe changed the subject. 'Wiseman thought you might be here and left you a message. He wanted you to know that he examined a higgler named Norton, and discovered that he was stabbed with a stiletto.'

'No surprise there,' muttered Chaloner through a mouthful of cake.

'He also found an additional six men and women in the charnel house who had suffered the same fate.'

'Probably higglers, too. But you did not answer my question: have you decoded any of Downes' message yet?'

Thurloe spoke reluctantly. 'One part was easier to decipher than the rest because it contained a name – Robert Blackborne.'

'I *knew* it!' exclaimed Chaloner, slamming his hand on the window sill. 'No Fifth Monarchist can resist embroiling himself in insurrection.'

'The inclusion of his name does not mean he is involved,' warned Thurloe. 'For all we know, Downes might have been telling Eleanor to report his findings to Blackborne as a man who could be trusted.'

'I was on my way to see him anyway,' said Chaloner. 'Hopefully, he will be at the Navy Office, but if not, his nephew Hewer will know where to find him.'

'I would accompany you, but I think it would be more sensible for me to continue working on the cipher. I am making progress, albeit slowly.'

'I know why Downes made it so difficult,' said Chaloner, finishing the last of Thurloe's food and wiping his hands on his breeches. 'Because Rye escorted Eleanor to the Tower, and Downes knew that Rye was a Fifth Monarchist.'

Thurloe looked doubtful. 'Did he know it? How?'

'You told me the answer to that yourself: Downes' particular friends were Simpson and Glasse, who lead the sect that Rye chose to follow. Clearly, one of them told him.' Chaloner prepared to leave, brushing crumbs from his clothes. 'I cannot see King Jesus being very impressed with any of them.'

'He will not be very impressed by men who eat their friends out of house and home either,' retorted Thurloe tartly. 'Well, do not stand there primping, Thomas. Go and see what light Blackborne can throw on this miserable affair.'

It was a long, hot journey to the Navy Office. Chaloner tried to hurry, but his earlier run had exhausted him, so it took more time than he felt he could spare to get there. He reached his goal eventually, sweating, weary and fraught with worry.

'Mr Pepys has gone to a wedding feast,' supplied Secretary Hewer, pre-empting the question he thought he would be asked. 'But I expect him back by—'

'Never mind him,' interrupted Chaloner. 'Where is your uncle?'

'He went to see my grandfather in Deptford,' replied Hewer, and an anxious expression suffused his face. 'They have been estranged for years, so I asked why he should visit him now, but he would not say. He looked unwell . . . '

'Unwell how?' demanded Chaloner. 'Frightened? Anxious?'

'Pale and worried, but resolute, as though he had come to terms with something terrible.' Hewer swallowed hard and looked away. 'I fear he may have some insidious disease, and went to heal the rift while he is still able.'

335

Chaloner's stomach roiled. Did Blackborne expect to perish in whatever mischief was unfolding, encouraged perhaps by the belief that he would not remain in his grave for very long? 'What else did he say? Tell me his exact words. This is important.'

'Nothing! He just said he wanted to make peace with his sire before it was too late.'

'Too late for what?'

'He did not explain, but I thought he meant too late for him, which is why I assume he has some sickness that . . . But you can ask him yourself. He will not tarry long in Deptford, because he has an appointment in Poulters' Hall later today.'

'Poulters' Hall?' barked Chaloner. 'Why there?'

'He is a member – he goes there to meet his friends.' Hewer grimaced. 'They had a great feast on Friday, and he was so looking forward to going, but the Navy Board demanded his help and he missed it. But did he complain? No, because he puts his country above all else.'

Chaloner closed his eyes, disgusted with himself. How could he have failed to discover that Blackborne was a member of the organisation that seemed to lie at the heart of all his mysteries? And what a pity the Navy Board had needed Blackborne on Friday, because if he had gone to the feast, Chaloner would have seen him there.

Speaking of friends,' he said tiredly, 'how well does he know Vicar Simpson and Vicar Glasse?'

'Oh, quite well, I should think. There are not many Fifth Monarchists left in London these days, so they tend to see a lot of each other. He mentions them to me occasionally.'

'What does he say about them?'

'Just that they share his beliefs about King Jesus. But why all these questions? I hope you do not think he is involved in anything untoward. There is no more loyal man in the entire city than my uncle.'

'Right,' said Chaloner flatly.

'The only other thing I can tell you is that after visiting Poulters' Hall, he said he intends to travel outside the city.'

'How far outside?' demanded Chaloner.

'To an egg farm near Willesden, although I cannot imagine why.'

'*Drinkell's* egg farm?'

'Drinkell, yes,' said Hewer, nodding. 'That is the name he mentioned.'

Chaloner thought fast. He was sure the Fifth Monarchists had decanted to a 'safe house' after he and Swaddell had confronted them in Allhallows, and where better than a place that saw very few visitors and had a strong perimeter fence?

Of course, this would mean that the Fifth Monarchists and Drinkell were in cahoots, which was a new development. He pondered the possibility. It would certainly explain why Drinkell had tried so hard to prevent Chaloner from meddling in Company business, and why he had objected to Williamson being told of Collins's belief that the agitators were professional rabble-rousers. Did this mean that Drinkell was a Fifth Monarchist? Chaloner had never heard him talk about religion, but that meant nothing.

He decided to visit Poulters' Hall at once, in the hope that Blackborne had finished his business in Deptford and would be there, perhaps meeting Drinkell. Then he could demand answers from the two of them together.

337

He trotted along Tower Street, looking for a hackney, feeling time running out like sand through his fingers. Then he heard his name called from a passing coach, and glanced around to see Swaddell. He leapt in and yelled to the driver to take them to Poulters' Hall with all possible speed.

'No, continue to White Hall as I ordered,' countered Swaddell, and showed Chaloner a note in the Spymaster's distinctive hand. 'There is a crisis, and Williamson says Montagu needs our immediate assistance.'

Chaloner's stomach churned with tension. 'Why? What has happened?'

'He is accused of murdering two men from the Buttery.'

'You mean the pair who died from eating heat-tainted food?'

Swaddell nodded. 'He is ultimately responsible for all the palace's victuals, and Bristol brays that if some of it was bad, then Montagu has blood on his hands.'

'It was the weather,' said Chaloner in agitation. He did not have time to waste on petty politics while a deadly plot was in the offing!

'Perhaps, but we cannot ignore a direct command from Williamson,' said Swaddell. 'And your Earl will agree. Montagu is his friend and he does not have so many that he can afford to lose one to Bristol's machinations.'

Angry and frustrated, Chaloner saw he had no choice but to see what could be done to exonerate Montagu before tackling Blackborne and Drinkell at Poulters' Hall.

Chapter 13

It was an unpleasant journey to White Hall, with the afternoon sun blazing in through the carriage windows. It was hot enough to make the leather seats painful to sit on, while any exposed metal had heated up enough to scorch careless fingers. As they clattered down Ludgate Hill, Chaloner saw children trying to bake fish on the super-heated cobbles. Usually they would be attempting to fry eggs, but there were none of those to be had.

'We do not have time for this,' he said for at least the fourth time since they had set off, taut with tension. 'Surely Montagu can fight his own battles?'

'Bristol's sly attacks on him these last few days prove he cannot,' replied Swaddell, all unruffled calm. 'He has been too badly damaged by the rumours, so stop grumbling and start thinking of ways to save him.'

They rode the rest of the way in silence, and arrived to find the palace in an uproar, partly because of the scandalous gossip about Montagu, but mostly due to the increasingly frenetic preparations for the next day's Adrian Masque. Servants scurried in and out of the Banqueting House with furniture and props, although

339

orders were followed with ill grace, and there was an overwhelming air of sullen defiance.

'Most of them disapprove of it,' explained Swaddell. 'Especially as it is scheduled on the eve of a predicted Second Coming. They fear for their souls.'

Chaloner led the way to the Lord Chamberlain's apartments, aware of hostile glares from the courtiers he passed – when the King had returned, his favourites had followed, so the entire palace now seemed to be populated by his Earl's enemies.

'Clarendon is the *real* culprit behind the Buttery murders,' one lady informed a crony, loudly enough to make sure Chaloner heard. 'Lord Bristol accuses Montagu of the crime, but we all know Montagu is Clarendon's pawn.'

Unwilling to waste time defending his employer to people who would not listen anyway, Chaloner hurried on, Swaddell a dark shadow at his heels. They reached Montagu's chambers, to find him sitting with Margaret Hay and Surgeon Wiseman.

'Here you are at last!' gulped Montagu in relief. 'Have you heard what is being said about me?'

Chaloner nodded. 'But I do not see how we can help.'

'You are right – you cannot,' said Wiseman with his customary arrogance. 'The Buttery men *were* poisoned, but no human hand was responsible. No divine one either, no matter what the fanatics claim. It was heat-spoiled food.'

'*We* know that,' said Margaret bitterly. 'And so does Bristol, but he would rather use the tragedy to attack Edward.'

'It is because of that broadsheet,' said Montagu, and shot Chaloner a sheepish glance. 'We decided we dared

340

not wait for you to compose one about Bristol, because he cannot open his mouth without braying something nasty about me, so we did it ourselves. Unfortunately, I think he knows it was us, and these vile accusations are his revenge.'

'What did you write?' demanded Chaloner, exasperated. Why had they not listened to him and abandoned their ill-advised scheme as they had been told?

'The truth,' replied Margaret defiantly. 'That he is unsteady, unreliable and dangerous, and that the country will never be safe until he is no longer in it.'

'I know we should have left it to you,' said Montagu wretchedly. 'But I was desperate to silence his malicious tongue before all these important people roll up for the masque tomorrow. Unfortunately, it was a terrible mistake, because it is obvious now that he will continue to slander me until I am driven from the King's grace.'

'And if Edward goes, there will be no one left to stand between Bristol and your Earl,' put in Margaret. 'So you *must* help us, Mr Chaloner.'

'But I do not know how,' objected Chaloner. 'Other than finding out exactly what the Buttery men ate to make them ill, although Wiseman is better qualified to do that . . . '

'I am,' agreed Wiseman. 'And I have already done it. The culprit was a batch of eggs purchased from a higgler who came to the Great Gate to hawk his wares. I suspect the rogue had hoarded them for days, waiting for the price to rise. Thus they were sold when they were past their best.'

'So the eggs were indeed poisonous?' gulped Montagu, horrified.

'Not poisonous exactly,' said Wiseman pedantically.

'But certainly unfit for human consumption. Itinerant traders rarely have the facilities to keep their wares at safe temperatures, which is why it is unwise to purchase them from anyone who is not licensed.'

'But I *had* to!' cried Montagu. 'The palace cannot function without eggs, so when a fellow appeared with ten dozen, of course I snapped them up.'

'Yet bad eggs reek,' said Margaret, puzzled. 'Surely the Buttery men would have noticed the stench and refused to eat them?'

'I have explained all this before,' said Wiseman impatiently. 'There is a stage between good and rotten when there is no unhealthy smell, yet they can still bring a man low. We call it egg fever, and it is not uncommon in the summer, especially if chicken droppings are left on the shells. Professional poulters wash them off at once, but higglers are less fastidious.'

'It is not your responsibility to buy eggs,' said Chaloner to Montagu. 'It is the Poultry Department's. So why did you do it?'

'Because the higgler refused to deal with them,' replied Montagu wretchedly. 'He would only sell to me in person.'

'Curious,' mused Chaloner, wondering if Bristol or one of the Poultry Department had guessed the eggs were unsafe, and had decided to use the higgler to strike a blow at the man they aimed to destroy. All were ruthless enough to have devised such a scheme, and none would care a fig that it might hurt the innocent.

'We will find this egg-seller and demand the truth,' promised Swaddell, although Chaloner thought it would be like looking for a needle in a haystack, given the number of them who had invaded the city. 'What can you tell us about him?'

342

'I was more interested in his wares,' replied Montagu helplessly, 'which *were* encrusted with droppings, now you mention it. Lord, what a business! I wish Hadie were still alive, because *he* would know the man's name. He was very knowledgeable about the illegal egg trade.'

'You knew Hadie?' blurted Chaloner in astonishment.

'He used to clerk for me occasionally,' explained Montagu. 'He was not a poulter himself, but was acquainted with men who were, because he was a member of their Company. He was as pitifully poor, but upright and kind, and I considered him a friend. Indeed, he did me the honour of lodging his will with me. I must see it executed soon.'

'You have his will?' Chaloner's thoughts raced as a solution to one mystery flashed into his mind. 'When did he make it?'

'A day or two before he died. He was—'

'W, I and L!' interrupted Chaloner urgently, and turned to Swaddell. 'The three letters he made with his fingers as he died. Not a name, but his *will*.' He swung back to Montagu. 'Where is it, sir? We need to see it at once.'

Frowning his bafflement, Montagu rummaged in a drawer and produced two sheets of paper, folded and tied with a ribbon. One contained instructions for the disposal of Hadie's worldly goods, which were to be sold and the money given to Wogan for the poor. The other was a report describing how certain people were conspiring to create a city-wide shortage of eggs. Chaloner and Swaddell read it quickly.

'So Hadie *did* write a letter about his discoveries,' breathed Swaddell, 'and he expected it to be made public in the event of his death. He taunted the killer about it as he died, and Elsie and Dorcas witnessed his assailant frantically trying to make him say where he had left it. And here it is, safely in the care of someone he trusted.'

'But why would anyone want eggs to become scarce?' asked Margaret, mystified.

'According to Hadie,' said Chaloner, tapping the letter with his finger, 'so that prices will rise and make the culprits wealthy. He says here that he aimed to demand answers from Crookey and Catline, because he suspected their involvement. Unfortunately, he was murdered before he could do it.'

'Then you must confront them,' said Wiseman, settling back and pouring himself a cup of wine. 'Because courtiers cannot be allowed to create food shortages. Or to meddle with free trade, for that matter. It will cause an uproar all over the city.'

'Well, gentlemen?' said Montagu. 'What are you waiting for?'

Chaloner and Swaddell hurried to the Banqueting House, hoping the men from the Poultry Department would be there, because neither wanted to squander time looking for them. However, Wiseman was right to say that Hadie's allegations would cause a tremendous scandal if they became public – and might even spark riots of their own – so the matter had to be addressed as a matter of urgency. Chaloner prayed that it would not take long, because he was desperate to turn his attention back to Blackborne and Drinkell.

'There they are,' said Swaddell, pausing at the door. 'Sampling the wine that will be served tomorrow. And the palace servants have gone to eat, so they are alone. Good.'

'We will probably end up arresting the lot of them,'

344

said Chaloner. 'Does Williamson have room for them all in his cells?'

'Unfortunately, causing a shortage of eggs is not an arrestable offence,' said Swaddell. 'All we can do – after we challenge them and demand answers – is refer the matter to the Company of Poulters.'

'*Murder* is an arrestable offence,' countered Chaloner. 'And I suspect they – along with Bristol – are responsible for what happened to the Buttery men. Then there is Hadie, stabbed when he was on the verge of exposing their plans.'

'None of this will be easy to prove,' warned Swaddell. 'The evidence is circumstantial. Moreover, if they killed Hadie, then it means they also dispatched Bowles, Hill, Downes, Eleanor and the regicides, but I see no motive for that.'

'We can ask them once they are in Williamson's dungeons.'

'Very well,' sighed Swaddell, seeing him resolute. 'I shall run and fetch troops from Westminster, because we will need help if we are to take them all into custody. Meanwhile, you can lock them in here, then stand guard to make sure they do not leave.'

'I will begin questioning them,' said Chaloner, loath to waste a minute when time was of the essence. 'Then, when you return, you can arrest them while I go on to Poulters' Hall.'

'Tackling them on your own would be a mistake,' stated Swaddell firmly. 'Just do what I say and wait until I get back. I will not be long.'

Chaloner ran to the guard house, grabbed the relevant keys, and secured the Banqueting House's doors. There

345

were only three, so he was able to finish in a trice. Unfortunately, Will Chiffinch and Lady Castlemaine saw him, and came to demand what he thought he was doing.

'It is for a surprise,' lied Chaloner, thinking fast. 'Bristol challenged my Earl to think of something to entertain the King, so he has. However, no one can see it in advance, or it will ruin everything and the King will be disappointed.'

He was astonished when they believed him, and not only desisted in their efforts to reclaim the keys, but offered to keep everyone else out, too. He dreaded to think what would happen when they learned the 'surprise' comprised the arrest of a lot of their friends.

Unwilling to stay with them while they bombarded him with questions, he hurried to the back door and let himself in, careful to secure it behind him again. Then he went to the main hall and took up station behind a tapestry to monitor his quarry, relieved when they all seemed content to continue drinking and showed no inclination to leave.

Everyone from the Poultry Department was there, including retainers – except Munger the clerk, who was doubtless working while they relaxed – so they numbered about twenty men. Chaloner knew Swaddell was right to urge him to wait, but he was sure he could prise something useful from them before the assassin returned with help. After all, as long as he had the keys, none of them could escape. What could possibly go wrong if he began his interrogation early?

'Perhaps *he* murdered the Buttery men,' said Catline slyly as Chaloner left his hiding place and walked towards them. 'I always thought he was dangerous.'

'Not as dangerous as you,' countered Chaloner. '*You* are the ones who arranged for the higgler to sell tainted eggs to Montagu.'

'Prove it,' challenged Catline, smug in the knowledge that no independent witnesses were there to hear what was essentially an admission of guilt.

Chaloner addressed the others. 'You are all in serious trouble, but if you answer my questions, I may be able to save you from the scaffold. You see, a document has come to light that implicates you in some serious crimes. The first is purveying, the second is a plot to drive up the price of eggs, the third is murder, and the fourth is insurrection.'

Several of the Poultry men exchanged uneasy glances, although Catline continued to regard him with contempt. Crookey settled for a mocking laugh, but even so, Chaloner saw concern flicker in his eyes.

'You are mad!' the Supernumerary Groom blustered. 'Murder and insurrection indeed!'

'This document *proves* your guilt,' stated Chaloner, aware that the Supernumerary Groom had not denied the first two charges. 'So will the ringleaders confess, or will you all hang for their misdeeds?'

'Ignore him,' ordered Catline, as his cronies began to mutter uncomfortably among themselves. 'This so-called document does not exist, so he aims to win a confession by trickery. Well, it will not work.'

'First, purveying,' began Chaloner. 'Crookey's remit is to secure cheap supplies, so that the rest of you can pocket the difference. However, he does it by coercing merchants into selling their goods at cripplingly low prices. That is illegal.'

'It is,' agreed Catline with a crafty smile. 'But no merchant will ever have the courage to accuse him of it in a court of law, so how will you make your case?'

'Several tradesmen have agreed to do it already,' lied Chaloner. 'And you may think the King will protect you all

347

from these charges, but condoning purveyance will lose him the support of his people. He will not risk it – not for you.'

'The people!' spat Mezandier. 'Who cares what they think? And who bleated to you about Crookey's tactics anyway? Was it Master Farmer? If it was, I shall kill him.'

'Go and fetch more wine, Mezandier,' ordered Crookey sharply, clearly aiming to be rid of the man before he brayed more incriminating remarks – Catline might believe a lack of witnesses to the confrontation would render any confessions inadmissible, but the Supernumerary Groom was becoming increasingly unsettled by Chaloner's confident accusations.

'Do not worry about Farmer,' Mezandier told him between gritted teeth. 'I will make sure he and the others keep their mouths shut.' He turned back to Chaloner. 'Besides, the King knows what we do, so you will walk away now if you know what is good for you.'

'So now you drag His Majesty's name into it?' flashed Chaloner. 'I cannot see him being very happy about that. Who else will you include? Bristol?'

'Bristol takes his cut,' shrugged Mezandier, fending off the colleagues who were anxiously trying to shut him up. 'And anyway, the laws against purveying are stupid – an infringement of our age-old rights.'

'The other three accusations are more serious,' Chaloner went on, giving Mezandier a contemptuous glance before addressing the others again. 'Conspiring to inflate the price of eggs, murdering Hadie when he tried to unmask you, and plotting rebellion.'

Despite his friends' increasing alarm, Mezandier refused to stop talking. 'We had nothing to do with those. Who is Hadie, anyway?'

Chaloner did not oblige him with an answer. 'Your recipe for syllabub requires a thousand eggs,' he continued. 'Not to mention the ones needed for the pies and tarts—'

'That syllabub will be remembered for years to come,' interrupted Mezandier gleefully. 'Especially as we shall serve it in that.' He pointed to the replica of the baptismal font and smirked. 'That will be a poke in the eye for all the papists.'

Chaloner was disinclined to remind him that the papists whose eyes were set to be poked would include high-ranking guests from France and Spain – people the King could not afford to offend. He continued with his charges, stretching the truth to see if Mezandier could be goaded into revealing anything else.

'We have witnesses who will swear in a court of law that you aim to become rich from manipulating the egg market with—'

'We do not have to listen to this,' said Crookey, coming to his feet in a way that told Chaloner he was now very worried. 'We are leaving.'

Chaloner watched him reach the door to find it locked. 'Thanks to the poulters you cowed, you will have all the eggs you need for tomorrow, while the rest of London watches with envy. Then two things will happen.'

'What two things?' demanded Mezandier, while Crookey began to haul on the door with mounting agitation.

'First, there will be an enormous surge in the demand for eggs, as fashionable folk want for themselves what is served at the King's masque,' replied Chaloner. 'And second, the shortage will drive prices through the roof.'

Crookey shrugged, feigning unconcern. 'Market forces – supply and demand. You cannot hold us responsible for those.'

349

'We can when you suddenly become wealthy from them,' Chaloner flashed back, wishing Swaddell would hurry up. 'And we have Hadie's testimony that you will. Exerting control over the egg trade was your idea and—'

'*Our* idea?' interrupted Mezandier, and laughed. 'It all came from the poulters! We merely consented to creating a greater demand for eggs. Besides, it will do no harm – eggs are underappreciated and there is nothing wrong with reminding folk of their value.'

'It *will* do harm,' snapped Chaloner. 'It will cause resentment among those who cannot afford them, and resentment leads to strife.'

'You exaggerate,' spat Mezandier. 'And we do not give a damn, anyway – not when we stand to make such a handsome profit. We regret nothing of what we have done.'

Catline scowled at him. 'You are a fool, Mezandier! Now he will persecute us even more vigorously, and it is only a matter of time before he uncovers some snippet of evidence we have overlooked. And that could prove very inconvenient.'

'He will not, because he will be dead,' declared Mezandier, whipping out his sword.

Chaloner only just managed to draw and parry the first blow. Sparks flew as their blades met. Then the others raced to join in, and he saw he had made a serious error of judgement in tackling them without waiting for help.

He dodged behind a beautiful 'medieval' table in the expectation that they would not risk damaging it by slashing at him, but Mezandier's blood was up. Catline bellowed his dismay when one lunge scored a deep cut across its polished surface.

'If you must dispatch him, at least *try* not to make a mess in the process,' he snarled. 'And hurry up before someone unlocks the door and comes in. We cannot afford for there to be witnesses.'

As one, everyone launched himself at Chaloner, who fought back using every trick he knew. He grabbed a tapestry and ripped it down so it fell over Catline, upended tables to form barriers between him and Mezandier, and lobbed jugs, goblets and plates at everyone else. But he was losing ground. Eventually, he was forced to take refuge behind the baldachin, with its handsome columns and ornate canopy.

'Stop, Mezandier!' screeched Catline furiously. 'If you nick *that* with your clumsy great blade, the paint will come off and everyone will know it is not real gold.'

Mezandier took no notice, and nor did the others. By silent agreement, they advanced on Chaloner from two sides at once. He prepared to sell his life as dearly as he could.

Chapter 14

Mezandier was just raising his sword for the killing blow when there came a snap of opening locks and Williamson's men poured in, Swaddell in the vanguard. Chaloner expected the courtiers to surrender when they saw they were outnumbered so heavily, but they continued to fight like lions. Crookey urged them on with increasingly desperate howls, aware of what they had to lose in defeat, although he was careful to stay away from the flailing weapons himself.

Then Swaddell managed to slip behind Mezandier. One hand snaked around the man's head, while the other ran a sharp blade across his throat. It happened so fast that Chaloner barely registered what had happened until Mezandier toppled forward, fingers scrabbling at his ruined neck.

Horrified by the loss of their most experienced warrior, his cronies let their swords drop to the floor in surrender. Eventually, Crookey was the only one who still held a blade, although he flung it away hastily when Swaddell began to advance on him.

'I yield,' he squealed. 'Please! Stop!'

There was a moment when Chaloner thought Swaddell would dispatch the Supernumerary Groom anyway, but he swung away at the last moment, and ordered the prisoners to kneel with their hands on their heads while his soldiers stood guard over them.

'We are favourites of the King,' shouted one, struggling valiantly for defiance. 'We will be free by nightfall, and then it will be *you* who is in trouble.'

But Crookey was astute enough to know that favourites changed with the wind, and that His Majesty was not noted for constancy towards his friends, as the Earl of Clarendon's current predicament demonstrated. He eased away from the others, eyes darting everywhere as he began to calculate the best options for himself.

'It will take more than a document and a few resentful poulters to convict these men,' he told Chaloner. 'However, I will provide what you need in exchange for my freedom.'

His cronies clamoured their disbelief, and he edged even further away, cringing but determined.

Swaddell regarded him beadily. 'Why should we trust you?'

'Why should you not?' countered Crookey, licking dry lips. 'Grant me my liberty, and I will help you prosecute the entire department.' He glanced at Chaloner. 'And Bristol.'

His erstwhile friends bellowed with renewed outrage, and he blanched at some of the threats that were issued, so Chaloner took his arm and pulled him outside.

'Talk,' he ordered curtly, once they were out of earshot.

'I will give you incontestable written evidence of purveying and price fixing,' said Crookey with a sickly smile. 'But not murder and rebellion, because we have nothing to do with those. I will swear any oath you ask, but that is the truth.'

Chaloner regarded him coldly. 'So what *can* you tell us?'

Crookey began to gabble, suddenly afraid that his efforts to save himself might not work. 'That I convinced Master Farmer at the Company of Poulters to do what we wanted, because he is weak and easily intimidated. I persuaded many others, too.'

He began to list them, and Chaloner saw his tentacles had reached far and wide, because a good three dozen tradesmen had been all but bankrupted by his antics.

'I know you ordered Farmer to give him ten dozen rabbits for the masque,' said Chaloner. 'But as to eggs, he told me that you source them directly from a country estate.'

Crookey had enough hubris left for a sneer. 'A country estate indeed! The truth is that we send our servants to Poulters' Hall, and they *take* what we need for free. Farmer dares not stop them, and if anyone else objects, Drinkell deals with them.'

'What about the plot to manipulate market forces?'

'That was all Drinkell's idea, too,' replied Crookey. 'He owns a huge farm, and stands to earn a fortune if the scheme succeeds. He has persuaded all the big producers and most of the medium-sized ones to stand with him.'

Chaloner was more interested in the allegations that had brought him racing to White Hall in the first place. 'Which of your rabble arranged for Montagu to be sold the tainted eggs?'

'Catline,' replied Crookey promptly, 'because he knew

354

it would please Bristol. And Bristol loves anything that will hurt your Earl and his allies.'

Chaloner thought about the stiletto killer, and the possibility that he was a hired assassin. 'Could Bristol have ordered Eleanor Montagu's murder, just to allow him to spread damaging rumours about her husband?'

'He might,' nodded Crookey, eager to say anything he thought Chaloner wanted to hear. 'He is ruthless.'

Unfortunately, suspicions were not evidence. Chaloner continued to press him, but while Crookey's testimony would allow his cronies to be charged with corruption and interfering with free trade, that was where his usefulness ended. Chaloner left him with a guard, and went to see what Catline would be prepared to admit now that the game was up.

'He escaped,' smirked one of the prisoners. 'He will run straight to men who owe us favours, so do not think we will be in your hands for long.'

'Take them away,' Chaloner ordered the guards, cursing himself for not noticing Catline's absence sooner. 'They are Williamson's concern now.'

The sight of so many courtiers being marched away excited a lot of attention and a good deal of alarm, so that Chaloner suspected the Poultry Department was not the only one to break the laws regarding purveyance. He wondered if it would frighten the rest into being honest – for a while, at least. Montagu was among those who came to watch.

'You can cancel the masque now its organisers are no longer here to oversee it,' Chaloner told him. 'It may help restore the King's tarnished reputation with his subjects.'

'But everything is ready,' objected Montagu, jumping smartly into the shadows when Bristol stalked past, agitation in his every step. 'And too many important people have been invited for us to back out now – high-ranking ambassadors, foreign princes, wealthy bankers. To tell them not to come would be a diplomatic disaster.'

'You think seeing the King wallow in syllabub is good for international relations?'

'Yes, if these emissaries are encouraged to join in,' replied Montagu, surprised that Chaloner should need to ask. 'It will be an experience none of them will have had before, so it must go ahead. I shall handle the final details myself, although the only remaining task of any significance is making the syllabub . . . '

'I do not think—'

'Obviously, it cannot be put together too early, or it will go sour,' continued Montagu, his expression distant as he calculated measurements and ingredients in his head. 'I had better make arrangements at once.'

'We just saved him from an accusation of murder,' said Chaloner to Swaddell, watching him hurry away. 'But does he thank us? Is he chastened by the experience? No! He is only interested in saving that wretched masque. All courtiers are as bad as each other.'

'Keep your voice down!' hissed Swaddell, glancing around in alarm. 'Besides, I imagine he is right to say there would be diplomatic repercussions for cancelling it now. We arrested the organisers too late in the day, I am afraid.'

Chaloner pondered what the confrontation had achieved. 'All we did was expose a few dishonest courtiers, but Crookey – the most corrupt and devious of them all – will go free in exchange for turning king's evidence.'

'He will go free,' acknowledged Swaddell, and his eyes turned beady. 'But who can say how long he will live to enjoy it?'

Chaloner did not want to hear more. 'We wasted time here at the expense of solving the murders and thwarting Thursday's trouble. We need to go to Poulters' Hall immediately. Hopefully, Blackborne will still be there, and he is at the top of my list of suspects now that we have eliminated Crookey.'

'No, we need to find Catline first,' argued Swaddell. 'I doubt he ran to "men who owe him favours" on behalf of his friends, and will be working out how best to reach the coast. We cannot allow him to escape.'

With ill grace, Chaloner followed Swaddell to the Poultry Department's headquarters, where the clerk, Munger, tearfully informed them that he had nothing to do with his colleagues' crimes. He had not set eyes on any of them that day, because they had gone drinking in the Banqueting House, while he did all the work in his sweltering garret.

'I told you all I knew about their antics when we talked the other day,' he said to Chaloner. 'They got rich on what they did, but they were too clever to leave any evidence of their felonious antics for me to find.'

Chaloner patted his shoulder reassuringly, and asked him to take them to Catline's lodgings, where a bemused servant was there to say that his master had dashed in, grabbed his valuables, and raced out again.

'Where has he gone?' demanded Swaddell. 'To Lord Bristol?'

The servant did not know, although Chaloner thought that Bristol was unlikely to harbour Catline quite so soon after the department's spectacular fall from grace.

'I suppose we will have to forget him, then,' said Swaddell reluctantly, as he and Chaloner walked back across the Great Court together. 'Pity, because I suspect that he, not Crookey, was the real power behind their department's crimes. Now he will slither away to France, while his cronies pay the price for his machinations.'

'I do not think he will run,' said Chaloner. 'He is no Crookey, ready to give up at the first hurdle. He will still be here. Moreover, do not forget that it was Catline who changed the date of the Adrian Masque when King Jesus was rumoured to be coming early.'

Swaddell frowned. 'Because his hams need to be eaten.'

'That is what he said, but palace victuallers know how and when to order food, even during heatwaves. I have a bad feeling that the masque and Thursday's trouble are somehow connected, and we need Catline to tell us how.'

'But we have no idea where to look for him.'

'Ask Williamson to find out from the prisoners,' instructed Chaloner. 'Tell him it is urgent, because the more I think about it, the more I know I am right.'

Swaddell dashed off a note, ordered a soldier to deliver it to Westminster with all possible haste, then commandeered a carriage to take him and Chaloner to Poulters' Hall.

The city wilted in the afternoon heat, and Chaloner promised himself never to complain about cold weather again. His clothes stuck to his skin, and he had constantly to blink sweat from his eyes. When they arrived, Poulters' Hall was silent and still, with none of the noisy hubbub he had seen the last time he had visited. He exchanged a glance with Swaddell, both knowing this state of affairs was ominous on a day when its freemen should have been doing business within.

They advanced cautiously. The front door was barred from the inside, so they went around to the back. There was a small garden, but the gate was latched shut, obliging them to climb over the wall. They jumped down into a yard that was blisteringly hot and carpeted in weeds. They hurried across it, glancing up at the windows as they went to see if anyone was looking out. There was not so much as a flicker of movement at any of them.

The rear door was also secured, but Chaloner was able to pick the lock. When it swung open, they peered into a kitchen that stank of wood smoke and old grease. The cooking fire was dead and the ashes cold.

They crept towards the main hall, listening intently for any indication that someone else was in the building. It was as silent as the grave, and the hall and its ante-chambers were deserted. They climbed the stairs, where the Company's officers worked, but no one was there either.

'This is not right,' whispered Swaddell. 'These places are never empty, especially during the week, and it is not so late in the day that everyone can have gone home.'

Chaloner led the way to the basement – the so-called pantry – where he had first met Elsie and Dorcas, and where Hadie's body had been stored until its burial. The place reeked of chicken manure, so strongly that Chaloner felt his gorge rise.

'Master Farmer!' exclaimed Swaddell, hurrying towards the bound, gagged and terrified man who lay on the floor.

'And Beadle Collins,' said Chaloner, bending to examine the insensible old man, and glad when he detected a life-beat in his neck. 'Someone has hit him over the head.'

'What is happening?' croaked Farmer, the moment Swaddell removed the rag from his mouth so he could speak. 'Why did he assault us?'

'Who did?' asked Chaloner urgently.

'Drinkell, of course,' hissed Farmer, as if the answer were obvious. 'Collins discovered that he had been doing sly business with White Hall. The two of them quarrelled, and Drinkell walloped Collins with a jug.'

'Did he wallop you, too?' asked Swaddell solicitously.

Farmer looked sheepish. 'He made me sit still while he tied me up. I would have fought back, but . . . well, he looked dangerous, so I wisely opted to comply.'

'Start from the beginning,' ordered Swaddell. 'How did Collins find out what Drinkell had done?'

'He has friends – servants – at White Hall, and one confided how the Poultry Department is working on a plan to force up the price of eggs.'

'Crookey told us that was devised by poulters,' said Chaloner.

'But not me,' squeaked Farmer. 'I admit that Crookey made me give him Company eggs for free, but I would *never* have agreed to manipulate the market. To be frank, I am not formidable enough to bring it about. Drinkell is, though, and I know Crookey and Catline always turned to him when I failed to meet their expectations.'

'So whose idea was it? Drinkell's, Catline's or Crookey's?'

Farmer looked frightened. 'Drinkell's. Oh, Lord! Now the three of them will kill me for betraying them, just like they promised.'

'Crookey will not,' averred Swaddell. 'He is in gaol, and Drinkell will soon join him there. What else did Collins find out?'

'That Drinkell has convinced all the large and medium farms to withhold their eggs until Thursday, when they will be sold to celebrate the Second Coming at a greatly inflated price. And they have done it! Just look around you. I have never seen this place so full.'

Chaloner peered deeper into the pantry and saw thousands of eggs in crates and trays, stretching as far as the eye could see. Drinkell and his associates had obviously been stockpiling them for days. Unfortunately, none had been washed, which explained the reek.

'So the heat has not put hens off their lay after all,' he said, turning back to Farmer. 'That was a lie invented by greedy producers to explain the sudden shortage.'

Farmer nodded. 'And everyone believed it.'

'But you must have noticed what was happening,' said Swaddell, and gestured around him. 'They cannot have put all these boxes down here in secret.'

'Well, they did,' said Farmer shortly. 'When the supplies dried up and the pantry was no longer needed for sorting, Drinkell ordered it locked. That was on Friday – the day after you first visited, Chaloner.'

Gradually, Chaloner began to understand what had happened. 'So the farmers withheld their stocks, but they reckoned without the higglers. There were more of these anyway, thanks to the agitators, but the paucity of legal supplies encouraged hordes more to try their luck. No wonder you were so keen to crush them! They undermined your plans.'

'Not *my* plans,' objected Farmer. 'Drinkell's – him and his friends at White Hall.'

Chaloner was not listening. 'Hadie worked out what was happening, and confided in his friend Bowles. Both were murdered to prevent them from telling anyone else, and so was Hill. Then the killer turned his attention to the higglers themselves. A number of them are dead, all stabbed with a stiletto.'

Farmer was horrified. 'Dear God! What has Drinkell done?'

At that point, Collins began to regain his senses, so Chaloner and Swaddell helped him up the stairs to sit in the hall. Farmer fetched him some wine, although he took a healthy swig himself before handing the rest to his beadle. As soon as Collins was able to speak, Chaloner plied him with questions. Unfortunately, the old man had little more to add, other than the fact that Farmer was innocent of everything except weakness and ineptitude.

'Does this mean that Drinkell is our killer?' asked Swaddell of Chaloner.

'Him or Catline,' replied Chaloner. 'Perhaps with Blackborne's connivance, as I still do not trust his role in this affair.'

'Drinkell and his friends will put their eggs on sale tomorrow – the eve of the Second Coming,' Collins was saying. 'People will pay anything for them then, not just because they are rare, but because they are symbolic of new beginnings.'

'Then I hope someone removes all the bad ones first,' said Chaloner, sure from the stench that a lot had turned. 'Or they will make people ill, as the Buttery men learned to their cost.'

'The ones sold will be perfectly safe,' said Farmer. 'We know what we are doing.'

Chaloner supposed he had to believe that was true. 'Where is Drinkell now?'

'At his farm, I imagine,' replied Collins, 'making sure Newdick collects every egg that has been laid, so as to maximise tomorrow's profits.'

'Blackborne is involved in this, too,' said Chaloner, and regarded Farmer rather accusingly. 'Yet another Company member.'

Farmer blinked. 'But Blackborne does not know the first thing about the egg business. He joined because he applauds our charitable work.'

'He is a Fifth Monarchist,' said Swaddell.

'So what?' asked Farmer. 'I am an Anabaptist and Collins is a Papist. A man's religion has nothing to do with what our Company does.'

'Could Drinkell be a Fifth Monarchist?' asked Swaddell.

'I sincerely doubt it,' replied Collins acidly. 'If he worships anything, it is mammon.'

'Has Blackborne been here recently?' asked Chaloner, speaking quickly because he was becoming aware again that time was fast running out. 'To visit Drinkell, perhaps?'

'Yes, he came about a week ago,' replied Collins. 'I remember, because he and Drinkell seemed an ill-matched pair for such a lengthy conversation – they chatted for hours.'

'But did he come today?' pressed Chaloner urgently. 'His nephew said he had a meeting here this afternoon.'

'I never saw him,' replied Farmer. 'Did you, Collins?'

The beadle shook his head. 'But I can tell you where he lives if you like.'

Chaloner turned to Swaddell. 'We will go there first, but I suspect we will find him with Drinkell at the farm.

We need to go to Willesden as soon as you can muster troops.'

Swaddell glanced at the window to see the sun was setting. 'If we want to catch these villains red-handed, we need to do it in daylight – to see *all* of them and observe *exactly* what they are up to. We will travel there tonight, but we will tackle them at dawn.'

Chaloner knew Swaddell was right, and that if they were to avoid Drinkell and his cronies – all the large producers and most of the medium ones, according to Crookey – slipping through their fingers under cover of darkness, it would be sensible to wait until the following morning. That did not mean he was happy about it, though, and he worried all the way to Blackborne's Pudding Lane house.

As they hurried along, he noticed that the streets were oddly empty for that time of day, and wondered if people were staying away from the taverns lest King Jesus really did appear on Thursday and had something to say about people who drank too much. Those folk who were out were unusually well behaved.

'Let us hope we can nip any mischief in the bud at Drinkell's farm,' he said, panting from the sharp pace he was setting. 'Although I still think we should go there now.'

'You were nearly killed at White Hall by rushing ahead without taking basic precautions,' said Swaddell curtly. 'Do not make the same mistake twice. I do not have so many friends that I can afford to lose one to stupidity.'

Blackborne's house was grand, suggesting that he had earned a fortune from running the navy for Cromwell. It was in darkness, so Chaloner picked the lock on the front door, while Swaddell shielded what he was doing by standing behind him. When it was open, the two of them slipped inside.

'It stinks in here,' muttered Swaddell, fumbling in his pocket for a candle.

'Bad eggs,' whispered Chaloner, more certain than ever that Blackborne was involved in Catline and Drinkell's scheme, especially when Swaddell's flickering candle revealed a number of eggs on the table. Some had been broken into dishes for examination, although Chaloner could make no sense of the scribbled notes piled by the side of them.

They searched the house quickly, but there was no sign of its owner. All they found was a letter from Drinkell, asking Blackborne to visit Poulters' Hall that afternoon.

'But Blackborne did not go,' said Swaddell. 'If he had, Collins and Farmer would have noticed him.'

'Not necessarily – it is a big place. Moreover, he and Drinkell would not have wanted to be seen together if they were up to no good. And now we *must* organise the raid on the farm, because they will all be there – Drinkell, Blackborne, Catline, the corrupt poulters, *and* the Fifth Monarchists who are using it as a safe house. You mark my words.'

Chaloner was in an agony of tension as he and Swaddell ran to New Palace Yard, where every window in Williamson's building blazed with light. They entered to see clerks hard at work transcribing rough notes from the prisoners' interrogations into written confessions. There was an air of fevered industry.

'This is a good sign,' said Swaddell. 'It means the villains have decided to cooperate. They will implicate Bristol, and we shall save your Earl yet.'

365

Chaloner hoped he was right. He followed Swaddell to the Spymaster's office, where Williamson sat behind his desk, a lantern casting eerie shadows on his sallow face. He glared at Swaddell and Chaloner as they walked in.

'I suppose you want my thanks for exposing dishonest dealings at the heart of White Hall,' he said curtly. 'But the truth is that you have created a lot of inconvenient waves. The Poultry Department men were doing no real harm, and arresting them all has annoyed some very important people.'

'They *were* doing harm,' countered Chaloner angrily. 'They were effectively stealing from the public purse, they poisoned everyone in another department, and some of them are likely involved in even more serious crimes.'

'You mean Catline,' said Williamson coldly, 'whom you allowed to escape. And that is highly unfortunate, because the others tell me that he was the ringleader. You netted the minnows, but let the pike swim away.'

'Did you ask the minnows where Catline might have gone?' asked Swaddell.

'Of course – they all think he is with Bristol. However, he is not, because I searched Bristol's house myself. Catline is not there, and neither Bristol nor his household knows where else he might be.'

Chaloner chafed and fidgeted impatiently as Swaddell provided his employer with a detailed account of all that had happened since he had last reported to him.

'You are right about Catline and the Fifth Monarchists,' said Williamson when Swaddell had finished. 'The prisoners confirm that he has indeed arranged the Adrian Masque to coincide with Thursday's mischief – whatever that might be. They say they do not know details of the scheme, and I am satisfied that they are telling the truth.'

'So now we have the proof we need to challenge the instigators of all this chaos,' said Chaloner to Swaddell. 'We must go to Drinkell's farm *now*, and stop them before this plot swings into action. Dawn may be too late.'

Williamson glanced at the hour candle. 'It will take me a couple of hours to reassemble the men – I sent them all home after the White Hall arrests, not imagining you would need them again so soon. You two go ahead, and I will follow as soon as I can.'

'That is not a good idea,' objected Swaddell, alarmed. 'At the last count, there were two hundred Fifth Monarchists in London. What if they have all gone to Willesden? And if Tom is right, and all the rogue poulters have joined them there . . . '

'Obviously, I do not expect you to start tackling them by yourselves,' said Williamson impatiently. 'But you can watch them and assess the situation, so we will know how best to act when I arrive. Do not glower at me, Chaloner. We would have arrested these damned fanatics already if you had not wasted precious time hounding dishonest courtiers.'

'But we did it on your orders!' Chaloner flashed back, beginning to lose his temper.

'I asked you to help Montagu, not depose an entire palace department,' snarled Williamson. 'But before you leave for Willesden, check Poulters' Hall again. It would be embarrassing to race off into the countryside if all our villains are hiding here instead.'

Chaloner thought it would be yet more wasted time, but Swaddell disagreed, and the coach driver listened to him. They arrived to find that Farmer and Beadle Collins had summoned every Company member they thought would be loyal to them, and were busily telling them

367

what Drinkell had done. Elsie and Dorcas were among them, Lester a faithful shadow at their heels.

'All these folk hail from the little farms,' Lester told Chaloner. 'Or else they joined the Company to support its charitable work. Elsie tells me that every large and medium-sized concern has been seduced by Drinkell on the promise of fabulous profits. She thinks such cooperation between them is a necessary precondition for Drinkell's plan to work.'

'Drinkell is a criminal,' declared Collins, overhearing. 'He will never be elected Master now – and I shall never be replaced as beadle.'

While they were talking, Chaloner penned a note to Thurloe, feeling he needed to be kept abreast of the situation, too. He asked Thurloe to go to Westminster immediately, and urge Williamson to hurry, because he had the uncomfortable sense that the Spymaster was not viewing the matter as urgently as he should.

'You do not trust Williamson?' asked Swaddell, reading over his shoulder.

'He was not particularly enthusiastic about our plan,' replied Chaloner. 'And he may decide his men are better deployed in the city, ready to quell any trouble arising from all these rumours about the Second Coming. Now I need an honest poulter to deliver—'

'I will take it,' said Elsie, holding out her hand. 'And Dorcas and Salathiel will go with you to Drinkell's farm. She knows it better than I do.'

'I would rather stay with you, my love,' said Lester, at once.

Elsie smiled. 'Help your friend, Salathiel. I will join you there as soon as I can.'

368

Chapter 15

During the journey to Drinkell's farm, Swaddell told Lester and Dorcas about the confrontation in White Hall, while Chaloner fretted that they might never arrive – the carriage was travelling so slowly that he felt he could walk faster. The problem was that the driver and his horses could not see. The track was pitch black, because dust from the city had risen to obscure the stars, and there was no moon to light their way. Moreover, it was swelteringly hot and airless, which made the coach an unpleasant place to be.

'I wish Elsie had not offered to deliver your letter,' said Lester unhappily. 'I do not like the thought of her out alone in the middle of the night.'

Chaloner wished it, too. He wondered if there had been something peculiar about her eagerness to oblige, and he began to worry that she and Dorcas were among those who aimed to make a fortune with Drinkell. The two of them claimed to have witnessed Hadie's murder, but what if they had actually been there to *help* the killer? Dorcas had told him what Alice the prostitute had seen, but had refused to let him speak to her himself. Who was to say Alice had not been invented to lead him astray? His concerns were exacerbated by the fact that Dorcas seemed oddly unconcerned about what they were preparing to do, whereas he and Swaddell were as taut as bowstrings.

'Perhaps you should get out here and wait for Williamson,' he told her, and tried to see her face, to judge for himself how his suggestion was received, but the inside of the coach was too dark.

'That would not be the best use of my services,' came the calm reply. 'Incidentally, did you know that Lady Montagu bequeathed some money to our Company in her will?'

Chaloner was wrong-footed by the abrupt change of subject. 'What . . . I do not . . . '

'She wanted it to be used to benefit poulters and hens alike,' Dorcas went on. 'Unfortunately, her husband says it has been stolen.'

'First by her groom and then by a Fifth Monarchist with gambling debts,' said Chaloner flatly. 'I doubt poulters *or* their birds will ever see any of it.'

After what felt like an age, Dorcas knocked on the ceiling to tell the driver to stop. They were perhaps half a mile from the farm, and she suggested walking the rest of the way, so as not to alert Drinkell to their presence. Then she led Swaddell, Lester and Chaloner off the road to a footpath that was barely visible in the gloom, although the night was lighter than it had been. The short summer night was almost over.

'How do you know about this track?' demanded Chaloner, eyes narrowed. 'You have only visited Drinkell's domain once – with us – and you cannot possibly have

370

spotted the path out of the coach window when we were all squashed inside together.'

'I came back the following day,' she replied smoothly. 'I have a professional interest in such places, and I felt Newdick's tour was too brief.'

'We do not need you to lead us there, Dorcas,' whispered Lester, wrinkling his nose as a hot breeze wafted an eye-watering aroma towards them. 'We can just follow the stench.'

'Hens only smell if their keepers practise poor hygiene,' retorted Dorcas. 'Mine do not stink, and nor do yours, Thomas. Salathiel took me to see them.'

Chaloner was uncomfortable with the notion of her in his home, but he held his tongue, as there was nothing to be gained by putting her on her guard. However, he would watch everything she did very closely, and if she made one hostile move, he would incapacitate her until the crisis was over. He followed her along the path, treading lightly, although he need not have bothered with stealth, given that Lester crashed along like an ox behind him.

Dorcas was wrong about it being only a short walk, and it was almost completely light by the time they reached the perimeter fence, which meant that surveying the farm under cover of darkness was no longer an option. Chaloner's anxiety intensified. Had she taken them on a more tortuous route deliberately, aiming to thwart them by stealing the advantage night conferred? Or had they just started the journey too late?

She was all for scrambling over the fence at once, but Chaloner insisted on watching the farm for a few minutes first, hiding behind a leafy tree.

The compound was devoid of people, although a

terrific racket emanated from the sheds as the chickens woke and began to call for their breakfast. He was puzzled: dawn was usually hectic for poulters, and Newdick and his staff should have been busy filling feed bins, mucking out soiled bedding and collecting eggs before they became fouled. Or was the place run with a bare minimum of staff, so as to maximise profits? Or, more likely, had the labourers been dismissed to prevent them from seeing what Drinkell was up to?

Chaloner led the way over the fence, where a quick search revealed that all the outbuildings were deserted, although a large number of wagons stood piled high with crates, and horses were tethered nearby ready to be backed into the traces. He opened a crate at random. Droppings adhered to most of the eggs within, and a glance at the sky told him that they would soon be in the full glare of the sun, which was no way to treat food that spoiled.

'I have never seen so many eggs,' Dorcas breathed, lifting the corner of a tarpaulin from what Chaloner had assumed were bales of straw, but which transpired to be even more ready-packed boxes. 'There must be tens of thousands of them, and as Drinkell only has three thousand birds, many of which are currently off their lay, some must be weeks old.'

And Drinkell planned to sell the lot at an inflated price, making himself a fortune, thought Chaloner, stunned by the scale of the operation. He was no expert in high finance, but he did know that people would pay a premium for a short period of time, after which there would be a glut, and prices would fall. Small concerns would likely be ruined, leaving the way clear for the larger farms to sell their sub-standard wares without competition from those providing goods of higher quality.

'I expected this place to be teeming with rebels,' said Swaddell, looking at Chaloner accusingly. 'Not to mention Drinkell, Blackborne and perhaps Catline. But no one is here. Your notion of the Fifth Monarchists having a "safe house" is wrong, and we are in the middle of nowhere when we should be back in the city.'

'They must be in there,' said Chaloner, nodding towards Newdick's house.

Swaddell drew a dagger. 'Then I suggest we find out, although I can tell you now that we will not discover two hundred insurgents and dozens of corrupt poulters inside – there is not enough room. We made a bad mistake by coming here.'

But Chaloner was beginning to sense that they had not. Newdick's house had all its windows boarded over, which Chaloner had originally assumed was to exclude the stench of chicken muck, but now he wondered if – like Allhallows church – it was to conceal whatever went on behind its doors.

'Wait!' he hissed, grabbing Swaddell's arm to stop him from surging forward. 'First, we are going to let the hens out.'

Swaddell regarded him askance. 'Why? Because you feel sorry for them? We do not have time for—'

'Freeing them will cause noise and confusion,' explained Chaloner tersely. 'And I have a feeling we are going to need it.'

Before the others could argue, he darted to the nearest barn and began to struggle with the gates. Lester hastened to the next one, while Dorcas ran to a third. Swaddell hovered uncertainly, not sure what to expect when thousands of chickens suddenly found themselves at liberty, and convinced that diversionary tactics were unnecessary anyway.

'They are not coming out,' he said sourly, when Chaloner returned a few minutes later. 'Yet more time wasted when we could be hurrying back to the city.'

'They will,' promised Chaloner. 'They just need to gain confidence. Look – the bolder ones are beginning to emerge already. *Now* we can go and see what is happening in the farmhouse.'

Swaddell and Lester followed him, but Dorcas insisted on staying behind to coax the rest of the birds out. Chaloner would have preferred to keep her where he could see her, but there was no time to argue, because the assassin was already flinging open the farmhouse door and striding inside, knives at the ready.

The main room was huge, comprising the whole of the ground floor, and contained nothing but a table and two chairs, which were lost in it. It should have been dark with all the windows shuttered, but several lamps hung from the rafters. Three men stood in the middle of it. Blackborne held a handgun, which was aimed at Drinkell and Newdick.

'I knew Jesus would send someone eventually,' said Blackborne, lowering the weapon in relief. 'These two rogues have been up to no good at all. Arrest them at once.'

There was a moment when no one moved, then Drinkell made a dive for the door. Chaloner stepped to block his way. Meanwhile, Newdick leapt at Blackborne, grabbing for the gun. With one smoothly flowing motion, Swaddell slid up behind the poulter and put a knife to his throat. Newdick froze in alarm, then slowly released his hold on the dag.

'Good,' said Swaddell, shoving Newdick away from him before disarming Blackborne. He tossed the pistol to Chaloner, who was startled to see it was not loaded.

'I am no killer,' said Blackborne softly, seeing his surprise. 'I only used it to keep them in line until God sent help.'

'Lester, stand outside and keep guard,' ordered Swaddell, and turned an exceptionally malevolent gaze on Blackborne, Drinkell and Newdick alike. 'Hands up, all of you, and tell us where your confederates are hiding.'

'If by "confederates" you mean my workmen,' said Drinkell, cutting across what Blackborne started to say, 'they only come every other day. It cuts costs and makes the eggs cheaper for the consumer. But I am delighted to see you! This lunatic is—'

'I guessed something unsavoury was unfolding here,' interrupted Blackborne, making a point of keeping his distance from the other two. 'Over the last few weeks, Drinkell and the other large-scale producers have stopped supplying eggs to London, causing prices to rise. They do not care that this creates hardship for the poor.'

'Why should I?' demanded Drinkell indignantly. 'I run a business, not a charity.'

Blackborne ignored him. 'He designed this farm to produce the highest number of eggs for the smallest possible expenditure. But chickens are also God's creatures, and this is *not* what He had in mind when He gave us stewardship of the Earth.'

'If God disapproved, He would not have made me so rich,' Drinkell flashed back. 'But enough of this sentimental nonsense. I am a busy man. I have—'

'Your confederates,' interrupted Swaddell sharply, as

conflicted as Chaloner regarding what to believe. 'Where are they?'

'When I arrived, Drinkell had three apprentices,' replied Blackborne. 'But he sent them to watch the road, so I took the opportunity to challenge him and Newdick.'

'You went to Deptford to make peace with your father yesterday,' said Chaloner, hopelessly confused about Blackborne's role in the affair.

Blackborne grimaced in exasperation. 'Yes, and I made a will, too – the things any man does when he knows his life will be in peril. You see, Drinkell invited me to Poulters' Hall yesterday, and I knew then that he meant to kill me. So, I came here instead, to confront him in a place where I had the advantage of surprise.'

'He is one of those mad Fifth Monarchists,' sneered Drinkell. 'Do not listen to him, Chaloner. He is insane – they all are.'

'I *am* a Fifth Monarchist,' said Blackborne with quiet dignity. 'And I long for the Kingdom of God. However, I doubt it will come tomorrow, no matter what my co-religionists believe. Something else will, though – something evil and vile.'

'What nonsense is this?' snapped Newdick. 'He is—'

'It is all to do with Drinkell's eggs,' said Blackborne, cutting across him. 'I examined some at home, and they were—'

'They are all perfectly healthy,' snapped Drinkell, so defensively that Chaloner suddenly understood exactly what was going on. 'I repeat: do not listen to him. He is a disgraced Parliamentarian, whereas I am a senior officer of the Company of Poulters. It should be obvious which of us is telling the truth.'

'It is,' said Chaloner. 'And it is not the man with crates

of dirty eggs sitting in the sun, ready to be sold to eager Londoners. As any chicken-keeper knows, unwashed eggs spoil quickly in the heat. You *want* people to become sick.'

The alarm in Drinkell's eyes betrayed his guilt. 'I do not!'

'The Buttery was a trial run,' Chaloner went on, as more became clear. 'Seventeen men were laid low with egg fever, and two died. It was a scheme devised by two regicides – Millington and Waller.'

'*What?*' whispered Swaddell, shocked. 'Steady, Tom! That is a wild leap!'

'Not really,' said Chaloner. 'Not now I have put all the pieces together. You see, Millington and Waller were famous for devising intricate plots for Downes and others to implement. They invented one using bad eggs as a weapon, but it was so "insidious" that they all vowed never to use it.'

'This is ridiculous!' cried Drinkell, although Chaloner could tell from his alarm that he had finally hit upon the truth.

'Somehow, Drinkell found out about it, and decided to deploy it here. To ensure its success, it was necessary to silence everyone who might understand what was happening: four regicides were killed in Switzerland, four more in prison, and then Downes himself.'

'You have no idea what—' objected Drinkell.

'But Downes realised what was going on before the killer came for him,' interrupted Chaloner, 'and he wrote letters telling trusted friends what was afoot. The Tower refused to deliver them, so he gave the King a chicken called Eghfeva.'

'Which sounds like egg fever,' put in Blackborne, and

smiled at Chaloner. 'You have it! I learned some of this from Drinkell himself a week ago. I got him drunk in Poulters' Hall, and we talked for hours – he revealed more than he should have done.'

'But the Tower got a pigeon instead,' Chaloner continued, watching Drinkell open his mouth to deny Blackborne's claim, although as Collins had seen the pair of them talking together, Chaloner suspected it was true. 'In desperation, Downes tried to use Eleanor Montagu to raise the alarm. We have his message to her.'

'Oh, Lord!' gulped Newdick, suddenly frightened. 'Do you? Does it name names?'

Chaloner was not about to admit that they still did not know what was in it, or that the only part Thurloe had managed to decode had said 'Robert Blackborne'.

'But to return to the Buttery,' he went on, 'the "higgler" who sold the tainted eggs to Montagu was you, Newdick. Or perhaps Drinkell. Either way, Montagu will identify the culprit and he will hang.'

'No!' cried Newdick in horror, and pointed an unsteady finger at Drinkell. 'He *told* me to do it. It was not my idea.'

'Shut up, you fool!' snarled Drinkell. 'Admit to nothing.'

'You brought me here last week to show off your farm,' said Chaloner. 'That and the subsequent invitation to the feast was not generosity – it was to keep me busy while an assassination attempt was readied.'

'You are right,' bleated Newdick, easing away from Drinkell. 'That is exactly why we stayed with you all that day – to get word about your meddling to the right people. And there *is* a plan to flood London with tainted eggs, so that when the Kingdom of God comes, no one will be in a position to fight it. I will tell you everything if you—'

He broke off when Drinkell lunged at him, although the assault faltered when Drinkell found himself at the end of Swaddell's dagger. Prudently, he backed away.

'Newdick is lying to save himself,' he said tightly. 'How can we give egg fever to everyone in London? It would be impossible.'

'Almost certainly,' agreed Chaloner. 'Although I suppose that anyone who does become ill will need care from those who do not, which will prevent a few more folk from trying to stop whatever you are planning. What is it? Another rebellion?'

'Of course not,' blustered Drinkell. 'I am a poulter, not an insurgent.'

'They aim to poison White Hall, too,' put in Blackborne. 'That is why Catline invented a recipe for syllabub that calls for a thousand egg yolks – *raw* egg yolks, which are more deadly than cooked ones. People will die – it will be mass murder.'

Drinkell tried a dismissive smile, although it emerged as a grimace. 'You exaggerate! A few people may become sick, but a day in the latrines never did anyone any harm.'

'What about a stiletto to the chest or in the ear?' demanded Chaloner. 'Will you argue that those never did any harm either?'

But he could tell from the bemused expression on Drinkell's face that the poulter had no idea what he was talking about. Blackborne understood what he was asking, though.

'Neither of this pair is clever enough to direct this terrible business, Chaloner,' he said. 'They have a paymaster. Do not ask me who, because they refuse to tell me.'

'Look, I am a wealthy man,' squeaked Drinkell, raising

his hands in alarm as Swaddell's blade pressed into his neck. 'I can give you so much money that you will never have to work again. All you have to do is walk away.'

'Who controls you, Drinkell?' demanded Chaloner, pleased when neither Swaddell nor Blackborne showed the slightest interest in the offer, much to the poulter's obvious consternation. 'The Fifth Monarchists?'

'Do you really need to ask?' came a voice from the door.

Chaloner whipped around to see Catline there, armed with a brace of pistols and with a veritable army of men at his heels. Most were junior courtiers, but there were also three apprentices – the lads Drinkell had sent to watch the road. With disgust, Chaloner realised he would have seen the boys if Dorcas had not insisted on getting out of the coach early.

'I thought you would have left the country by now,' said Swaddell, eyes glittering dangerously as he lowered the blade from Drinkell's throat. 'You should have done, if you had any sense.'

'Oh, I shall be safe enough here,' drawled Catline with a smirk. 'Especially once you are not around to cause problems.'

Chaloner cursed himself for paying so much attention to Drinkell that he had failed to notice what might be happening outside. He, Swaddell and Blackborne were disarmed and made to stand against the wall, while Drinkell and Newdick hurried forward to greet the newcomers with relief. Then Lester was dragged in, struggling between two captors.

'Sorry, Tom,' he muttered sheepishly. 'They crept up on me.'

He did not mention Dorcas, and Chaloner saw he expected her to stay hidden, to warn Williamson when he arrived. By now, though, Chaloner knew she would do no such thing. He was also aware that Elsie would never deliver his message to Thurloe, so that the chances of rescue were all but non-existent. Then his attention was caught by Newdick.

'I did *not* betray you!' he was wailing. 'It was a ruse to buy time. I never—'

Catline shot him, showing no more emotion than he would to killing a fly. Then he turned to Chaloner.

'I hoped we would meet again,' he said, even as the blast of the dag still rang in their ears. 'You and I have a score to settle.'

'Williamson is on his way as we speak,' declared Swaddell. 'You cannot—'

'Actually, he is not,' interrupted Catline smugly. 'He received a message from you explaining that the Fifth Monarchists are hiding in Clarendon House – that the Earl is the mastermind behind all this trouble.'

'Clever!' said Drinkell gushingly, although Chaloner noticed that his gaze kept straying to Newdick's body, clearly wondering what sort of men he had thrown in his lot with.

'Williamson will never fall for it,' said Swaddell dismissively. 'For a start, he knows my writing.'

'Oh, there is nothing on paper,' gloated Catline. 'I spun the tale to your wife, and she will give him the message. He will believe her, because she is such a sweet soul.'

Swaddell made a strangled sound in the back of his throat at the notion of Catline near Ursula, while Chaloner experienced a stab of despair as he realised that Williamson *had* swallowed the bait, because he should have arrived by now if he was coming. So should Thurloe, which meant that Elsie had indeed betrayed them. He glanced at Lester, wondering if he had drawn the same conclusions.

'Your plan will not work,' warned Blackborne, valiantly struggling to remain defiant. 'Half the eggs will smell so bad that no one will touch them, while most of the rest will be safe. You cannot possibly organise things so that *every* egg is toxic.'

Catline shot Drinkell an accusing look. 'You said you could.'

'I can,' blustered Drinkell, although he looked nervous. 'I have timed everything to perfection. You know I have. It is why we kept having to change the date of the Second Coming – so that the eggs would be at the stage when they will do the most damage.'

Chaloner regarded Catline with distaste. 'So while Drinkell incapacitates London, you think you will do the same at the masque.'

Catline smirked. 'Everyone will want to taste my syllabub – we have whipped up anticipation to fever pitch about the new recipe.'

'Yes,' acknowledged Chaloner. 'But now there is a warrant for your arrest, you cannot go to White Hall to make it. Montagu has taken over your duties, and as the rest of your department is in prison, there is no one left to tell him what to do.'

'You forget our clerk. Poor Munger was never part of our plan, but he knows the recipe. He will be helping Montagu as we speak, desperate to cooperate in the hope of keeping his job.'

Chaloner shook his head, amazed that Catline should

382

think such a preposterous scheme would work. 'But everyone knows the formula is yours. They also know it was you who brought the date of the masque forward to tonight, and it will quickly become obvious why. You will never get away with it.'

Catline waved a dismissive hand. 'No one at White Hall is intelligent enough to put all that together – especially once they are either dead or sick from egg fever. Then Bristol will arrange for my colleagues to be released, and we shall step in to run the country.'

Chaloner gaped at him, wondering if he was in complete control of his wits. The man was brash and confident, but his belief in such a silly scheme revealed him to be credulous and imprudent. Could such a person really convince wealthy poulters, mad Fifth Monarchists and indolent courtiers to work together? Suddenly, Chaloner was sure he could not. So, who could? Bristol, because he had bigger ambitions than merely being restored to the King's good books?

'Do you hate the King so much, then?' Swaddell was asking, as stunned as Chaloner by the man's aspirations. 'You made much of the fact that you are one of his favourites.'

'I am,' shrugged Catline. 'However, his affections are inconstant, as the Earl of Clarendon can attest. I want a more stable position, with me in a greater position of power.'

Swaddell raised his eyebrows. 'I doubt you will ever be—'

Catline aimed his second pistol and pulled the trigger. It happened so fast that the assassin had no time to flinch. Luckily, the weapon flashed in the pan.

'Pity,' muttered Drinkell sycophantically, although he

was patently unnerved by Catline's penchant for shooting people in cold blood. 'I am tired of hearing his voice.'

Catline tossed him the guns to reload. 'Never mind him – he is nothing. Listen! The others are here at last.'

There was a commotion outside, after which a dozen more men crammed themselves into the house. They were Fifth Monarchists, and Chaloner was not surprised to note they were led by Vicar Simpson. He *was* surprised to see Glasse with them, though, having assumed the greedy cleric would have taken the opportunity to vanish with Eleanor's gold. He looked hard at Simpson. Surely, such a wild and eccentric man could not be the plot's instigator? Was it Glasse, then, pretending to be venal and cowardly to ensure no one would suspect him of greater things?

'Thank God!' cried Blackborne when he saw his co-religionists. 'Terrible things are happening here, Simpson. You must tell these men to—'

'Oh, shut up,' bawled Simpson. 'You have never really been one of us – too moderate by half. We are here to help King Jesus to his throne, and we do not care how we do it.'

Chaloner's heart sank as yet more Fifth Monarchists arrived and milled around outside. There were not two hundred of them, as he and Swaddell had feared, but combined with Catline's followers, they numbered upwards of sixty, which meant that he, Swaddell, Lester and Blackborne would be able to do nothing but watch as the plot swung into action.

'You cannot do this,' said Lester hoarsely. 'It will hurt thousands of innocents.'

'And King Jesus will not condone murder,' put in

Blackborne desperately. 'Listen to me, Simpson. You know I am right.'

'Anyone who dies today will rise in glory tomorrow,' bellowed Simpson with a shrug. 'Assuming they are worthy, of course. And if they are not, well, they do not deserve to live anyway.'

'Then why bother with this plan at all?' demanded Blackborne. 'If the Kingdom of God really is at hand, you have no need to give anyone egg fever.'

'The Kingdom of God!' spat Catline. 'You are mad!'

Simpson bristled. 'King Jesus will appear at dawn tomorrow, just like Docility Gander foretold, and I shall take my rightful position in White Hall. Christ will want me close, so I can tell Him which sinners should be blasted into oblivion. You will be the first, Catline, and Drinkell will be next.'

Catline curled his lip. 'Unless you want to greet your King Jesus with a bloody great hole in your chest, you will keep your lunatic opinions to yourself.'

Simpson blanched. 'But that would damage my coat! My body will rise uncorrupted, of course, but the Bible says nothing about clothes, and I cannot meet my Lord imperfectly attired. Now, does anyone have any ale? It is hotter than the devil's cauldron outside.'

Catline regarded him warily, clearly wondering if the Fifth Monarchist was making sport of him. After a moment, he grabbed Drinkell's shoulder and hauled him to one side for an angry, low-voiced discussion. While they were busy, Chaloner tried to turn Simpson against Glasse, in the frail hope that he might be able to use any resulting discord to his own advantage.

'Did Glasse tell you what he did, Simpson?' he called. 'After murdering Wogan in cold blood, he did the same to Rye and Vernon, although Vernon lived to tell the tale.'

'Vernon is alive?' gulped Glasse in alarm.

'Yes, and he will testify to your crimes in a court of law.' Chaloner addressed Simpson again. 'Meanwhile, Wogan's body will be found buried in *your* churchyard, but it will not be Glasse who is accused of killing him. It will be you.'

'Nonsense! I am a saint – one of God's chosen,' declared Simpson grandly. 'No one will dare point fingers at me, so stop blathering and repent of your sins while you can.'

'Speaking of sins, which one of you killed Downes and his friends?' asked Chaloner. 'Not to mention Bowles, Eleanor Montagu, Hadie, Hill and a host of higglers.'

'None of us,' hollered Simpson indignantly. 'We were all together when Bowles died, Catline and Drinkell included. We were discussing which Fifth Monarchist beliefs would most appeal to Londoners.'

Yet more became clear to Chaloner. 'I wondered why so many people were willing to accept your bizarre theology. You selected the most appealing parts, but kept quiet about the rest?'

Simpson shrugged. 'It worked, especially the bit about everyone being equal. All paupers like hearing that, although it is untrue, of course. For a start, no one is equal to me.'

'We know you are one of the Pudding Lane agitators. You disguised yourself at first, and you chose your venues with care, but my landlord's servants heard you speak openly in Allhallows on Saturday.'

'Because, by then, I realised that everyone likes what I say,' blared Simpson. 'God will not allow—'

'Who was the other? Not Glasse, because he would never risk himself so.'

'It was Vernon, Tom,' said Swaddell quietly. 'An educated man whose profession grants him a natural authority. He also cares about the poor, which is why he and Wogan were friends.'

'Yes, he helped,' hollered Simpson. 'But I did it better, and God must be delighted with me. But hark! Is that the tramp of holy angels I hear outside?'

'No,' said Drinkell, breaking away from Catline to glance towards the door. 'It is the man who will make an end of you, now that your usefulness to him is over. And good riddance, you damned fanatic!'

Simpson blinked. 'But I am needed to usher in the Kingdom of God!'

'You are insane!' spat Catline. 'And I cannot tell you what a trial it has been to work with you. Thank God it is nearly over. You will go the same way as all the others who stand in our way.'

Before Simpson could reply, several sets of footsteps rattled on the ground outside. Then someone appeared in the doorway, and, for a moment, all they could see was his silhouette. Then he stepped inside the room.

'Wogan!' cried Chaloner in astonishment.

Chapter 16

For several moments, all Chaloner could do was stare at the regicide, who was flanked by Vernon on one side and Docility on the other. At their heels was a group of grim-faced mercenaries, all armed to the teeth. Catline and Drinkell greeted Wogan with wary respect, and Chaloner felt a great wave of exhaustion wash over him as he struggled to comprehend what was happening. Swaddell and Blackborne looked equally stunned, and so did the Fifth Monarchists, with the exception of Glasse. There was a hard, cruel expression on Wogan's face that Chaloner had not seen there before.

'Are the dead walking already?' breathed Simpson unsteadily. 'We must go to White Hall at once. King Jesus will—'

'Glasse did not really kill him,' said Chaloner tiredly. 'I thought at the time that Glasse's response to Wogan's questions was disproportionately violent, and I was right. Glasse "murdered" him because the pair of them were afraid you would speak out of turn – it was the quickest way to shut you up.'

'Wogan gave Glasse some pre-arranged signal,' put in

Swaddell. 'The word "enough" probably, which he spoke three times. Wogan's so-called demise left him free to work unfettered. It also served to prevent us from viewing him as a potential suspect.'

'Yes, you are quite right,' said Wogan briskly. 'When I offered Thurloe my assistance, it was to find out what *he* knew about my plans, not to demean myself by acting as your helpmeet.'

'Wogan was appalled when you forced him to go with you to interrogate me,' said Glasse smugly. 'And so was I at first– there was a terrible moment when I thought he had changed sides.'

'No chance of that,' said Wogan tersely, and turned to the Fifth Monarchists. 'Lay down your weapons and stand by the wall with the others who are a thorn in my side.'

'Wait a moment now,' objected Simpson indignantly. 'We are all working together to usher in the Kingdom of—'

'We used you,' interrupted Catline harshly. 'Do you not understand that yet, fool? We took what we wanted and now you are superfluous to requirements.'

'He is right,' said Wogan dispassionately, as the Fifth Monarchists exchanged glances of incomprehension and dismay. 'Your role in the affair is over, so stand by the wall or I shall shoot you where you stand.'

He looked so deadly that Chaloner wondered why he had ever considered the possibility that the man was capable of remorse. He had a sudden, vivid memory of regicides in his uncle's house, listening to Wogan arguing a point with fierce and uncompromising passion. Such men did not change, and he experienced a surge of anger against Thurloe – he had always trusted the

389

ex-Spymaster's judgement, but it had been horribly wrong this time.

When the bewildered Fifth Monarchists had been disarmed and prodded into a line, Wogan turned to Vernon. 'Go and make sure no one else is skulking about.'

The physician beamed his delight. 'Of course, dear friend. And I must say it again: I cannot tell you how glad I am that Glasse did not kill you.'

'But he very nearly killed you,' said Chaloner, aiming to cause dissent again.

Vernon waved a dismissive hand. 'All forgotten and forgiven now that we are within sight of our mutual goal.' He smiled at Wogan again. 'I am so full of joy that—'

'Yes, yes,' interrupted Wogan irritably. 'I know – you have brayed it at least a dozen times already. Now go and do what you are told.'

With an uncharacteristic bounce in his step, Vernon hurried out, taking two of the mercenaries with him. Chaloner wondered how the physician could be so effusive in his affection when it was painfully apparent that it was not reciprocated. When Vernon had gone, Wogan glowered at Chaloner.

'How could you and Thurloe think I would abandon my beliefs? I am a man of principle. I do not blow in the wind, and it is insulting that you thought me a weakling, blubbing about repentance and redemption.'

Chaloner looked at Wogan, aware that everything about him had changed – his clothes were finer and neater, he stood taller and more defiant, and his eyes blazed as madly as any of the Fifth Monarchists'. Chaloner had never seen a man so completely transformed. Then his eye lit on the weapon tucked into Wogan's belt. It was a stiletto.

'A man of principle?' he asked contemptuously. 'You murdered nine of your fellow regicides, Eleanor Montagu, Hadie, Hill and God knows how many higglers – including Bibie, your own landlord.'

Wogan shrugged. 'It was necessary. I regret none of them.'

'Hadie,' said Swaddell suddenly. 'Glasse mentioned that Hadie once helped you to serve the paupers' broth – he was so impressed by your charity that he left everything he owned to you in his will. I suppose he recognised you as he died and—'

'He did,' interrupted Wogan shortly. 'And then claimed to have outlined all my plans in a letter to a trusted friend. Well, even if he did, it is too late to make a difference now.'

'You think you are a talented assassin,' taunted Swaddell. 'But you allow your temper to guide you. Rage led you to smash all the eggs in Bowles' shop – and you did the same in Enfield when you killed Norton – but it was a mistake, because it made us realise that their deaths were unnatural.'

Wogan declined to answer, and instead rolled up his sleeves in readiness for getting down to business. One forearm bore a distinctively shaped bruise – one that had been made with the flat of a sword. Chaloner nodded to it.

'You attacked Lester and me in Pudding Lane, but we drove you off with ease. You scuttled away and were too cowardly to try again.'

Wogan regarded him with dislike. 'I did not "scuttle". I made a tactical withdrawal because I was outnumbered. But you will not escape this time.'

'Your murder spree began with the need for secrecy,'

said Chaloner in distaste. 'You dispatched the regicides to make sure none of them raised the alarm when the plot swung into action, and you even decided Eleanor Montagu was a risk.'

'She was,' retorted Wogan. 'I knew Downes had guessed what was afoot when his guards described how he had suddenly started to write letters. And when I heard he had sent that woman a book . . . well, she had to go. Rye told me how to get at her.'

'You were never part of Downes' cabal,' said Swaddell, 'so how did you find out what Millington and Waller had devised?'

'He heard it from the four who lived in Switzerland,' said Chaloner, when Wogan made no reply. 'He told me himself that he had been to Vevey.'

He had mentioned going to Jersey, too, where Millington and Waller had been incarcerated. Chaloner was disgusted with himself for not making the connections sooner.

Wogan gave a small smile. 'The idea was brilliant, and I knew the moment I heard it that I had to put it into action. And I shall – today.'

'You were brave to accompany me to the Tower,' said Chaloner, thinking the audacity of it beggared belief. 'The place where you murdered Downes. What if someone had recognised you as "Father Tyme"?'

'I was disguised both times, so the risk was small,' replied Wogan dismissively. 'I was far more concerned that Downes might have left something in his cell to give me away.'

'Afterwards, you said that the guards admitted to letting others in to visit Downes, besides Father Tyme and Eleanor Montagu. That was a lie, to muddy the waters.'

'And you believed it, just like you believed me when I said the Fifth Monarchists were no rebels – your interest in them was growing tiresome, so I had to nip it in the bud.'

'You did tell us that,' acknowledged Chaloner. 'But it did not stop us from—'

'And Thurloe was just as credulous,' Wogan interrupted disdainfully. 'He happily trusted the reports I sent to convince him that I was a changed man. He forwarded them to Williamson, who accepted them, too.'

'Because the information in them was accurate,' objected Swaddell. 'They allowed us to arrest a number of radicals who represented a serious threat.'

'That was you?' asked Simpson in an uncharacteristically small voice. 'Some good people were executed as a result of those raids.'

'A necessary sacrifice,' said Wogan shortly. 'It is a pity, though, that Thurloe's spies told him that I was in the city in the first place, because the effort of deceiving him has been a strain.'

'You should have watched me more closely in the Tower,' said Chaloner, unwilling to let him think he had won on every count. 'Because I *did* find something in Downes' cell. There was a message in that secret hiding place by the—'

'Liar!' snarled Wogan. 'You found nothing – I was watching.'

'It described your plot and all it entails. It will never work, so give up while—'

Wogan gave a sharp bark of disbelieving laughter. 'We all would have been arrested by now if that were true. No, the truth is that you have reasoned everything out far too late. Nothing can stop me now. And do not expect rescue, because none will be coming.'

'He is right, you know,' murmured Swaddell, as the regicide strode away. 'It—'

'No talking,' snapped Glasse, brandishing a pistol. 'The first man who speaks will be shot. And so will the second and the third.'

Chaloner could see he meant it.

There was nothing Chaloner and the others could do as long as Glasse and a number of hard-eyed mercenaries held them at gunpoint. Defiantly, one of the Fifth Monarchists began to chant a psalm, but his friends thought better of joining in when he was shot after the first verse. Outside, Wogan issued order after order to his men, and Chaloner could hear the egg-laden carts begin to leave for the city. Inside the crowded farmhouse, the heat began to build, and everyone sweated uncomfortably, guards as well as prisoners.

Suddenly, Drinkell gave a dismayed shout, and through the open door Chaloner saw that a lot more hens had finally ventured into the open. Hundreds were on the loose and they were getting in the conspirators' way. Drinkell rushed out, and frantically began trying to herd them back inside their barns, but the task was impossible.

After a while, Wogan returned to the house, accompanied by Glasse, Catline, Docility and a red-faced, frustrated Drinkell. Glasse smirked at the Fifth Monarchists, making Simpson seethe with impotent rage, while Catline reserved his gloating for Chaloner and Swaddell. Neither gave him the satisfaction of acknowledging it.

'You did not know that Wogan was a murderer when you first agreed to work with him,' said Chaloner to

394

Glasse. 'I saw your shock when you realised he was the one who had dispatched his fellow regicides.'

'No one cares about regicides any more,' said Glasse dismissively, then glanced uneasily at Wogan. 'Present company excepted, of course.'

'Two plots, one purpose,' mused Swaddell. 'One involving Drinkell, Catline and eggs; the other using the Fifth Monarchists to foment unrest and uncertainty.'

'The radicals' part is finished,' said Drinkell, glancing at them with dislike. 'So we summoned them here for disposal. We cannot have them getting in the way later.'

Wogan was looking at Chaloner. 'Your uncle illustrated how heavenly portents can be used to good effect, so Docility provided some for me. All were designed to add credence to the Fifth Monarchists' vision of the future.'

She laughed. 'It was fun playing the role of mystic. I can scarcely credit how readily folk believed me. Flying dragons and talking swans indeed!'

Blackborne glared accusingly at Wogan. 'And the Fifth Monarchists' remit was to spread word about an imminent Second Coming, so that everyone will put any disturbances down to that, rather than the start of whatever regime you want to impose on us.'

'Precisely,' said Wogan. 'Although most will not care at first, because they will be too sick with egg fever. By the time they do, I will have reinstalled a republic and things will revert to how they were in Cromwell's day, only better. No one likes this debauched King, so he can go the same way as his father.'

'He can,' agreed Drinkell, although his attention was outside, on the hordes of hungrily milling hens. 'And no one in the city will be in a position to stop us.'

'No one at White Hall either,' put in Catline.

'This will never work,' warned Blackborne. 'It relies on massive numbers of people falling ill, but you over-estimate what tainted eggs can do. I conducted experiments at home, you see – spoiled eggs *can* lay a man low, but it is very time-specific. Only a fraction of yours will do what you hope.'

'He is lying,' said Drinkell, when Wogan glared accusingly at him. 'I am the expert here, not him. The eggs *will* do exactly what I have promised.'

'I shall enjoy watching White Hall suffer,' said Catline, and grinned at Chaloner. 'I have arranged for some syllabub to be sent to Clarendon House, so do not think your Earl will escape unscathed.'

'If you show your face at the palace, you will be arrested,' Chaloner pointed out. 'So you will not be "watching" anything.'

Catline laughed tauntingly. 'The masque requires everyone to be in fancy dress, so I shall be safely disguised. No one will recognise me until it no longer matters.'

'Go,' Wogan told him. 'It is time you were in position. You, too, Drinkell.'

'But my birds,' objected Drinkell. 'I cannot leave them out. They will lay their eggs all over the place and I will lose money by—'

'*I said go!*' snarled Wogan, so fiercely that Drinkell flinched in alarm. 'And remember that I do not tolerate failure. If you disappoint me, I will kill you.'

Drinkell and Catline disappeared quickly, both clearly unsettled by the threat. Moments later came the clatter of wheels as a carriage bore them back to the city. Chaloner felt his stomach churn. How could he stop the madness when he was a prisoner? And even if Blackborne was right, and only a few people fell victim to egg fever, he had not forgotten that two of the Buttery men had died from it.

'You have perhaps eighty mercenaries, courtiers and poulters here,' said Swaddell. 'Not nearly enough to subdue London, even if half the city and all of White Hall is suffering from egg fever. You are—'

'Two friends will join us today, and good Parliamentarians will flock to support them like flies to honey,' said Wogan smugly. 'We will not be only eighty for long.'

'Ludlow and Love,' surmised Chaloner, remembering how worried Thurloe had been to learn they were at large.

Wogan inclined his head.

'This scheme has been doomed from the start,' said Swaddell, regarding the regicide contemptuously. 'You did not anticipate the sudden increase in higglers when the poulters started withholding their stocks, which meant that eggs were not as scarce as you expected them to be.'

'I have dispatched the worst offenders,' said Wogan. 'And when I find the rogues who encouraged them to ply their trade, I shall kill them, too.'

'One was Vernon,' said Swaddell, eyes glittering vengefully. 'He really does care about the poor, which is why he gives them free medical care. It suggests you never confided your real plans to him, because if you had, he would not have gone out agitating.'

He did not say the other culprit was Simpson, who gave a discreet sigh of relief.

'I do not believe you,' said Wogan, although Chaloner could see the uncertainty in his eyes. 'Glasse – take them outside.'

'Shall I shoot them?' asked the vicar eagerly.

397

'They are too many, and we cannot risk an escape. I have something else in mind.'

Chaloner and the others were herded into one of the now-empty barns. The previous occupants were everywhere outside, pecking, flapping and generally getting underfoot. He was gratified to see they hampered everything Wogan's men were trying to do.

Once the prisoners were inside, Wogan closed the door and a heavy bar thumped into place to secure it. Chaloner peered through a crack in one wall, and saw the mercenaries begin to pile kindling against the walls, while Glasse stood by with a flaming torch.

He yelled a warning to the others, then embarked on a desperate hunt for another way out. There was none, and he was sure the place would ignite quickly, because not only was it tinder-dry after so many hot days, but it was full of combustible materials like straw, manure and feathers. Meanwhile, Simpson was bellowing through the door.

'Vernon! I see you out there. Will you let this lunatic burn us alive? We are your friends! You and I encouraged the higglers together in the interests of fairness and . . . ' He trailed off, suddenly aware that this was something he should not have mentioned.

'You will not be harmed,' Vernon called back, although even from a distance, Chaloner could see he was bewildered by the turn of events. 'Wogan has promised—'

'It *was* you?' demanded Wogan, shocked. 'I thought they were lying.'

'Of course it was me,' said Vernon, frowning. 'Who did you think it was? You and I are fellow champions of the downtrodden and poor, and encouraging Londoners to rebel against wealthy companies is right and just. You are a charitable man who—'

'I was "charitable" because it was the only way I could stay in London without being arrested,' snarled Wogan, exasperated and angry. 'Do you really think I care about paupers and beggars? It *pained* me to have to feed them, and I am glad the money came from you and not from me – I found the hoard in your cellar.'

Vernon gaped at him, while Chaloner recalled Simpson mentioning such a cache after Bowles' funeral in Allhallows. 'You stole my savings? But—'

There was a sharp crack as a gun was fired, followed by the sound of a falling body. Simpson howled his dismay, which was a mistake, because it revealed where he was standing. A second shot rang out, a bullet punched through the door, and the Fifth Monarchist crumpled. His fellows screamed and scattered in all directions.

'I said I would kill the agitators, and now I have,' said Wogan in satisfaction. 'Glasse – light the fire.'

Fortunately for the prisoners, the barn was harder to ignite than anyone had anticipated. The kindling went up in an impressive blaze, but far too fast to catch the building itself, which, although as dry as a bone, was constructed of old, very sturdy timber. Furious, Wogan ordered his minions to bring more straw from a nearby compost heap, but it was filthy and heavily impregnated with stinking manure, so neither the mercenaries nor Catline's courtiers appreciated being told to tote it around. They obliged, but so slowly and fastidiously that scant progress was made.

Meanwhile, the freed hens were causing havoc, and everything was taking longer than it should. Wogan grew increasingly frustrated, screaming commands at the mercenaries, who transpired to be ill-disciplined and lazy, and the courtiers, who had been more obedient when Catline had been there to keep them in line. He was losing control of the situation, and he knew it.

Inside the barn was pandemonium. There were no flames, but smoke billowed thickly, making the air difficult to breathe. Some Fifth Monarchists were trying to kick down the door, while others prayed in loud, insistent voices. More practically, Swaddell, Blackborne and Lester were working their way along the walls, methodically testing each board for weaknesses.

Chaloner opted to investigate the ceiling. He upended a long perch and used it to climb up to the rafters. To his relief, the roof was poorly made – Drinkell had cut costs there, too – allowing him to punch a hole through it. He scrambled out and lay flat, half expecting to be shot at, but no one was looking at the roof – a few mercenaries guarded the door, ready to gun down anyone who burst through it, while the rest were collecting straw.

'This way,' he hissed to the others. 'Quickly!'

He hauled Swaddell and Lester up beside him, and left Blackborne to organise the Fifth Monarchists. He slid down the far side of the roof and landed lightly, before darting for cover, scattering hens as he went. Swaddell and Lester were hot on his heels.

At that moment, there was a yell from Glasse, who had spotted prisoners scrambling across the roof. Wogan bellowed an order, and the mercenaries began shooting at them. Blackborne did not flinch, but several of the others dropped back inside the barn, while the rest froze in terror.

'We cannot watch them being picked off!' breathed

Lester, as one radical toppled from the roof with a sharp cry of pain. 'We have to help them. But how?'

'By smashing the eggs on the remaining wagons,' determined Swaddell. 'Wogan will order his men to stop us, which will give at least some of the fanatics time to get away.'

'Go!' ordered Chaloner. 'I have another idea.'

Swaddell and Lester ran for the carts, while Chaloner made for the huge grain silo. A large handle acted like a tap, so he opened it as far as it would turn and stood back as feed began to gush out like water. Starving hens immediately started to flow in from all directions, and he saw two mercenaries stumble as they fought to keep their balance in the feathery tide. Meanwhile, Wogan had spotted Swaddell and Lester by the carts.

'Those are just a fraction of the thousands that will be sold today,' he jeered. 'You cannot stop what I have started, so give up and die like men.'

'Gold!' bellowed Blackborne, who had found a place on the roof where he was safe from musket balls. 'Eleanor Montagu's treasure. Glasse was going to keep it for himself, but I have it here.'

'You do not!' cried Glasse angrily. 'I put it somewhere safe.'

'Did you?' demanded Wogan, eyes narrowed. 'When were you going to tell me about it? I have itched to lay my hands on that ever since I learned it was under her pillow. It was my second mistake, the first being to put a book on her chest to make her death look natural. I did not realise I had grabbed Downes' peculiar ramblings.'

'Who wants some?' yelled Blackborne. 'Come on! You could be rich.'

The mercenaries exchanged hesitant glances, and their

inattention allowed several Fifth Monarchists to slither down the back of the barn and run to safety. Then there was a metallic tinkle and a coin landed nearby. It was closely followed by another.

'Wogan will kill you once your usefulness to him has ended,' Blackborne shouted. 'So take the gold and leave while you can.'

Livid, Wogan blasted wildly at the roof with his pistols. 'Keep firing, damn you!' he roared at his men.

But the mercenaries' attention was on the coins. One man darted forward to scoop them up, at which point Blackborne tossed down several more. With a jubilant whoop, the other soldiers surged towards them.

'No!' screamed Wogan furiously, tossing aside the spent guns and whipping out a sword. 'I will kill—'

There was a sharp report as a weapon was discharged. He staggered, and gazed in astonishment at the blood that seeped from a wound in his leg. Everyone else scattered, looking around wildly to see where the shot had come from. Chaloner knew: he had spotted movement behind a bale of straw. It was Dorcas, who immediately began to reload.

Wogan saw her, too. Oblivious to or uncaring of his injury, he began to run towards her, sword at the ready. She glanced up, then frantically tried to work faster. In her terror, she dropped the powder horn, losing vital seconds as she fumbled to pick it up again.

Chaloner knew Wogan would run her through before she could shoot him again. With a sharp stab of understanding, he saw he had been wrong about her: she was not on the side of the conspirators, but had been patiently biding her time, waiting for the moment when she could make an actual difference to the outcome – and she would have done, had her aim been true. The realisation meant he could not allow Wogan to murder her.

He hurtled forward. At the sound of his footsteps, Wogan started to turn, but too late. Chaloner crashed into him, sending him sprawling and the rapier cart-wheeling from his hand. They both scrambled towards it and, reaching it at the same time, began to grapple.

Chaloner was not sure how long he wrestled with Wogan on the ground. He was distantly aware of the roar of flames as the barn finally caught alight, and of hens flapping everywhere in panic. He heard Swaddell and Lester doing battle with courtiers, and knew fights were breaking out among the mercenaries as Blackborne lobbed coins for all he was worth. Dorcas had abandoned the gun and was fighting Drinkell's three apprentices with a stave.

But five against eighty were hopeless odds, and Chaloner knew it was only a matter of time before he and his friends were locked in another barn with kindling around the outside. Then there was a screech of warning from Glasse, and Chaloner saw others racing to join the fray. It was the Fifth Monarchists, wielding makeshift weapons grabbed from the outhouses – hammers, pitch-forks, axes and even part of a plough.

'For King Jesus!' one bellowed. 'And for poor Simpson, too!'

'Good men!' howled Blackborne in fierce delight. 'I knew you would choose the right side in the end. For King Jesus and the war against the ungodly!'

The fanatics were a fearsome sight now they were armed and their blood was up, and several mercenaries turned tail and ran. Others followed when one wall of the barn collapsed, showering them with burning cinders.

Blackborne slid off the roof and rolled clear, yelling encouragement as more of his co-religionists hurtled into the mêlée.

'Coaches!' came Dorcas's horrified voice. 'Look! Coaches are coming!'

Chaloner tore his eyes from Wogan just long enough to see she was right. Carriages were approaching fast, their wheels and the hoofs of horses raising great clouds of dust in their wake.

'It is Ludlow and Love!' yelled Wogan, punching Chaloner away and staggering triumphantly to his feet. 'Just as they promised.'

Chaloner grabbed him around the legs, dragging him to the ground again. If *he* was going to die that day, then Wogan would die with him.

'It is Elsie!' cried Lester, as a woman leapt from the leading vehicle and raced towards the skirmish brandishing a handgun. She was followed by men in the buff-coloured jerkins that identified them as Williamson's troops.

Wogan stopped fighting to gape his shock – shock that intensified when Thurloe alighted from the next coach with warriors of his own – old Parliamentarian intelligencers who had remained loyal to him and who were very good in a brawl. The ex-Spymaster carried no weapon, but his presence alone was enough to make some courtiers and mercenaries give up the fight.

'There will be no rebellion today,' he announced firmly, fixing Wogan with the expression that had caused many a traitor to quail in his boots. 'Ludlow and Love are no longer in the country. They have denounced your venture as madness and slithered away.'

'It is true,' said Williamson, who held a dag in one

404

hand and a sword in the other. 'They came because you bragged about a foolproof plan, but when they learned what it entailed, they knew it would never work. They will be halfway back to Vevey by now.'

'You lie!' snarled Wogan. 'If you had been in a position to hold that sort of conversation, they would be arrested, not going home. Do not try to deceive me.'

'Downes told them what was afoot,' Thurloe went on. 'Despite the Tower's interference, he did manage to get a message to them. Perhaps Eleanor Montagu sent it for him. Who knows? Regardless, Ludlow and Love will not be coming.'

'*No!*' screamed Wogan, staggering to his feet. 'The plan *will* work! Millington and Waller were geniuses. The King will die today. You know—'

Williamson raised his gun and pulled the trigger. Wogan was dead before he hit the ground.

'He had a knife,' shrugged the Spymaster, when Chaloner gaped at him. 'He was going to stab you with it.'

Chaloner knelt to feel for a life-beat, recalling what had happened the last time he had last seen Wogan 'killed', but he could tell from the size of the wound that the regicide would not be rising from the dead a second time. He opened his mouth to accuse Williamson of barefaced murder, but then it occurred to him that Wogan had just been given a far kinder death than the one he would have faced if he had been arrested and tried.

'I saved your life,' said Williamson, watching Chaloner sit back on his heels to stare down at the man who had instigated so much chaos. 'There is no doubt in my mind that he was about to stab you, and any witness here will agree.'

'I am sure they will,' muttered Chaloner, thinking that – other than Thurloe – everyone watching was in the Spymaster's employ, so would 'see' whatever he told them.

Williamson gave a small smile of satisfaction. 'Well, consider my heroism payment for dispatching Eleanor's murderer. In other words, I am no longer under any obligation to find Lester a ship.'

Chaloner blinked his disbelief, but before he could argue, Swaddell ran up.

'We have work to do,' he said briskly. 'Catline and Drinkell are still at large and intend mischief with their cartloads of rotten eggs.'

'We had better stop them, then,' said Williamson.

Chapter 17

There was no time for Chaloner to reflect on his escape from what had seemed like an impossible situation. Pandemonium still reigned, with chickens loose everywhere, the barn burning uncontrollably, and a host of courtiers, rogue poulters and mercenaries still to round up and place under guard.

'You must have passed the coach carrying Catline and Drinkell on your way here,' he said to Thurloe. 'And all their carts.'

'We passed a lot of vehicles,' said Thurloe. 'Word has spread that King Jesus is expected tomorrow, so some folk are going to meet Him, while others are fleeing for their lives. We would have been here sooner if the road had been less crowded.'

'Even so, you took far longer than you should have done. What kept you?'

'The moment Elsie gave me your note – the poor lady was half-fainting from sprinting so hard the whole way – I summoned a few loyal friends, and we all hurried to see Williamson, as you instructed. He had just received a panicky visit from Swaddell's wife, saying that rebels were in Clarendon House.'

'A ruse by Wogan,' said Chaloner. 'Do not tell me Williamson believed it?'

'He did, and it took an age to convince him otherwise. We set off eventually, but Wogan had set an ambush – insurance against us ignoring his trickery and coming here anyway. We were on our guard for such an eventuality, but thwarting it and securing the perpetrators cost us more time regardless.'

'I thought Elsie had betrayed us when you failed to appear. Dorcas, too, because she seemed suspiciously calm for what we were about to do, and I felt she stopped our coach too far away from this place.'

'You should be glad she did, or it would have driven right into that ambush, and I doubt you would have come out alive.' Thurloe glanced to where she was sitting on a bale of straw, white-faced and shaking now the crisis was over. 'She is a very brave lady, who fought just as hard as anyone in that mêlée.'

'Yes,' acknowledged Chaloner. 'I was wrong about her and Elsie. All I hope is that Lester never learns what I thought, because he will not appreciate me believing ill of the woman he intends to marry.'

'He will not find out from me.'

Chaloner looked around, still struggling to rally his reeling wits. 'Where is Docility?'

'She escaped,' replied Thurloe. 'Back to the city, I imagine, ready to make sure the plan proceeds more smoothly there than it did here.'

Chaloner noticed that it was not Williamson who was overseeing the rebels' capture, but Swaddell and Blackborne. Dorcas pulled herself together and went to help Elsie with the chickens, Lester acting as a willing, if inept, assistant. While they worked, the Spymaster sat on an upturned crate and watched. He had never been a particularly inspiring leader of troops, preferring instead to oversee operations from his Westminster lair, but Chaloner felt he should make at least some pretence at being in charge.

After a moment, Blackborne bustled up to Thurloe with businesslike authority, revealing the man who had run Cromwell's navy with such impressive efficiency.

'You, Chaloner, Swaddell and Williamson must go back to London,' he said briskly, 'because Catline and Drinkell cannot be allowed to succeed. Choose two dozen soldiers, and leave me the rest. I will make sure this horde plays no further role in the mischief, and you can collect them at your leisure later.'

Swaddell agreed at once to the plan, and detailed twenty-four men to cram themselves into three of the carriages. Then he, Williamson, Thurloe and Chaloner jumped into another, and their drivers turned them back towards London.

They made poor time, because Thurloe had not been exaggerating when he had said the roads were crowded with folk travelling in both directions. In addition, the horses were tired from the outward journey, so the drivers struggled to make them canter, even when they reached the more open stretches.

As they crept along with agonising slowness, Swaddell told Thurloe and Williamson about the encounter with Wogan in more detail, while Chaloner thought about the people who would suffer if Drinkell and Catline carried out their plans. Neither knew that Wogan was dead, so had no reason to stay their hands. He found he did not care what happened in White Hall, feeling that anyone debauched enough to jump in a vat of syllabub deserved whatever he got, but he did mind that innocent Londoners were about to be harmed.

'When we arrive, Thurloe and I will take half the men and look for Drinkell in Poulters' Hall,' he told Swaddell. 'You and Williamson take the rest and tackle Catline.'

'But Drinkell has the potential to cause a lot more damage,' argued Williamson, 'and it will take *my* authority to stop him, along with you, Swaddell and the bulk of the soldiers. Ergo, Thurloe must handle White Hall on his own – which will likely be more effective than blundering in with an army anyway. The palace guards will help.'

'No!' cried Chaloner, appalled.

'He is right, Tom,' said Thurloe quietly. 'Drinkell must have recruited a lot of fellow poulters if he aims to distribute spoiled eggs all across the city, and it will take every one of you to stop him. Besides, I still have friends at Court, so do not worry about me.'

But Chaloner was uneasy, suspicious that the Spymaster was willing to put the health of the city above that of his monarch.

'You do not want to save the King yourself?' he asked, thinking it was out of character for the Spymaster to pass up an opportunity to curry royal favour. Or did he think Thurloe would fail, and wanted to distance himself from the repercussions?

Williamson eyed him coldly. 'I just told you – Drinkell is the more serious problem, so that is where my duty lies.'

Chaloner's disquiet intensified, but the decision had been made, so there was nothing more he could do except fret as their carriage rumbled far too slowly towards London.

It was late afternoon before they reached the outskirts of the city. Chaloner was all for jumping out and running the rest of the way, but Thurloe convinced him to sit tight – that there was no point in arriving too hot and tired to do anything useful.

'Do you believe we can stop Drinkell?' he asked of Swaddell, daunted by the magnitude of the task that lay ahead.

'It will depend on how many other poulters he has convinced to join him,' replied the assassin soberly. 'But we can do one thing to reduce the number of casualties: Wiseman said the risk of egg fever is much reduced in cooked eggs, so we shall send some of our men out to act as criers, warning folk not to eat them raw.'

He ordered the driver to take them to Poulters' Hall first, then deliver Thurloe to White Hall. Chaloner jumped out while the coach was still moving, followed by Swaddell. Williamson alighted with more dignity. Thurloe leaned out of the window and grabbed Chaloner's arm, pulling him close so he could whisper in his ear.

'Be careful, Tom. White Hall is not the only place where snakes nest.'

'You mean him?' whispered Chaloner, glancing at the Spymaster, whose face was unusually pale, and who only watched as Swaddell directed half the men to different parts of the city, to spread their message as widely as possible.

'I mean anyone,' replied Thurloe, and with that, the carriage rattled away, tearing his hand from Chaloner's wrist.

There was no time for reflection, as the remaining soldiers had readied their muskets and drawn their swords. Swaddell gave the order to advance. The front door was locked, and Chaloner was about to suggest going around the back when one soldier stepped forward, took aim, and kicked it open.

The main hall was deserted, but the rear of the building was a hive of activity as crates were hauled up from the pantry and carried into the yard. Several wagons were waiting to be driven away, while others formed a queue that ran down the lane and disappeared around the corner. The poulters faltered when they saw armed men bearing down on them, and Chaloner could see the guilt in their faces. Some began to howl for Drinkell, although a lot more began to do battle.

The man in question came hurtling up the cellar stairs to find out what was happening. When he saw Chaloner and Swaddell, his jaw dropped in shock.

'You! But—'

'Wogan is dead,' interrupted Chaloner. 'And so is your plan.'

'Liar!' Drinkell turned to a monster of a man with a shiny bald head and blunt, pugilistic features. 'Uley? Kill them.'

The giant lumbered forward with a furious roar, wielding the biggest broadsword Chaloner had ever seen. Chaloner whipped out the rapier he had taken from a dead mercenary at the farm, aware that it looked alarmingly flimsy by contrast. He stepped forward to parry Uley's blow, and felt the shock of it vibrate through his whole body.

'Shoot him!' Swaddell bellowed at Williamson, who

had ducked behind him when Uley had begun his advance. 'Quickly!'

'I forgot to reload,' gulped Williamson. 'And I left my other weapons in the coach.'

Chaloner heard no more, because all was suddenly chaos and confusion, as more poulters poured from the pantry wielding an eclectic array of weapons. There were far too many of them, and Chaloner saw with despair that his side was going to be over-whelmed.

Confident of victory, Drinkell hauled some of his people away from the fighting, and directed them back to loading up the carts. Out of the corner of his eye, Chaloner saw another full wagon trundle away. Then Uley skidded on a broken egg, and Swaddell was on him in a flash. Drinkell gasped his shock as the giant fell to the assassin's blade.

'Surrender!' shouted Swaddell. 'Your champion is defeated.'

Unfortunately, Uley's death only encouraged the rest to fight harder than ever. Chaloner's arms burned with exhaustion as he battled with every ounce of his strength, tackling two or three poulters at once. Williamson stayed behind him, and gradually, they were forced backwards, until they reached the corridor that led to the hall. It was easier for Chaloner to fight there, as it reduced the number of poulters who could attack him at the same time.

'What is happening?' came a tremulous voice that was instantly recognisable as Beadle Collins's. 'Let us out at once!'

Chaloner risked a quick glance to his right, and saw the door to the kitchens had been secured with a sturdy bar.

413

'Williamson, open it!' he gasped.

The Spymaster obliged, all fingers and thumbs, while Chaloner kept their attackers at bay with great sweeps of his sword. The moment the bar was off, the door flew open, and out shot Collins gripping a heavy ladle and Farmer with a chair leg. Behind them were three dozen poulters who had remained loyal to their Master; they had armed themselves rather more sensibly, and brandished knives, meat cleavers and spits.

'Forward, men!' cried Collins, a savage grin splitting his wrinkled face. 'Show these rogues what the *cream* of our Company can do.'

He tore into the thick of the mêlée, and at first, Chaloner thought he was just eager to do battle. Then he realised the beadle was aiming for Drinkell. Step by step, the old man struggled through the milling mass until his quarry was in range. Then he raised his ladle and brought it down with all his might on Drinkell's unprotected head.

'Your leader is dead,' bellowed Williamson, which was the first useful thing he had done all day, as far as Chaloner was concerned. 'Lay down your weapons.'

'You heard him,' bawled Collins, giving Drinkell another belt for good measure, although it was clear that he was hitting a corpse. 'Surrender, or die like this filthy traitor.'

Seeing the odds now stacked against them, Drinkell's people began to do as they were told. Chaloner left Swaddell to deal with them, and ran into the yard, where one poulter was in the process of making his escape, lashing his horse for all he was worth. Chaloner surged forward and hauled him from his saddle.

414

'How many carts have already gone out?' he demanded. 'And where are they going?'

'Twelve!' bleated the terrified rider. 'Four each to the three main markets. But Poulters' Hall is only one of Drinkell's caches. He has others all over the city.'

Chaloner's heart sank at the sheer scale of the operation. He dragged the man back inside, and shoved him with his confederates.

'You are in charge,' Swaddell told Collins. 'Lock this rabble in the kitchens and guard them until I return to escort them to Newgate.'

The old beadle gave a military-style salute, delighted to be entrusted with such a task. Chaloner turned to Farmer.

'You and your people *must* prevent Drinkell's eggs from being sold, or your Company is going to be blamed for poisoning an entire city. Find his caches and destroy them.'

'The soldiers and I will help,' said Swaddell, and drew Chaloner aside; Williamson followed. 'You must hurry to White Hall, Tom, lest Thurloe needs you. All our efforts will be for nothing if His Majesty is poisoned with bad eggs.'

'True,' agreed Williamson, his customary hauteur restored now the danger was over. 'All manner of rebels will crawl from under their rocks to chance their hands if we lose our King. Not Fifth Monarchists, perhaps, given that they seem to be on our side now, but all the other lunatics who think they know how to run a country.'

'Come with me,' said Chaloner. 'It is your job to protect him.'

'My job is to prevent rebellion,' countered Williamson loftily. 'And as soon as I have finished here, I shall go to

Pudding Lane, to make sure no stray agitators are waiting to bray their own twisted versions of the Kingdom of God.'

'He is right, Tom,' said Swaddell. 'Now, go!'

As there were no free hackney carriages, Chaloner leapt on to an occupied one. He pulled its startled passenger from his seat, and ordered the driver to take him to White Hall as fast as was humanly possible. It was a matter of life and death.

'The King's death?' asked the driver coolly, not moving. 'Because if that is what you aim to prevent, you can walk.'

'The palace needs to be ready for King Jesus,' barked Chaloner, too fraught to think of a more plausible excuse.

'Then hold on tight,' declared the driver, eyes agleam. 'You can count on me.'

There followed perhaps the most terrifying journey Chaloner had ever made in a coach. Rarely were more than two wheels on the road at the same time, and corners were taken with such reckless abandon that he was sure they would overturn long before they reached their destination.

But arrive they did, and Chaloner alighted on unsteady legs. The horse stood with its flanks heaving and its head bowed as it fought to regain its breath. Chaloner started to pay for the ride, but the driver waved the money away.

'I did it for King Jesus.'

Chaloner hared through the Great Gate, hoping the man never learned how he had been deceived. Once inside, he skidded to a standstill and gazed around in horror. The yard was chocked full of carriages, as hundreds of guests arrived for the Adrian Masque.

Everyone had entered into the spirit of the occasion by donning fancy dress, although some people's notion of what was worn in the twelfth century was bizarre, to say the least. Almost all involved masks, which made identifying Catline – or Thurloe, for that matter – impossible.

Driven to desperate measures, Chaloner grabbed a guest who did not look too important, and relieved him of hat, cloak and mask at knifepoint, then locked him in a pantry with the threat of a blade in his gizzard if he tried to raise the alarm. Then he hurried towards the Banqueting House, aware that the masque had been going for some time, and that he might already be too late to prevent disaster.

The Banqueting House was unbearably hot, even though all the windows were open, and it was more tightly packed than he had ever seen it. The babble of voices was deafening, and the racket was exacerbated by the troupe of 'medieval' musicians, who made a colossal racket with their drums and screechy pipes.

Not caring whom he jostled, Chaloner tried to force his way towards the replica baptismal font, aiming to see if it was filled with syllabub, but so many people were clustered around it that it was impossible to reach. Then a servant emptied a bucket of something yellow into it, and the way the closest onlookers attempted to step back as it dripped over the sides told him it was already brimming.

Several of the King's favourites had taken the best places in front of it, standing on a large platform that raised them to the point where their knees were level with its rim. Chaloner supposed it had been built to facilitate easy access for when it was time to go a-wallowing. They surrounded a man dressed as Adrian the Fourth, and Chaloner did not need anyone to tell him that this was His Majesty, choosing to play the star of the show.

As he watched, a servant in a monk's habit arrived with another pail of syllabub. It was Catline, betrayed by his sinuous gait and hands that shook with excitement. He set the bucket down, scooped some of its contents into a goblet, and held it out for His Holiness to try.

'No!' howled Chaloner, although the music and thunder of strident voices were so loud that he knew neither the King nor his companions would hear him. 'Stop!'

Frantically, he tried to fight his way forward again, but there were just too many people, and he made no headway at all. Then he noticed a 'bishop' join the King's circle, his face obscured by the veil that hung from his wide-brimmed hat. Chaloner recognised the slight figure and dainty gait immediately. Thurloe! The ex-Spymaster ascended the platform and then pretended to trip, hitting the Pope hard enough to knock him off balance.

Horrified, Chaloner watched as the Pontiff stumbled against the font, arms windmilling wildly. Then, almost in slow motion, in he went, toppling over the edge with a great wet splat. Syllabub flew in all directions, causing those closest to duck away with shrieks of shock.

All that could be seen of the hapless Vicar of Rome were two frantically waving legs. His cronies darted forward to pull him out before he drowned, but the syllabub made him slippery, and by the time they managed to set him back on his feet, he was gasping for breath and covered in bright yellow slime from head to toe.

The music stopped, and the roar of conversation ceased as everyone waited in taut silence to see what would

418

happen next. The Pope stood choking and gagging, his finery hanging in oily folds around him and his tall mitre sadly askew.

Then someone began to laugh. The Pontiff turned towards the voice, and forced what may have been a smile, although it was difficult to tell through the eggy froth.

'Your Majesty,' he croaked. 'It is my honour to amuse you.'

'You do, Bristol, you do,' guffawed the King, striding forward to poke him playfully in his syllabub-coated ribs. Bewildered, Chaloner saw he had been wrong to assume the monarch would snag the top role for himself, and that His Majesty had chosen to dress as a cardinal, instead. Judging by Catline's posture – rigid with stunned disbelief – he had made the same mistake.

'Good,' said Bristol tightly, as the King walked in a circle around him, grinning all the while.

'What a sight you are, man!' His Majesty exclaimed, eventually coming to a standstill in front of the hapless nobleman. 'Well, I shall not be eating any of *that* later, not now you have been in it with your boots on. The plan was for us all to go barefoot.'

'But sire!' blurted Catline in abject dismay. 'We have worked hard to make this for you, and eggs are so rare. You *must* try it!'

The King swung around, and even from a distance Chaloner saw the animal cunning in his eyes – the same cunning that had allowed him to survive when there were so many plots against him. 'Must I? Then *you* drink some, and show us how delicious it is.'

Catline swallowed hard. 'I . . . have an aversion to eggs, sire.'

'What a pity,' said the King, and nodded to a pair of

minstrels, who hastened forward to lay hold of Catline and pull off his mask. 'Had you eaten some, I would have known you were innocent of this plot against me. You refused – ergo, you are guilty.'

Catline's face was white with shock as he was hauled away. He opened his mouth to deny the charge, but closed it again when one of his captors jabbed him with a knife. The King turned to Montagu, who, somewhat inexplicably, was wearing a toga.

'Get rid of it,' he ordered, nodding at the syllabub. 'And send for Wiseman. I suspect Bristol will have need of him later.'

He strode away, his entourage chattering excitedly at his heels. Chaloner looked back at Bristol, trying to read his expression. Was it mystification because he had no idea what was going on? Or alarm lest Catline named him as a fellow conspirator? But it was impossible to tell, even if his face had not been coated in yellow goo.

'Come, Tom,' breathed a familiar voice in Chaloner's ear. 'We should leave before either of us is recognised.'

'I assume it was you who warned the King,' said Chaloner. 'But how did you get close enough to speak to him?'

'I told you – I still have a few friends in White Hall,' replied Thurloe. 'Even so, this is no place for us. Come. We should see if Swaddell and Williamson need help.'

Legs unsteady, Chaloner followed him out into the sultry night air.

Epilogue

When Londoners woke on Thursday morning, it was to find that nothing had changed. At first, there was dismay that a perfect world had failed to materialise yet again, but they were used to broken promises, and it did not take them long to shrug off their disappointment and return to their daily lives.

Many of Drinkell's eggs did reach the markets, but they did scant harm – the unhealthy ones were either discarded because they stank, or they were cooked to the point where they were safe. Wiseman reported a mere handful of egg-fever cases, none of them fatal, leading Chaloner to suppose that it was more difficult to poison a city than Millington and Waller had appreciated.

'It is a pity that dosing the Buttery men achieved such spectacular results,' the surgeon said. 'It gave your villains false confidence. Of course, the fact that Catline fed them raw eggs in a posset helped – cooked ones would not have done nearly so much harm. But the scheme could *never* have worked on an entire city. Your rebels were delusional.'

'Yes,' agreed Chaloner. 'They were.'

*

Two days later, on a beautiful late-summer evening, Chaloner finally finished dealing with the aftermath of the plot and went to report to Thurloe. The ex-Spymaster was in Lincoln's Inn's garden, relaxing on a bench under a shady beech and savouring the coolness after the heat of the day.

'I do not think I can live in London any more,' said Chaloner, sitting next to him. 'I am tired of thwarting one rebellion, only for another to take its place, and I do not like working for the Earl.'

'Nor would I,' averred Thurloe. 'But what would you do instead? You cannot go home to Buckinghamshire, because the last thing your family needs is another mouth to feed – and they will be in desperate straits without the money you send them every month.'

'I could earn just as much from music,' said Chaloner. 'Wren tells me there is a vacancy for a violist in the Chapel Royal, and has offered to recommend me for it.'

'Then you should let him,' advised Thurloe. 'But before you exchange your sword for a bow, tell me what you have been doing since we last parted ways.'

'The only conspirator not accounted for now is Docility Gander,' reported Chaloner. 'All the corrupt courtiers from the Poultry Department are in prison. Wogan, Drinkell, Catline, Glasse, Rye and Crookey are dead. So are Simpson and Vernon, although they were unwitting tools in Wogan's hands.'

'Catline, Glasse and Crookey are not dead,' countered Thurloe. 'They are in the Tower.'

'They saw what their future held, decided they did not like the look of it, and took their own lives. At least, that is the official story. Personally, I find it hard to believe that all three contrived to cut their own throats.'

'Swaddell,' murmured Thurloe in distaste, 'so that details of the plot will never be made public in a trial. Williamson allowed me to speak to them all on Friday, and I can tell you that none were suicidal then.'

'You visited them?' asked Chaloner in surprise. 'Why?'

'To ask a few questions that have been nagging at me – such as why Glasse agreed to "murder" Wogan when it hardly cast him in an admirable light and later forced him to flee for his life.'

'What did he say?'

'That Wogan made him do it and he was too frightened to refuse.'

'That may be true,' said Chaloner. 'Wogan transpired to be as cold and ruthless as anyone I have ever met.'

'I should never have believed his protestations of remorse,' said Thurloe ruefully. 'But he was so convincing. The reports he sent about several very dangerous insurgents were excellent, but it transpires that he betrayed people who had sworn allegiance to him – he sacrificed them without a qualm to convince me of his sincerity.'

'Even now, it is hard to believe that he killed so many people – Downes and eight other regicides, Eleanor Montagu, Hadie, Hill, Bowles and a still-undetermined number of higglers. Then he shot Simpson and Vernon, and tried to burn the Fifth Monarchists alive.'

'Speaking of Downes, I finally managed to decode his message to Eleanor. It was so complex that I think his expectation was that she would pass it to the intelligence services without ever knowing what it contained. She could never have unravelled it, you see – it took me days, and I have years of experience with ciphers.'

'Why did he make it so difficult?'

'Almost certainly to protect her – if she was ignorant

423

of its contents, he hoped that would be enough to keep her safe. Unfortunately, he underestimated Wogan's ruthlessness.'

'So what did it say?'

'Exactly what we thought it would – details of the plan devised by Millington and Waller.'

'So why was Blackborne's name mentioned in it?'

'Because, as I surmised when I first saw it, Downes recommended him as a good man to trust. Mine was in there, too.'

Chaloner thought again about the plot. 'I find it difficult to imagine how Wogan thought it would work. Even if Drinkell and his poulters had managed to make enough people ill, most would have recovered, at which point they would have fought back.'

'Wogan genuinely expected them to rally behind Ludlow and Love once they arrived,' explained Thurloe, 'although I think he overestimated how delighted folk would be to see them. They were influential rabble-rousers in their day, but their stars have waned since.'

'I would not have thrown my lot in with them,' averred Chaloner. 'Despite the fact that I would far rather have a Commonwealth than this debauched King and his useless government.'

'That is treason, Thomas,' said Thurloe mildly. 'You should watch your tongue. Incidentally, Catline told me that Wogan aimed to deploy the intelligence services heavily once he and his fellow conspirators were in power – using its spies to root out and silence dissenting voices. I wonder what Williamson will say about that when I tell him.'

'Well, Swaddell will be appalled. He may be an assassin, but he has his principles.'

'I doubt Catline, Crookey and Glasse would agree,' said Thurloe drily. 'But on a brighter note, Eleanor's fortune will be used for what she intended.'

'It has been found?' asked Chaloner, surprised. 'I know Blackborne did not have it on the barn roof – he used his own money to distract Wogan's mercenaries.'

'Glasse told me where he had hidden it in an attempt to buy his freedom. The Company of Poulters will use it to transform Drinkell's farm into a place where better egg-producing methods can be devised – ones that benefit poulters *and* their hens. Dorcas and Elsie are to have charge of the venture.'

'Lester will wed Elsie next week.' Chaloner shook his head in wonderment. 'Who would have thought it? He never seemed very interested in marriage before.'

'I am sorry Williamson failed to get him another ship. I know for a fact that he tried, but his request was flatly refused. He was shocked to discover that he does not have the power and influence he thought he did.'

'Fortunately, Blackborne was able to help. The King invited him to White Hall to give an account of his role in thwarting Wogan, and while he was there, he put in a word on Lester's behalf. He knows a good seaman when he sees one.'

Thurloe smiled. 'Then perhaps we shall survive the war with the Dutch after all, because I shall certainly feel safer with Lester patrolling the high seas. Incidentally, I hear that Bristol is recovering. I do not like the man, but I am glad I am not responsible for giving him a fatal dose of egg fever.'

'His illness has given my Earl a much-needed respite, along with the claims in the pamphlet "the Paladin" wrote about him. Montagu and Margaret Hay were far more brutal than I would have been, and exposed all manner of unsavoury things about him. When he is well enough to return to Court, he will find his reception very cool.'

'I am glad they avenged the lies he told about Eleanor. She was a good woman, and Bristol had no right to use her in his selfish schemes.'

'No,' agreed Chaloner. 'She realised that the Fifth Monarchists had suddenly become much more dangerous, and tried to draw everyone's attention to it with her broadsheets. It is a pity we did not heed her warnings, because then none of this would have happened.'

'Speaking of Fifth Monarchists,' said Thurloe, 'do you know where they are? I understand there was no sign of them when you and Swaddell returned to Willesden to collect all the prisoners that Blackborne was guarding.'

'They were unwitting helpmeets to Wogan's scheme,' replied Chaloner. 'Blackborne was right to let them disappear, and I suspect the fright they had will encourage them to keep their radical theology to themselves from now on.'

'I hope you are right,' said Thurloe. 'Because I should not like them to try again.'

Chaloner grinned suddenly. 'I shall never forget Bristol toppling into that syllabub! I still laugh whenever I think of it.'

Thurloe also smiled at the memory. 'Pushing him in was enormously gratifying. Would that I could do the same to all White Hall's useless sycophants.'

At that moment, one of the Inn's youthful porters arrived to say that there was a lady at the gate, waiting for Chaloner.

'Dorcas,' said Chaloner, blushing. 'I offered to take

426

her to the Foxhall Pleasure Gardens to see the fireworks tonight. I did not think she would accept, given my coolness towards her on the way to Willesden, but she seems ready to forgive me.'

'Go,' said Thurloe. 'You deserve to be happy, and you and she have at least one thing in common: you are fond of chickens. You could both do a lot worse.'

A little later, in the small hours of Sunday morning, a shadowy figure slipped down Pudding Lane. Swaddell and Chaloner had been so busy rounding up treacherous courtiers and dishonest poulters that their hunt for Docility had been fleeting at best, and she had had no difficulty in eluding capture. Eventually, she reached Skiner's Coffee House, where a man was waiting outside for her, cloaked and hooded against recognition.

'Well?' he demanded. 'Did you collect them all?'

She nodded. 'I buried them in the garden. They will never be found there.'

He made an exasperated sound at the back of his throat. 'I told you to burn them! Fire is the only way to make sure they never see the light of day. Do it tonight. And when you have finished, leave the city and never return. If you are not gone by tomorrow, I shall send my assassin after you.'

'Yes, sir,' said Docility with barely concealed anger. 'As you wish.'

The Spymaster turned on his heel and stalked away, cloak billowing behind him. Docility was not the only one who was disappointed that Wogan's plot had failed, because Williamson's unsuccessful attempt to secure Lester a ship had exposed the unpleasant truth that he was less important – and certainly less appreciated – than he had thought. He knew he deserved better, and wished Wogan had come to him sooner with his offers of riches and high-rank in a new government, because then he could have made sure the scheme had worked.

In the end, he had only been able to hinder Chaloner and Swaddell in trivial ways – sending them to White Hall when they had wanted to confront Drinkell, delaying his own arrival in Willesden until it should have been too late . . . Indeed, he would not have gone at all if Thurloe had not appeared and demanded it. There had been one wild, desperate moment when he had considered dispatching Thurloe and denying the man had ever arrived that night, but the ex-Spymaster had come in company with a dozen of his former spies. It would have been impossible to conceal that many deaths, especially as they all would have fought back, resulting in a pile of corpses that not even he could have made disappear.

But it was over now, and all that remained was to make sure no one ever learned about his role in the affair. The worst moment had been at the farm, when he had been convinced that Wogan was going to say something incriminating. It was fortunate that his dag had been loaded when he had needed it.

When Williamson had gone, Docility padded silently to Fish Yard, where she opened the gate that led to a back garden. She had worked for Farriner before Wogan had recruited her to his cause, and was grateful to the kindly baker for accepting her back into his service when he heard she was unemployed.

She scowled into the darkness when she recalled Williamson's order for her to disappear. She had very nearly been in government, so no mere Royalist politician was going to tell *her* what to do! Moreover, she had no intention of leaving the city she loved.

Trying not to make a noise, she scraped away the scrubby soil and retrieved the incriminating papers – letters from Ludlow and Love, the list of people who would have been executed once Wogan was in power, and his outline for a new regime that included Williamson. When she was sure she had them all, she slipped into the bakery. As she had hoped, the oven was still hot, with the fire banked beneath it.

Moving silently, so as not to wake Farriner and his daughter sleeping above, she began to burn the papers – or some of them at least. The ones implicating Williamson she would keep, and woe betide him if he threatened her again.

Her bitterness intensified with every flame that consumed the documents. Wogan had come so close! If no one had interfered, Drinkell would have distributed the eggs, the King would have jumped in the syllabub, and a new republic would have been installed with her in a position of great power.

She blinked away tears. She missed Wogan, and was outraged that he had been shovelled in a mass grave on Drinkell's farm, along with all the others who had died there. She had gone to visit it the previous day, and had been appalled to discover the burial mound covered in chickens, all busily scratching for worms.

Through her tears, she saw that one of the burning pages had dropped into the pile of faggots that Farriner kept at the side of the oven. The continuing hot weather meant the faggots were unusually dry, so they ignited at once.

Swearing under her breath, she kicked the pile over so she could stamp out the flames. Unfortunately, they caught the wood shavings that were scattered across the floor each night to keep the shop smelling fresh. Before she knew it, the entire room was ablaze.

She screeched her alarm, coughing as smoke billowed around her. Farriner and his daughter heard her cries, and, muddle-headed with sleep, stumbled down the stairs to see what was happening. By then, flames were licking at the front door, trapping all three of them inside.

'Upstairs,' yelled the baker urgently. 'We will escape over the roof.'

It was easier said than done. The house was several storeys tall, and Docility had never liked heights. Farriner clambered across to his neighbour's roof, pulling his daughter behind him, but Docility could not bring herself to follow, not even when flames burst into the attic and she felt them sear her back. All she could see was the dizzying fall in front.

'Come on,' howled Farriner, leaning out as far as he could to offer her his hand. 'It is not far and I will help you. Hurry!'

But Docility could not do it. As the flames engulfed her, a distant part of her mind wondered how this could be happening when, by rights, she should be sitting in White Hall with Wogan. Minutes later, she was dead, the first fatality in one of the worst catastrophes ever to befall the city.

Historical Note

The year 1666 was an eventful one for Britain, which was still reeling from the effects of the plague, not to mention two decades of civil unrest and a king whose hold on the throne was still tenuous. Omens about the dreaded year with three sixes were taken seriously, and *The London Gazette* recorded all manner of them, including turkey-egg-sized hailstones, a rain of fish in Kent, and a pyramid of fire in the sky over Southampton. Contemporary broadsheets went even further, and contain reports of blood-filled cisterns and streams, coffin-shaped clouds, and numerous reports of talking animals and birds. *The London Gazette* also recorded news about Pope Alexander VII's failing health; he was said to have started sleeping with a coffin in his bedchamber to remind him of his mortality, and died a few months later.

It was also a bad time because the country was at war with the United Provinces of the Netherlands, with most hostilities taking place at sea. The Four Days' Battle was in June, during which the youthful and inexperienced Admiral Berkeley was killed and his flagship, HMS *Swiftsure*, captured. Some records show a Captain Lester as *Swiftsure*'s master.

In August, the British fleet returned to port, to refit and revictual. Later that month, the Navy Office, including Clerk of the Acts Samuel Pepys, was summoned to White Hall to explain why it was taking so long. Pepys's diary records the meeting, and also describes his delight with the new purple upholstery that was being installed in his closet. All through that summer, rumours abounded about the status of both fleets – in or out of port – with the country living in constant fear of invasion.

On 19 and 20 August came an incident known popularly as Holmes's Bonfire, in which the daring Admiral Robert Holmes burned a Dutch merchant fleet, along with the village of West Ter-Schelling in the province of Friesland. The attack on a civilian settlement appalled the United Provinces, so when London was engulfed by the Great Fire two weeks later, it was seen by the Dutch as divine retribution.

Robert Blackborne had been the leading navy official during the Commonwealth, and Pepys regularly consulted him for advice, although it seems Blackborne's extreme Puritan views prevented him from being appointed in any official capacity. There is some suggestion that he may have been a Fifth Monarchist, although the evidence is unreliable. Blackborne's nephew was Will Hewer, who began his own distinguished naval career as Pepys's clerk.

Most of the other characters in *The Pudding Lane Plot* were also real people. John Bowles the grocer died on 21 August 1666, and Daniel Norton died eight days later. Mrs Gander lived in Fish Yard, as did John Bibie, Widow Noest, and Thomas Farriner the baker. The Rainbow Coffee House was owned by Thomas Farr, and Samuel Speed sold books from the back of it. Fabian Stedman may have been a printer, and was a famous early bell-ringer. The landlord of the King's Head tavern on Fish Street Hill at this time was Robert Cradock, and the Sunne's landlord was Thomas Padnoll.

A number of regicides did die between 1664 and 1666, and two of them – Gilbert Millington and Sir Hardresse Waller – breathed their last within a few weeks of each other in Mount Orgueil Castle, then a prison, on Jersey. However, I have taken some liberty with dates. Millington was probably still alive in August, while the exact date of Waller's death is unknown. John Downes only fades from Tower of London records after November 1666. However, by this time, all the regicides were ageing men living under stressful conditions, so a spate of deaths among them is hardly surprising.

John Dixwell fared better than most: he fled to New England and assumed a new identity, where he lived out his days in peace. Edmund Ludlow, regarded as one of the most dangerous of the king-killers, lived until 1680, and Nicholas Love until 1682; both died in Vevey, Switzerland, which attracted a lot of British political and religious exiles. Thomas Chaloner had died in exile in 1662.

Thomas Wogan, another regicide, was captured at the Restoration and imprisoned in York. He escaped, and eventually fetched up in Switzerland, too, where he met up with Ludlow. There are unsubstantiated rumours that he returned to Britain to foment rebellion, but he disappears from the records in 1666.

London was stuffed to the gills with religious radicals in the 1660s, including members of the peculiar sect known as the Fifth Monarchists. One was John Vernon, a Parliamentarian army officer, who was exiled in 1661, but who flagrantly lived in London and practised medicine;

433

he died in 1667. Another was John Simpson, vicar of Allhallows the Great, who allowed his church to be used for illicit gatherings; he was well educated and a fiery orator, but was unsteady in his opinions and had lost the confidence of his fellow 'saints' before his death in 1662. One Mary Lane was buried in his church, although she was never a smuggler. Other Fifth Monarchists include Thomas Glasse (died 1666), a Baptist minister who lived in London with Vernon; John Rye (died 1667), a writer of inflammatory tracts; and one 'Mr Skiner' who sold coffee.

The Worshipful Company of Poulters is an ancient foundation that controlled the sale of poultry, small game and eggs. Its Master in 1666 was Symon Farmer, and his Renter (junior) Warden was William Drinkell, who became Master himself in 1672. The Company beadle from 1640 to 1671 was Charles Collins. Most freemen were male, but two women appear in the records: Elizabeth Henwood (1670) and Elizabeth Eades (1680), called Elsie and Dorcas here to avoid confusion between two women with the same first name.

One of the Company's remits was to regulate a business that produced a lot of nasty smells, waste and noise. One man who did not follow the rules was Henry Newdick. He lived on Gracious Street (Gracechurch Street) in 1684, and decided to keep live poultry in his cellar. His neighbours complained, and he received an official warning.

Another problem the Company had to contend with was higglers – unlicensed traders – who flouted the rules about when wares could be sold, where and for how much. A Mr Hill was hired to tackle them in 1658. Other Company members at the time were James Hadie and Richard Pheasant (who was later a Master himself).

Edward Montagu was the Earl of Manchester. His fourth wife was Eleanor, who, rather oddly, was the step-mother of his second wife. Montagu was her fourth husband; her third had estates in New England. When Eleanor died, Montagu married Margaret Hay. He had been a Parliamentarian general during the wars, but declared for the King at the Restoration, and was rewarded by being made Lord Chamberlain.

The Poultry Department at White Hall was responsible for providing the King and his Court with birds, small game and eggs. In 1666, its clerk was James Munger, its Sergeant was René Mezandier, and one of its grooms was Henry Catline. Jeffrey Crookey was appointed Supernumerary Groom on 6 July 1662. Syllabub really was one of Charles II's favourite foods.

Richard Wiseman was Surgeon to the Person, and Will Chiffinch was called the Pimpmaster General by Londoners, because he supplied the King with female company. His wife was named Barbara. Lady Castlemaine was the King's mistress during the early 1660s, and bore him several children.

The brilliant but quixotic Earl of Bristol had tried to impeach the Earl of Clarendon in 1663, but his plan had backfired, causing him to flee the country to avoid charges of lying to the House of Commons. He returned in 1666, and promptly took up where he left off. His campaign to blacken Clarendon's reputation eventually succeeded, with the help of others who felt the Earl had outlived his usefulness. Clarendon was exiled in 1667, and lived the rest of his life in France. Matthew Wren, cousin to the more famous Christopher, was Clarendon's secretary from 1660–1667.

Joseph Williamson supervised the intelligence services.

He was a talented civil servant, but not a very good spymaster, and had a reputation for being aloof, arrogant and unfriendly. By contrast, John Thurloe had been an outstanding spymaster, a post he combined with being Secretary of State.

On Monday 27 August 1666, *The London Gazette* recorded an incident where Dutch prisoners of war tried to set Bristol alight with faggots stored on the quayside. A few days later, in the early hours of Sunday 2 September, a blaze in Thomas Farriner's bakery in Fish Yard, off Pudding Lane, became the four-day inferno known as the Great Fire of London. The first casualty was Farriner's maid, whose name is not recorded.